The fisherman's DAUGHTER

The Fisherman's DAUGHTER

a novel

MELINDA SUE SANCHEZ

Covenant Communications, Inc.

To *L'amore Mio*; I'd fight through any war to be with you.

Acknowledgments

FIRST, I MUST ACKNOWLEDGE THE amazing people of southern Italy, who awed me with their stories of bravery and perseverance during WWII. The war invaded their country right at their doorsteps, and so many of them lost loved ones and suffered atrocities. I was particularly awestruck by the everyday "housewives" who traded in their aprons for rifles or worked as spies on their bicycles, carrying messages hidden in their clothes and delivering them under the noses of the Nazis.

I want to thank Kirk Shaw and Kathy Jenkins of Covenant Communications for loving *Fisherman's Daughter* from the moment they read it—and for snatching it up.

I have to thank my sister Julie for giving me my first typewriter and being my personal cheerleader; my precious daughters, Morena and Siciley, for dragging me to workshops and opening doors I never dreamed were there; ANWA for its wonderful people, chapters, conferences, and connections; Pam Goodfellow for lessons that changed my life; Cindy Williams for always kicking me in the pants; Karen for having my back; my dad for his sweet support; and my mama for passing down her writing abilities.

And finally, I have to thank my hunky man for making Italy and my entire life full of extra magical purpose, constant faith and support, and absolute joy. I love you for forever, *marito mio*!

Chapter One

THE STEADY SLAP, SLAP, SLAP of my skirt against my shins gave rhythm to my steps as dust landed like sifted powder on the tips of my leather shoes. Graceful hills rolled beside me, divided by long rock walls and row after row of olive trees that stretched their scratchy limbs to the sky. I raised my face to bask in the warmth of the sun, happy for a chance to visit Franca again, and I caught a glimpse of someone unfamiliar in a nearby pasture.

After three years of Nazi occupation, I knew better than to seek out a stranger, but I slowed my pace. The man moved back and forth, but the wall between us blocked my view. Curiosity overran my caution. I crept up a small knoll and ducked my head under the branches of a tree to get a closer look. An old wooden wagon sat in the middle of a grassy field, the bed sagging beneath a pile of limestone and lava rocks, while a young man with curly black hair stacked more rocks inside and whistled into the afternoon breeze. As he turned to gather another load, my knees loosened beneath me. I'd been friends with neighborhood boys in my seventeen years, but none had a face like this young man. His dark profile shot a tingle to the tips of my fingers as a warm breeze played with the hair at the nape of his neck.

The trunk of an ancient fig tree abutted the fence. I moved behind it and chanced another peek into the pasture. The young man was gone, the wagon of stones like a scenic painting just a few yards away. It did not seem possible he could have vanished, to have disappeared the moment I'd seen him, but the field sat quiet and empty.

I took a careful step around the tree trunk into the open, stretched my neck over the top of the wall for a better look, and he stood up right in front of me, each of his hands gripped around a large rock. His black eyes widened at the sight of me before the corners of his mouth lifted in a broad smile. "*Buon giorno.*"

I swallowed air and stepped backward onto rocks that tipped and rolled under my feet. Seconds ticked like minutes before I hurried a few paces down the road and smoothed my stride. I fought the impulse to look back and failed; I flipped my braid behind my shoulder for one quick peek and . . . there he stood atop the fence, watching me.

He smiled. "*Mi scusi . . . Signorina*, you have not been sent to spy on me, have you?"

My face burned and I turned my back to him. I quickened my pace and winced when he called to me again.

"Wait a minute, *Signorina*; I am new to Sicily. I was only trying to greet you, to say *buon giorno.*"

The tenor of his voice vibrated under my skin and I hastened my step, but the chance he could be an enemy who would retaliate against my rudeness demanded a response, so I called over my shoulder, "*Buon giorno.*"

A breeze cooled my face when I made it around a bend where a row of cypress trees blocked me from the young man's view. I focused on the crunch of gravel beneath my shoes.

A flock of swifts darted above the wildflowers along the side of the road, and I eased my breathing to a slower pace. The man in the field did not look like a Nazi, but I knew better than to be sure at just a glance. To see someone load large rocks into a wagon can simply make one curious. I had not intended to be seen. And when I hurried around another bend, I determined to never give the incident, or the dark stranger, another thought.

* * *

The next morning I leaned back against a mountain of netting while seagulls announced another feast would soon be lifted from the belly of the sea. Papa's fishing boat, thick with painted layers of cobalt blue, rocked me across ripples of waves on the wood slat that spanned from side to side and had served as my seat for almost two decades.

I breathed in the mist that rose from the silky Mediterranean and studied my father's face; the creases around his eyes looked like a fan had been pressed against the top of each cheek. He caught me watching him and winked at me, and I remembered the days as a child when I had wished my eyes were not dark and ordinary. I reminded Papa of this and he laughed.

"You have your mother's brown eyes, Marianna, soft and dark as a mother doe's."

"As a child your blue eyes seemed like a miracle to me, Papa, like the saints had kissed each one when you were born."

A horizon of low hills painted a background for my father's rugged shape. He frowned and shook his head. "Blue eyes are the result of German ancestry mixed with our Italian—something I am not so proud of these days."

Nerves prickled at the base of my neck. I crossed myself and said a quick prayer as Papa patted my knee with a callused hand. "The sea and our country still belong to our hearts, *Carina Mia*." His eyes dulled to ash. "But you are thinking of our Bruno, no?" The shriek of a gull cut through the air and a grasshopper flew up from where it had been hiding in the bottom of the boat. The bird plunged from above and snatched the insect in its beak.

My chest tightened and I looked away. "I want to stop it, Papa, to keep Bruno from having to go back. There has to be a way."

Papa's eyes drooped at the corners. "I know, *Carina*."

Several gulls dove at the top of the water and pecked at the fish that had escaped the net or flipped out of the boat during our last catch. I found a shell and threw it in their direction, breathing easier when the gulls scattered and flew away.

Papa patted my knee. "You usually have joy in your eyes when you come with me. We have pulled in a few nets now. Go ahead and swim before we go."

"It will scare the catch. You work too hard already."

He shook his head with a tsk of his tongue. "Swim, Mari. My own little fish is more important than all the slippery ones in the sea."

Waves splashed against the side of the boat and sent water droplets into the air before they landed back on the surface with the ping of tiny bells. Perhaps the sea would ease the worry that had rooted itself in my chest. "I will swim for a few minutes, but I am coming back to help you bring in the last net."

I slipped my shoes and dress off, down to my black bathing costume, and dove into the sapphire ripples. I kicked my legs with gusto and pushed myself far from the boat. The hush of a thousand tiny knots hitting water whispered behind me; my father had raised his strong arms, thrust them out in an arc, and cast the fishing net on the sea.

I flipped on my back and floated in the peace of the familiar sounds, yearning for the days when Bruno and I were young, swam for hours and pumiced our feet on the sand as we ran. The only time I could out-guess my brother in any challenge was in the water, especially when my best friend Franca and I teamed up against him. The sea had been our favorite playground since childhood and now served as a brief refuge from the threats that hovered over my family.

The surface of the water covered me like a ceiling of emeralds and jade while I kicked my feet and cupped water into my hands with each stroke of my arms. I stretched out and dove deep, letting the pressure on my ears shut out the world up above. My hair streamed down my back and whipped like a rudder through the current. My muscles tingled and burned before I made my way to the shore and tiptoed through a patch of lava rock.

I lay down on a beach strewn with tiny bits of seashell. The sun crept up and breathed the first hints of her fire onto my skin while clouds sailed overhead and beckoned me to climb on their billowy backs. I rolled over to bake the other side of my legs, the sand pillowing my cheek.

When the morning slipped higher into the sky, I climbed up a craggy hill, grateful for the calluses that protected my feet. Slender blades of grass bowed to the gusts of wind, sweeping the valleys before me. Gentle slopes rolled into rows of twisted grapevines, bending toward the earth with their corpulent fruit.

I inhaled the fertile haze that floated in the air and gazed over the vale to the city of Siracusa, an ancient queen who had withstood wars and plagues for more than two thousand years. She stood in her majesty, spires and gargoyles towering like sentinels above her cobbled streets while pigeons and doves nested in her terracotta tiles. Once again, she was occupied by an army bent on owning her and destroying the freedom of her citizens. The wind dried my teary eyes until the screech of seagulls drew my attention back to the sea.

Papa's boat bobbed on the water. He pulled in a load of fish and small octopi, opened the mouth of the net, and let them flip and tumble into the boat. Worry for the strain on my father made me shiver; he was more tired every day and sick so often. I slid down the rocky hill and hurried to the dock to meet him.

The heavy scratch of wagon wheels on gravel approached from a distance, and my shoulders relaxed when our hired man, Aviano, rode up.

The clomp of Aviano's weathered boots on the pier dulled against the spongy softness of the wood. He pulled his hat back, exposing gray hair and deep furrows around his eyes. "*Signore* De'Angelis, you and Marianna can return home. I will get this catch loaded and taken to market for you right away, no?"

Gratitude for Aviano filled my heart as Papa tossed my dress to me and stepped from the boat onto the pier. I slipped the dress over my head and covered my wet suit.

"Mama did tell me she needed my help today, Papa . . . and we can have lunch together."

Papa lifted his arms in protest. "I have work to do. You and your mother worry too much."

"What is so bad about your wife and daughter wanting you to be at home with them?" I shook my hand in the direction of home. "*Andiamo*, Papa, let's go. You know we cannot keep Mama waiting."

He dropped his head and mumbled protests behind me while we walked up the pier. Our old wagon creaked under my father's feet as he climbed up and gripped the reins of our horse, Tesoro. "Come, Tesoro my friend, we have lost the battle once more."

I leapt up beside him and shaded my eyes with my hand. "What a magical day, Papa. Aviano will go to market to sell the fish, and you will become richer even while you rest."

"Rest. Bah, you and your mama worry, worry, worry. But I know when I am out-voted."

A deep growl and cloud of dust rose over the landscape; a convoy of trucks, their doors stamped with black swastikas, passed in front of us like a pack of wolves headed for Siracusa. Tesoro stomped and whinnied, and Papa's face blanched white. The reins slipped from his hands. I grabbed them and called to Tesoro over the din. "Shhhh, *Amico Mio, calma . . . calma. . . .*"

At last the trucks disappeared. Papa sniffed and laid his scratchy hand over mine. "Do not let them frighten you, Marianna. We survived the last war; God will provide the way through this one."

A gray pallor still haunted his face. I leaned in and kissed his whiskered cheek. "We will say prayers tonight, Papa. And we will block the war from our minds for a wonderful meal and afternoon with Mama." I swallowed the bitterness left in the wake of the trucks and clicked my tongue to set Tesoro on our way.

The rest of the trip home was peaceful, the songs of the gulls fading in the distance as the road curved in front of the tall stone walls of our farmhouse.

My mother stood in the kitchen in her purple paisley dress and cooked on the cast iron stove, her dark hair pulled up in a smooth twist on her head. I wrapped my arms around her waist from behind and squeezed. "Thank you, Mama, for having me go with Papa this morning. The sky was the most beautiful it has ever been and the sea rocked me like a baby in its arms."

Mama laughed quietly and turned to face me. "Eh, I am not sure a young woman of almost eighteen could be considered a baby, but I am happy for you, sweet Mari. Did you catch many fish?"

"Well . . . I think Papa sacrificed a few to let me swim, but we still had a good day."

She touched my nose with her tapered finger as my father stomped into the room and sat at the table. "The bigger sacrifice is at market today."

Mama waved a wet cloth in the air. "So much complaining." She wiped the countertop with the cloth. "I have spoiled you is the problem; maybe you do not appreciate the time with your wife like you should."

Papa stuck out his lower lip and held out his hands, palms up. "What spoiled? Aviano does not call in the customers at the market like I do. We lose money. But I am being ambushed by my family and even my hired man once again."

My mother's eyes softened when she looked at my father. "Ambushed? Aviano is lonely and bored since Adele died. I sent him to find you because he needs work to stay busy and to earn wages."

I reached for a stack of dishes in the cupboard above the sink and carried them to the table. The porcelain plates rang a muted chime against the thick wood when I set our places. "Mama, you can mention to our neighbors that *L'Amici di Carita* still needs many donations of food. We are also searching for new members to help since the Germans have made so many of the boys enlist. We can hardly call ourselves The Friends of Charity if we have no friends, can we?" I swallowed the lump in my throat when I thought about the neighbor boys who had been a part of us; some were only fifteen yet had been forced into military service—even into battle.

My mother's face had paled at my words, so I quickly changed the subject. "I will see to the animals before my bath then come and help you finish lunch."

I unhitched Tesoro from our wagon and led him to his stall for feed. I patted our mare, Matilda, as I passed by her stall. She moved like we were one when we took our rides in the valleys; Tesoro, for all his brute strength, let me lead him like a lamb. Our two milk cows lumbered behind me to the barn each evening and reminded me of my mother's aunts—wide hips rocking back and forth, their bellies round and soft. Aviano did the milking most days, but I fed them all.

I grabbed the bucket of dried corn from inside the shed next to the chicken coop. The chickens, who had escaped the enclosure yesterday, scurried in behind me as I walked through the wire door to toss them a treat. I held the door steady to keep it from smacking against two strutting hens who were always the last of the brood to catch up and whose pale green eggs had the richest flavor. A dozen chickens pecked at the ground and stood at my feet in anticipation of their meal. Bruno always laughed at my "pets" that flapped their wings and perched on my extended arms eating the corn right from the palm of my hand. I had sneaked fertile eggs into my room more than once as a child just to watch them hatch.

After all the animals were fed, I hurried back to the house. Twenty minutes later, I'd finished my bath, and my braid lay damp and heavy down my back. Mama uncorked a dark bottle she took from the pantry, and the well of a crystal dish turned gold as she poured it full of olive oil. She glanced over her shoulder at me.

"I forgot to mention—on your way to Franca's sometime, you may see the Scalvone's grandson, Massimo. He just arrived on leave from the mainland to help his grandparents with their farm."

I felt my face flush. The young man who had caught me looking at him in the field the day before must have been this grandson.

My mother placed the olive oil back on the shelf. "The women in town said to tell you he is very handsome."

I coughed away the tickle in the back of my throat and grabbed a handful of silverware. "Ah, Mama, the women in town are like a hundred mothers clicking their tongues at me when I fish with Papa; they think my skin is too bronzed to attract a man." I laid each utensil in its place on the table before I put my hands on my hips and lowered my brows at my mother. "And you sound like Franca; she says I should swoon and pine for men like she does. But I have Bruno, and a brother is the only young man I care to be around. If I need more male attention, perhaps Bruno and Laura's baby will be a boy."

And perhaps it would be better to walk another way to the Chessari's home and avoid the Scalvone's field. I grabbed a steamy loaf of bread from the stove and tossed it back and forth between my hands so it wouldn't blister my fingers. "It is much more important to me that we find a way to get the Nazis out of here, Mama. *Madonna Mia*, have you heard the stories at the market about how many people died in Africa? We . . . I need to do something to help."

I placed the loaf of bread on the table. Mama walked up and lifted my chin with her hand. "You give me such pride in all you do, *Carina*. But you cannot stop the war and sacrifice your future because this insanity is upon us. You will never be able to end or justify any of it, my daughter. And you cannot protect or save everyone. Perhaps you worry too much."

I pressed my cheek against my mother's before I went to the cupboard for more dishes. "I do not worry more, or work any harder than the people I love."

Mama sighed and tossed her dish cloth over her shoulder before she filled the bowls I brought her with rigatoni. Papa came back into the room and the three of us sat together while the steam from the pasta filled our noses and its thick buttery flavor filled our mouths. I looked at my mother across the table, and Papa's words on the boat echoed back; her eyes were "soft and dark as a mother doe's."

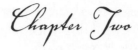

THE FAMILIAR CLINK OF HEAVY dishes on marble could be heard all the way from where I stood barefooted in our garden the next afternoon, and I knew my mother was back at work in the kitchen. My feet sank into the warm, moist soil as I stepped between each row of vegetables and picked a basketful of lettuce and cucumbers for an evening meal. The smell of olive oil and bubbling pasta sauce swirled through the yard and beckoned me into the house.

I cranked the handle at the well, and the bucket rose to the surface. A sheet of clear, cold water spilled over the edge and I washed the vegetables, using the rest of the water to rinse my feet and hands before I headed to the kitchen. The moment I entered the house I stopped in my tracks with a sigh; Uncle Mimmo and Aunt Pasqualina sat in the kitchen. They had already spent three weeks with us and now, after only a few days' reprieve, they had come back to "help."

As soon as I'd placed the vegetables on the counter by the stove, my uncle started his tirade again, his plump face red as an overripe tomato ready to burst. His eyes bulged and his bald head shook while he pounded the kitchen table with his thick fist. "Mussolini betrayed every Italian born on this sacred continent; we are halfway through 1943, and we are still trapped under the Nazis. He stabbed us in the back with his promises, sold our souls, and condemned us all."

I wondered with dismay how many times my uncle could repeat the same frustrations that did nothing but spin in circles. Papa sat next to him and my aunt at our kitchen table and bobbed his head in support of Uncle Mimmo.

Aunt Pasqualina pushed her silk scarf back off her head and pulled the lower lid of her left eye down with her finger. "Mussolini has the eye of the devil, and may God curse him for it. Mimmo did not want to tell you, but this morning when he was helping you, he pulled up his first net and there were five dead fish in his catch. *Five*." She shook her head with a moan, her thin face creased in a deep frown. The lace trim of a handkerchief poked out of the sleeve of her black sweater at the wrist; she pulled it free and wiped her nose. "It is a sign, dead fish first thing in the morning. That evil man has cast the eye of the devil on all of us."

I forced back a smile and laid down the knife I used to slice the cucumbers. I tsked my tongue. "If the war has us all so upset that we are afraid the devil is cursing fish then maybe it is time for us to do something about it."

Uncle Mimmo slapped his hand on his forehead with a moan. "Once again she speaks of uprisings." He waved his hand at my father. "Adamo, can you finally convince your daughter that peasants and fishermen cannot defeat the devil?"

Papa shrugged his shoulders and stuck out his bottom lip. "But who is to say that we cannot defeat him?"

I held onto the back of his chair. "You are right, Uncle; if Hitler and Mussolini are the devil then we have God on our side. With God at the head of the army, we can and will win."

Uncle Mimmo covered his face with his hands then tipped them back, palms up. "Such an innocent you are, Marianna. You make it sound so easy. We are not in God's army; Mussolini forces us to be Nazis."

My muscles stiffened all the way up my spine and I blinked back tears. "We are not and never will be Nazis."

My mother left the food on the stove and patted Aunt Pasqua's bony arm. "Perhaps we have worried enough about war for today. But. . . ." She laid her hands on her heart and looked at my uncle. "Mimmo, you are Adamo's brother. You have helped us so much. You are a hero. But you must not feel you have to move in for a while just because Bruno will be gone on duty; we have Marianna and Aviano. And you know how Pasqua fears that the Germans will take your home and use it for their headquarters. Please do not stay away from your safety in Sortino."

Aunt Pasqua smiled almost shyly. She rose from her chair and hugged my mother. Uncle Mimmo stood too and held out his arms to my father. "Ah . . . such words of love. I do anything I can for my little brother." The two of them embraced and patted each other with gusto on the back.

Normally I would have laughed inside at my mother's gushing efforts to send my aunt and uncle on their way, but the news that they may move in with us hit me like a hammer. I was still trying to reclaim my breath when Bruno and Laura walked in. Relief and gratitude buoyed my sinking heart.

I hugged Bruno, then grabbed Laura by both of her hands and kissed her cheek. "You look beautiful as a mama, Laura. You have had a good week, no?"

She laid her hand on her rounded belly and smiled. "Not so good this week. But I feel the baby stretch and kick me clear into my ribs now. It is very strong, I know."

I hugged them both again. "Oh, I can hardly wait to be an aunt. I will come and help you any time you need." The joy over their baby did not thwart for me the anguish about my aunt and uncle possibly moving in with us.

Bruno looked with concern into my teary eyes and whispered something in Laura's ear. He nodded his head at me and then toward the back door. I looked at my parents and my aunt and uncle. "*Scusatemi* . . . I forgot to feed the chickens."

Aunt Pasqualina sat back down at the table, the deep crease back in her forehead. She pointed her finger at me. "Wait a minute, Marianna. Where are you and your brother going? You are always on the go, and you are the reason we came back. We came to remind you it is time for you to find a husband before all the good men are killed in the war. The way you fish like a boy with your father and run the countryside on your errands for the poor is going to ruin your chances. You do not need to be in the middle of soldiers and a war. You have a duty to settle down so your papa will not worry about you when he is so tired."

She shifted her focus to my father and pointed at him. "Adamo, she is your daughter. You tell her where her duties lie before she worries you to death."

Mama and Papa shook their heads no, and Papa opened his mouth to speak, but Uncle Mimmo waved his hand in the air with a tsk of his tongue. "Pasqua, you have your own agenda. Talking about Mussolini and the Nazis is far more important than a marriage. So is helping with the fishing until my brother is feeling better. Besides, Adamo said he wants her to choose or even go to America for more schooling. Leave the girl alone."

Aunt Pasqua shook her finger at her husband. "Higher education is for vulgar girls who do not obey their husbands and offend God. You are her uncle and must know Marianna is almost eighteen. I was sixteen when you married me. She must marry before she becomes too independent. She is turning wilder every day out on her bicycle and horses and even out on that boat like she is not even a woman. She does not spend enough time in the kitchen. What kind of a man will want her?"

The temperature in the room seemed to spike by thirty degrees while my aunt and uncle argued about my future and Papa waved his finger back and forth at both of them. "We are proud of our daughter and all the help she gives the poor. . . ."

Bruno spoke above the melee. "Mama, Papa, everyone, I have not had any time with Marianna. If you will excuse us to be late for dinner, I would like to go with her on a walk."

Papa winked at me and smiled. "*Si, si*, take your time and enjoy the evening."

I spun around and bolted out the back door, Bruno right at my heels. I gulped in air to calm my temper as Bruno came up beside me. I looped my arm through his. "Before you and Laura arrived, Uncle Mimmo was shouting so loud Mussolini himself probably heard and is on his way to arrest us. And if Aunt Pasqua gives me one more speech about marriage, I will run away to a convent."

Bruno chuckled while we walked through the yard to the road in front of the house. I leaned against my brother and poked him in the ribs for laughing at me. He kissed the top of my head. "All will be well, Mari. Mama and Papa are not bossy and superstitious like the other relatives. And who knows? Maybe God will provide a miracle, and Uncle Mimmo and Aunt Pasqua will leave."

"That is what I am praying for. I love them, but *Madonna Mia*, I've gotten thinner and thinner just from escaping the kitchen so much when they are here. And when I do stay I cannot eat; my stomach ties into a knot with all that doomsday talk. Why has everyone lost hope? We should be discussing what we can do to help or stop the war, not how we are all going to die at the hands of Hitler."

The wind kicked up, salty and fresh, as if the foamy Mediterranean had cleansed it of the smoke and debris of war before whipping it back to shore. The trees shook their leaves overhead while Bruno kicked a speckled rock and a cloud of dust flew up on the toe of his leather shoe. Each time we caught up to the rock, he kicked it out in front of him again.

"You have always wished you could be tough, Mari. Remember the time we threw rocks into Uncle Mimmo's fish pond from behind his barn? You were mad as a badger when you could not throw the rocks all the way to the pond."

"It was humiliating. All I could do was gather the rocks for you." I stepped in front of Bruno and kicked the speckled rock all the way down the road.

Bruno laughed. "See what I mean? Always wanting to be tough."

I locked my arm through his and gazed up at his handsome face. He had Mama's dark eyes and Papa's unruly hair, cut short for the military. I was grateful that we lived in the verdant countryside with quiet fields between us and our neighbors. These were the only moments we could grasp for fun or peace; not just the absence of enemy soldiers or relatives bombing the Germans with their pounding fists, but sweetness and reassurance floated in the air when I was with Bruno.

My shoulders relaxed while daylight slipped down toward the mountains and passed its duty to a vibrant moon. Before I knew it, we were at the edge of the Chessari vineyards.

The Chessaris owned what seemed like miles of land that covered the wide valley in thickets of grape vines divided into rows, some vines so tall you could walk beneath them. Now that Bruno had married Franca's sister, Laura Chessari, the guest cottage in the back of the vineyard was their new home. Someday, after we could awake from the nightmare of war, the estate would be Bruno's full-time work.

The gnarled trunks of the vines lifted the thick foliage like umbrellas overhead while the fruit hung in clusters of rubies. The moon bathed the landscape in twilight. The grape leaves turned silver and cast shadows on the powdery earth below. Bruno snapped fruit from a vine, hopped atop the rocky wall, and held his hand down to help me up. I jumped up beside my brother, and he gave me some of the grapes.

No matter how tightly I had squeezed my lips as a child, juice still dripped down my chin and onto the front of my clothes every time I bit into the grapes. Many times I had stood at the sink behind our house and scrubbed my stained blouses with soap, soda water, and a brush while my mother checked my progress with consternation. But playing with the juice-filled fruit had always been an irresistible affair for Bruno, the Chessari girls, and me.

The encroachment of war cast a spell on the vineyard when Bruno popped the grapes between his front teeth and challenged himself to shoot a stream of juice farther and farther, a game we had played since childhood. A chill crawled up my arms when the dark stream spewed from his mouth and soaked like . . . watery blood into the ground in front of him. The muscles in my throat tightened until I could barely speak.

"Is there anything that can be done so you will not have to go into battle again, Bruno? You will be fighting side by side with the Nazis. It is insanity to fight, to possibly lose your life under the rule of a monster. I have heard that more and more of our people are secretly joining the partisans. Mussolini says the partisans are traitors, but maybe they are our last hope. If you stall your departure somehow, we could find a way that you can at least serve on the right side."

Bruno's eyes tightened when he stared straight into mine. "No matter how I feel about it, I could never risk joining a secret rebel army. If I disappeared, the Nazis would come for Laura first, then they would find the rest of you. They have my name and our address on rosters or papers. There is nowhere for us all to hide and no place truly safe. I have to go. I am as much a prisoner as the men in the camps."

My muscles slacked. "When do you leave?"

"I report to Messina in two weeks."

The grapes were too bitter now. I dropped the last two to the ground and watched with blurred vision as they rolled down the embankment.

Bruno jumped from the wall and helped me down. He put his arm around me. "Marianna, please do not cry. I will fight every soldier who gets between me and my home. I will come back. I promise you."

"I know you will do all that you can, but what if it is not enough? There has to be a way to overthrow Mussolini, to refuse his power and betrayal. I cannot bear our helplessness."

He squeezed my hand. "Are you still frustrated that you cannot throw the rocks?"

"Maybe . . . but I am not a child anymore. Who says I cannot throw them somehow?"

A deep frown creased his face. "Do not do anything foolish, Marianna. No more talk of rebels or armies. I will fight for the both of us."

"You need to concentrate on your own safety. I will not be foolish." I forced a smile and hugged my brother. "Besides, we are in the countryside away from all the arguments and battles, no? What would the soldiers want with a winery or fisherman's house?"

Chapter Three

FABRIC TARPS HUNG OVER ROW after row of long wooden tables of vegetables, fruits, and meats. The covering offered shade but stifled the air with the pungent odors of fish, plucked chickens, and the rusty stench of butchered meat clutched in the claws of metal hooks. Mama and I stood inside our booth, the tables loaded with the catches of the day: cod, octopi, anchovies, and calamari. To keep the flies at bay, we waved a stick with a ribbon tied to the end over their shiny bodies.

While relieved that Uncle Mimmo and Aunt Pasqualina had gone back to Sortino, I was filled with worries. Papa was ill again, his handsome face even thinner this morning. My mother and I had to sell our fish at the open market. It was my second home, but I would rather catch than sell fish any day.

The women always haggled with me about the price, so I shook my head no with a tsk of my tongue when I heard any hesitation in their voices. I wanted to surprise my worried father with a purse full of coins when we returned. Sometimes when a customer offered a low price, Mama said my name very quietly so no one could hear but me. I'd turn to her, and if she lifted one eyebrow, then I knew that particular *Signora*, on my mother's signal, would get the bargain she hoped for.

When the sun tilted toward the top of the sky, the freshness of the fish had reached its limit and our work was done. I carried a big white bucket to our table, scooped out a handful of salt, and poured it over the pan of shimmering anchovies. Mama and I grabbed the cod by their tails and whipped them back into a bucket, then carried all the buckets and pans of leftovers to our wagon to take to the poor and homeless.

When all of our supplies were loaded and cleaned, Mama and I tipped the wooden water barrel we kept in back of the wagon and ran water over our hands. I lathered the lavender soap my mother made every spring all up and down my arms and cleaned beneath each fingernail. With a scrub of my face and brush through my hair, I hopped up in the wagon while Mama finished her cleaning.

I reached for Tesoro's reins, looked behind me, and inhaled sharply in surprise; the elderly *Signora* Scalvone had just exited the market and was headed straight for us, her hand gripping the arm of her grandson, Massimo. My chance encounter with him at the pasture had been so brief he would probably not remember me. But I scanned the plaza for somewhere to go before they came closer and I had to find out. All of my friends and the other vendors were busy packing their wares or were still occupied with customers. Mama still dallied at the back of the wagon. I checked over my shoulder again; the Scalvones were getting closer.

I jumped down from my seat and busied myself with Tesoro's harness. I readjusted the straps and tightened the buckles, watching my surroundings only from the corner of my eye. *Signora* Scalvone stopped at the back corner of our wagon, where she grasped Mama's hands and kissed her cheeks. Mama patted the woman's rounded shoulders. "How are you today, my dear neighbor? And who is this handsome young man you have with you?"

Their conversation muffled when I moved to the other side and crouched down to inspect Tesoro's hooves. Then my mother's voice called out loud and clear, "Marianna, our neighbors would like to say hello to you."

It was a long walk to the back of the wagon. I swallowed the dryness in my throat and avoided the gaze of the grandson, but courtesy required that I raise my eyes when the *Signora* introduced us. "Massimo, this is the lovely Marianna De'Angelis, the *Signora's* only daughter."

Massimo reached out his hand to shake mine with a wry smile and a lift of his dark brows. "What a pleasure Miss Marianna, but have we not met before?"

A flame sparked beneath my skin and I bit my tongue. I averted my gaze and focused on the ornate scrolls carved in stone above the windows of a nearby church. I did not put out my hand.

Mama inquired about *Signore* Scalvone and the length of Massimo's visit, and I lost the battle between my pride and the magnetic force of the young man beside me. While he chatted with my mother, I darted a glimpse in his direction, startled by what I saw: eyes framed in black lashes, irises dark as coal, a whiskered jawline carved in alabaster.

Mama talked of the weather and the health of the *Signora* and her husband until they all shook hands in farewell. I had kept my eyes busy observing Tesoro, the buildings, the clouds. I finally faced them again and Massimo smiled, his full lips parted over perfect, white teeth. My head took a swim and I stepped backward on the cobblestone.

"*Mi scusi*, I have to drive the wagon."

I gulped in the air that had eluded me and lost my footing on the step of the wagon when I tried to climb up. A firm hand gripped me by the elbow.

"Be careful; this city is full of enough injuries."

I looked back at Massimo, shocked that he had kept up with me. I almost tripped again before I climbed up and slid down onto my seat. He stayed beside the wagon, a brown fedora gripped in his hand. "*Signorina*, I did not mean to startle or frighten you the other day at my grandparents' pasture. It was nice to meet a neighbor, after all."

I was being ridiculous; he was only my neighbor. I forced myself to meet Massimo's eyes and smiled. "It was very nice to meet you too." I gripped Tesoro's reins to steady the twitch in my hands.

Massimo slipped his hat back on his head and tipped it down with his fingers. "Perhaps we will see each other again sometime. *Buon Giorno*, Marianna."

"*Buon Giorno* . . . Massimo."

He took his grandmother's arm and they walked away. The pressure on my chest eased. Mama climbed up beside me and patted me on the knee.

"The Scalvones and their grandson will be eating dinner with us next Sunday afternoon."

An itch prickled up my spine. "They will? Only one week from now? When did you invite them? Before I was standing there? Why? I am . . . not sure that is a good idea, Mama."

My mother lifted one eyebrow. "Oh? And why would that be, Marianna? You are usually so happy to have friends for dinner."

My mouth ticked at the corners; when my mother lifted her eyebrow, she already knew the answer. I struggled for words. "Well, the Scalvones are old and it is so hot outside. I worry about them traveling to our home in the heat of the day."

She patted my leg. "Such a thoughtful girl. You can help me take very good care of them."

Tension pinched at my shoulders, and I looked down at the reins in my hands. Mama rubbed her hand on my back.

"You do not have to live the life of a nun to help your community or family."

"Bah—not a nun, just a citizen who has more to do than swoon over handsome men."

"So you think Massimo is handsome?"

"Mama . . . please."

"All right then, give Tesoro the lead so we can get the fish to your friends and hurry back to Papa."

The words my mother had spoken refused to quiet in my head, and my elbow burned all the way home where Massimo had touched me.

* * *

For five days in a row, Aviano and I fished and vended at the market while Papa rested. The tomatoes would be overripe and falling from the vines if Mama did not bottle them this week, so she stayed at home to finish the task. Standing at the steaming pots of tomatoes had seemed a chore when I helped her each year, but today I would trade it for my father's good health.

The world seemed strange in the mornings on the way to the sea— quiet, as if the birds held their chatter and the bees their harvesting until Papa rode by and sang or whistled again. My palms had grown a new layer of calluses, and my shoulders ached at the end of every day.

We stopped at a church so I could light a candle and pray every morning on the way to market; the moments inside the chapel were a small tonic that gave me hope. Aviano was not religious; many times he said that the day his wife's spirit left her body, it took his spirit with it. He waited in the wagon, snorted his tobacco, and gazed straight ahead while I ran inside for the daily ritual.

I was thankful for Aviano's company when we entered town. The German guards snarled at the public more often since their massive loss in Stalingrad the previous winter, especially when their troops surrendered to the Soviet Union in May and to Britain in North Africa the very next day. I filled my prayers with gratitude for these defeats. If Hitler and Mussolini lost then maybe Italy would be free, my brother would not have to leave, and so many others could return home.

The business at the market gave me a chance to see many friends and stay informed on loved ones now cast across the continent. It was sunny above the tarps of the booths. The bins and baskets of watermelons, sweet cantaloupe, and peaches so ripe they sprayed juice into the air with every bite, were not nearly so plentiful as in years past. But even with supplies depleted or stolen by soldiers, the farmers managed to harvest another day's fruit from the trees and vegetables from the fields. Many donated their leftovers at the end of the week for our *L'Amici di Carita*.

Five-year-old Liliana Leva kept me company at the market. Fresh slabs of pork hung on hooks from the wood frame of her family's booth two stations down. Many days the Nazi officers confiscated the Levas' meat before they had a chance to sell it. The poor family sometimes sold only pieces of remaining pork to the public and went home almost empty handed.

Liliana's father swatted at the flies that swarmed for their dinner while his two oldest sons played games and chased each other, their uncombed hair like pieces of hay poking out of the bale. *Signora* Leva had recently given birth again, and her husband carted the rest of the children to the market every day to give her rest. Such a helpful man was the talk of the market between the women when their envy, longing, and jealousy bounced his status from revered husband to a silly man who babied his wife.

The crowds had died down. Aviano ate an apple on a bench under his favorite elm in the plaza while I tended to the last trickle of customers. I had known Liliana from the time she bulged and grew in her mother's womb. Now she sat on a milk crate inside of our booth, her dark head bowed over a plate of pasta, boiled eggs, and olives she ate with her fingers. I sat on my own crate and folded my arms across my knees as I watched the little cherub who was my friend.

"How is your mama, Lili? Is she well?"

She lifted her head at an angle to see me from beneath long bangs and scrunched her dark eyes, deep in thought. "She is home letting the baby suck milk from her chest. He is hungry a lot."

I stifled a laugh, pulled out a fresh sheet of newspaper, and wrapped five fish into a package. Lili had finished her food and watched me tip a bucket of water and wash my hands. "Step up on the crate and let me smooth your hair for you, Lili. I bet your mama did not have a chance to fix it for you this morning."

Lili put her dish on the table and climbed on top of the crate in a blue dress, the bow in back tied extra snug to make it fit. She smiled at me and I dipped a cloth into the bucket to wash her face and greasy fingers. I did not have a comb, so I used my hands to untangle the dark hair that twisted and snagged down the little girl's back. I wet my fingers and ran them down the length of her hair, then divided the sections and braided it nice and neat. Lili turned around on the crate, wrapped her arms around my neck, and kissed me on each cheek with pink rosebud lips. I laughed and kissed her back then worried when she looked past me and her eyes widened in fear. She jumped from the crate as two German guards approached my table.

"*Me ne devo andare*, I have to go to Papa right away."

Lili scrambled off, and the guards loomed in front of me, faces stoic, the starch in their gray uniforms long spent. I inhaled extra air and held my head level. "May I interest you in some fresh fish for your meal today?"

The shorter soldier smiled, but his companion stared and held his lips tight like he had swallowed something bitter. His slow, steely gaze scanned down my body and stung like icy daggers on my skin. I flinched when another soldier shouted from the other side of the market, his voice like the boom of a cannon. The taller soldier sneered at me, shouted something in German back to their comrade, and both of the soldiers stalked away.

I leaned against the table in relief and rubbed my neck where it throbbed at the base. I looked around for Lili and spotted Massimo Scalvone looking at me from a fruit stand three rows away. A nervous tingle stirred in my chest and I jumped when a nearby motorcycle roared past the market.

Massimo nodded his head in salutation, and I lifted my hand in a small wave before he turned and purchased a watermelon from a woman in a black scarf. He took a step my way, then stopped and turned in the other direction and left. He had been at the market every day this week, but each time had waved or nodded at me, hesitated, and then gone the other way. A battle between relief and disappointment each time he left surprised and unsettled me. I had plenty to do and worry about without thoughts of Massimo bothering me. Still, he had been so friendly before, almost anxious to talk to me. But now he kept his distance.

I picked up the fish I had wrapped for the Leva family and held my other hand cupped around my mouth. "Liliana. Come back, *bambina*, and get your package; I wrapped some fish for your mama today."

Lili ran to me, her bare feet making little pitter-pats on the cobblestone before she jumped up in my arms.

"*Grazie*, Mari. I have to run to Papa if soldiers come close. I think he is worried they will try to steal me. He said some soldiers steal children if they are Jews, but I am not a Jew—just my friend Anika is and they already stole her."

Horror for Anika and her family gripped me. Anika Lenni was Lili's age. I did not know her family but had seen her quiet mother shopping in the market while Lili and Anika played with their rag dolls at the Levas' booth. *Signore* Leva told me the Lennis were dairy owners until the Germans had taken the father away. They later confiscated their home and land. *Signora* Lenni had lived with her three children in one of the alleyways, forbidden to go home or to stay with any families who knew them. We had given her fish every day and refused the coins she offered from a shaky hand. When they disappeared, I had assumed it was to go stay with family or that they had found somewhere to live. Now I knew that tiny Anika with her shiny black eyes was gone. Her mother and brothers must have been taken too.

My arms weakened, and I lowered Lili back to the ground. I crossed myself in prayer, and Lili tilted her head with a frown. "Why are you praying, Marianna?"

I knelt on the gritty cobblestone and held her by her shoulders. "Listen to me, *Carina*. You are very smart to run to your papa and you must always listen to him. Most people are good, but some men and even women are very bad. If you are ever in trouble and you cannot find your papa, you hide. Hide just to be extra safe and careful. *Hai capito*? Do you understand, Lili? We will say prayers that your friend Anika will be back, so do not worry."

Her eyes were big as the moon when she nodded her head up and down. I hugged her and brushed off my knees when I stood. The day seemed stifling hot now, and I had no more desire to sell fish. Today I would take an extra turn by some of the destitute families on the way home and give them all the fish I could.

Sadness swelled with the breeze that lifted the tarps like parachutes overhead. It was time to go home. The morning sales had been slow, but I still had earnings to show Papa. Aviano returned, and we started the chore of packing the leftover spoils. In spite of my conflicted feelings, I could not stop my eyes from searching the aisles for the return of Massimo Scalvone.

Chapter Four
MASSIMO

I WAS A RUNAWAY TRAIN. A fool. My eyes refused to look away every time I saw Marianna De'Angelis, and the perspiration from the heat of the day could not validate the sweat on my palms when I caught myself watching her again.

I surrendered to the excuses I made for going to the market—as if my grandparents were in daily need of fresh produce or meat when they lived on a farm.

I was blessed, doomed, and damned from the moment I saw her for the first time. I had seen something, someone watching me while I loaded the rocks in the pasture. The dark silhouette, almost hidden behind the tree, had moved forward. I'd ducked for cover behind the pasture wall and grabbed rocks to defend myself.

What I had thought was a spy lurking behind a tree peeked over the wall, and the illusion of an enemy melted into the graceful face and liquid eyes of an angel. Huge grin on my face, heart kicking, I'd had only seconds to take in her beautiful image before she darted away.

Perhaps the daughter of a nearby farmer or fisherman, a lost lamb—whoever she was, I'd jumped atop the wall to find where she had gone in the flash of an eye only to catch her in retreat and decidedly unwilling to heed my call. When she'd rounded the corner behind a group of cypress trees, the weight of my disappointment surprised and frustrated me. I'd jumped down from the wall with resignation—it was for the better. Beauty or not, friend or foe, she'd had the wisdom to escape me. I walked back to the wagon to finish my task and tried to dismiss the rumble in my chest that came from more than the passing of war planes overhead.

Now here I was again, only today I was the spy. Dinner at her home tomorrow would be a torture that could break my will. Marianna's braid cascaded like a wide black ribbon of silk down her back. When a little girl jumped into her arms and kissed her cheeks, I felt her satiny skin on my own lips and laughed out loud at myself for being an idiot. Luckily the woman who sold the watermelons made small talk and looked up as if she was in on the joke.

"You need only one watermelon, *Signore* Scalvone?"

I broke my focus from Marianna. "Excuse me? Oh, *si, si*, just one today, thank you. And please call me Massimo."

The woman smiled, smoothed her hair, and opened her palm. I paid for the fruit and bristled in alarm when two German soldiers walked toward the De'Angelis's booth and the little girl with Marianna ran away. The soldiers' stop was brief but I continued to amble through the market in search of more fruit until it seemed certain they would not return. Marianna looked pale when they left, and she leaned against the table of her booth. She lifted her chin, looked at me, and I nodded my head. I took a step in her direction and stopped—a German soldier stood alone at the other end of the market and stared me down. My suspicions mounted; someone had been sent to watch me. The lives and safety of so many hinged on my every move. My own family stood in jeopardy over my simplest mistake. I was an idiot to be this close to Marianna.

I took my ridiculous watermelon and forced myself to leave the market without passing the fish stand.

Chapter Five

MARIANNA

~⚬~

THE MOMENT WE ARRIVED HOME from church the next day, my mother put me to work in the kitchen. I chopped vegetables and then stirred the marinara sauce, plump with chunks of ham, before I put the big black pot of water for the pasta on to boil. Olive oil floated on top of the water and swirled like a kaleidoscope as the clear liquid turned to steam. I opened the squeaky door of the stove to stoke the fire, my face already so warm in anticipation of the Scalvones' arrival that the flames almost scorched my cheeks.

A pitcher almost slipped from my hands when Papa sneezed in the next room, and I'd dropped two eggs out in the coop when a fussy hen jumped from her roost. My mother's brow creased when I told her what happened. "My goodness, Marianna, if the Scalvones do not arrive soon I am worried you will catch the house on fire."

I grumbled in frustration and my mother's eyes softened. My father sang in the other room in a way that would have usually made me laugh. I put the bowl of grated parmigiano on the table. "Papa not so loud; today is the Sabbath."

I did not know what that had to do with him singing, but I yearned for peace and quiet. I squeezed my eyes shut in frustration that my mother had invited the Scalvones to dinner. So many things needed to be done—helping my parents, watching the war, and working all I could to help our neighbors and country. I certainly did not need to worry over people who made me feel uncomfortable.

I heard Bruno and Laura talking to someone outside, someone with a rich, familiar voice. I almost dropped the stack of plates I was carrying to the table. "*Managia*," I mumbled in frustration. I set the plates down, grabbed a white napkin, and stuck it in my pocket.

I glanced out the big side window to the garden. No one was in sight. I slipped out and ran across the lawn to the well. I pulled up a bucketful of cold water, took a deep drink, and dipped the napkin inside. My face was instantly cooler when I wiped it with the wet cotton cloth. The sweet cry of birds and hum of bees at work in the flower bed brought me back to myself. I was home. I could do this.

I came through the back door and made my way to the parlor. *Signore* Scalvone and his wife sat side by side in two high-back chairs and smiled like little wrinkled children with their arms folded on their laps. The *Signore* and Massimo stood when I entered, and I nodded at them without meeting their eyes. My nerves eased when I saw my brother and his wife on the settee. Laura pressed her cheek against mine when I leaned down to greet her. I slipped into a chair next to my mother.

I willed my eyes to stay away from Massimo, but they betrayed me over and over. He wore a yellow shirt with baggy brown trousers, and the depth of his laugh stirred the air and brought back the nervousness that had eased at the sight of Bruno and Laura.

The conversation soon turned to the hopelessness of war, and I rolled my eyes at Bruno. At the first hint of a break in conversation, he spoke up. "Marianna and I should give Massimo a tour of our property before dinner."

I wished I was sitting next to my brother so I could pinch him.

Massimo smiled. "That sounds like a nice idea. *Grazie*, Bruno." He patted his grandfather on the leg, and *Signore* Scalvone grinned.

I had always thought *Signore* Scalvone was delightful and kind. He wore black pants, a black sweater, and a black beret with a white cotton shirt. He chuckled in a raspy voice, "You young pretty ones go and enjoy yourselves outside. You do not need to worry today about ugly people in the war and all their evil threats. The sun is warm and happy; go and bask in it."

Signora Scalvone's eyes squinted in a supportive smile that did nothing to calm me when I followed my brother and Massimo outside.

The day seemed especially warm as we followed the winding path beside our garden to our barn. I let my brother play the host and tell Massimo about himself while I listened. Tesoro whinnied when we entered the barn, no doubt anticipating a snack. I reached into a bucketful of carrots I had pulled for him and Matilda that morning and handed some to Tesoro. I kept my focus on my horse's silky nose while he ground the carrots, and my hand was soon emptied.

Bruno introduced Massimo to our mare, Matilda, and our two milk cows. I could not imagine anything we could show Massimo that he had not seen many times at his grandparents' farm but he looked around with interest. He patted each cow on her scruffy head and told the cows it was very nice to meet them. Veins rippled beneath the skin of his hands as he moved them slowly and smoothly down Matilda's shiny black coat.

I cleared my throat. "Um. . . ." Both men looked at me with interest. "I already gave Matilda her treat this morning. I think we should go back to the garden area and sit on the chairs."

They followed me toward the house, their casual conversation about horses a chance for me to remain quiet. Although I tried to hurry my steps, the two of them stayed right behind me as I crossed our lawn, the grass so thick beneath my feet it was cool even in summer. The yard slanted down toward multiple rows of vegetables and the three wooden lawn chairs grouped under the shade of a bushy olive tree. I made it a few steps ahead and sat down on one of the chairs with my legs folded to the side. I needed a chance to catch my breath away from Massimo's presence. They walked toward me, and I spoke up. "I am a bit thirsty. Perhaps the two of you could go see the well and bring back a bucket of water so we can have a drink."

Massimo did not seem to hear me. He opened his arms as if embracing the garden before him. "Ah, now this looks like an oasis, a bit of paradise."

I detected a glimmer in my brother's eye. He pointed to the chair nearest me. "Well, thank you, Massimo; our mother loves her gardens. You should enjoy it a moment. Make yourself comfortable by Marianna, and I will go and get the water."

Bruno whisked away before I could argue. I looked over at our guest when he sat down beside me, and the warmth of the afternoon crept up my cheeks. Words had never escaped me before I met Massimo, and now my thoughts spun like a top. I kept my head bowed and smoothed the wrinkles in my skirt. Massimo leaned forward and rested his elbows on his knees. "You seem very interested in the ground today, Marianna."

I lifted my gaze and forced myself to meet his eyes, but Bruno returned from the well before I could unlock my tongue. He handed Massimo his cup of water. "So tell us about your life in Foggia, Massimo—your family, where you have been, everything."

Bruno handed me my water; I gulped it too fast, and I coughed. "Please pardon me; I need to help with dinner. The two of you can visit, and I will see you in the house."

I stood to leave, and Massimo jumped up. "I would like to help in the kitchen as well."

My breath escaped in a small puff. "Oh, no, please do not bother yourself; you are our guest today."

Massimo wrinkled his brow with a teasing smirk. "Well, then, it would not be nice to deny me my request, would it?"

I hesitated and nodded my head. "Um . . . no, I guess not. It would be very kind of you to help."

Bruno faked a little cough and grinned. "I think it was unfair to feed Tesoro his carrots in front of Matilda. I will go finish feeding her. If Laura asks, tell her I will be right back."

I glared at Bruno for abandoning me again, but he strolled away with a wave. I was on my own and alone with Massimo. I reached down and checked for a phantom pebble in my shoe, then gave a polite nod toward the house for him to follow.

When I opened the back door, my anxiety eased at the familiar green walls of our kitchen and the sight of my mother at the stove. Her hair was pulled up in an elegant knot, her dress covered by a worn apron tied around her waist. Massimo entered, and Mama's eyes registered surprise at the sight of us alone.

"Welcome again, Massimo. Please seat yourself here by the open window and relax if the parlor is too warm."

A chair scraped the wooden floor as she pulled it from the table and brushed it with the towel from her shoulder. Massimo stepped forward and lightly touched her on the arm. "Oh, please, do not bother yourself, *Signora*. I offered my services to your lovely daughter. I often help my grandmother in the kitchen."

I winced a little at the sideways glance she gave me before she smiled and answered him. "*Che bravo*, what lucky grandparents to have such a grandson in their home. How long is your visit?"

"Just for the summer. I am on leave and here specifically to help my grandparents; although they are taking such good care of me, I worry I am becoming spoiled and will never want to leave."

Mother tsked her tongue. "No, no, Massimo, I have passed their pastures at least twice this week and have seen you hard at work."

Massimo shook his head. "Please, *Signora*, do not be giving yourself delusions about me; they are devoted grandparents and repay me well above anything I could do for them."

His eyes were black as the olives from our trees, and they actually twinkled. I hoped my mouth had not gaped open while he was speaking. It did not seem possible that anyone—any man—could be this handsome and sophisticated and be standing in my kitchen. I wondered where he really came from and what he really was. There had to be more to his story; people just did not look this beautiful, speak this eloquently, and come to help cook in a kitchen of plaster walls and wooden floors. It seemed absurd to even look at him.

I sat down to wipe the spots from the glass goblets when my mother offered Massimo a chair right beside me. I stood and headed to the counter piled with vegetables. "Let me finish the salad, Mama, while you and Massimo visit."

Massimo did not take the chair my mother offered him. He followed me to the counter. "Oh, no, I was sincere in my offer to help."

He reached for the lettuce before I could. I stared down at the tomatoes and cucumbers and suddenly had no idea how to prepare a salad. He looked at me with a question in his eyes. "Do you have a bowl or platter for this?"

He held out the lettuce with a gentle smile, and I caught a glimpse of a dimple in his cheek. I was grateful when I heard my voice. "Yes, of course we do."

I reached above the sink, pulled down a porcelain platter, and put it on the counter. I grabbed the lettuce from Massimo and started tearing it into small pieces until I heard his low chuckle and he clasped his hand over mine. "You are a fierce little salad maker, *Signorina*. The poor lettuce is helpless in your hands."

A fire ignited on my skin where he touched me. The heat moved up my arm to my neck, my face. I stopped breathing altogether.

Papa's voice boomed into the room, and I jumped with a quick intake of breath. Papa looked right at Massimo. "Please come quickly, your grandmother has taken ill and she is asking for you."

We hurried into the parlor where *Signora* Scalvone lay back on our couch, her skin pasty and white. Her husband fanned her face, and Laura held her hand. Mama rushed in with a wet cloth and a glass of water.

The *Signora* tried to smile. "I am so sorry to interrupt your dinner, Camilla, but I think I had better go home."

We all nodded and reassured her we understood while disappointment lowered like a shadow on the room. I patted the *Signora* on the hand before Papa and Massimo helped her, half carrying her to the Scalvones' truck in front of the house. Massimo sat at the wheel while his grandmother laid her head against the back window between him and her husband. *Signore* Scalvone's face was somber when he waved goodbye to us from the passenger window.

The truck roared to life and they were gone in an instant. I watched the lights on the back of the truck until I could no longer see them.

* * *

Mourning doves announced the arrival of another June dawn through my bedroom window the next day. Papa had insisted that he fish with Aviano this morning. I stretched and lingered on the soft cotton sheets of my bed. Bright coral rays streamed in the window and lit up the floor. Today I would gather food and supplies from *L'Amici di Carita* with Franca and the others and take them into town.

I dipped my hands into the basin of fresh water I had carried up the stairs the night before and washed my face. A breeze came through the window and stirred my curtains from their slumber. I laid my towel on the floor, undressed, and stood on its thick rough fabric. A plump sponge swelled in the cool water that took my breath as I scrubbed it down my skin.

An hour later I sat in the saddle on Matilda's back and urged her into a full gallop through a field of wild daisies. It was easy to walk to the Chessari home, but this week my family had enough extra food to fill Matilda's saddlebags and tie other bags to them as well. The salted fish and vegetables were too much to carry myself, and a brisk ride on my way to Franca's was irresistible on such a brilliant morning.

The sun winked from behind a bank of clouds and scattered purple and gold shadows on the ground. A path led up the side of a nearby hill, and I diverted my plans for a moment and nudged Matilda toward the ascending trail with the click of my tongue. "Come, Matilda; let us reach the top by the count of ten."

Matilda stretched her neck forward and loped up the modest mountain. My skirt fluttered like butterfly wings against my thighs while Matilda leapt over rocks and landed on patches of grass and cracked soil in our assent. The sun had brushed the clouds aside before we came to rest on a wide summit that overlooked the valley. Breathless and exhilarated, I slid from Matilda's back and slipped my shoes from my feet to feel the grass with my toes. No matter the heartache of war, the love of my country filled my heart as I breathed in her air.

The rumble of horses' hooves echoed through the valley; someone approached at a healthy pace on horseback. Closer scrutiny revealed familiar black curly hair and wide, muscular shoulders. The rider reined the horse to a stop, and his deep voice resonated up the serpentine pathway.

"Is there room up there for two?"

Massimo Scalvone. The man was a phantom sent to haunt me. Before I could answer, he was on his way up the hill on the back of the Scalvones' buckskin horse. I glanced around for refuge, but Matilda had carried us as near the top as she could. I was trapped. I steadied my breath.

Massimo leapt with the ease of an expert from the back of his horse, led it by the reins the last few steps, and stopped in front of me. His eyes had grown darker. He smiled, and the nerves of a blushing schoolgirl gripped me by the stomach. A breeze stirred through Massimo's hair, the salty air turning musky with his scent. "Good morning, Marianna."

I was surprised that my voice worked. "*Buon giorno*, Massimo . . . of all the places to see you." He stood there quietly smiling for one second too long. I cleared my throat. "Please tell me, how is your sweet grandmother?"

"Much better, thank you." He stood beside me and looked out at the valley and the Mediterranean. "She tends to do too much for her age and has these tired spells that force her to catch up on her rest. By the way, I seem to find you in the most unexpected places—deserted roads all alone, the market, the top of a hill."

Matilda nuzzled my shoulder and, thankful for something to do, I reached in her saddlebag for an apple. Massimo stood with his hands in his pockets and watched me feed Matilda until my chest tightened. I avoided those black eyes of his and patted Matilda on her neck. "Well, my father is a fisherman, so I grew up in the market. But much to my Aunt Pasqualina's dismay, I do like a life that it not so predictable. So Massimo, you are here on leave . . . and what did you 'leave' behind?"

He chuckled. "Oh, I cannot tell you all my secrets at once. Where is the fun in that?"

I sighed. "The war has made this world full of secrets. I grow tired of them."

The wind augmented its pace and his eyes clouded. "So do I." Massimo's horse shook his head and stomped his feet in a restless dance.

I jumped. "Oh, I am sorry I did not offer a treat to your horse. He seems a little put out with me."

"I have a feeling his frustration is less about apples or carrots and more about your mare. He may be a gelding, but he knows a beauty when he sees one."

We'd had horses since I was a baby, but a blush flooded my face nonetheless. The horse had no consideration for my feelings; he whinnied deep in his throat and rubbed his nose against Matilda's neck. I managed a smile but did not meet Massimo's eyes. "Could I offer him some carrots?"

Long strands of my hair whisked and fluttered in the wind. Massimo caught a runaway curl with his fingers and tucked it behind my ear. I hugged my arms to my chest, and he dropped his hand and cleared his throat. "Absolutely, carrots it is."

I reached into the bag, gripped the largest handful of carrots I could manage, and held them out to Massimo. His fingers brushed my palm when he took them. He fed his horse and patted it between the ears. "In regards to the war, are you not afraid to be galloping in the countryside alone?"

I shook my head with relief for the change of subject and gestured toward the colorful patchwork of the landscape. "I cross the valleys rather than the roads all I can. This is my home. And Franca and the whole Chessari family is just a mile away." I watched his serious face while a smile tugged at the corners of my mouth. "And I am not alone."

The awkward mood seemed to lift. His smile sent an ache deep into my belly. He covered his heart with his hand in mock sincerity. "So if we are viciously attacked by the enemy, I shall be your protector."

I straightened my shoulders. "If you like, but my horse is pretty ferocious, and I am not afraid."

Matilda munched on a patch of green grass, and I hoped Massimo did not detect the tremor in my voice. He stood half a head taller than me, and I looked straight up into those obsidian eyes to reassure myself I was foolish to be so nervous. Massimo grinned, and no reassurance came—just a magnetic wave that rippled over my skin.

He lowered his brows and pointed at Matilda's saddlebags. "Yes, she looks like she would be great protection. And either you have a lot of snacks for your horse in those bags, or you are planning a rather large lunch today."

My shoulders relaxed. "Oh, those? My friend and I started a group last year to take supplies to people stranded and living on the streets. In fact, I should go; my friend Franca will wonder where I am. We need to be at St. Olivia's church in an hour to put our supplies together and go on deliveries."

"The old abandoned church? You are not meaning to go into town with just the two of you, I trust?"

The picture of the dwindled numbers of our volunteer group flashed through my mind before I answered. We had started with almost twenty members, but as the Nazi army and strength diminished, they took younger and younger men and forced them into battle. Some of the parents would not let their boys help our group anymore for fear they would be taken by the soldiers. Our numbers lessened every week while families hid their young sons in the countryside.

I blinked and straightened my shoulders. "No, no, our group will meet at the church and we will travel the rest of the way to town together."

Massimo shook his head. "You are fierce, Marianna De'Angelis, all the way to your core."

The quiver he caused in that core defied any validity to his words, and I forced a smile. "I just want to help, to do something to make things better . . . I wish I could do more."

I sounded so sure, so in control, when in truth I felt like a damsel from one of Aunt Pasqualina's absurd romance novels next to him. Massimo would not break his gaze from mine. He reached for the wild strands of my hair again, and I swayed like the branch of a willow.

I'd had enough. Massimo opened his mouth to say something, but I climbed up into Matilda's saddle and tugged the hem of my skirt down to cover the lacey edges of my slip before he had time to speak.

The leather stirrups against my bare feet reminded me of the shoes I had left on the ground. I looked down at Massimo, and he lifted the shoes up and gave them to me. Worried about the shaky status of my nerves, I did not stop to put them on. I gripped my shoes in one hand, Matilda's reins in the other.

"Thank you, *Signore* Scalvone . . . it was nice of you to stop by." I kicked my bare feet into Matilda's sides, and she charged down the hill.

Chapter Six

MASSIMO

I watched Marianna rush away—the dance of her hair as she descended downhill on the shiny back of her horse, the cloud of earthen powder behind the horse's hooves like fairy dust in her wake—and I knew that fate had won. No matter the danger, no matter the outcome between Axis and Allies, I had lost the battle to stay away from her.

But there was more than just the threat of my death at risk—the lives of too many depended on me.

Marianna made it to the bottom of the hill and galloped away into the distance. I climbed up on my horse and cursed my weakness. Cursed the powers that kept me away from her. Massimo Scalvone, you are a fool.

Chapter Seven

MARIANNA

FRANCA CHESSARI HAD ALREADY FILLED and loaded the back of a long wagon with pails of water before I arrived. She blew a dark tendril of hair from her eyes and grinned at me as I approached her after putting Matilda in the stables. The saddlebags of food hung over my shoulders and arms.

Franca's hair curled in tight coils from the bottom of her tresses to the crown of her head. I had pulled on the curls and watched them spring back many times. Her nose was generous like her father's—"very striking," her mother called it—but her large, deep eyes and full-lipped smile blended her features into a lovely picture. She wore her favorite color again today, a green cotton dress that flared out at her slender waist. Rings of sweat circled under her armpits.

I placed the food from the saddlebags in the wagon and hugged Franca. "Excellent; we have many baskets of vegetables and fruit this week."

Franca pulled up a cloth and showed me a basket of bread as well. Ten different families had donated goods and dropped them off here at the Chessari home for us every Thursday since we had started our group more than a year ago.

I wrapped my arm around Franca's waist and gazed at the cornucopia of food. "Why are we using a wagon instead of your truck?"

Franca groaned in frustration. "Since my father left, the soldiers have become more brazen; they took our car and all but one of our trucks two days ago. Mama is afraid we will be stopped by soldiers and harassed and that the last truck will be confiscated. She hid it in the garage of the guest house out in the vineyard."

I patted Franca's shoulder. "They would take food from a baby's mouth if they wanted to."

"Of course they would. Mama also insisted that one of the workers ride with us until I told her that Guido and the boys would be at St. Olivia's to meet us before we go on into town."

"Thank goodness for Guido or we might be shut down by now."

After I filled the last two pails with water, we were loaded in the wagon and ready to go. Franca whistled, and the two chestnuts at the head of the wagon pulled at their harnesses and stepped onto the road. The hindquarters of the horses swayed back and forth while their hooves thumped against the baked earth in rhythm. We were on our way at last.

* * *

The walls of St. Olivia's abandoned church cracked and crumbled. Vines and grass twisted up through the rocks, and the garden in front looked like a cemetery of skeletal trees and decayed vegetation. An alabaster Madonna stood on a pedestal in the middle of the courtyard, the carved smile on her face feigning happiness in the forsaken gardens. Franca and I walked inside the church to find the rest of our group.

Giuseppe, Leonardo, and Carlo could have been brothers—even thirteen-year-old triplets, they were so alike. Their tangled crops of hair, luminous eyes, and clever smiles were each a reflection of the other. They sat in tattered chairs at a table with Leonardo's grandfather, Guido. The boys jumped up when we arrived and our irreverent voices, raised in loud celebration of our abundance of goods, threatened to stir any dead in the abandoned cemetery outside. Surrounded by food, clean water, and stacks of cloth for bandages and blankets, we were a wealthy band in the midst of war.

I looked at my friends and the supplies they had brought to add to ours, and happiness filled my chest as if the doors had been flung open and the first breath of spring rushed in. We had not been able to gather so much in weeks. I clapped my hands. "We are as rich as King Midas! Let's hurry and get it all loaded."

The boys sprang to their feet; grabbed buckets of summer squash, tomatoes, and linens in their arms; and scurried to the wagon outside. The church became a whirl of the six of us hurrying back and forth.

Guido was a reed in the wind, a long brittle branch that I was sure would snap if he bent to lift a heavy bucket. The seventy-nine-year-old grandfather of Leonardo, he would not allow us to call him *Signore* Lecce when he helped our group. "This is a youth group, no?" he had teased.

We all nodded in curiosity.

"That makes me young when I am with you, then. So you must call me Guido."

He winked each time he said it, and if we slipped with a *Signore Lecce*, he stopped us with a tsk of his tongue. So we called our white-haired member Guido, and he smiled every time we did.

The abundance of supplies looked like the makings of a grand picnic when we finished loading and stopped to get a drink of water. The boys chased each other around the garden before they raced to the wagon. They climbed over each other's backs for the best seat, and a wrestling competition ensued.

Guido carried the last bucket of grain and playfully swatted Leonardo on the head. "*Andiamo tutti raggasacci*—time to be on our way, wicked boys."

Franca and I sat arm in arm on the front seat of the Chessari wagon and led the group in song while Guido led the horses. The boys balanced on the sides of the wagon bed, their feet placed carefully between baskets and pails that sloshed water on their dusty feet when we bounced over bumps and ruts in the road.

Just a couple of miles into our journey, I recognized a German jeep loaded with four Nazi soldiers headed in our direction. I held my breath when they slid to a stop beside us. Two soldiers stepped from the jeep. They pointed their rifles at our chests as if we were the enemy and narrowed their eyes with suspicion. A wiry soldier with a weak chin pursed his lips before speaking in German-accented Italian.

"What is it that you think you are doing on this road? And where did you get all of this food? It looks like you have been stealing."

I bit back my frustration before I could answer, but Guido spoke up quickly.

"We gathered it all from our homes and neighbors and are making a delivery to some relatives in town—just a bit of pity for the poor. May we offer you hard-working soldiers some fresh fruit and vegetables?"

The soldier sneered, lowered his rifle, and yanked the reins from Guido's hands. "You cannot distract or bribe us with an offer of your rotten food. Everything belongs to the Führer anyway. You own nothing. Get down from this wagon."

He pointed toward the back at Leonardo. "And you, the tall one, get out of that wretched wagon at once. Why are you not in the military fighting the enemy?"

Leo leapt out the back of the wagon and stood in place like an obedient child. I grabbed the reins, gripping them tight in my hands to suppress the urge to jump down and defy the soldiers. Franca sat like a statue beside me, her arm looped stiffly through mine. I forced myself to remain silent, to hold my temper and lower my eyes as if in submission when I looked at the soldiers.

The soldier pecked at Guido's chest with his sinewy finger. "Indolent men like you should be shot by the side of the road. The Führer needs bravery and sacrifice. Get in the jeep before I have you whipped in front of your pathetic women."

Guido hung his head down, bobbing it back and forth as if in deep disappointment. "I am afraid that I am so aged and worthless you would not want such a burden to be a part of your valiant army. I am seventy-nine years old; even my wife says all of my useful years are behind me."

The soldier's eyes glimmered like those of a snake focused on its prey. His long, skinny neck jerked forward and he spit in Guido's face. Guido stood still, the gob of saliva sliding down his wrinkled cheek while he stared at the ground.

The soldier marched toward Leo, the metal of his boots clinking with each stomp of his feet before he stopped. He knocked Leo's beret from his head, then scooped up a handful of dirt from the road. "You lazy boy, are you too afraid to fight for your country? Do you hide behind old men and worthless women because you are gutless and *stupido*? Eh?"

He puffed up his cheeks and blew the handful of dirt into Leo's face. Fury struck me like a lightning bolt, and I sprang to my feet while Leonardo coughed, gagged, and rubbed his eyes with his hands. The soldier slapped and pushed him until he fell to the ground and hit his head on a rock. "Maybe we will take you into custody right now, baby boy, and your mama will never know what happened when you do not show up for pasta tonight. Get up."

I started to jump from the wagon, but Guido caught my movement from the corner of his eye and shook his head no. I took deep breaths to calm my anger before I did something that would cause us more danger.

Leonardo held his tears but shook so hard I could hear his teeth rattle together when he wiped the dirt from his lips and the blood from his forehead. He wobbled back up and stumbled over beside his grandfather. "I . . . I tried to enlist, but they sent me away for being too young, Sir. I am only thirteen."

The soldier growled and kicked him in the shin so hard Leo cried out and fell to the ground again. The soldier glared down at the crumpled boy. "Stop your lies, deserter."

In spite of Guido's warning, I jumped from the wagon. I ran to the back and pulled out a basket of homemade bread. "Sir, what the young man is telling you is true; he is barely older than a child. We have fresh bread here. You soldiers work so hard to protect us, you must be so hungry. Please . . . eat."

I put the basket down, ran back, and grabbed a bucket of water. I dipped a ladle inside and thrust it toward the soldiers. Water spilled and dripped down the side and beaded on the powdery dirt on the ground.

Leonardo slipped back inside the wagon and crouched down with Giuseppe and Carlo while two of the soldiers snatched loaves of bread. Franca retrieved a bandage from the back and wrapped Leo's head while I spoke to the soldiers.

The last soldier, his hair so blonde it looked white, climbed from the jeep and took the ladle from my hand. He drank, dipped the ladle again, poured the water over his head and I noticed a long, red scar that ran all the way from his eye to his jaw. He shook the droplets from his hair and ignored me completely when he walked back to the jeep and climbed in. He looked over at the soldier who had harassed Guido and Leo. "Come on, Voight, you've had your fun. I want to get back to headquarters."

I could see by the scowl on his face that he was not too happy with Voight. His words went unheeded as Voight shoved Guido toward the front seat of the wagon. Guido climbed up and sat down, and the soldier marched back beside me and grabbed hold of my braid, jerking my head to the side.

The white-haired soldier stood up inside the jeep. "Leave the girl alone or I will report you."

Voight stared into my eyes as if considering his options, then glowered at the very blond soldier. "Shut up, Weimer, you do not outrank me." He yanked down on my braid so hard my head wrenched back and I was staring straight up at the sky. The muscles in my neck strained, and my heart thumped in my throat like a trapped animal's. The low hum of an approaching vehicle filled me with hope and trepidation at the same time. The soldier still held my braid tightly, and I could not look to see if more enemies had arrived. The vehicle skidded to a stop just a few feet away, spewing rocks at our feet.

Voight let go of my hair and shoved me to the ground. I landed hard on my stomach and tasted dirt. "Keep your mouth shut and do not move or get up or I will shoot all of you." He stepped on my braid and pinned my head to the side.

Rocks ground into my cheek as the door of what had sounded like a truck opened and closed and someone climbed out. Footsteps scratched in the gravel and stalked toward Voight before a deep voice spoke. "Perhaps I may be of service?"

I almost choked on the dirt I inhaled when I recognized Massimo's voice. I wanted to cry with relief.

Voight snapped at Massimo. "Who the hell are you and what do you want? Why are you out here alone in a truck like this? Are you a deserter?"

Massimo's voice was calm and cool above the sound of rattling papers. "I believe my papers will explain everything. You and your men are interfering with orders. I am aware of the movements of these six individuals and do not appreciate you getting in the way of their assigned task."

The soldier grabbed the papers and stepped off my braid, but I did not dare stand.

I looked up as Massimo reached his hand down for mine and he lifted me to my feet. I looked into his eyes and saw them soften before he let go of my hand and locked a flinty stare back on Voight. "The *Signorina* will not be harassed anymore, and these people are to continue to their destination with my supervision."

Voight mumbled and spat out his reply in German. Then, much to my surprise, he shoved the handful of papers back at Massimo, turned on his heel, and marched back to his jeep, his face red with rage as they screeched away.

The wave of relief knocked the wind from my lungs, and I had to grip the side of the wagon to keep from falling. Massimo took hold of my arm and led me past the wagon to his truck. "Climb inside, Marianna; I will tell your group that we are all going back to the church."

Ripples of cold sweat ran down my back. Massimo helped me inside the truck, and I sat down with relief and watched my comrades through the window. When the dust behind the Nazis' jeep faded farther into the distance, everyone jumped down from the wagon. Massimo shook hands with the boys and Franca, then talked to Guido and patted him on the shoulder.

Franca put her arm around Guido and led him back to the seat of the wagon. Leonardo climbed up first and extended his hand to help them up. He sat between them and wrapped an arm around his grandfather while Franca took the reins. I wiped at the gritty tears on my cheeks and blinked back the burn in my eyes.

Massimo climbed in the truck, and the rigid manner he had held with the Germans eased. He reached in his pocket and handed me a handkerchief. "The Nazis are gone, at least for now. I am unsure whether you are all the bravest souls or greatest fools I have ever seen for trying to go into the city full of Germans with no one but an old man, young boys, and two women. A wagon of teenaged boys with fresh food and water in Siracusa? The Nazis look for new recruits everywhere and snatch up any good food. You may as well dangle a worm before a school of fish. Are you injured?"

He searched my eyes for an answer, and I shook my head no, embarrassed that I could not stop my tears. Franca turned the wagon around in front of us. The boys in the back sat quietly and did not wave with their usual exuberance. I looked at Massimo when we did not follow them. He nodded his head toward St. Olivia's.

"I told your friends to go behind the church where they would not be seen. I want to watch for a moment; I do not trust those men and want to be sure they are not looping back around."

"You saved our lives, Massimo. How can I . . . we . . . possibly thank you enough?"

He shook his head and squinted his eyes while he watched the road through the truck window. "I wish I had been there sooner to stop them. They behave like animals instead of men. I saw them pass by my grandparents' place and remembered you had mentioned St. Olivia's church. I worried that they may intersect your path, so I used my grandfather's truck to come and check."

The engine rumbled to a start when he turned the key, and I could not suppress my curiosity any longer. "Those soldiers listened to you; they left so fast and did not even ask questions. Why?"

The force of Massimo's foot on the accelerator lurched the truck toward the church, and the high-pitched protest of the engine echoed off the rock walls that lined the pastures on each side of the road. The muscles in his arm strained when he shoved the stick shift into place, the gears higher, the truck faster.

Rocks popped and pinged inside the wheel wells, and the birds that pecked for bugs and worms on the sides of the road took flight at our approach.

Eyes fixed straight ahead, Massimo gripped the gear shaft until his knuckles turned white and exhaled through his teeth like it was his first breath since the Nazis drove away. "I am . . . only concerned that everyone is unharmed and that you feel safe."

I gripped the handkerchief he had given me. "I am not harmed or afraid anymore; I know I am safe with you."

He shook his head in frustration, leaned back against the seat, and eased up on the accelerator. "That kind of trust, such innocence, can get you killed in an instant. Never take chances. You are safer if you stay away from . . . all soldiers . . . even me."

I shook off his counsel without hesitation. "You seem so angry. Why do I have to stay away from you? We are fellow Italians—neighbors. Even though you are forced to serve with the Nazis, I know that you are not my enemy."

He tightened his hands into fists around the steering wheel. "No, I am not your enemy, but there is risk in being around me just the same. When I take you back to the church, you must go home immediately."

I thought of the families that waited for us and for the food and water we would bring; the Silvanna family, the Turisi couple sitting around their fire. I knew I had to get these supplies to town no matter the risks. But the thought of going without Massimo now seemed daunting. "So you will not help us, then? I must deliver the supplies to those helpless families today, even if it is the last time I ever can. I cannot leave them there waiting, the little ones hungry while they wonder where we are."

"You do not have any choice."

"Those families, the little children, do not have a choice . . . but I do. Do not worry, Massimo; I am sure you scared those soldiers away for good."

We had reached the church, but instead of pulling around back like he had told Franca to do, he stopped at the front doors. Massimo scowled. "The way you look the adversary in the face is a death sentence. I am telling you it is too dangerous. You must go inside and tell the others you have no choice but to go home. Promise me that is what you will do."

I climbed out of the truck and leaned in the window. "Thank you for all you did today. I owe you my life. We all do, and I know that. Please do not worry about this any further."

I hurried to the church doors before he could stop me. I heard the truck engine shut off, the slam of the door, and the smack of Massimo's boots against cobblestone as he marched up behind me.

"You are going on a suicide mission. I will not just stand by and let you go."

I stood on shaky legs, stared straight into the depths of Massimo's eyes, and tried to gather enough breath to speak. "I personally know two of the families to whom we take food; they were regular customers before the war tore their lives apart. Two old people, four little children—they watch for us."

He threw his head back with a curse and clasped me by the hand. He opened the door of the church and marched me inside. The damp air cooled my skin, which had grown warm in the truck with Massimo. Giuseppe and Carlo rushed up to greet us with grins on their faces while their arms waved in the air in praise for our rescuer.

"*Bravo*, Massimo. *Bravo*, Massimo. *Bravo*, Massimo!"

An owl perched in the rafters ruffled its feathers at the volume of their chants and flew out a hole in the roof. Leonardo, Franca, and Guido sat at the table. A look of astonishment covered Franca's face when she spotted Massimo's hand clasping mine. Massimo let go and stood at the head of the table. He pulled back a chair and gestured for me to sit; he grimaced when I refused. Giuseppe and Carlo still chanted his name, and he waved his hand for them to stop.

He tried to smile. "I appreciate your gratitude, but truthfully you are the heroes here who have been risking yourselves for all of these many months. I do not mean to take charge of your brigade, but since all my efforts to convince Marianna that these trips to town are too perilous have failed, I do have a suggestion for how we can do this in a way I hope would be safest."

My mouth fell open in shock. I thought he had come in to tell the others we had to give up and go home.

Franca lifted her hand with a frown. "It does seem that the risks are just too great. What good would it do to help some if one of our own is lost in the process? We cannot understand why the Germans are so against our help; Mussolini sided us with them. But they have become more and more of an enemy. What can we do?"

Massimo nodded his head and folded his arms. "The soldiers do not like to see the people on the streets receive help; they believe they would not be living there if they were not guilty of a crime against the regime, that it is their own actions that put them there. But they are not aware of what one brigade does from another. I will go with you this time. If we are stopped, I will tell them I have been ordered to deliver supplies and your group has been directed to assist me."

I placed my hand on my heart. "You could get past them again? Convince others to leave our boys and Guido alone?"

"I have the paperwork that could make it possible. And if it does not work, I will persuade them."

I swallowed the knot that had lodged itself in my chest when he pulled a pistol from his boot. The boys whooped and hollered with excitement, but I was clutched by the same nausea that I had the first time I saw weaponry in my brother's hands.

Perhaps we would have a chance to protect ourselves with Massimo's help, to keep these young boys, an old man, even Franca and me from becoming victims in our own streets. But any force we had to use could so easily be turned back to us tenfold. Nausea grew to a burn that crept up my throat. Massimo seemed to read my thoughts, and he looked into my eyes and nodded his head in reassurance. Gratitude for his help overcame my fears, and I reached out my hand to shake his.

His hand clasped mine, and the set of his jaw eased. "What you are trying to do for these people may feel good to you, but it is . . ."

I lifted my chin to protest, and he shook his head. "*Va bene*. Let's just get this done and get you all home."

Massimo looked at our diminished charity group and smiled in spite of the tension I saw in his eyes. "Marianna has convinced me to help you today, but I have to tell you it is against my best judgment to do so. The anger in the German army is out of control, and anyone can become a victim of it. The war is not going as they planned; their losses are mounting, and they want everyone to pay for it. I will go with you today but strongly insist this be your last trip. Your next confrontation with the soldiers could be much worse than it was today."

Guido pointed at Leonardo, who slumped against the table with the bandage wrapped around his head. "My grandson is injured and no matter how much I wish to help, I must say I am still weak in the knees. I am so sorry; we may have no choice but to go home. But we do not have a way back; we all came in Franca's wagon."

Franca's eyes were magnified by tears. "Mari, I have to take them all home. Before you walked in, Guido was shaking so hard it scared us all, and Leo is nauseated. We will pass Giuseppe's and Carlo's houses on the way back, and their families will know something is wrong if they do not come home when they see us."

Our team had dissolved within a matter of a minute. A crumbling mosaic of Saint Peter, his eyes mortared in eternal sorrow, looked down on me in pity from the archway above Franca's head.

I stood next to Leo. "You were brave out there today. I know you and your grandfather need to rest." I looked at Franca and the boys and tried to steady the quiver in my chin. "Maybe we have done all that we can. The rest of you need to go, and that leaves only two of us." I looked at Massimo and held my breath.

He sighed out loud. "Marianna and I can use my truck. I will take her to make the deliveries. I agree the rest of you have done all that you can for now and do not need to worry; your friends will receive their help. If you see any soldiers, they may not bother you since you will not have supplies in the wagon, but keep the boys sitting low in the back and go directly to your homes."

Franca stood and clasped the collar of her blouse in her fingers. "I am not sure it is proper for the two of you to be alone together."

I felt my face redden before Massimo chortled. "You are right, *Signorina*, but hungry people, suffering children—perhaps nothing about this war is proper. You have my word; I will treat *Signorina* De'Angelis with respect."

He turned and faced me with a wry smile. "It looks as though you are in jeopardy no matter what you do. This day turns more dangerous by the minute. Let us get the supplies into the truck the fastest way possible before any soldiers come back around."

I nodded my head and headed outside, more nervous about getting back in the truck alone with Massimo than I could be over the threat of soldiers.

Chapter Eight

I HAD NEVER NOTICED HOW small the cab of a truck was before. When we jostled on the unpaved roads, my leg almost bumped against Massimo's hand on the gear shift. He asked about my family and when I turned my head to answer, his face seemed just inches away.

Only a few jeeps and trucks passed as we rumbled over the rutted cobblestone into the city. The soldiers paid us no attention, and the fear in my head quieted. No doubt the truck in which we rode drew much less notice than when we had come by horse and wagon.

Siracusa had always been alive with the scramble and buzz of her citizens on errands in the daytime and strolling her streets in the evenings. Now people peeked out the curtains of their windows rather than taking the evening walks as they had before. The neighborhood seemed completely deserted until we neared the area where several of the homeless had set up lean-tos or makeshift homes along the sides of buildings.

We rounded a long, winding curve into a lower part of the city and saw the Turisi's camp. The elderly couple sat hunched beside a circle of bricks that surrounded their tiny fire. Blankets draped across rope and tied from one building to the next formed the tent in which they had lived for several months.

I recognized the same gray shawl *Signora* Turisi wore draped around her shoulders every time we visited. Her husband was a small man of quick wit and high cheekbones that made his eyes look squinted even when he was not smiling. The two of them ambled over to the truck when we pulled to a stop and they recognized me. Dressed all in black, *Signore* Turisi tapped his beret with his fingers in a friendly salute until he saw Massimo step out in his uniform. His eyes widened in trepidation until I held up my hands in reassurance.

"Please do not fear, *amici*. This is Massimo Scalvone, a family friend and someone we can trust. He is helping me today because the rest of *L'Amici di Carita* could not come."

Massimo shook their hands. "Marianna has spoken with great affection and respect for you. This is a privilege to meet you." My old friends smiled and relaxed at Massimo's gentle manners.

Massimo lifted a pail of water from the back of the truck and carried it to a table made of wooden boards laid across rocks. The pink-rimmed eyes of *Signora* Turisi lit up when she saw the fresh, clean water. She squeezed Massimo's arm and walked him to their fire. She pulled him down to sit on a bucket that had been turned upside down beside her. She reached into the pocket of her dress, pulled out a photo, and placed it in Massimo's hand.

"You look like our grandson." She looked at her husband. "*Guarda*, see, look at his chin*, marito*, it is just like Antonio's."

Signore Turisi sat down on the other side of the fire and bobbed his head up and down in agreement. Massimo gazed at the photo. "I could never hope to be as fine-looking a soldier. You must be very proud."

The *Signora* placed a cup in Massimo's hands; he patted her hand in gratitude and gulped what I knew had to be a watered-down version of makeshift coffee. The heavy weight that pressed on my heart lifted, if just for those few moments, at the joy on the old woman's face.

Signore Turisi's eyes filled with tears when he saw the supplies we had brought them. He gripped my hands in his. "*Siete angeli di Dio tutti voi* . . . you are angels, angels from God . . . *grazie, grazie*."

"Dear *Signore* Turisi, you and your wife are the angels who have sacrificed so much. I only wish we could give you . . . or do . . . more. You need food to keep your strength up so you can welcome that grandson home someday soon."

He rubbed his chin with a weak smile. "My wife makes me shave everyday just in case he comes home." His tired eyes almost twinkled. "I am awfully happy to see that clean water."

I swallowed the pinch in my throat, amazed at such happiness because of a bucket of water. We hurried to hide fruit and vegetables beneath the blankets that made up their bed so that soldiers or thieves would not see them. Daylight slipped further away, and I wished I had more time to visit with the Turisis. I broke off a chunk of bread before hiding the rest of the loaf and placed the piece on the table near their fire pit.

Signora Turisi held onto Massimo's arm. Bulging purple veins ran beneath the onion-skin surface of her hand. Massimo patted it. "I am certain my grandparents' extra bedroom would be more comfortable than the home you have constructed here. Please bring your things and come with us."

Signore Turisi shook his silvery head. "Oh, no, son, I will tell you what we told your friend, Marianna. We helped a neighbor who was Jewish and had our home taken away for it. Now the Germans watch us. We would be a danger to anyone who took us in."

Their story stabbed me like a knife once again. I looked at the Turisis' camp. Tomorrow this food may all be gone, stolen by others living in desperation; taken by bandits who would sell it for exorbitant prices or confiscated by soldiers. Helpless once again, I hoped that at least my friends could eat their fill, or that if it were taken it would still somehow end up helping someone who truly needed it. I placed an extra blanket around the shoulders of the old man, kissed the *Signora* on each creased cheek, and gestured to Massimo that we best be on our way.

* * *

The setting sun reflected off the stone of a nearby building and cast a yellow glow over the family sheltered beside it. The Silvana family had made a wall out of rocks on the side of the building and lived between the two walls. A string tied between a metal hook in the wall and a wooden post at the end of the rocks held laundry that dripped into puddles on the ground. The children ran up to the truck as we arrived and stretched their hands out for food and to be lifted into our arms.

Signora Silvana held a basket of laundry at her hip. She set it down and wiped her hands on her apron as she walked up to greet us. Her three sons jumped onto the tailgate of the truck, and she shook her finger at them. "Only take what *Signorina* De'Angelis tells you to. Not everything is for our family."

They all answered in unison, "*Si*, Mama."

I walked back to the boys, my throat tightening at the sight of their dirty faces and unkempt hair. I pointed to the baskets they could each have. "Here, Marino, take the squash, it will last a long time and we have plenty. And Nicola, make sure the tomatoes are out of the sun; they are very ripe already. Salvatore, you can take the peaches."

They took to their tasks like eager puppies, yipping in celebration at the sight of fresh fruit. The weight of the day lifted. Massimo smiled at the boys and stashed the buckets of water behind an extra wall the family had constructed to hide their supplies.

Three-year-old Eleonora ran up to Massimo, her hair black as the ash from Mount Etna. Her knee socks, full of the dust of the day, sagged around her ankles. She patted Massimo on the leg, and he reached down and picked her up. He grabbed a peach from Salvatore and placed it in Eleonora's grubby palm. Thick juice dribbled down her chin with every bite, and I searched for the basket of clean rags.

I handed a piece of torn sheet dipped in water to Massimo, and he wiped the little girl's mouth. He danced with her still in his arms and sang a song that made her giggle and hold tight around his neck. His voice overpowered the pigeons that cooed from the eaves of the building, and they scattered into the air. The song ended, and Eleonora nestled her head against Massimo's neck, the stubble of his whiskers catching the wisps of her hair. He patted her, his hands huge on her tiny back, and I realized I had been staring.

Massimo witnessed the moment my glimpses turned into a gaze when he lifted his head and caught me watching him. He kept his eyes locked with mine, even when Eleonora scrambled down from his arms. I stared back as if paralyzed. Massimo's eyes softened as if a mist had surrounded the two of us, but after mere seconds he scowled and turned away.

A tap on my shoulder made me jump.

"Marianna, only God and *i santi* can repay you for this help." *Signora* Silvana held her hands toward the sky as if in prayer, a gesture that shook me from my confusion over Massimo's cold scowl. I forced a smile and hugged the *Signora* in reassurance, startled by the prominence of her shoulder bones. I grabbed some peaches and handed one to each of her children, who gathered like ragged ducklings around her skirt.

I tore a loaf of bread into pieces and gave one to Eleonora when she ran up beside me. I handed the largest piece of bread to their mother and closed her hand around it when she tried to refuse. "Please, *Signora*, you do not need to thank me. You have supported my family for years by buying our fish at the market. We are all helping each other. Please, eat what you can. How will you help your children if you have no strength?"

She sat on the ground with a sob, and I crouched down beside her and reached for her hand. Her eyes were ringed with fatigue, her skin taut over her cheekbones while her hair hung in a thin braid down the back of her tattered dress. I led her to a chair, dipped a cloth in a bucket of clean water, and handed it to her. She sat and wiped her face while Massimo stayed busy by the truck. I stood behind her and rubbed her shoulders.

"Someday, *Signora*, I will convince you to come and stay with us. I know you fear the soldiers, but perhaps they have stopped watching you. The Germans are so preoccupied these days, I am sure they would no longer bother you."

She shook her head no with a sniffle. I patted her shoulder. "I will be back to help you if there is any way I can. The danger of coming into town has escalated, and it may be a while. Hold onto everything you can to feed your family and try to find extra. I will not forget you if there is anything I can do."

Signora Silvana stood, and we embraced. Massimo and I stacked everything we had brought behind their wall just as the sunset deepened from gold to burnt ocher. Our goodbyes were brief, sealed by a vow I made to myself that I would somehow soon find a way to get them into a better shelter.

* * *

The trip back home was stifled in silence. Massimo glared at the road as if his eyes would set it afire, his forehead furrowed, his shoulders stiff. I tried to think of anything to say, but his sudden coldness and withdrawal bound my tongue. Minutes ticked by, and I could not sit still; I tapped my foot against the floorboard and smoothed my skirt with my palms several times.

"Did I do something offensive, Massimo? Are you angry with me?"

He looked at me, tension still locked in his face. "No . . . no, Marianna. It is my entire fault. You? You have done nothing." He glanced at me and tightened his hands on the steering wheel. "And I am a fool."

My quick intake of breath echoed in my head. "Whatever you are, whatever it is that is bothering you, you are no fool, Massimo."

Pain pinched behind my eyes while I watched him drive, but he would not look back at me or speak anymore. I was grateful for a reprieve when we arrived at my home. I slipped out of the truck with a brief thank you for his help. He barely smiled before speaking in a clipped tone. "You are welcome, *Signorina*. Please, take good care of yourself."

I stood on the grass and watched the red lights on the back of his truck fade into the night.

Chapter Nine

LUSH PLANTS AND TREES COOLED the courtyard in front of the Chessari home. Franca opened the heavy, carved front door; her dark hair curled extra tight and springing in all directions. She reached for my hand and pulled me inside. "Come in. Come in, Mari. I am anxious to hear about the deliveries yesterday. I had bad dreams about those soldiers all night."

I could not contain a smile. "Is that what curled your hair? And the deliveries went well, so do not worry."

She tsked her tongue. "Do not make fun. I slept with my hair wrapped in rags all night to get this curl for the dance tonight. What do you think? It looks good, no?"

"Of course it does; you look like a stage actress from America, it is so full and wavy. Every man you see at the dance will be enchanted and want to sweep you away."

Franca's eyed narrowed. "Not good, Mari; if my mother heard you, she'd dip my head in water. She has been so upset since our episode yesterday she won't let me go farther than our front courtyard. Luckily she is in her parlor. Laura is here taking a nap before she goes out to the cottage to wait for Bruno to come home."

"I meant to say that you look lovely with your hair so full. It catches the sunlight through the window."

She grinned, and I put my purse down on the table in the foyer and walked behind her to the top of their stairs. "Franca, I did not tell my parents about yesterday. I was too afraid to upset Papa. Thank heaven Laura is doing well with the pregnancy now and resting. Where are the twins?"

She answered me over her shoulder. "Since they recovered from influenza they have been unstoppable. Mama put them to work in the garden. I told her you were coming and that we had to get ready for the dance, or she would send me out there too." She stopped halfway down the long hall to her bedroom and gripped my hand in hers. Her dark eyes sobered.

"Mama sent our man Tigo to check on Guido and Leonardo, and he found them well and rested, although Leo is scratched up and bruised. I am forbidden to go on any more deliveries. I am afraid our *L'Amici di Carita* is doomed, or at least I have done all I can."

A knot tightened my throat and I swallowed hard against it. "Yes, I know that yesterday was too dangerous. I am still trying to think of a path we could take to keep helping people, but every idea I come up with hits the same wall."

Franca squeezed both of my hands in hers. "But we can be thinking about what to do and still have a nice time at the dance tonight, no?"

To see neighbors and friends at a dance honoring our soldiers could be a tonic of comfort. A sense of hope buoyed my spirits, and I squeezed Franca's hands in return. "Maybe all is not hopeless, and we will find a way to sneak the supplies to people. For tonight, let's celebrate and cheer for our soldiers. I am determined to be there for Bruno no matter the opposition."

Franca did a little hop in front of me, a huge grin on her face. "This morning *Signora* Orlandini came by to visit my mother, and I heard her say that Giovanni and GianCarlo are here on a brief leave and are going to the dance. They are both so handsome. Who would ever dream that God could create perfection twice in one family like that? They will need our support at the dance also, no?"

I grinned at her enthusiasm until her brows lowered in thought. "But Mari, what of that Massimo Scalvone? He is *bellissimo*, and you were with him all that time yesterday. The way he rescued us was so heroic, and he took you with him personally. I think he cares for you."

A flush flooded my face, and I covered my cheeks with my hands. Franca tsked her tongue. "*Madonna Mia*, I knew it. You want him. I hesitated to ask for fear you would run like a filly the other way like you always do from men. And now look at you—your eyes are open so wide you look like you've been caught in one of the boys' rabbit traps. You are so determined to be independent, Marianna De'Angelis. But I do not care if you do not want to hear it—there was *magica* in the air when the two of you were side by side at the church yesterday."

I sighed, stalked off to Franca's bedroom, and slumped down in her floral-printed chair. One mention of Massimo's name, and a fire had ignited in my chest. But the memory of his withdrawal and dark silence in the car smothered the flames. Franca walked behind me into the room, a scowl of suspicion on her face. "Tell me."

I shrugged. "He . . . he was very kind and helpful to the people. But we did not talk very much. That was all."

Franca shook me by the arm. "Then why are you so red in the face? Maybe you are sick. Or are you a little lovesick?"

I caught my breath when she said the word *love*; Massimo's gaze had fused with mine like the sun soaking into my skin, until he had frowned and looked away abruptly. His silent withdrawal on the trip home, the danger of war, my family in need . . . I had to refocus; this was no time to think of anything else. Tears gathered in my eyes. "Franca, do not say that."

"I am teasing you, Mari. You worry so much. Massimo is gentle, kind, brave, and so handsome with his thick, curly hair. His eyes could melt the snow on the Alps in the middle of winter. He watches you. I could feel your feelings for each other like a heartbeat in the room."

I sat taller in the chair. "No, no, no, Franca. Remember we have loved ones to protect and help. How can I think of anything or anyone but my family and our country at such a time as this?"

Franca's eyes were deep pools of concern. "Love does not wait for the war to end, *l'amica mia*, it must be embraced before it is torn from our arms."

Her words pierced me like an arrow and made it difficult to swallow. I placed my hand at my throat, and Franca squinted her eyes with a tsk of her tongue. "Very well; I will let you get away with your self-deception. For now."

I pretended not to notice her wry smile before she waved me over to her side. We climbed up on her tall feather bed and propped ourselves on pillows across the white tufted bedspread. Rose-scented talcum powder sat on her nightstand and permeated the air with its sweet perfume. Franca fell back on her pillow with a sigh, her curls making a fan around her smiling face. She looked at me with a shine in her brown eyes.

"So how long can you stay today?"

"I can take my time and even ride with you to the dance. Mama is not certain that Papa will feel like going, and she thought I needed to go."

Franca bolted up. "Of course we need to go. I was thinking today about how important the dance is and our duty to support it."

I laughed. "You, *l'amica mia*, were thinking about dancing with handsome soldiers."

"Buh . . . *Va bene*, who . . . me? Very well, then, I will prove to you that I know the real reason for the dance, even the title."

"Which is?"

She sat back beside me and placed her hand on her heart. "*Forza Italia.*" She smirked in triumph and then sobered. "I know about the real things too, Marianna; I know the governor of Siracusa planned this dance to celebrate our country and to show our soldiers we sustain them no matter what side they must fight on. They need support from all of us, no matter the reasons. Perhaps even more."

I hugged my friend. "I am sorry if I mocked you. You are so good for me. Like a light in my dark worries."

That light snapped back on in her eyes, and she grabbed both of my hands and squeezed them in hers. "And you make me face the dangers when I want to run away." She hopped up in excitement again, the heaviness gone. "You are forgiven. And I have the perfect way for you to show your loyalty to Italy and the soldiers."

I smiled. "I feel too afraid to ask."

She continued undaunted. "I was wondering if it might be nice for you to try something different or, um, new for the dance. Not anything too big, but something I have been trying to get you to do for a while."

Franca's eyes seemed to plead with me. "What I mean is, would you mind if I helped you get ready? You could borrow a dress of mine just for a change and maybe we could try a different style for your hair?"

I looked at the floor, then back at the hopeful face of my friend. "Sure, Franca, why not?"

Franca lept off the bed. "Oh Saints be praised, Marianna, at last we get to fix you up. Hair, cosmetics, jewelry, and one of my fancy dresses. I think I have died and gone to heaven."

She hugged me and squealed with joy. Franca's exuberance made me laugh. "I did not say that you could put me through a torture ritual."

I had never been as well dressed as Franca, and my suntanned skin from mornings in Papa's boat was far from feminine compared to hers. She was already at her closet, which was much larger and definitely fuller than mine. I swallowed hard while she pulled out dress after elegant dress and laid them on her bed with a happy hum.

I held up my hand. "Wait, wait, wait—how about something nice but not too fancy?"

Franca rolled her eyes. "Very well, *va bene*, do not panic. But my goodness, do you realize how gorgeous you will be? You will have every man, boy, and soldier in the room with their heads spinning. Look at this heavenly dress I will be wearing. Can you believe it?"

She picked up a gold dress and actually twirled around the room, her stocking feet sliding on the white marble floor.

"It is beautiful, Franca; you will look like a *principessa*. I do not mind borrowing a dress, but I do not know about wearing cosmetics."

Franca sang and danced around the room until she heard me and stopped short. "You have said no to cosmetics a hundred times already. We are almost eighteen, and you have never even tried lipstick for heaven's sake. I can hardly get you to look at a magazine with me unless it's about the war."

"The magazines and papers show us what is going on. And you know I have to see where Bruno might be sent and if there is any way we can stop him from having to fight with the Nazis. And I never said anything against lipstick; it's just that I have never used it."

My voice was a little raspy from the image of Bruno in battle. Franca sat on the bed beside me and put her long, slender arm around me, her smile now sweet and sincere.

"He will be protected, Mari. We will stop by the church every Saturday and light every candle for him."

I knew we could never afford that. Franca's family vineyards here and up north had been prosperous, so money had not been a problem for her before, but I loved her for her support. "*Grazie*, Franca." I hugged her, comforted by her confidence. "Now show me something, my friend, and I might give it a try. Maybe I will let you do something *meraviglioso* with my hair. And since I have been so unwilling in the past, I will let you use cosmetics on me too."

She jumped to her feet and clapped her hands. "Oh, I think I have the perfect thing—it is light pink and the top layer is shear and billowy. It sweeps above your ankles when you dance."

I gasped for breath when she pulled it from the closet and held it up to my view. "Ohhh . . . Franca, it is lovely."

* * *

Dinner came quickly and stayed lively around the Chessari table. Laura was dining with Bruno at their cottage home before the dance while Franca and I joined her mother and brothers.

Franca's eyes lit up when she addressed her mother before we sat down to eat. "Mama, Marianna is going to wear my pink chiffon, and we will have an additional surprise in a little bit."

Her mother tilted her head. "Oh, and what would that be, *Carina*? You two have a scheme in mind once again?"

"No, nothing like a scheme, Mama." Franca winked at me. "Just a beautiful plan for Mari—you will see."

Her twelve-year-old brothers seemed fixated on how much pasta they could shovel into their mouths until Dominic lifted his head and raised his eyebrows. "Is it a secret plan? Can we help?"

Damiano lifted his head with a jolt. "*Si, si*, we love to help with secret plans. Come on, Franca, *dai*."

Franca sat down and scowled at her brothers. "You two have no idea how to do this plan; this is just for young women, so you would make a mess of everything. Play war outside and plan your spy tactics."

The boys frowned, shrugged, and went back to twirling their spaghetti around their forks.

After dinner Franca grabbed me by the hand and tugged. "Come now, Marianna, your artist awaits."

* * *

An hour seemed like two before Franca finished my extensive toiletries. She stepped back wide-eyed. "You look like a woman, Marianna."

I stood in my white nylon slip and touched my lips carefully with the tips of my fingers. The mauve-colored lipstick, applied so delicately by Franca, was moist and smooth, not at all odd or unpleasant as I had thought it would be. My hair fell full and soft down my back, and when I tipped my head back it swung in long, loose curls below my waist. The perfume she had sprayed like a mist on my skin rose up sweet and floral to my powdered nose.

I did not know if Franca was right, if I looked like a woman, but I knew I felt like one. I pulled the silky dress over my head and the satin lining rustled as it slipped down my hips and brushed above my ankles. I twirled around the room, my stocking feet sliding across the marble floor.

Chapter Ten

I HOOKED MY ARM THROUGH Franca's to help settle the butterflies doing dives and flips inside my stomach as we walked into the dance hall. Cars and wagons pulled to the curb behind us in constant succession to deliver guests to the door. It seemed the entire population of Siracusa had burst out of their homes and filled the world with new life. Dominic and Damiano dashed ahead of us before we reached the doors, the back of their curly black heads the only thing we could see as they ran into the hall. Franca's mother hurried around us to keep up with the boys.

The dance hall made up the heart of an elegant hotel in town. Marble pillars lined each side of the room like the muscular arms of a giant lifting the roof two stories high above everyone's heads. Painted cherubs covered the ceiling, their bows pulled back and pointed at us from billowing clouds.

Multiple lanterns hung suspended from pillar to pillar, illuminating the shine on the wood floor and bathing the air in an amber glow. A big band played on a stage at the end of the room, where an enormous Italian flag covered the wall behind them.

The music swelled and picked up tempo. Hundreds of people, dressed in their finest, gathered in groups along the sidelines. The toll of war sprinkled like black pepper throughout the crowd as so many wore black to mourn and respect the deaths of family members.

A line of friends and families danced hand in hand and kicked their feet in synchronized rhythm down the long passage. Some broke free and promenaded in front of the crowd, raising their arms to the ceiling to cheers of "*Viva L'Italia.*"

I found my parents seated with a circle of friends—Papa, his eyes puffed up with fatigue but still handsome in his finest suit, and Mama, glowing in a cream-colored gown with pearls around her neck and dangling from her ears. Mama listened intently to something *Signora* Chessari said beside her, and I felt sad for Franca and Laura's mother; like so many times of late, the extended business trips *Signore* Chessari took in the north left the *Signora* alone for weeks at a time.

Papa opened his mouth in awe when he saw me. He squeezed my hand and kissed me on the cheek. "I have never seen such beauty; you look like a seraph, *Carina*."

"*Grazie*, Papa. You are *bellissimo* in your suit. I am very happy that you could come tonight."

He smiled, and Mama patted the empty chair next to her. I sat down, leaned in to my lavender-scented mother, and kissed her smooth cheek.

"I have never seen you more elegant, Mama. I am proud of my beautiful parents."

My mother touched my hair. "And you have become a woman tonight; I think our little starling has turned into a swan." Her eyes glistened with joy, but her words carried an edge of sorrow.

I laid my hand on hers. "Thank you, Mama."

Laura sat on the other side of me next to her mother, her eyes reflected in the blue of her dress, the curve of her growing pregnancy concealed under a lacy wrap. I walked around the table beside her and pressed my cheek against hers and raised my voice over the music. "Where is that brother of mine? Please tell me he is not on patrol tonight or has not abandoned you."

She shook her head. "He went to speak with his comrades for a bit while I visit with your parents, *non fa niente*, I do not mind at all."

I stood and made my way around the circles and shook hands with the neighbors. Nerves tingled on the back of my neck when I spotted *Signore* and *Signora* Scalvone at a nearby table. The desire to look for Massimo pulled me like a riptide, but I could not find the courage to look around the room for him. My legs held steadier as I forced my focus on others and searched for him from the blurred edges of my vision.

I finally walked over and shook hands with each of his grandparents. "Ah, you two look *bellissimi* tonight."

Signore Scalvone shrugged his shoulders. "*Grazie, Signorina*, it is not so easy to look nice all in black." His eyes lit up. "So I break the rules."

His wife frowned but he looked back at me with a twinkle in his eye. "Do you know, *Signorina* Marianna, why I wear all black to mourn the dead, but I insist on my white shirt?" His eyes squinted and sparkled in mischief.

I smiled and shook my head no. "I am afraid you will have to tell me; you have me puzzled."

He chuckled and pointed his crooked finger at his black beret. "Because black is for the dead." He pointed at his white shirt. "But white is for the living." He pointed his finger straight up and raised his voice with enthusiasm. "We are surrounded by death, but there is still a resurrection."

The man's spirit was contagious. I squeezed his bony shoulder and laughed. "You have the kind of attitude that we all need these days, the white shirt in the middle of all the dark worries. Thank you for that."

The women had curled their hair into tight curls or rolled it under like the actresses in America that Franca had shown me in a magazine. The men strutted around the room in loose linen suits, buttoned shirts, and suspenders, while their hair gleamed with hair crème.

A man jumped on stage with his accordion and the members of the band all cried out in unison, "Polka!" The accordionist's fingers moved with precision on the keyboard, and the accordion bellowed a fast-moving polka through the room. Franca and I joined one of the lines that whipped around the hall and called out "*Viva L'Italia*" on cue. We cheered with the crowd, holding up our hands to the flag in salutation of our beloved nation and soldiers. Renewed hope for my country filled my heart.

The guitars and drums slowed the tempo to a melancholy tune. I spotted Bruno in his uniform and beret standing by a wall with a group of soldiers. He signaled me to come over. I held out my hand and he grasped it and hugged me. "I think we need to dance at least once this evening, dear sister."

Tears filled my eyes with pride and love for my brother in his respectable uniform, the gentle look on his face. We walked out to the dance floor, and he shook his finger at me in mock sternness. "No tears, Mari; we are celebrating our inevitable victory and I need your smile tonight."

"No, we are showing our love for our country and the men we love, even if they must fight with the Nazis. But I will do my best. . . . You do look handsome, Bruno. You are a man now, a husband and in a few weeks a father." I took a breath. "Soon you will be a heroic soldier in the battles again."

"I will always come home to you as a big brother, no matter what else I am. Never forget that."

Bruno lifted his brows in a smile and squeezed my hands. "Now let us dance, because the rest of the night belongs to Laura."

The tuba bellowed from the stage in a rhythm that made me want to march in a parade. Drums and trumpets joined in, and Bruno threw me out in a spin. The hem of my dress fluttered, and the crowds went by in a blur. Franca had insisted I wear shoes with at least some heel, and although they were new and a bit unnerving, their rhythmic clip against the wood floor added to my ability to move my feet to the music.

With mock sophistication I swung my hips back and forth to the music until Bruno set me on another whirl. I came to a stop with my back to Bruno and looked up into the sidelines of people. Massimo Scalvone stood amongst the crowd, his dark stare focused straight on me. Bruno grasped my hand and pulled me back around. I finished the dance in a frenzy of jitters, frustrated that I should be so nervous because of Massimo. I darted my eyes to the side to watch for him as we left the floor, unsure if I hoped to see him or hoped I would not.

The fast pace of the dance and tension in my chest made the room a bit unsteady, and I leaned into Bruno. "I am so thirsty; can we get something to drink?"

The band leader announced the next number, and Bruno shook his head. "I need to get back to Laura and our parents; you go get some punch, and we can meet up later."

Bruno kissed me on the cheek and went to find Laura. I took a quick breath, kept my eyes focused straight ahead, and walked toward the long tables of refreshments covered in lacy white tablecloths. Heaped with creamy desserts and lined with cups of punch, the banquet tables did not depict the sad state of war at all; in the countryside, dairy cattle and fresh food were, thankfully, still available.

The music softened to a waltz, and people crowded the floor while I reached for my punch. The sweet juice soothed my dry throat, and I dared a glance into the crowd for Franca. I spotted her in the middle of waltzing couples. The sparkle of her gold dress radiated on her face as Giovanni Orlandini led her to the graceful melody. I smiled in anticipation of the stories I knew would gush from my friend after the dance, sipped at my punch without tasting it, and—

"*Mi scusi, Signorina*, may I have this dance?"

I jumped and almost spilled my punch at the resonance of that voice. Massimo stood beside me, his mouth curved in a smile. My heart beat like a baby bird's in the palm of its captor, and I nodded my head in mute assent. I finished the rest of the punch in one swallow; Massimo took my cup and placed it back on the table before he led me to the dance floor.

I lifted my hand to his shoulder, barely touching the fabric of his shirt with my fingers. I hoped he did not hear my breath escape when he placed his hand on the small of my back. He opened his other hand and I laid my trembling fingers on his palm. His fingers closed over mine, and the sudden dryness in my throat made it hard to swallow. I followed Massimo's lead around the dance floor, and he leaned down to my ear.

"You look rather lovely tonight, Marianna."

Confusion and the tingle of nerves refused to let me raise my head, and I said, "Thank you," to his shoulder. He let go of my hand for just a moment, placed his finger under my chin, and lifted it. "Please forgive me for being so ill-tempered last night on our way home from the food deliveries. I think I was feeling a bit tired. Do not worry—I do not bite, I promise."

He was wearing a light blue shirt that made his skin glow and somehow made the room spin. I had almost lost my voice just looking at him. I had been so sure I would keep my distance if I saw him after his remote silence the evening before. But he looked at me warily, his brow creased as if his effort at frivolity was much more difficult than he could admit. My humor and patience rallied. "You say you do not bite? Well, maybe I do." Much to my relief, I felt a smile on my face even though my voice quivered.

Massimo laughed out loud, and his chest shook and brushed against me. He spun me around and actually winked at me. "Well, then, maybe *I* should be a little bit afraid of *you*."

The wink stirred a wisp of defiance and I inhaled deeply, lifted my head a little higher, and stared into his eyes. "Maybe you should."

He chuckled again despite the tension that returned to his eyes. The song ended, another began, and Massimo kept his fingers wrapped around mine.

"The breeze is usually so nice this time of evening; would you like to step outside with me for a few moments? If I observed correctly, there is a terrace overlooking a courtyard just outside the doors."

I nodded my head, anxious for a chance to break from the crowd and gain control of the flush that kept flooding my face. "Yes, that would be nice."

The opportunity to catch my breath eluded me when Massimo kept his hand against the small of my back. He led me outside, and I realized we would be alone. Crickets sang in chorus through the balmy air while moths fluttered around the torches that lined the stone balcony.

Massimo walked me to a concrete bench that overlooked garden boxes and a fountain of mermaids spewing water from their mouths. My muscles gave a little jerk when he sat down beside me. The flames of the torches reflected in Massimo's eyes, and a moth fluttered past me and dived into the fire.

He cleared his throat. "I want to apologize again for my foul mood yesterday, Marianna. I find my position here to be almost unbearable at times. I have always seen my path so clearly, have known exactly what I was to do and never questioned my integrity or my strength—until now."

"Massimo, no matter what your moods may be, in the short time I have known you, no one could ever convince me you do not have integrity or strength."

He stared at me with such intensity I felt the heat from the torch behind him. He shook his head. "That is not the first time you have defended me. Thank you for your kind words. But I cannot help but question myself when it comes to what I truly desire . . . and the things I know I must do."

I clasped my hands together. "As a soldier under Mussolini, Massimo, how could you not feel wretched because of what you must do at times?"

"Yes, the battle on the field is brutal in more ways than one. Yet at times it is what one must do as a man that is the biggest trial of all."

"I do not pretend to understand all a soldier must feel, but at times you talk as if I can have only half of the puzzle pieces. There are twists and conflicts in your words."

"Twists in my words?"

"You said you find your position here unbearable; I thought you were here on leave, that your position was helping your grandparents?"

He was quiet before he sat up straighter; the corners of his mouth twitched. "Of course it is. That is the truth. I want to give assistance all I can."

"Then I want to ask you again; when you helped my relief group on the road, when we were in danger from those Nazis, they actually obeyed you after they saw your papers. Why would they do that?"

He scowled as he pushed his hair back off his forehead with his fingers, "Ah, yes, what would anyone do in this war without their 'proper' papers? If only I could write my own papers—my life—the way I want to. I cannot even explain my actions." Frustration sparked in his eyes.

"*Va bene*, you cannot tell me all things, or perhaps you feel you cannot trust me. Let me assure you that you can."

He laid his hand on mine. "If there were anyone I would want to tell everything to it is you; I know I could trust you. I could . . ." He leaned in as if he would kiss me. "You draw me in like a bee to nectar. God grant me strength to stay away from you."

He stood and took me by the hand. "I'm being ridiculous. I would not blame you if you turned me down, but would you dance with me one last time?"

The words shocked me and sounded so final, his tone so fatal, while his declaration and the gentleness in his voice melted my misgivings into a puddle at my feet. I gripped my fingers tightly around his. "Yes, I will dance with you."

The band played a soft and melodic tune when we went back inside. Massimo drew me close to him, and I took a deep breath, catching the scent of sandalwood from his skin. The sureness of his steps and the strength of his hand on my back held me steady while the room spun on an axis. He held my other hand tightly in his.

A wall of mirrors captured and framed us in another world. I raised my chin to see our image and looked right into Massimo's eyes. His tension and angst from earlier was gone, replaced by a hazy heat penetrating through my skin. The thump of my heart pounded against him; I opened my lips for breath and a puff of air escaped them when Massimo intertwined his fingers with mine and pulled me closer.

The music swelled in a crescendo of violins, and Massimo lowered his head and pressed his cheek against mine, the stubble of his whiskers prickling at my skin. "Marianna . . . you would be the cause of any man's conflict. You are so very brave and . . . breathtakingly beautiful."

I turned my head the tiniest bit, and Massimo brushed his lips against mine. I matched my lips to his, and everything disappeared but the warmth of his mouth.

The music ended, and Massimo pulled back. He took me by the hand and led me to the side near the crowd. His voice was low, shaky; the tension was back in his eyes when they glanced past mine. "For the last time, please forgive me. You must go back to your family, Marianna. I am so sorry; goodnight."

He turned and left before I could reply. I stared at his back, unable to move while rejection and confusion collided in my head. The room seemed stifled and still until I jerked out of my trance and went out the side door back onto the veranda. I glanced down at the garden to calm my trembling and leaned my shoulder on a marble pillar. I breathed through my nose and held my fingers against my mouth. The sky was black as ink, the stars almost swallowed in the depth.

The clicking of heels grew louder behind me; Franca rushed up and took hold of my hand. "I saw everything. Your face looks pale even in the torch light. Come, sit down on this bench." Franca sat beside me and held my hand. She patted it when I stayed silent. "I can give you only one minute to catch your breath until you have to tell me everything."

Before I could think of a reply, the patio doors burst open and a mass of people flooded out. The shrill shriek of whistles rang from inside the dance hall and sent a shock wave across my chest. Franca grabbed my hand and yelled above the shouts of the passing crowd.

"Something is really wrong; we'd better go to the car. Hurry!"

People ran past in a frenzy and yelled that Nazi soldiers had come to arrest the crowd. My chest burned with panic. "My parents, Bruno and Laura. . . ." Massimo. . . .

Franca's eyes widened like a frightened foal. "Of course, I am coming with you. Go, go, go."

I pushed my way against and through the crowd into the building, making sure Franca was behind me. The whistles had stopped but people still scrambled out the side doors. Some tripped and fell while others cowered and froze in their seats or huddled together in the corners. A line of German soldiers stood on the stage, the band members still in place behind them, their instruments gripped in their hands.

A tall German soldier marched to the microphone, his boots against the hollow floor like the blow of hammers through the spacious room. He blew his whistle in short bursts and snapped his fingers at the soldiers lined up behind him. They immediately marched to the back of the stage, ripped the Italian flag from the wall, and tore it to pieces with their bare hands—some used knives they pulled from their boots. A cold burn of anger made me shiver. I grabbed Franca by the hand and we held on to each other.

Tears were rampant. Men and women, young and old, buried their heads into the chest of the nearest loved one, everyone's faces grim and taut in suppressed resentment. My knees were weak but my back held me straight against such bullying—such an evil lust for power.

The soldier in front had not moved, his stone face chiseled in a sneer. "The display of the Italian flag is a flagrant disregard of the law. The flag of our beloved Führer unites us all and is the only flag you will see or display ever again or you will be executed for treason. This assembly will cease immediately. If you do not return to your homes, you will all be under arrest."

His guttural German accent smeared his words with hatred that seeped under my skin. The room was a whirl of whispers, cries, and gasps as people headed for the doors. Franca and I ran to the place we had last seen our family near the front stage. I caught a glimpse of Bruno ushering our parents, Laura, and her mother and brothers out the front door. I called to him over the crowd, but the noise of the room swallowed my cries. A large brigade of soldiers ran in from a side door into the hall, gripped their rifles by the butt and the barrel across their bodies, and used them to push the crowd out the doors.

People gripped and grasped at each other to keep from being separated as they stumbled and pushed each other toward the exits and away from the cold metal of weapons pressed against their backs. I caught a glimpse of the stage; the man with the accordion crouched and hovered over his instrument while a soldier held a baton above his head and screeched in German. My heart dropped into my stomach as we were herded out the doorway and past another line of soldiers; they were Italian soldiers, their rifles at the ready against their own countrymen. I stared right into the eyes of some of them. Either they were puppets at the end of a string, or their hearts had turned to granite.

Franca nudged me from behind. "Say nothing, Marianna; go, quick, keep moving."

People in carriages and automobiles honked their horns or slapped the reins of their horses to get away in a hurry while Nazi soldiers pointed their rifles at them. There was no sign of Massimo or his grandparents, and I hoped they had gotten away. I looked in vain for my parents' wagon, the Chessari car, or any of our family members.

Franca pulled me behind a courtyard wall. "Wait here just a moment; maybe our family will come looking for us."

"It is too dangerous to stay here; we can run all the way home if we have to. We need to go now." I reached for Franca's hand to pull her away from the wall when Bruno rounded the corner. Relief washed over his face at the sight of us. I hugged him and held onto his hand as he pulled us into a run.

I scratched my knee and tore the hem of my gown when we climbed the outside wall of the courtyard. We ran across the grass in the dark to the Chessaris' car. All of my family and Franca's were there, and I was relieved my parents had abandoned our wagon in favor of the faster vehicle. Franca and I squeezed in the back while Bruno got behind the wheel. He jammed his foot on the gas pedal, and rocks spewed behind us from under the wheels. "Do not worry, Mama and Papa, I will have a worker drive me back in a bit when the soldiers are gone, and I will drive the wagon home. We've been through this type of thing before, and all will be well."

My father's head lay back against the seat, the flash of passing headlights illuminating his pasty white color against the black leather upholstery.

Traffic was still backed up, and we had to slow down. Franca's twin brothers whooped and hollered when we passed the soldiers in front of the dance hall. "*Auguri Nazi scemi, abbiamo vinto noi*—good luck, you fools, we are still the winners!"

Elisa Chessari grabbed her son by the shoulder. "No, Damiano, we are moving too slowly—they will hear you."

Dominic answered first. "We won, Mama, we got away. We hid in the car in back of the building and did not let them force us to leave the girls. Damiano and I thought of the plan. We are so much smarter than those German *scemi*."

The headlights of a car behind us showed the grim look on *Signora* Chessari's face. She raised her long finger to her lips. "Shh . . . So you did, but you know the dangers."

The boys' shoulders slumped. Franca had told me her brothers wrote their father often of their plans to thwart Hitler and Mussolini. She also told me that unbeknownst to them, their mother never mailed the parts about their war strategies and rebellion for fear the letters would be intercepted and put the family in danger for treason.

The trip out of town took longer as people, carriages, and vehicles jammed the roads. I sat wedged between Franca and my mother. The car quieted for the remainder of the trip home, the sniffles from Laura in the front seat next to Bruno the only sound. I rested my head on Mama's shoulder, my anger over the Nazi threats seething in my stomach and my mind swirling with the memory of Massimo's kiss.

Chapter Eleven

AN UNSPOKEN TREPIDATION LAY LIKE a blanket on the countryside. The ensuing week had been quiet, subdued. Hired laborers and neighbors carried on where moods were tense, faces somber, and glimpses over the shoulder frequent. Shutters and curtains closed earlier in the day; trips to town became a group affair.

Despite the fearful end of the dance, Papa seemed a bit more energetic and fished every morning with Aviano. I stayed close to home, cooked, and gardened with Mama and read for hours on the grass next to our pond.

I was grateful Uncle Mimmo and Aunt Pasqua were not here. At least for the time being we could focus on peace and reassurance. When the visions of the soldiers at the dance rose up, I fought the Axis in my head and refused to let their tyranny take my courage or defeat me. Yet the war still bombed and hacked its way across the continent and the world.

My personal conflict was more persistent; alone in the garden or lying across my bed at night, I watched the moon rise and turn from an orange globe to a silver beacon while I relived the moments with Massimo. His hand on my waist, his musky scent, and the taste of his lips all assailed me, bombarded my thoughts and held me captive no matter how I battled.

His abrupt departure the night of the dance remained a mystery and I replayed the scene in my mind with confusion and a knot of pain at the top of my stomach. It had been a week. News from town and the market had been especially quiet while the silence between our home and the Scalvones' farm hummed in my head.

There was something wrong that was threatening in Massimo's life, but he refused to tell me what it was. My thoughts were a whirlpool of conflict and fear. I stopped reading many times beside the pond and just stared into the sky.

Sunday morning I looked in vain for Massimo and his grandparents at mass. My mother worried about the *Signora* since her bad episode at our home and the stress of the raid. While I prepared the afternoon meal, she and my father went to the Scalvones' to check on them; I tried not to dwell on the fact that they may see Massimo.

Chapter Twelve

MASSIMO

I HAD CONFRONTED THE ENEMY face to face with more bravery and self-control than I had Marianna De'Angelis. Only the worst kind of creature would go near a woman—an innocent woman—and put her life in danger because of his own desires.

I'd fought like a madman back through the crowds the night of the dance to make sure she made it out of the hotel safely when the German soldiers raided. I watched her scale a wall and dash to her neighbor's car. Only then could I run back to my grandparents' truck and hurry them home. But when I'd danced with her, kissed her, I'd almost given in and jeopardized everything. Guilt had been my constant companion since then; I knew the rules—the role I had to play and the risks if I pursued Marianna.

Now her mother and father sat in my grandparents' living room, their kind faces creased in concern for my grandmother and their sincerity about to make my determination to stay away from Marianna snap.

Signore De'Angelis smiled, and the white lines of the crow's feet around his eyes disappeared. "Massimo, during these difficult times we must all stick together to support one another. We cannot let one assault by the enemy keep us down or hiding in our homes. We have known and loved your grandparents like family far too long. That makes you family, and you are to return with us for an afternoon meal without hesitation."

I opened my mouth to give one more excuse when my nonna laid her soft hand on my knee. "*Per favore*, please come with us, Grandson. Our time together is so short."

I shook my head in defeat and force a smiled of reassurance for my grandparents and our guests. "Of course, I would love to dine with you today."

Chapter Thirteen

MARIANNA

THE THOUGHT THAT MY PARENTS may return with news about Massimo set my nerves on edge. Fresh air swept through the kitchen from the open window, stirred the hair at the nape of my neck, and sent a shiver of expectation across my skin. The clop of horses' hooves coming from a distance almost blended with the rhythm of the knife as I chopped peppers into thin slices.

Our old rooster strutted in front of our house like a guard dog. He crowed, and I knew my parents were home. The front door opened and Mama's voice echoed down the hall. "Friends, please come and make yourselves at home in the kitchen; I am certain Marianna has everything almost ready." I turned to the stove before they got to the kitchen and stirred a pot of pasta as they came into the room.

Mama led our guests in and pulled out the chairs from the table. The stooped figures of *Signore* and *Signora* Scalvone shuffled in, and Massimo came in behind them. The steam from the pot rose like a cloud over my face and took my breath before I fanned it away.

Massimo stopped under the archway of the kitchen entry as if hesitant to enter. He leaned against the wall and shifted his feet while mine stayed cemented in place. I stirred the pasta sauce for several minutes without looking up. When I gained my courage, I glanced at Massimo. He nodded his head in my direction with a nervous smile and walked over to the marble counter beside me where I had just chopped the peppers. "I believe I owe you a salad, *Signorina* De'Angelis. I was a terrible assistant and abandoned you in the middle of the task the last time we were here for dinner."

The sting of his abrupt departure at the dance rose up again. I bit my lower lip. "Well I understood your reason for leaving . . . that time."

My voice trailed off despite my determination to sound strong. "Your grandmother was ill."

I quickly stepped away to catch my breath and headed to the table. I patted *Signora* Scalvone on the shoulder. "I am so glad you are well today, *Signora*. I do not cook as well as my mother. I am afraid you will all have to tolerate my efforts."

I shook *Signore* Scalvone's hand, and he grinned. "No matter how old I am, I know a good pasta sauce when I smell one. It will be *delisiosa*, I know."

Papa tended to the horses and carts outside while Mama set the plates on the table. I had no choice but to return to Massimo's side and prepare a salad with shaking hands. Time turned back, as if the Scalvones had never left the first time they had come to have dinner with us.

I breathed in deeply and set the basket of greens within Massimo's reach. "I suppose I will let you take care of the lettuce, Massimo. I remember you preferred that task the last time."

Massimo hesitated before he reached for the leafy vegetable, his smile sheepish. "A lot has happened between us since then, has it not?"

I stared at his mouth as he spoke, an urge to press my fingers over my lips.

"Yes . . . yes, a lot has happened. . . ."

Massimo held the leaves of romaine still in his hands without looking at them, his gaze locked on mine. He swallowed hard. "I was grateful to see that you made it safely out of the dance."

"You saw me?"

"Yes, I had just reached my grandparents' table when the Germans arrived. I got them to the truck and ran back to check, to see that you were safe."

"I . . . thank . . . there was no need; you had said your goodbye."

Tension creased the corners of Massimo's eyes. He placed the bunch of lettuce back on the counter and took me by the hand. "I wanted to . . . Marianna . . . I cannot. . . ."

I blinked hard and looked away. "I know. You keep saying that you 'cannot,' but it is all you say. So maybe I 'cannot' either."

He pushed his hair back with his other hand. "I need to talk to you; there are reasons—"

Papa's voice bellowed into the room. "*Carina Mia*, our guest is working in the kitchen again? The war has truly turned this world upside down. Please, Massimo, I insist you come sit beside your grandparents."

At the sound of Papa's voice, Massimo lifted his hand from mine, exposed my skin to the cooler air of the room, and headed toward the table. "Do not worry, *Signore* De'Angelis. If the world was free to focus on kitchen chores instead of war every day, then perhaps the human race could regain its dignity once again."

Papa lifted a glass of water while he patted the chair beside him for Massimo to sit down. "To kitchens, salads, and the more important things in life."

Massimo lifted his own glass of water. "And nothing could be more important than family or all of those we love."

I tore at the lettuce myself and tossed it into bowls before I glanced at everyone at the table.

Mama smiled at the Scalvones. "You have quite the generous and wise grandson; it is obvious he desires to do some good in the world, even if it means helping his hosts in the kitchen."

Massimo's grandmother smiled back at my mother before she patted Massimo's cheek with her wrinkled hand. "Oh, yes, you would never know he grew up being waited on by servants, would you? He works harder than anybody we have ever hired, and he does it for free."

Massimo set his glass of water down and shook his head. "Oh, no, Nonna, I do it for your almond biscotti."

The room filled with the echoes of everyone's laughter but mine. I dished the ravioli into our blue china bowls with a tremor in my hands. Steam danced across the tops of the dishes, and I lifted the lid from the simmering pot of pasta sauce and dipped the ladle inside.

Signora Scalvone still laughed from the table. "Yes, our Massimo's fiancée is a very lucky girl to have him; I hope she realizes that. She is the daughter of a general, a very high-ranking general."

My hands froze on the ladle. A hot bubble rose to the top of the thick sauce and exploded, splattering the red pulp all over the front of my white blouse. The word *fiancée* pealed like a bell through the room. My ears rang while I reached for a dish towel and tried to wipe the scalding sauce from my clothes. But it was no use; it only spread farther across my chest.

I kept my head lowered, turned away from the stove, and looked toward the table. "Excuse me; I seem to have made a real . . . mess of myself. I need to change."

Signora Scalvone's announcement glued me to the floor for one more brief moment before my head lifted of its own will. I looked at Massimo.

His eyes were huge, glazed over, and as black and empty as the pit of my stomach. He opened his mouth as if to speak and shook his head back and forth.

I heard Massimo get to his feet, the voices of friends and family calling behind me, but had no idea what anyone said as I bolted out of the room and up the stairs.

* * *

I kept my focus on my family when I came back downstairs several minutes later, my emotions pounding at my temples like a hammer. Relief eased the pain when I saw Bruno and Laura at the table.

Papa patted my hand and smiled. "There you are, all nice and cleaned up. I like this pink blouse even better than your other one anyway."

I glanced up into the deep eyes of my father. "Thank you, Papa."

I could not look at Massimo. He was quiet and much more serious. His hesitant attempts at humor or to engage me in conversation landed flat at my feet. I made an excuse each time to look another way or leave the table to get something we needed.

My father kept the conversation moving. "We are determined to let our Marianna be the first *Siciliana* woman to cross the ocean and attend an American university when the war is over—perhaps even in New York City if she wants to."

I perked up a little at the mention of university—of any escape—and out of the corner of my eye, I saw Massimo look at me.

Signore Scalvone waved his weathered hand and shrugged his shoulders. "You just cannot keep these young ones under your wing like you used to. The world is growing bigger. It is time to end this wretched war and go find adventure." He winked at me and grinned.

I sat a little straighter as Papa went on. "We do not know how we would get her there with the oceans filled with battleships for now, so she is stuck in her mother's kitchen, studying at the library and working with this old fisherman for now." Papa patted his hand on his chest.

Bruno tore a piece of bread from a one of the loaves then set it back in the middle of the table. "I do not know what a woman does with a degree, except for teaching or nursing, but Marianna will find something wonderful—I have no doubt."

I managed a small smile at my brother. "Thank you, Bruno. You know some have said that you can be excused from military duty in America if you are attending university."

Bruno gave me a meaningful look. "Well, like I have said many times, who would defend our country if we all went to America? I will conquer the war, and you conquer the university."

Massimo frowned. "How safe can it be for a young woman alone to attend an American university? I could understand if a father were concerned about his child going off and running to America with bombs flying through the air."

My muscles went rigid. "Well, since there are no children here and no one of your concern, then you can rest easy and go on with your life knowing that anyone you sincerely care about is safe." I wanted to bite my lip to keep the edge out of my voice, but I could not stop myself.

He folded his napkin and laid it on the table without looking away from me. "I do not believe anyone is safe these days—certainly not young women, not even me . . . at least not anymore."

My mother stood. "All right then, please everyone go relax in the parlor while I prepare some coffee and dessert for us." She took me by the elbow as we all stood. "Marianna, would you please stay and assist me?"

"I was wondering, *Signora* De Angelis, if I might borrow your daughter for a few moments?" We both spun around at the sound of his voice and looked at Massimo. He put his hands in his pockets, his eyes wary.

My mother's eyes were soft and gentle when she looked back at him. "Yes, of course you may, Massimo. Mari, perhaps you should show him the pond, if you and Bruno have not already?"

My spine stiffened. I did not answer my mother.

Massimo turned to his grandparents. "Please feel free to return home if you need to; I will enjoy the walk home a little later."

They both nodded and waved on their way to the parlor. "See you soon, Grandson."

WITHOUT A GLIMPSE TO SEE if Massimo was behind me, I marched out the back door and headed across the grass. I opened the gate between two pecan trees that led to the pond and let it swing shut as I entered the flower garden. When it did not latch, I guessed that Massimo followed close behind.

The gate opened into a garden full of my mother's rainbow of flowers. I reached the stone paving that circled the pond and sat on a black wrought-iron chair while the lowering sun cast the garden in hazy color. Butterflies dipped down for a drink from the deep green pond and sent tiny ripples across the surface, but I gave them only a glance.

Massimo sat down in a chair across from me, leaned forward, and rested his elbows on his knees. I looked at his face in spite of myself—at his smooth skin, the faint shadow of facial hair above his mouth and across his jaw. I had just built a wall of defiance, and now the quiver in my abdomen was back again. An ache spread through me; this face, this young man, was in another world now and would never have anything to do with me. The reality hit me that I had wanted him to have everything to do with me—had hoped, had dreamed without letting myself face it until now. Now all chance was gone.

I feigned new interest in the butterflies while a flood of tears crested behind my eyelids and the weight of Massimo's stare threatened to push me down in my seat.

"I do not blame you if you hate me, but I also know that mercy is one of your attributes. Could I have just a few minutes of that mercy, Marianna?"

My voice was locked in my throat, but I nodded my head.

Massimo concentrated on the ground in front of his feet before taking in a deep breath and looking up at me. "The first time I saw you, the day you were peeking at me from around the tree, I thought you were an apparition or someone sent to spy on me. When you darted away, I jumped up on the wall in an instant to find you and realized you were more than an apparition—you were real and beautiful. But it was more than that, something I could not describe."

The haziness of the day must have seeped into my mind; his words spun around in my head. Massimo stood and picked a flower from the mossy edge of the pond and began pulling at the petals with his fingers while he paced, his eyes dark and somber.

"I watched you until you rounded the corner, confused at the vague sense of loss when you were gone. I reminded myself of my situation and pushed my sanity back into place. Yet, fool that I am, I found myself thinking of you."

The tremor in my chest over his words was cruel. My own body betrayed me with hopeful reactions while loss, anger, and disappointment pulled me down like an anchor.

A light wind rustled Massimo's shirt sleeves and the hair at the nape of his neck. "Although it is a small community, I was still surprised to see you at the fish market. Your shock at seeing me and your apparent nervousness amused me—while your defiance stirred me. I found myself drawn to you and could not quit looking at your beauty."

I stayed unmoving and unmoved in my seat while Massimo paced across the stone pavers, his face drawn and serious.

"I followed you up the hill that day on my horse knowing once again that I was an idiot. I tried to dwell on your youth, your innocence. Nothing helped."

I stood, opened my mouth to say something, but Massimo dropped the flower to the ground and held up his hand. "Please, if you would just let me continue, let me fully explain, maybe you will not think the very worst of me. I am so sorry. . . ."

I sat down and gripped my hands together, the metal chair warm against my back while I looked at the man who made me want to run and hide.

"That day when the Nazi soldier had you pinned to the ground I wanted to kill him to protect you and had no choice but to go with you to be certain you were safe. What ignorant irony—being seen with me, by the wrong people, could be an even greater danger to you. I knew that day that my attraction to you was out of control.

"I pushed myself away and built a barrier that I told myself I could never cross. But the time for the town dance had arrived. My grandparents so wanted to attend, to see their friends and feel like the world was normal again. I knew I had to take them. I had thought of you incessantly but tried to push back the hope that I could see you again. I made a plan; if I saw you there at the dance, I would stay away."

Massimo stopped pacing and stood just a few steps away by the pond. "The sight of you set my heart pounding like a school boy's, Marianna. I watched you from behind the crowd until I could not stand it anymore, and when I asked you to dance and was touching you, I finally faced how much I had been longing to . . . it was like falling into a fire as I held you and kissed you. I berated myself for being a selfish idiot and walked away. I should have known better . . . I had no business. . . ."

I stood straight up and walked over to the pond, standing before Massimo. Confusion made my every breath tremble. I blocked out the pounding in my head, a thick coating in my throat, and worst of all, the tears I could barely contain as I stared into his beautiful, unattainable face. A wall of anger and frustration rose up to protect me.

"Why are you telling me this?"

His jaw muscles tightened and he took a deep breath. "There is no simple answer to that."

My mind ran as rapidly as my heartbeat. "You obviously love someone and want to marry her; you cannot mean the things you are saying. I do not even know what you are saying, what you can possibly mean. Am I supposed to feel better or find you valiant because your feelings have been so difficult? When all along you kept the simple fact that you are marrying someone else a secret? Do you think that if you 'dwell on my youth' you can play with me, take the things you say to me as a passing game for amusement? As if I am too much of a child to matter or understand?"

Massimo's eyes widened and he shook his head back and forth. He lifted his hands, palms up. "No—no—no—please, Marianna, let me explain. There are things I am not supposed to say, secrets I am to protect."

He reached for my hand but I pulled it away. I hated that I could not stop my voice from shaking; even my hands trembled now, and I folded my arms and curled my hands into fists against my sides to still them. In spite of all of my defiance, I was still aware of a power that surrounded Massimo and threatened to pull me in.

I moved one hand over the ache in my chest and steadied a wave of dizziness. "I cannot imagine why your engagement must be such a secret; your grandparents knew. Maybe you should go now. I am not a child who must be kept ignorant of danger or protected like an imbecile for my own good. Regardless of what you may think, I am a woman, and I have a life and plans just as you do."

I wanted to run toward the house, throw the gate open, and rush through it. But somehow, in spite of everything, I knew that this time it would latch behind me, that there would be finality in that closing. I could not do it. The sun slipped behind the edge of a mountain, and a new breeze rushed up through my hair and cooled my feverish face. Crickets began their evening songs along with the distant cries of seagulls.

A shadow of vulnerability washed across Massimo's face and flattened the luster in his eyes. He slowly reached for my hand, his voice almost a whisper as his fingers interlaced with mine. "You are right. No more secrets. If you will just hear me out, I am going to tell you everything."

The warmth of his hand loosened all of my limbs and made me want to curl into a ball to protect myself. I eased out the breath I had been holding and blinked back the pressure behind my eyes as I let him guide me back to the chairs. I sat down and caught my tears with my fingers. I could not look at him, did not know if I even wanted to. I had never asked for this, was happy before. Free. Now this man had walked in, and my life sat on an invisible cliff.

Massimo swallowed hard and sat down across from me again, clasped his hands together, and leaned forward. He sat silent for so long that I shifted in my seat. "Tell me, Massimo; perhaps we both need you to say it."

He gazed at me in earnest. "I am going against my father's warning and the threat of a very dangerous man in order to tell you the full story."

He blew out a breath before he began. "But I want you to know why my grandmother said what she did today and the real story of why I am here. Perhaps even why I have acted the fool, although there is no excuse."

I nodded my head but could not smile to reassure him before he began.

"I come from a different life than here. We are a political family in Foggia; my father is a high-ranking government official. Most of my father's people come from here, but he left home at eighteen for an education and a career in politics. He always wanted to be a leader, to be one who made a difference, who helped Italy be a better country. He still does."

I kept my eyes on him. His head hung down at times, although his words sounded so sure, like something he should be proud of. He sat up a little straighter.

"My father has been in government for all of my twenty-one years and more. There is a bond there between my father and me, closeness I have always treasured and depended on. My mother is from Milano—black hair, an elegant woman." Massimo's eyes lit up at the thought of her. "I cannot remember a time that she was not wearing lipstick as red as her roses that line our drive. Entertaining political guests and hosting large, important parties has been her full-time job through all the years I can recall.

"My sister, Nicla, is three years older than I, and we had the duty since we were children to stand beside our parents in elegant dress and smile politely while we endured the cheek pinches and *baci* of hundreds of old women at government parties and balls."

I could not help but be touched by the vision of Massimo as a little boy in formal clothes at the mercy of doting old women. Massimo's lips twisted before his brows lowered once again. "And then the war arrived. Mussolini joined Hitler and the Axis, and the elegant guests turned into solemn and angry men in secret meetings behind locked doors."

The moist, briny fragrance from the pond hung heavy in the air, the mist clammy on my skin.

"From the beginning, because of the evil intent in Hitler and Mussolini, my father has worked—behind the lines, you might say—to protect our country against them, against the Axis. There are those who agree, who work with him and risk everything to do what they can to save Italia. And there are those who lust for blood and circle like salivating demons around anyone whose loyalty to the Nazis is questionable."

Massimo's eyes narrowed as he grimaced, tapping his fists against the arm of his chair. "One particular day, a few months ago, my father called me into his office. His brow was beaded in sweat and he looked as if all life had been drained from his face. He told me that the man who had just left, a General Barberi, had come to enlist him back into the military to be a commanding officer. He told me he would have to serve directly under Barberi and Mussolini for the Nazis."

Massimo's tone was crisp, bitter, and lined with rage as he spewed out his story. "General Barberi is an extremely powerful and treacherous man, the instrument in hundreds of deaths and thousands more arrests of our own countrymen. My father is a highly sought-after and respectable political figure. Barberi knows that enlisting my father on his team would win him great praise and would endow him with more power and authority.

"That alliance would be unbearable for my father, so he refused it. Until—" Massimo stood and pushed his hair back, paced back and forth with his hands in the pockets of his trousers. He stopped and stared straight at me. "Barberi told my father that he had enlisted spies who had been watching him, and they had uncovered and followed my father's secret work—his organization of Italian Partisans and their movements against the Axis."

The crickets seemed to lurk in the bushes around us, their evening songs turned into warning whistles. Massimo shook his head slowly back and forth, his face contorted in disgust.

"That is not all. As if this danger for my father was not bad enough, that slithering snake Barberi constricted his coils even tighter."

He was quiet so long I finally whispered, "What did he do?"

Massimo laughed bitterly. "Barberi has a daughter, a young conniving blonde daughter, named Fatima whom I had met at parties in our home. Barberi boasted that this girl had been watching me for some time, claimed to have fallen in love with me, and was determined to have me for a husband."

A shiver burned my skin at the mention of the woman who would have Massimo, while he shook his head and took deep breaths in disgust. "Barberi looked straight at my father and told him that he knew he worked as a connection for the Italian Partisans—that the Partisans were now backed and supplied by the American OSS, and that made him a full-blown traitor. He waved a paper in my father's face—a list of the others in government who work under my father against Hitler. Some of them are my family's most beloved friends."

Massimo rubbed the back of his neck and paced on the pavers in front of me until I thought he must be exhausted, his shoes crushing the tiny white flowers that popped up through the cracks. He held up three of his fingers. "Barberi listed three things that my father must do. One, he had to stop working with the Partisans; two, he had to come quietly into military service as Barberi's assistant; and three, he had to make me marry the daughter. Only then would Barberi burn the list of Partisans and prevent our entire family from being arrested as traitors."

I became conscious of an ache in my shoulders and realized it was from gripping the arms of my chair so tightly. What a fool I had been—a silly child playing with hopeless infatuation in the middle of a war. My heart fell, and I covered my face with my hands while the evening cries of the gulls in the distance echoed in my head.

"When? How soon do you have to marry her?"

Massimo threw his arms up in frustration and turned my direction while his breath escaped between his teeth. "I do not know, but it is likely to be soon. The thought of it makes me rage inside like a volcano. My father has tried everything he can up to this point to find a safe way out, but to no avail. I have no choice—Barberi told him the Nazis would come for my mother first, then the rest of us. I will do what I have to do for the safety of my family. I would sacrifice my own life if I had to."

"Is there anyone here who can help you? Any connection you could make to get yourself and your family out of the country?" Before I could finish my question, I remembered how widespread his father's connections must be as a Partisan. Without ever meeting him, I knew Massimo's father would never escape if it put others at risk.

"If only we could, and take all of those at risk with us. There are far too many. My father is not one to be bullied or to see his family threatened and his son used in such a way, but the solution takes time—and time is running out."

"I am a lieutenant in the military, and before I came here I was assigned to protect Foggia. The minute General Barberi set this trap, my father became a madman, determined to find a way to stop him. He sent my mother in secret to stay with my sister and her husband in Switzerland to keep her out of the crossfire. He started paperwork to put me on leave from duty and get me out of Foggia in hopes the girl would forget her ridiculous infatuation—or we could at least stall plans for the marriage. He then set his sights on his endangered comrades."

Massimo sat down, his shoulders slumped in defeat. "I worry every day that he may sacrifice his own safety to protect the rest of us."

I knew about sacrifices; even though we did not want to support Italy's alliance with Germany, my own brother refused to find a way out of fighting with our army because of the danger to our family—especially to Laura—if he did not go.

There were so many willing to die for the sake of protecting their families. Devastating sacrifices were being made because of a madman. Visions of my friend Enzo popped into my head—his gapped-toothed grin on the playground when we were kids, the stare-down we had at our first dance when we were both too afraid to walk out on the floor after he asked me to dance.

At school Enzo was nicknamed "the bird boy"; after windstorms he gathered the baby birds that had been blown from their nests and hand-fed them until they were big enough to be set free. Once during a summer storm he fell from a tree and broke his arm while trying to put a baby bird back in its nest.

Last year he came home in a casket from France, his entire midsection missing after he fell on a grenade to save his comrades.

I stared at the blurred ground until Massimo spoke again. "I thought I might discourage the Barberi girl myself, but every time I saw her and tried it was obvious she was used to getting what she wanted and expected to turn me her way regardless of what I thought or felt."

It was almost comical that Massimo would think spending time with this girl might discourage her—that he could be that blind to his own beauty, the strength about him that made a woman want. It only made him more desirable. Pain drained through me again. The clouds drifted toward the horizon, and Massimo huffed in exasperation.

"I played a polite role, and before I knew of it my father had secretly arranged military leave for me. He made the needful status of political connections here in Siracusa and my grandparents sound imminent and dire and announced that I would have to spend a few weeks here helping them through a 'crisis.' We tried to keep the engagement and the whole evil plot silent, but before I left, word spread to my grandparents that I was engaged. General Barberi sealed my fate and insisted I give Fatima a ring in front of a ballroom full of people the night before my departure."

The vision of a ring on Fatima's finger constricted like a band around my chest. I closed my eyes against it while Massimo continued.

"We have stayed silent about my repulsion to the girl for safety's sake. Barberi believes his plan is foolproof, that he has our cooperation and that his power is intact—it is better for now that he live in his delusion. Even my grandparents believe I am happily engaged. Of course, they know nothing of the evil in this family or the danger my father is in. They are very old; it is better that they do not know."

I rubbed my hands up and down my arms to ward off the chill of his story. "Massimo, are you safe being seen anywhere but at your grandparents' home? Did you put yourself at risk that day you helped us on the road and went with me into the city?"

He held his palms up to stop my concerns. "No, I wanted to help you. I had to know you were safe, no matter the risk. And at least those ridiculous papers state that I am here under 'protection,' so that allowed me to help. However . . ." His eyes locked into mine. "Barberi is a snake. I know he's had me watched, at least in town. If word were to reach him that I have been seen with a beautiful young woman . . . there could be serious danger in that."

I squeezed my eyes shut again and let my head tip back against the metal chair, unable to block out Massimo's words while I tried to think of a way to help him. He continued with his story and I fought the urge to stop him, not sure if I could take anymore.

"My father used his connections to make me an officer in the military. Under his authority I am here on a special assignment that is not to be interfered with. It is all a mockery and designed only to keep me out of harm's way until we find an escape or I marry Barberi's daughter. That is how I had the paperwork to make the Nazis leave that day. Mussolini himself signed those papers. What a disgusting lie. I have been nothing but the ludicrous pawn, a deceitful idiot and coward hiding in the countryside while my father sweats and risks his life to find our way out.

"But if I return now I would have to marry the girl soon, or I would risk putting my father and many others in worse danger. His letters only tell me plans are in motion, to trust him, and that I must stay here for now for both of our sakes. Each day I wait to hear from him or the military with an assignment, news, or orders. But as time passes I realize that my fate—this sham of a marriage—is inevitable, that I will be that little boy again who had to entertain my Papa's guests in the hardest role I have yet to play."

I had to hold my breath and look away from Massimo to keep the sobs in my throat at bay. My eyes stung as the tears gave way. "I know that you are telling the truth. I am so sorry for your pain, for the danger for you . . . and . . . your family."

The setting sun glistened on the sweat of Massimo's forehead, and he rubbed his eyes in fatigue. I knew his powerlessness must feel like an anchor around his neck. I stood, took his hand, and led him to the pond.

"Here, kneel down and splash some of the water that trickles over the rocks on your face. It will help you feel better." I sat on a wide, flat stone next to the pond while Massimo used both hands to wash his face in the water. He shook the droplets from the front of his hair, sat on the grass next to me, and the ache to touch him made me tremble. Massimo watched me and ran his fingers down my cheek before letting his hand fall back in his lap.

My eyes were wet again, but now I had no desire to catch and hide the tears. His pain was mine. As hope waned, I realized how much I had wanted him, that being near him had created a part of me I never knew I needed. All of my foolish stubbornness blew away with the leaves across the ground. I watched them tumble helplessly in a blur until Massimo spoke again.

"People are asked to do so much more in this war—have their lives, bodies, loved ones, and freedom ripped to shreds right before their eyes. I have endeavored to help my grandparents to the best of my ability since they have honest need of assistance. And I have wanted to make my time mean something and do what I can. All was in motion until I saw you, Marianna. An arrow pierced me at the sight of you . . . and no matter how much I have fought it, I have let you take root in me."

He knelt in front of me, lifted my chin, and looked into my wet eyes. "The most beautiful of rose buds in my mother's garden cannot compare to you; soft, elegant, glowing with beauty and grace."

His eyes were filled with tears, and they burned with sincerity. He stood and took my hand, lifted me to my feet, and slid his arms around me as a gentle wind twirled in ribbons around us. My heart danced in joy to be held like this, trembled at what it might do to me when he left. I ran my hands up his back, embraced and breathed in the fresh scent of him while he pressed his cheek to mine.

"My life is in such limbo, Marianna, such distress. I can offer nothing but a promise that I will not use you, mistreat you, or endanger you in any way anymore by being near you. I was compelled to tell you my story, because . . . because from the moment I saw you I felt you were a part of me. I wanted you to know the truth, and knew I could trust you with it."

I could feel his heart pulse against my breast. Strong. Steady. He pulled his head back, looked in my eyes, and lifted his hand to my cheek.

"You pull me in like the tide, but I have no choice but to go the other way. I have to stay away from you to keep you out of this nightmare, to keep you safe. You deserve your life, your freedom, your dreams."

He brushed his lips across my jaw, holding them against my cheek for the briefest of moments. "Goodbye, Marianna. I will think of you . . . for the rest of my life." His hands slid down my arms before he stepped back and turned to go. I stood paralyzed, staring at his back as his feet pressed down the thick, dark grass with each step he took away from me.

Chapter Fifteen

PRESSURE SWELLED IN MY HEAD with each footstep that Massimo took until it erupted with a tremor that rippled to the ends of my fingertips.

"Massimo!"

I darted across the grass and reached for his hand. "I cannot watch you walk away from me again. I cannot do it."

He stopped, eyes wide in astonishment.

I fought the quiver in my voice. "It is too late. You have come into my life. I can decide what risks I will take, of whom I will or will not be a part."

My chin quivered, and I clenched my teeth to stop it. The wisdom of my parents flowed into my mind, empowered me. "Why should evil men be allowed to have all the control they want over us? They may block the oceans with fiery barges and fill the skies with wrath, but I will not let them possess my soul."

I pressed my fisted hand against my heart. "I will not let them decide who I will love. This war may even kill me, but it will never own who I am or what and who I want." I breathed deeply to steady my shaky breath.

Massimo stared back at me. Seconds passed, his jaw still locked. The red fire of the sun reflected in his eyes when he took me by the shoulders. "What an arrogant fool I am. Heaven help me, what a complete fool I am."

I was not finished yet and took a deep breath "I will nev—"

Before I could finish, Massimo stopped my words with his mouth, his lips covering mine with such strength he left me barely enough room to breathe. I gasped for air through my nose, and my mouth gave way to his. He kissed me with an urgency to match the power of the threats held over our heads. I kissed him back. I let every wall I had built around my heart crumble at our feet.

His shirt glided along his skin as I slid my hands up his back and over his shoulders. He kissed my face, along my jaw, and more gently on my eyelids. I slowed my breath when he pressed his lips at my temple and held me against him. "Marianna De'Angelis. All this fighting, the nightmare and power of war, and you are my undoing. You have the strength and courage of armies, smell like honeysuckle, and taste like nectar."

My skin flushed in the cool evening air. The tenderness of his words amazed me and held me spellbound. I brushed my lips against his, soft as butterfly wings at first, then relishing the fullness and warmth of his mouth; I glided into another wave of his kisses and the wonder of being held in his arms.

The evening calls of frogs lent music to the garden. The breeze slowed, soothed, and Massimo held my face in his hands. "We must discuss this, Marianna; as much as we may rail against this war, it is still breathing hatred and threats down our necks. Even your family could be at risk because of any association with me. No matter what we feel, we may have to stay apart."

I buried my face into his chest and closed my eyes, but he lifted my chin and made me look at him. "Remember, sometimes I am sure I am being watched in town. I do not want you in any danger, in any pain." He brushed his thumb across my lips and bent and kissed me again before he took a step away and held onto my hands. "If we were seen together and word was to get back to Barberi. . . ."

I tightened my fingers between his. "Can we appear only as friends to everyone? Good neighbors? My papa's health is shaky at times, and he needs help. You could come to our home to assist us, no?"

Massimo stood silent a moment. He turned his head and looked into the horizon, his eyes far away. My breath burned in my chest until he looked back at me. "Marianna, I will not use you or deceive you. I want to break away from this hold Barberi has on me, but for now I have no choice. I do not know what I might have to do—where I will go—when or if I would ever be able to return. I may have to go through with the marriage."

He let go of one of my hands and shoved his hair back off his forehead. I reached for his hand and clasped my fingers around it. "I know it is terrible right now. I do not expect you to have any answers. I trust you. Let me be with you, Massimo, while we work and wait for a miracle. To help you during this time would mean so much to me . . . even if I can do nothing else."

From across our property my father called my name. I stepped into Massimo's arms again and molded myself against him. "Do not go away."

The mourning doves cooed and looked down from their swaying nests as he caressed my face with his hand. He exhaled loudly. "We would have to be so cautious, and we could see each other only once in a while."

I grasped at the hope his words gave me and nodded my head in agreement. Papa called louder now, his voice sounding more insistent. Still clinging to one of Massimo's hands, I raised my voice to reach our house. "Coming, Papa."

I walked backward one step at a time, never taking my eyes from Massimo's. "I will be at the market on Saturday. If we cannot see each other before then, *ti prego*, please, please come and meet me."

I turned to run for the house and Massimo grabbed me by the hand. He spun me around to face him, his lips inches from mine, his breath warm and moist. "The Greek theatre—I will come for you at the market, and we will escape under the steps in the lion's den."

He smiled at last and closed the distance between our mouths.

* * *

I floated, drifted, and dreamed through the week, reliving that night by the pond with Massimo a hundred times a day. The balmy air of the sea was his breath on my skin, every breeze the stroke of his fingers though my hair. The nuzzle of Tesoro looking for an apple or carrots against my palm swept me into memories of Massimo's warm, musky skin and scratchy whiskers against my face. Each fruit on the tree was deliciously fragrant, and the vegetables I picked in the garden were plump and ripe.

Nervous expectancy became my constant companion in the days before the Saturday market. I sat in my room the night before, looking out my window at a moon that shone with such magic it made my skin tingle.

* * *

The next morning was half gone when I looked up across the plaza and saw Massimo approach the market. My stomach compressed into knots by the time he stopped in front of the butcher, two booths down. Massimo leaned against a post, one hand in the pocket of his beige linen trousers, a black fedora on his head pressing rebellious curls against his neck. He gave me a sideways glance, pulled the hat down low, almost covering his right eye, and winked at me. I stuttered and lost count of the change I was giving our customer.

Massimo nodded his head toward an alleyway next to the market and walked away. When the flow of shoppers abated I sat on a wooden crate and exhaled extra loudly. "Mama, I am so bored; can I go visit a friend?"

Mama's brow wrinkled. "Of course, *Carina*. We will be here another two hours at least, and business is slow. Enjoy your time, but be very careful and do not leave the market alone."

I lept from my seat in anticipation and scrubbed my hands in our bucket of soap and water. Then realized I may appear too anxious. I forced myself to walk casually when I left, feigning interest in the familiar booths along the way.

Two rows of palazzi lined the alleyway around the corner. Massimo leaned against the wall, his hat down over his eyes. He lifted his chin and the brim of his hat and peeked out at me with a teasing smirk. I covered my mouth to hide the ridiculous grin I could feel on my face. Massimo grabbed me by the hand, and we ran down the cobblestone alleyway. Dogs barked from windows above while sheets flapped and waved from clotheslines strung between the buildings on each side of us.

We hurried to two horses Massimo had waiting for us and made our way outside of town to an amphitheater built by the Greeks hundreds of years before. It always made me breathless to be here—the vast open arch of stadium, the granite seats that climbed in rows toward the turquoise sky. Dark, musty passageways that once held shivering Christians waiting to be fed to the lions or gladiators ready to fight lay hidden like hollow tombs below the seating. Grass and weeds intertwined and twisted around any crack in the stone, their roots like gnarled fingers gripped in blood-tainted soil and ancient rock.

A hot wind gusted, and a crowd of wildflowers waved in welcome across the theatre floor. Today the theatre was all ours, a place where I could look into mesmerizing eyes that by some miracle wanted to look back into mine. Here I held the hand of a man who in my mind could have sat in the highest, most privileged box as an emperor in days gone past.

We huddled on the lowest row, heads close together as if the birds hovered to steal our whispers and carry them to the enemy. Massimo broke the spell and lifted his brows with a smile. "Let's walk below in the lion's dens."

"You know they are supposed to be haunted. We will have to watch for ghosts and spirits."

Cool air blew from the mouth of the tunnels. We hurried inside. Rays of sunlight shot through small windows cut between the seats above us—the windows where ancient spectators watched ravenous lions or frightened soldiers pace in anticipation of their fate in the arena. I felt the gazes of their ghosts and lifted my hand up toward a shaft of dusty light. Massimo roared like a lion behind me, and I shrieked and ran into the darkness. He laughed and grabbed me around the waist, turned me around to face him and brought his mouth down onto mine in a glorious kiss. The dankness of the den was banished by the sweet scent of his breath.

I pressed my face into Massimo's neck and sighed while he rubbed my back with his hand. "What am I going to do with you, Marianna?"

I bumped my nose against his cheek. "I will figure out what to do with myself; our real worry is what to do with *you*."

His shoulders seemed to relax but he pulled me closer. "When the end of this insane war finally comes, you are what I want, all I hope for."

I was dizzy with wonder that he could feel so much for me. He leaned down and skimmed his mouth gently across my lips and along my jaw. My breath came in soft sighs until he spoke. "Time is a cruel monster; will your mother be concerned about you?"

"Not for a bit, but I do not want her to worry."

Massimo pulled me by the hand back into the brilliant sunshine. The slant of the shadows confirmed the rapid passage of time. I pulled back on his hand. "Not yet, it has hardly been an hour. There is time before we have to go."

We sat on the bottom row of the stadium again, the rock seats warm beneath us. I slipped off my shoes and let my bare feet slide on a patch of spongy grass. "It seems impossible so much brutality could have happened in such a beautiful theatre."

"It is the kind of place Mussolini or Hitler would use for their brutality now if they could."

The air whistled through the stone walls. "Do not say that, Massimo—do not even think of that; recite a quick prayer for safety."

I crossed myself and he smiled but shook his head. "No one is listening to God these days."

Tears gathered in my eyes. "We can, no matter what anyone else does, we can listen. . . . We can try."

He slid his arms around me and pulled me closer against him. "How amazing you are. How strong and mighty for such a gentle thing."

I shook my head. "My mother says I am just stubborn."

Massimo threw his head back and laughed, and I reached my hand up and covered his mouth. "I happen to believe the things I say, and I would and will fight for them if I have to."

His laughing stopped and his eyes darkened. "I know you would, and I would want to be there to protect you, to take you away from any danger."

"You cannot do that. You have to fight hard enough just to protect yourself. That is all I want you to think about."

The warmth of summer could not stop the chill in my veins over the thought of Massimo fighting the enemy. I shivered, and Massimo pulled me onto his lap and held me. I leaned in and kissed him in amazement that I could. His full, warm lips soothed my fears, made my heart beat for all new reasons. I touched his cheek with my hand. "Let's just live here. It could be our own place. The rock walls would protect us."

Tiny black flakes swirled in the breeze around us and landed on my dress. Even from miles away, Mount Etna spewed once again, showering her bursts of power on us in bits of black ash.

Massimo wiped a powdery piece from my cheek. "Life has a way of finding us, even here."

My heart had slowed to a hard, heavy rhythm. "Why does it feel that way to you? So hopeless and futile?"

"Too many years of politics in our home, I presume. My parents are kind and honest, yet brutality still prevails. They—especially my father— are in grave danger for doing what is right."

"But we are not finished fighting yet. There has to be hope, even victory. I know there is."

I stood up in front of him and held his hands. "We are here in an amazing theatre that is now considered a work of art. The beauty and peace of it is wonderful and real, even though at one time vile people used it for things of horror and agony and the innocent died by the thousands. Things change, good comes back and conquers."

He looked away as he had that night at the pond. I put my hands on each side of his incredible face and turned his head to look at me.

"Massimo, we will win. Perhaps God allows evil people to condemn themselves with evil acts, but I know goodness and virtue will prevail. We have to believe that." Strength drained from me. "If we do not . . ." It was difficult to speak past the sob in my throat. "If we do not . . . we can never be together."

Bees hovered and hummed over the flowers that pressed through the rocks beside us. Massimo stood and pulled me into his arms, embraced me so close I could barely breathe. He kissed me on the temple. "I will believe that we can win. Because for you, I would do anything."

Hope eased the tension in my throat. "We will do it together."

Massimo bent his head to kiss me, and I caught a glimpse of a dark figure on the steps across the theatre. I stiffened, and Massimo looked up in alarm.

"What is it? Did you see something?"

"Over there, a man on the steps. He saw me look at him and is climbing down now on the other side."

Massimo turned, saw the man, and took me by the hand. "Walk quickly but as casually as possible toward the horses. We will run as soon as we are out of his sight."

The soft buzz of the bees turned to an alarm in my head before we had made it to the horses and galloped away. We reached the edge of town and reined the horses in behind an abandoned building. Moss hung from the end of a dripping faucet, and a dead sheep lay bloated and stiff under a tree.

There had been no sign of the man behind us. I jumped down from my horse as Massimo dismounted from his. I ran into his arms. The grim crease in his brow filled me with new apprehension.

"Massimo, he was probably just a lonely man who wanders or goes to the theatre looking for a place of peace."

Minutes ticked by before he nodded his head. "We'd better give it a few days just to be safe. When does Bruno leave?"

The answer lay like an anchor on my chest. "Six days from today, June seventeenth."

Massimo rubbed his hands up and down the length of my arms. "I will come to you late that night at the pond. If someone is watching me then perhaps he will have grown bored with my lack of suspicious moves and I can get away. If for some reason I cannot come . . . do not try to find me; it may not be safe."

My breathing eased; at least he still wanted us to meet again. I would hold on to that. We found our way back to the market and he walked me to the end of the alleyway. I relished the scratch of his whiskers when we kissed goodbye and pressed the scent of his skin deep into my memory while hope and fear battled in my breast.

Chapter Sixteen

JUNE SEVENTEENTH ROSE OVER THE mountains in the east no matter how hard I held my breath to keep Bruno's departure at bay. My parents and I stepped into our wagon in somber moods on our way to the Chessaris' to accompany Bruno to the dock—the dock that held a battleship that would carry my bother away and within the reach of men determined to kill him. Men who would seek to drain his precious blood into the waters that swirled around his ship.

The wagon wheels slammed in ruts and potholes left behind by rain and the rolling tracks of tanks as we traveled into the city of Siracusa. My mother and I huddled together with the Chessari women: Laura, Franca, and their mother. Our scarves, pulled down low, concealed our tearstained faces from the stares of the Nazi soldiers along the road. I longed for the comfort of Massimo and was grateful we planned to meet by the pond later that night.

We passed the church where Bruno and Laura had been married months before, where Bruno's face had been lit and ecstatic before Father Gambarotto. He'd seemed so manly, so tall and striking in his pressed uniform and polished black shoes. Laura had looked like a princess in her white satin dress, a handful of yellow daisies clutched in her shaky hand, a few pinned in her honey-brown hair. Her eyes were misty during the vows, her skin aglow in a soft pink flush.

I had known Bruno loved Laura for years. It had taken the encroachment of war and Laura's tears to move her parents into consenting to their marriage; their attempts to protect her from being a potential war widow were all in vain. Franca and I had stood at the front of the church close to Laura, our hands clasped together as devoted bridesmaids while our other hands gripped our own cluster of yellow daisies.

Now I gripped Franca's hand for the strength to tell Bruno goodbye. The moment of farewell was devastating; I held my face against his cheek for as long as I could. "Hurry home . . . hurry home . . . I will be there to help Laura and the baby until you return."

Bruno nodded his head and, unable to speak, kissed me on the forehead. He held Laura until the last possible moment then boarded the massive ship and waved from the bridge while the wind carried our cries and tears to him. The Mediterranean churned black around the edges of the ship and carried my brother out into her depths until he was only a shadow on the water.

Papa and *Signora* Chessari helped a sobbing Laura back into the wagon, and we rode silently as the stones beneath the wagon wheels toward home. My chest seemed ready to burst. I pulled the scarf from my head, buried my face in its silky folds, and wept.

* * *

There were ghosts in the breeze. Spirits hovered and whisked the tops of the grass into a frenzy as they flitted and dashed over the ground. I shivered and hugged my knees to my chest, anxious to see Massimo's silhouette against the deep gray horizon. Despite my constant watch, it was the snap of a twig that told me Massimo had arrived at last. I rushed into his arms and sobbed into his chest, reminded of the times Bruno had comforted me all through our childhood. Massimo lifted my chin with his finger and wiped my face with his handkerchief.

"Bruno will return. I have it on good information that his ship may never leave the Mediterranean. Mussolini is nervous because of the uprisings against him and is hesitant to let our people go far. Your brother may be needed on the home turf to keep the Italians in line."

While relieved at the idea, I still shuddered at the vision of gentle Bruno fighting or even pointing a gun at his own people. "He told us that many troops were headed to Northern Italy for 'home security.' I hope you are right; if only he could be in Italy somewhere."

I'd taken a quilt from the closet in the hall before slipping out the back door to meet Massimo at the pond. I spread the quilt on the grass, and Massimo and I laid down side by side. Massimo stretched his arm out under my neck as a pillow. Clouds chased each other across the moon. The wind fanned the leafy branches above us and blessed us as we lay in each other's arms below.

The soft pink of dawn glowed behind the mountains before I could tear myself from Massimo's arms and run back to our house; the promise that we would meet again was like a beacon that lit my path.

* * *

On June twenty-second, my eighteenth birthday, Bruno had been gone only five days. I rose from my bed to the sweet scent of almond cake that diffused its scent through the stairway and lifted like a heaven-sent cloud to my room. Anticipation filled my heart.

Saturday at the market Massimo had come directly to our booth to purchase fish for his grandparents. He had passed me a note saying he would be waiting for me at lunchtime in a nearby abandoned building. Mama had extended her hand to Massimo with warmth in her eyes and invited him to attend my birthday celebration. His acceptance had been polite and kind. He had held his composure while I, on the other hand, had grinned with joy from behind my mother.

At last the day had come. Chores flew by and a ride on Matilda's shiny back over the hills made my blood and heart race all the faster. I whistled to the birds that gathered and swayed on wind-powered branches and set Matilda at a trot for home.

My father sat in the barn, handsome in his brown linen pants and suspenders. A fishing net lay spread across his lap while he threaded a thick needle through the latest tears and repaired the damage inflicted by the thrash of fins. He looked up when I led Matilda inside, and the sly grin on his leathery face betrayed the fact that he had a surprise for my birthday. I kissed his cheek and perched on his netted knee to hug him around his neck. His eyes twinkled, and he rendered his best version of *Buon Compleanno* for me in a raspy voice. Joyous anticipation filled my heart— not of gifts, but of a celebration where I would be among my loved ones.

A large crowd of family and friends would not be possible; danger increased every day for civilians. As the Nazis war efforts faltered, their tempers flared. It was not safe to travel far. But Massimo would be here, and Franca's mother had said their family would come or she would at least bring Franca by motor car.

A telegram from Laura and Franca's father—*Signore* Chessari, who was still in the north—assured us that he had tracked Bruno down. Bruno was still in Italy and would be for a while. Perhaps Massimo had been right;

the reason for the change in Bruno's orders may lay in the nervousness of Mussolini. The Italian people were fed up with him and the Nazi party. His speeches had become so angry and defensive that even his previous allies were turning their backs on him.

At last the sun drifted low, and the fluttering of anticipation began in earnest. Massimo would soon wind through the back pastures from his grandparents' farm, and we would meet at the fence.

In my bedroom I danced my way to the dresser, sang, and undressed. I filled a plump sponge with lavender-scented water from a white porcelain bowl and reveled in the stream of it as I washed it down my skin. I combed through my hair, left it long and flowing around my waist, slipped on my chemise, put on my green flowery dress with the lacy collar, and hurried down the wooden stairs in soft leather shoes.

The house was quiet. Through the large picture window in the kitchen, I spotted my mother in her garden, where she inspected the smooth, round tomatoes with her long-fingered hands. Vines of sweet peas cascaded down the walls behind her. Without a sound I made my way through the front door and around the other side of the house toward the fence. I sighed with joy at the sight of Massimo coming across the thick, green pasture where our horses and cows grazed.

I ran to him when he rounded the final row of trees and scaled the rock wall that divided us. He laughed and caught me in his arms, kissing me as hungrily as I did him. My birthday was complete, but must be shared with the rest of the family.

We walked hand in hand toward the house for as long as we dared. My fingertips held his until the last possible moment when we entered the backyard and were forced to pull away. Massimo waited beside the chicken coop while I went inside.

Aunt Pasqua sat at the table while my parents cooked and prepared food at the counter and the stove. Steam billowed above a platter of cream-covered pasta smothered in calamari. Birthdays were a day free of chores in our family. Papa wore Mama's spare green apron and assisted her with the cooking. I chuckled. "Papa I believe the sight of you looking so lovely in Mama's apron is my best birthday gift of all."

My father laughed, but Aunt Pasqualina, her black hair streaked down the middle with gray, looked at me and squinted her eyes. "You look bright pink in the cheeks, Marianna. Camilla, have you checked her for scarlet fever? It spreads like a demon during a war and kills people by the thousands."

Mama shook her head at my aunt while she wiped her hands on a dish cloth. "Ah, Pasqua, if we thought Marianna was sick we would have warned you not to come for her birthday. Rosy cheeks are a sign of good health and vigor—Mari is happy and healthy."

Aunt Pasqua stood and reached across the table, placed her wrinkled palm on my forehead, and scowled. The front of her black sweater dragged across the butter dish as she checked my cheeks and forehead for any sign of fever.

Uncle Mimmo walked in the room, spotted his wife's messy sweater, and his cheeks plumped up in a grin. He spread his arms, palms up, and gestured toward the butter smeared across the fuzzy angora. "*Ma che peccato*, Pasqua . . . what a shame. Look at the mess you are making on your sweater."

Aunt Pasqua's thick brows furrowed deep; she ignored her husband and lowered her hand from my face. "Hmm . . . she does not feel feverish but is definitely flushed. What were you doing before you came in here, Marianna? Were you out chasing around with those chickens of yours you call pets?

"Have you finished the quilts we started last winter? You will never be ready to furnish a home with so few blankets and tablecloths the way you live outdoors. And if a proper man or soldiers were to come calling, what would they think seeing you riding on a horse like a boy?"

Her sweater painted butter along the edge of the table with each sweep of her hand. My mouth twitched with the urge to grin but I stood and grabbed a napkin. "Slip off your sweater, Aunt, and let me help you with our messy butter. And thank you for your concern; I will try to be more diligent and careful."

Thank goodness she had switched her focus to my father's health, berating him for doing too much before Massimo knocked at the front door. I placed the sweater on the wash tub by the back door and scurried to the front room.

Franca entered in front of Massimo, her eyes bright with excitement when she saw me. "Mama could not make it, so one of our hired help brought the boys and me in a work truck. Laura has been a little too tired these days, and Mama put her to bed to rest. But I am so glad I could still come."

I embraced my friend and kissed her on each cheek. "I will miss your mother and my dear sister-in-law. Thank the saints you could come or it would not seem like a birthday at all."

Massimo stepped through the threshold from behind Franca, clasped my hand, and tipped his head in a slight bow. "So nice to see you, Miss De'Angelis. I apologize for the absence of my grandparents; they were not feeling well this evening."

If Aunt Pasqualina had been in the room and witnessed the heat that flooded my face when Massimo took my hand, my source of "scarlet fever" would have been revealed. The noise from the kitchen drew us in, and we gathered with the others for our dinner. Papa carried loaves of bread to the table as Mama kissed Franca on each cheek and held her slim shoulders. "God be with our Laura and your dear mother. Is your mama well? I should have told you to bring the twins along."

Franca scrunched her face. "Well, I am afraid I had to take it upon myself to bring them, since my mother and Laura were indisposed."

The moment Franca finished her sentence, a loud whoop from her twelve-year-old brothers sounded from the back yard and had us all turning toward the window. Franca covered her lips with the tips of her fingers in concern. "I am sorry I did not check with you before I brought them, *Signora* De'Angelis. Thank you for tolerating all their noise."

Franca placed a small box with a shiny gold ribbon on the table, and the light in her eyes dulled a bit. "Papa could not come either; he is still gone up north on more business. I do not know why the vineyards are having such problems that he must be gone so much in the middle of a war. Mama is distressed because of the danger, but she tells us that Papa's work is even more important now. Perhaps Mussolini likes our wine. *Mama mia*, my mother is a patient woman."

The smack of the back door banging against the kitchen wall made me jump. Twelve-year-olds Dominic and Damiano flew into the house and landed with a thud on the kitchen floor; their arms and legs tangled and flailing like octopi. Franca rushed over and pulled the twin on top up first. "Such an entrance, you wild boys. Dominic, you apologize to the De'Angelis family right now."

Dominic's face turned serious. His identical twin brother sprang to his feet behind him, and they both bowed their dark heads. Franca popped them on the back of their heads. "Dominic, Damiano, say you are sorry for the rude way you blasted through the door."

A simultaneous "Sorry!" blurted from them both. Papa laughed and reached his hand out to each boy. "Welcome to our home, young men. You make me lonely for my boyhood days. Now sit right down and eat your supper. That is an order."

A platter of pasta steamed in the middle of the table, and we all headed for the chairs. Franca sat on my left, and I had to feign nonchalance when Massimo sat down on the other side of me, causing a ripple of joy to race up my spine. Everyone obeyed Papa's command, and we filled our plates with warm pasta.

While we ate, conversation centered around the summer harvests, the catch of the morning, and the health of Massimo's grandparents. I kept my attention toward Massimo paced with that of all of our guests and did not look his direction as often as I longed to. Mama and Papa cleared the plates when we finished our first course, then placed a salad before each person. Uncle Mimmo sat next to the twins and chuckled with glee over their exuberant conversation at the other end of the table until Damiano's voice rose to a near shout.

"That is right, *Signore*, Mussolini and everyone else is doing this war all wrong. Dominic and I have worked hours on this, and we have got the war all figured out. They need to quit shooting at each other first and use our strategies." He bopped himself in the forehead with his hand and rolled his eyes. "If they would just use their heads."

Franca shook her head at her brothers. "I am sure Marianna does not want to talk about the war at her birthday dinner, boys; let us all eat in peace."

Papa grinned. "Thank you, Franca." He turned toward the twins, their dark hair still spiked in rebellion from their wrestling match on the floor. "And boys, if you want to write down your solutions to the war on paper, I will deliver them to Mussolini himself."

Damiano leapt to his feet. "We have got it all written out in code in our fort at home. We will be glad to translate it for you."

Uncle Mimmo's cackle resounded through the rafters overhead, and my shoulders relaxed. If my uncle could laugh, then perhaps the subject of war would not suffocate the joy I was feeling with my loved ones. I smiled at my uncle and then jumped when Massimo's foot tapped mine under the table. I took a drink of water and carefully bumped my foot against Massimo's pant leg. No one seemed to notice anything amiss until a small gasp escaped my lips; Massimo had slipped off his shoe and placed his stocking foot on my bare toes.

Aunt Pasqua pointed her bony finger in my direction. "You see, Camilla, her face is bright red once again. I am telling you, birthday or not that girl had better go to bed before she falls gravely ill."

My cheeks caught fire as everyone stared at my face with wonder and concern. Massimo continued to eat his salad with ease and rubbed his foot slowly on top of mine. I could not breathe, much less talk or eat.

Mama ate quietly but her eyes darted back and forth between me and Massimo. "Oh, Pasqua, I am sure Marianna is just excited for her special day. Adamo and I will clear the salad plates and bring out the gifts while we have our fruit."

Papa was the only one who wore a frown. He watched Massimo and lifted his brow. "Yes, Camilla, good idea. Massimo, are you finished yet? I would not want to interrupt your . . . meal."

Massimo wiped his mouth with the cloth napkin. "Yes, Sir, I am quite finished. Gifts would be a lovely idea."

"Good; could you help me carry them from the other room?" Papa stood and walked around the table, and Massimo stood quickly to join him. Papa glanced down at Massimo's feet. "Do not forget your other shoe. It must have slipped off during dinner."

Massimo flashed a glance in my direction then looked down at his mismatched feet. "Oh, yes . . . goodness . . . how did that happen?" He put his shoe on and quickly laced it. "I will be glad to help you, Sir."

Mama cleared her throat, and Aunt Pasqualina continued her grave survey of my by now deep crimson face. I looked into the liquid eyes of my mother for mercy, and she turned toward my aunt. "Pasqua, I could use some help with the cake; we will have it in the parlor if Marianna would like."

I nodded my head and sighed with relief when they left the room.

The twins talked in depth to each other at the other end of the table, their eyes lit with excitement. Franca gripped my hand, and I was surprised to see her eyes were wet with emotion. "Oh my goodness, Massimo is quite wonderful. I hope for the very best for you, Marianna. He looks at you with a caress in his eyes."

I almost choked on the grip of panic in my throat. "Oh, Franca, please do not say that . . . I cannot . . ."

Before I could finish my sentence, my father entered the room, the golden light of the lanterns overhead glancing off a few paper-and-ribbon-wrapped gifts in his hands. His deep voice broke my reverie with a boom. "Here we are, gifts for our birthday girl."

Massimo came in behind my father, a package wrapped in thin parchment tucked under his arm. He sat back down beside me. I opened my gifts, careful to spare the paper. Mama had made me a lovely flowery dress and had tatted the white collar and edge of the sleeves in delicate lace. Franca gave me two books, and Papa gave me a sun hat and winked at me when I opened it.

"That is so your Aunt Pasqua cannot complain that your face gets too brown on the boat with me."

Aunt Pasqua clucked her tongue at Papa and shook her head. "Adamo, you indulge her."

My hands shook a little when Massimo handed me the package from beneath his arm. "My Nonna wanted to make you something for tonight."

I untied the paper, peeled it back, and revealed a crocheted purple shawl folded neatly inside. I lifted it to everyone's view, and Massimo cleared his throat. "Nonna said that you love to read, and this will keep you warm in the evenings when the weather goes cold."

I looked in his eyes for just a moment. "Please tell your grandmother thank you for me. It is so soft and lovely. I will wear it every night this fall and winter."

After we had all enjoyed the almond birthday cake, Papa stood and spoke with raspiness in his voice. "We wanted to save this last gift to finish the evening for our little girl who is now a woman."

He pulled a small box from his pocket and handed it to me. I lifted the lid and looked down at a beautiful blue cameo on a gold chain laid on shiny satin. Mama tipped her chin up. "Look on the back of the cameo, *Carina*."

I turned the cameo over and read the inscription on the back: *Marianna*. I looked up and around the room full of family and hugged my tearful parents. "Where did you get something so exquisite in the middle of the war?"

Papa smiled. "We have a handy connection. Franca's father, *Signore* Chessari, had it made for us on one of his trips up north. It is nice to have such wonderful friends."

Everyone looked at Franca and her twin brothers, who let out a whoop of approval for their father's good work. I smiled at Franca. "If I do not have the chance to thank your father, you must tell him how much this means to me."

I showed it to Massimo, happy that he'd sat beside me again. I hugged and kissed each person in the room on their cheeks. The chain was cool and secure on my neck, and the cameo rested perfectly above my heart.

After everyone had left I ran upstairs and placed my gifts on my bed. I slipped on the new dress mama had made and inhaled her lavender scent that permeated the fabric. Papa read by the light of a lantern in the parlor, and Mama brushed her hair in her room. I slipped by and out the back door in a breathless rush.

Massimo sat on the bench by the pond in the soft light of the moon and rose to meet me. His arms came around me and he kissed me. I pulled away to catch my breath and laid my head on Massimo's shoulder, his chest against mine like the heat of a bonfire.

He was quiet—so quiet that I lifted my head to look at him. He kissed me softly, his eyes concealed in the dark. "While I waited for you I had time to think. I had my nonna crochet that shawl for you to keep you warm when I am gone. We must never forget that I will have to leave."

I covered his mouth with my hand and held it there. "It is my birthday. You are not allowed to ruin it."

He kissed my fingers and chuckled when I moved them away. He pressed his cheek against mine and caressed the other side of my face with his hand, running his fingers along my neck.

"Yes, it is your birthday, so you win this battle, *l'amore mia*. The day after tomorrow I will work in the pasture again. But I do not know if you could slip away to meet me there; your parents seemed a bit suspicious tonight."

It was my turn to laugh. "Who knew that a missing shoe could say so much?"

I slipped one of my feet from my shoe and ran my bare foot up the side of Massimo's leg. Massimo gripped me tighter around the waist. "I have to see you soon. If you can get away, you could come and help me in the pasture. I doubt anyone would bother to sit in a field to spy on me."

I turned my head and kissed him with relief that we would be together another day. "I will be there."

Chapter Seventeen

I LAY WIDE AWAKE THE next morning before the rooster had a chance to wake up the day. Hiding my relationship with Massimo from my parents haunted me. It was not in my nature to sneak around or to lie to them. But if he and I were discovered and they were questioned, it would be safer for them if they knew as little as possible. I had seen the way my father looked at Massimo when he saw his missing shoe at my birthday party. And my mother's glances were longer and more pensive every time he came around.

The ticking of the clock on the kitchen wall grew loud while I sat with my parents around our table at lunchtime. Rain poured in heavy drops that plopped on the panes of the kitchen window. I watched the chickens chase the bugs that came up from the ground for a fresh drink, their crops plump and purple on their necks. Massimo's name was so loud in my head I was sure my parents could hear it.

I wiped my mouth with a napkin and held my chin steady. "Papa, Mama, do you trust in me? *Perché* . . . because I need your trust now more than I ever have before."

Papa laid his hands on the table on each side of his plate and looked right into my eyes, the depth of his gaze a mirror for my conscience. The corners of his mouth lifted in a gentle smile. "Massimo was missing a shoe under the table last night." The clock's ticking seemed to slow while Papa and I looked at one another. He cleared his throat. "Your mother and I have discussed this. We see he is a good young man. A good man that is marrying another. We have never questioned your heart, Mari, and we do not need to now. But we question his."

My ribcage tightened like a corset had been cinched around it.

"Massimo's life . . . his . . . situation with the girl he is supposed to be engaged to is not what it seems. He is not deceiving me. This war holds so many prisoner and in deceptive ways. But I cannot say more."

Mama's eyes were moist as she pressed the palms of her hands together, her fingertips pointed toward heaven as if in prayer. She rocked her steepled hands back and forth in supplication. "This sounds like it could be dangerous, Mari. We trust you but we do not trust the war. People do such terrible things."

"But I do not do terrible things. And neither does Massimo. I promise you that he is honest and good. He's just . . . in a difficult situation."

My parents looked at one another, reading each other's thoughts, and I held my breath as if under water. Just before my lungs burst, my mother spoke. "You must promise us you will be very careful."

Tears of relief and comfort flooded my eyes. "I will, Mama. I promise I will be overly cautious in all I do."

We all stood and embraced while the downpour of rain lightened to a sprinkle outside.

* * *

The sky seemed as happy as I was the next morning; the sun shimmered while a few fat, lazy clouds floated adrift on the horizon. Trailing vines poured like waterfalls over the walls of the pastures while lizards darted through the cracks between the rocks. The rain the day before had washed the world clean, and new freedom eased the pressure in my chest since telling my parents all I could about me and Massimo.

I galloped on Matilda's back toward the Scalvones' pasture. My bathing costume was tight under my dress and held the moisture of the humid morning against my skin long enough to cool me as the wind rushed past.

My hair flapped like the fan of a palm on my back with each stride of Matilda's legs across the grassy ground. Massimo was at work by now, waiting for me to come through the gate for a stolen day together. After work in the field, we could slip away to the shore for lunch and then cool off in the sea.

Massimo led his grandparents' gelding as it dragged a plow across the field and churned up the ground. I could smell the pungent soil even before I led Matilda through the gate, removed her bridle, and set her free by a watering trough near the trees.

Massimo stopped and smiled when he saw me, his teeth white in contrast to his dark, unshaven jaw. "It is about time you got here; I cannot possibly get all this done without my inspiration." He pulled me in, and I wrapped my arms around his waist; the dampness of his shirt pressed against my skin. The faint scent of soap filled my nostrils when I bumped my nose against his neck. He lifted my chin and kissed me, his mouth lingering with mine.

He waved his hand over the area he had been working. "I am having some difficulty with my plow today. It must have been too dry last spring; even with the rain yesterday, the ground beneath the topsoil is too hard, and the prongs do not go deep enough."

"When I was a little girl and the ground was too hard, Papa had me sit on top of the plow to give it the weight to dig deeper."

He grinned and pointed at the plow. "Climb aboard your chariot, *Signorina* De'Angelis." I laughed as he picked up the handle for the plow, and I climbed on top of the wood platform that covered the blades and prongs. I held onto the sides to steady myself, and Massimo clicked his tongue at the horse to get him going. The ground churned beneath the plow and rocked it like a boat when the horse picked up its gait. I held tight to the frame beneath me while Massimo held the plow in line.

The blades churned through the soil and cut it like thick chocolate cake. It was working. I laughed out loud and urged the horse to go faster. "*Andiamo, andiamo.*"

The horse picked up his gate, and Massimo hollered in exhilaration. "Bravo!"

I looked over my shoulder at Massimo just as the sky flipped upside down. My arms and legs flailed in the air before I hit the ground and rolled to a stop with my face planted in the earth. The plow must have rammed against a buried rock and pitched me off the platform. Before I had time to pull myself up, Massimo was on his knees beside me. He gripped me by the shoulders and rolled me over. "Marianna, are you all right? Are you injured?"

I blew the dirt from my lips and brushed the rest from my mouth before I burst into laughter. The worry on Massimo's face gave way to relief, and I could not stop giggling. He sat down, still holding me by my shoulders, and gave way to his own mirth. I picked up a handful of moist soil, reached up, and rubbed it into Massimo's face.

He brushed it away and rolled me from his lap back onto the ground. Before I could get away he had grabbed handfuls of dirt and tossed them on my back. I jumped to my feet, bent over with laughter and loaded my hands with grimy ammunition that I launched at his chest. He ran up in front of me and gripped me by the wrists with one hand, dropping a moist dirt clod on top of my head. Grit spilled down my dress, and I screeched over the top of Massimo's laughter. I jumped forward in an attempt to land in Massimo's arms. He lost his balance, and we tumbled and rolled over the top of each other before we came to a stop.

Massimo lay on top of me grinning. I kept my eyes closed to keep the dirt out of them and blew into Massimo's face. He rubbed his dirt-smeared cheeks back and forth on mine, the whiskers and sandy soil rough against my skin. I screeched again, and his mouth came down on mine. We kissed, intertwined like the roots of the crops that would grow beneath us, and laughed with our lips pressed to each other's.

Massimo touched the tip of my nose with his finger. "I could work all the time like this. I think you should come 'assist' me every day."

I lifted my head as if for a kiss, and when he lowered his mouth to meet mine, I gripped a handful of soil and dropped it on his back. He rolled off of me onto the ground and I leaned over him, my tangled hair like a veil on each side of his face. "Do you surrender, Lieutenant Scalvone?"

He lifted my hair back over my shoulders and pulled me down to kiss him. "*Signorina* De'Angelis, I surrendered the moment I laid eyes on you."

* * *

The ground disappeared beneath us when we raced our horses to the shore at lunchtime. I flew from Matilda's back the same time that Massimo jumped from his gelding, and we ran into the gentle waves, the clear water washing the dust and clumps of soil from our clothes, hair, and skin. Massimo wrapped his arms around me; I toppled underwater and came up smiling, the taste of saltwater tangy on my tongue. The sun glistened on Massimo's skin and sparkled in the drops that fell from his hair. I floated like a sea nymph in his arms, the cry of a pelican like the call of a bugle over the waves.

For lunch I shook out the blanket I had tied to Matilda's saddle, snapping it in the wind before it floated down on the rocky sand. We sat on top, cooled our throats with water from a canteen, and ate the *panini* and apricots I had brought with me.

Massimo stretched out on his back on the blanket and I lay beside him, holding his hand. I closed my eyes. Massimo rolled to his side, took my face in his hand, leaned down, and brushed his lips across my cheek and down my throat. His mouth cast a spell on my skin, burning my lips and neck where he touched me. I touched his face, his whiskers scratchy in my palm, and kissed his mouth. It was flavored with the sweetness of apricots. I wrapped my arms around him and pulled him over me. The wind blew warm over the top of us.

Massimo pulled back and sat up. I caught my breath and reached for him. "What is wrong?"

"I cannot do this. To love you, to have you the way I want to and then have to leave . . . is impossible. I will protect you from that kind of pain . . . no matter how difficult."

He took hold of my hand, and I gained some composure. "You do not know yet. Maybe you won't have to leave. Perhaps your father . . ."

He tightened his grip on my hand before he looked across the water. "It has been too long; something must be wrong, or I would have heard something—anything—from my father by now. That is why I must keep reminding us both of what is real. I will have no choice but to set you free for the life you ought to have. You deserve love—love you do not have to hide. Children. A home."

I opened my mouth to protest and stopped; the hum of a bumblebee grew loud, covering the soft cry of birds and breeze until it grew into a roar overhead. They were German fighter jets, four of them on their way to Siracusa. My muscles went rigid. Our freedom was twisted around the fingers of an evil man who controlled Massimo—and now me as well—like helpless puppets.

Massimo leaned back on his elbow beside me. He caught the tears on my cheeks with his fingers and kissed my eyelids. "No matter what happens, I love you, Marianna. I will love you and no other for as long as I live."

"I love you too. I did not want to for fear it could crush me, but it has only made me stronger." The waves nipped at the sand near the edge of the blanket, and I sat up. "Why, oh why, is General Barberi so obsessed with you and this insane forced marriage? He does not sound like the kind of man who would care about his daughter's feelings."

"I do not know all the reasons, but I have realized this must have nothing to do with love or infatuation on Fatima's part anymore; maybe it never did. The Nazis are failing in the war, and Italy and its leaders could be left in ruins. General Barberi has committed terrible war crimes and may be in danger if the Germans lose and he is caught by the Allies. He will need to escape and have the funds to disappear. My father is very wealthy, and Barberi may be looking for a way to get his hands on the money."

"Why wouldn't Barberi just make your father pay him to stay silent about his Partisan dealings? Why bother with a marriage to his daughter?"

Massimo sat up and rubbed his hands up and down my arms when I trembled. "Remember, he wants the political esteem and gain for now because my father is so highly connected in the government. And he probably wants all the money—not just bribes—someday soon."

"But even if you are married to his daughter, the money will still belong to your father."

"I will inherit most of it, and there is a lot of it. Barberi will not hesitate to eliminate my father when he stands in the way of the wealth."

I tried to follow his logic. "Still, just because you are married to his daughter doesn't mean he can get his hands on it."

Massimo's voice lowered. "He can if his daughter is widowed. He would take all he wanted from her."

Hope drained from me, taking all warmth with it, and I knew there was more than one way to die in this war. New tears poured down my cheeks, and I wiped them away with a swipe of my hand while the planes grew smaller in the distance.

"You cannot marry her. It is a death sentence. We have to run. There is no choice now. We have to run."

He shook his head. "No, Mari. You know I cannot and I will not. You know why, and you know that love is not safe in war. Nothing is. I will do what I have to."

"And if you do, I will not move on, Massimo. You cannot make me. I will wait until you are free. I will be here if it takes all eternity for you to find a way out of Barberi's trap. I am yours already, and we both know that, no matter the physical restraint, obstacles, or distance. I will wait until the day I die."

He gripped his hands on my arms and stared into my eyes. "Do not talk about dying, Mari. Never, never talk about dying."

I buried my face in his neck, and my voice strained past the knot in my throat. "Then do not talk about leaving."

"I will not talk about it again—not until the moment we have to say goodbye."

Two days later there was a knock at our front door.

Chapter Eighteen

I CLOSED MY EYES FOR one second and willed that the person at the door would be nothing more than a neighbor or *Signore* Aviano coming to deliver the mail—not German soldiers sent to find recruits or steal from us. The hinge of the door squeaked as I eased it open.

Massimo stood on the stoop in full pressed uniform, a sheen of sweat on his pale face. A flicker of alarm grew into a flame when he stepped inside, his arms like dead weights in response to my embrace.

I forced myself to speak. "Tell me—tell me quickly, Massimo."

He stared straight ahead at the faded pictures on the wall. "I have received a telegram . . . from General Barberi. . . ." Massimo's voice cut its way through the ringing in my ears. "My father has been arrested in Foggia. He is being taken to Palermo to stand trial."

He finally looked at me, his eyes black and dull. "He is charged with treason for conspiring with the Italian Partisans, the British, and the Americans."

The floor moved beneath me, and I leaned against the wall while Massimo stood still as a statue. "No one Mussolini has tried for treason has lived. They have all been executed. Barberi could intervene; he could vouch for my father. But he suspected I was here just to stall, to hide from him and his daughter." His voice lowered. "He sent someone to watch me and they have seen us together, in spite of our attempts at secrecy."

An icy wave flooded my chest. The man dressed in black at the Greek theatre; perhaps he had watched us several times. I could not speak, could not make Massimo's words or the information find a place in my mind. I heard the ping and scratch of the shovel where my mother worked in the garden. We expected Papa anytime from the market for lunch. The pot of water I'd placed on the stove must have come to a boil by now. Everything had been normal just one minute ago—safe . . . hopeful.

Massimo paced in front of me, his shoulders tense, his hand gripped around his beret. "Mussolini will listen to Barberi, but the only way he will spare my father's life is if I go into custody and cooperate immediately with them."

The clock in the hall chimed a brassy tone. Massimo held me firmly by the shoulders. "You and your family could be in terrible danger. I do not know if they know who you are, but they could easily find out. Barberi is on his way to Siracusa with his daughter, Fatima, and he has the power to arrest all of you—to have you executed or, worse than death, taken to a prison camp."

My breath came in choppy gasps. "No, no, no, it cannot happen this way. You cannot go like a lamb to the slaughter. Surrendering to him is suicide. We will all be in jeopardy no matter what. It is a useless sacrifice."

His expression did not change. "It is my fault; I knew what my job was when I came here. I knew the danger, the risk when I met you. I have betrayed my father, condemned him. I have put you and your family in peril every time I have even looked at you."

I could not stop the pounding in my throat or my mind from racing in a desperate search to stop him. "No, Massimo—please, please wait. We will find a way. Listen to me. He will not win—Barberi cannot take you."

He let go of my shoulders and I grabbed his hands. They were stiff and icy despite the warm day. He slipped his hands from mine and placed his beret on his head. "I am to report today for duty to a German officer at headquarters in Siracusa. I will be under his direct command and house arrest until Barberi arrives. The wedding will take place almost immediately. I do not know where I will go after that."

Massimo lifted his hand to reach for me but let it drop. "If I do not report immediately, Barberi will send someone after me. I could be under his surveillance right now. I do not care what happens to me, only what happens to you and our families. Think of them, Marianna, and what could . . . what we know would happen. Your parents, my grandparents, and my father will die if I do not go. Maybe everyone we know and love. Every minute I spend with you becomes more dangerous."

The air lay like an anvil on my chest. I stepped in front of Massimo, reached for his face, and laid my shaky palm against the stubble on his cheek. "Massimo, this is not the answer. If Barberi wants all of your father's money, he will have your father killed anyway once you are married to his daughter; he might even have you killed right away. You know he will."

Massimo tightened his jaw and focused back on the wall behind me. He closed his fingers over my hand and pulled it away from his face. "You may find a way to escape if I buy you all some time."

Massimo's stare pierced like an arrow straight through me. "As soon as it is done, when the . . . ceremony . . . is done, I will take Fatima and leave. I will go far away to take away any focus Barberi has on Siracusa and my loved ones here. I want you to go somewhere and hide, at least for a while. If your parents cannot or will not go, then stay safe; stay in the countryside. Never go anywhere alone."

My head swam and I leaned toward Massimo. He finally reached for me—held me against him with an iron grip. I lifted my chin and he kissed me hard and frantically all over my face and mouth.

His words numbed my lips and fingertips and I could barely kiss him back. He took my arms from around him and opened the front door, "I will always love you . . . and only you."

A group of chickens scattered from the front stoop when the door opened, their feathers flying in alarm. My heart plummeted to my feet and I gasped for air. I was in a dream—a nightmare—and I could not wake up, no matter how I screamed inside.

I grabbed him by the arm. "Massimo, you and I will run. Our families will hide. We will go find your father and help him escape. We can find some of the Partisans with whom he worked."

He shook his head, his face like stone. "I have to go."

He lifted my hand off of his arm and headed out the door. The room spun, and I landed, engulfed in horror, on the floor. I rocked back and forth and pressed my hand against my chest to stifle the burn in my lungs. Before I knew what I was doing, I had bolted out the door after him. My dress whipped around my knees and dust flew up around my feet as I ran up behind him, crying his name over and over and begging him to stop.

Chapter Nineteen

MASSIMO

I MARCHED DOWN THE LONG, winding road away from Marianna, toward Siracusa and a future I could no longer control. The steady rhythm of my feet stemmed the rage that threatened like a volcano in my gut. I heard the crunch of rock and gravel as Marianna caught up to me. Over and over her pleas punched me like a fist. I locked my jaw and stared at the road, focusing my eyes on where I had to go. If I looked at her, lost focus on each determined stride I took, I would stop—grab her up in my arms and never stop running.

But my father's face haunted my every move. Marianna's safety, and the safety of her family and mine, depended on every step I took closer and closer to what I must do. So I kept walking. The pressure built. Mari pulled on my shoulders, wept against my arm, and begged me to listen. Every plea was the blow of a hammer on my will.

Her face, that glorious face that would pull me apart for the rest of my empty days, looked up into mine and pled with me, made a promise to let me go if I would stop for one last minute. My body reacted by instinct, and I pulled her against me and kissed her with all the fury and desperation I had locked inside. I would never win this war—the one that raged with passion for this woman.

She lept into my arms when I turned to her; her sobs were muffled against my neck.

I brushed the hair back from her face and tried to soothe her into reason, but there was nothing I could say. This was the end; I knew it and so did she. She kept her face buried in my neck and continued to weep against me. I laid my head on hers and ran my hands down her back, memorizing the feel of her hair, the rich sweetness of her skin. With a jerk she lifted her head and looked at me with wide eyes.

"Massimo, we will get married. . . ." She slid from my arms and grabbed my hands. "We can marry secretly, and then your other ceremony would never be real. We could give it time . . . until . . . you could find a way to give Barberi money, and then we could all get away."

I tried to pry my hands away before we both let insanity take hold. "Mari, I would never leave you that way. The secret would be discovered, and you would be taken away. I must go, and I must go now."

A vice tightened around my heart, and I turned back toward the city once again. She cried and clung to me, but I kept walking until she sighed and fell backward on the ground.

Her mother had come at a run toward us. She ran faster when she saw Marianna fall in a heap, crying out and kneeling beside her daughter. "*O, Carina, cosa c'e?* What is the matter? Shh . . . shh . . . shh. . . ."

I looked into the face of her mother while she held a weeping Marianna; guilt kicked me in the stomach. "Please, *Signora* De'Angelis, may God forgive me for the pain I have caused. I love her, but this is the only way I can protect her, your family, and mine. May you forgive my wretchedness and keep her well. It would be better if you got away, at least for a month or so. Watch for the enemy and speak of this to no one. As far as you know, I was just the neighbor's grandson who helped them for a while—nothing more."

She nodded her head and kissed the top of Marianna's head.

I helped them both to their feet, held Marianna for the last time, and watched her wrap her arms around her mother for support when they walked back toward the house.

Mari turned to me, her face white as alabaster. "I will be here, Massimo. I will never move on. Come and find me, no matter how much time it takes or what obstacles stand in the way."

I nodded my head, watched her turn to go, and then forced myself to go down the road away from her.

* * *

A dull roar grew loud in the distance and a German jeep, the black swastika like a poisonous spider painted on the door, came around the corner and skidded to a stop in front of me. A tall German soldier jumped from the back and saluted me with the *Heil* Hitler I so despised. I did not salute back and just stared him in the face. He pulled a paper from his pocket and shook it open.

"Massimo Giovanni Scalvone?"

I nodded my head.

"I have been instructed by General Pinuccio Barberi to take you into custody and hold you there until the arrival of the proper authorities."

I strode straight toward the jeep. The armed guard folded his paper and marched up behind me, the clink of metal on his boots like the rattling of chains.

Chapter Twenty

MARIANNA

THE SMELL OF LAVENDER SOAP woke me first, and I knew my mother was near. Matilda whinnied, the sound of it echoing as if far away. I opened and focused my eyes on the yellow ceiling of my bedroom. I sat up with a gasp. My mother sat alone in the rocking chair beside me.

I gripped the edge of the sheet that covered me. "Did Massimo come back?"

She shook her head slowly back and forth, and I fell back against the mattress, turned toward the wall, and pulled my knees up against my chest.

* * *

Gusty breezes pushed the fields of wildflowers toward the ground, wailed through the trees, and dried my tender eyes. Papa and I jostled toward the rocky shoreline to the steady rhythm of Tesoro's hooves plodding over soil and rock.

The rough shelves of lava rock scratched under my feet before we reached the pier and climbed into our fishing boat like hundreds of times before. I'd failed to be brave and told my parents about the trap that held Massimo the night before. Their tears fell as well as mine. But there was no way we could help.

Seagulls dipped toward shore, expecting another feast and unaware that the master at the humble helm grew more fatigued as the days droned on without mercy and that his passenger barely heard their cries. Endless waves jostled me, knocked me into the sides of the boat, and bruised me. Papa's brow furrowed.

"Why are your feet not braced? You will be purple within minutes."

Papa's face looked blurred through my tears. I leaned back on the old scratchy netting and covered my eyes with my arm. Papa tsked his tongue above the cries of a passing pelican. "Marianna, the day of miracles is not finished. Germans fill our towns, deceived by their own grandeur, but the beautiful sun rises and the mountains retain their majesty."

He shook me by the knee, and I lifted my arm from my face with reluctance. One quick glance into Papa's kind blue eyes and unbearable sorrow threatened to swallow me again. He spoke with such faith, such courage, yet the deterioration of his health showed what the stress of war was doing to him.

I turned toward the empty sea. "Yes, Papa, the land lives on. And the Germans own it."

He shook his head back and forth with another tsk of his tongue. "Look at me, *Carina*."

I forced myself to face him, grateful that I saw strength beneath the fatigue in his eyes. He lifted his shoulders and held his hands out, palms up. "We make such fools of ourselves when we believe a human being can really own anything. We each own only this." He slapped his heart with his rough hand. "Not the failing body of an old man, but the soul . . . the heart. You have Massimo's soul and he has yours, no matter what some greedy man with a gun tries to tell you."

I sat up on the wooden seat and a wave of hopelessness rose again. "I own his soul while another woman owns the rest of him?"

Papa took me gently by the shoulders, and the scent of salty sweat and the homemade peppermint candy he always kept in his pocket filled my nose. It would have comforted me under different circumstances. The memories of peaceful hours spent rocking beside my father on this boat seemed hazy, miles away. Papa squeezed my arms. "This girl, this daughter of the general, will own nothing, even if she takes every penny from his family. There is no truth or victory in evil . . . or in slavery."

Pain squeezed my throat. "And if Massimo has children with her? Do I still own his soul? An empty father for innocent babies? This war would kill them too."

His grip tightened on my shoulders. "Look at me—now, Marianna. Those things have not happened. Do not ever speak that way again or live a nightmare of your own creation. You are a fighter . . . fight until you have conquered this. I do not care what tragedies occur—you must never surrender to this war or let it have you. You have been the one to tell us all that we must not give in, even if it is just finding some sort of strength and meaning for ourselves. Get back on your feet, *Carina*."

Tears dripped from my chin but I nodded my head up and down. "All right, Papa, I will."

He shook me gently. "Promise me that no matter what prevails, you will not let the war conquer you."

"I promise you."

Chapter Twenty-One

MASSIMO

GENERAL BARBERI ARRIVED THE DAY after I was picked up by his minions on the road. He had me taken to his office before I saw Fatima. The room was dark, the red velveteen curtains pulled shut except for the smallest gap where dust motes floated down through a slash of light that landed on the marble floor.

Barberi turned on a desk lamp as I entered the room, and I blinked my eyes to see him. The lamp emitted a yellow light that turned Barberi's skin green and deepened the dark shadows on his face. He had the features of a bull—flared nostrils, tiny eyes, and a smirk that made my muscles itch to wipe it off his face.

He sat in full uniform behind a huge black desk and pointed to a chair on my side. "Massimo, sit down, my boy. It has been so long since I have seen my soon-to-be son-in-law, and I am anxious to hear any news you would like to share with me."

He opened the desk drawer in front of him, lifted a handgun from inside, and laid it in front of him on the desk. I remained standing, reluctant to begin my act of obedience despite the obvious threat.

Barberi patted the top of the desk with his hands on each side of the gun, and the smirk on his face stretched into a sinister grin. "Sit down, please. I want you comfortable while you give me the report of what you have been doing since you left us a few weeks ago. I have a feeling, in the end, it is going to be exactly what I want to hear."

I sat down across from him and gripped my hands together to keep myself from diving for the gun. Barberi interlaced his fingers over the top of the weapon and leaned forward. "Plans are in motion for the wedding. I am so anxious to see you and Fatima happily married. While the two of you honeymoon, I may even find a way, and the time, to visit my old pal Mussolini. You see, unless I make a personal visit or phone call to him soon after the wedding, your father is scheduled to be executed. So my health and well-being must be of the utmost importance to you."

He stood and slipped the gun into a holster on his side and walked to a tray of liquors and glasses. My eyes followed his every move, and I held my breath steady while rage burned in streams down my back.

Barberi poured himself some brandy and gulped it down. "I am sorry, Massimo; I would offer you some, but I think it is important that you have your wits about you while we discuss important things."

I did not move a muscle. "I assure you I am quite lucid. I know exactly what is going on."

He moved back to his desk and sat down. "My, what an intelligent man; Fatima is even luckier than I thought." He gulped down another shot of brandy. "So, tell me, Lieutenant Scalvone, have you been missing my Fatima, and are you as anxious as she is to get this marriage solemnized? Because if you are not, if my daughter tells me she is not happy, then I may not be able to ensure your family's safety—or yours—and that would be a terrible shame."

"I never before realized that my well-being was such a priority to you. I assumed that you were just the doting father."

"I am going to ignore any of your futile hints at hostility. They are rather pathetic."

I sat motionless in my chair, afraid that if I opened my mouth again it would set my muscles loose and I would lunge for his throat. Barberi pulled a folder from a desk drawer and looked at the papers inside with a tsk of his tongue.

"Well, well, well . . . trips to the Greek theatre with a little tart named Marianna De'Angelis—oh . . . and a few sneaky visits to see her in the night."

He closed the folder and his eyes glared red in the dim light. "I do not mind that you have used a local peasant to satisfy yourself before marriage. But that is all finished now. Completely finished, or your little mistress and her family will have to be brought in for some very thorough and quite uncomfortable questioning. So tell me, are you ready to be the faithful husband?"

The burn had risen into my eyes as I stared him down. I curled my hands into fists below the level of the table and swallowed the acid that had risen in my throat. "We do what we must sometimes, however distasteful."

Barberi lost the smile and sneered at me. "I will not tolerate your disobedience or any mistreatment of Fatima. Have I made myself quite clear, Massimo?"

My jaw locked into place. Barberi took the gun from the holster and pointed it at my head. "I am anxious that we communicate very well. I would hate to have any misunderstanding between us since we will be family so soon. You will be my new son, after all. So unless the vision of your father standing before a firing squad has lost your interest, what is your answer? Are you anxious to marry my Fatima?"

I stood up as the blood rushed to my head. "I will not fight you."

He laid the pistol back on the table, the smirk back on his face. "Good."

* * *

The hotel room where I was being held was a mausoleum, a crypt where I would be kept until the moment of my death—the moment I would say *I do* and Fatima would be my wife. I was forbidden to leave the room, while Fatima was free to visit and play the part of the devoted fiancée. I made a plan to tolerate what I had to; I would smile on cue and make excuses that my regard for her was too high to show my affection until the vows were solemnized. Then, God willing, my father could be released and I would find a way to escape.

The memories of my times with Fatima in Foggia were still vivid in my mind. Even then the sound of her voice grated layers of my skin to the bone. In social gatherings she'd made jokes about the casualties in the war and appeared bored by stories of the poor or wounded. She'd admired my mother's art collection with greed in her eyes and given our servants orders like she was a part of our family.

My sister, Nicla, and I did not have pets when we were children. But a feral cat with a thick silver coat found its way into our gardens several times through the years. When she stretched and purred on the lawn, we hoped we could pet her and feed her scraps from the table. But just when we reached out our hands to feed her, she would narrow her eyes with a flash of ferocity and tear into our skin with her claws. I still had the scars on my hands.

In social settings, Fatima danced and laughed like a debutante at a ball. She stretched and purred against me with a sultry glint in her eyes one minute; the next, she pinched my arm if I said something that displeased her or my attention strayed away from her. Each time I thought of Fatima, the burning sting of cat scratches rose up all over my skin.

Chapter Twenty-Two

MARIANNA

ALTHOUGH I KNEW THE THREATS that Massimo warned us about were real, we could not leave as he wanted. Papa's fatigue and illness became chronic and kept him in bed. He moved as slowly as a child learning to walk. Each day his eyes were weaker and puffier, his face drawn and sallow.

As a child I was sure there could never be a world without the daily bob of my father's boat on the horizon of the Mediterranean and the briny smell of a fresh catch growing fishier as the day warmed. Papa smiled and kept assuring us all that he would soon be back on the sea, but we all prayed for a miracle while more and more of the fishing responsibilities were transferred to me and Aviano. My arms and shoulders ached until they burned while we worked, but I had no time to give them relief.

New information traveled down the booths at the open market; despite the scorn toward religion by the Nazi party, the Santa Lucia procession to honor our patron saint would be allowed to take place the next week. Franca, Laura, and I made a plan to march with the crowds. We would carry dedicatory candles and walk in our bare feet behind the statue of the saint in hope that our sacrifice would bring the blessings we craved for our loved ones. We would march for Bruno and Papa. And, in my heart, I would sanctify my sacrifice for Massimo.

We were all aware that Laura's feet swelled and throbbed by each evening, but she refused to let anyone march for Bruno in her stead. When we tried to convince her, she accused us all of heresy, sure that God would not let her or the baby be harmed while honoring one of his holy saints. In the end we all agreed she would march and that Mama and *Signora* Chessari would wait at the end of the procession in the Chessaris' truck to take her home immediately. It was risky; the truck could be confiscated for military use, but it was a risk we would have to take.

The day of the procession arrived. The lacy hem of my skirt brushed across my ankles with each step I took to the beat of somber drums, the cobblestones warm beneath my bare feet. A tatted scarf covered my hair and tapped rhythmically against my lower back. I grasped my procession candle while its flame battered against the breeze and fanned waxy black smoke into my nostrils.

Dour clergy robed in black carried the statue of Santa Lucia on a platform on their shoulders. The ornate statue, draped in gold shimmering cloth, rocked back and forth to the beat of drums—ceramic piety atop a throne piled with gifts, money, and desperate appeals for mercy scribbled on notes and letters. Hundreds of people lined the streets, waved handkerchiefs, and crossed themselves when the procession passed. Some pressed against the wrought-iron rails of their balconies overhead and leaned over to toss flower petals down on the patrons. Many cried and prayed out loud.

Nazi soldiers perched like vultures in silent watch from several balconies overhead, their weapons tight in hand.

Franca and Laura walked beside me. Tears dripped from Laura's chin and tightened the knot in my chest for my brother. Franca and I took turns at Laura's side, one hand gripped tight to a three-foot-long candle, the other beneath Laura's elbow to support her as best we could.

I prayed fervently to drown my thoughts lest I think of Massimo. There had been no news, no reprieve. For all I knew, the day may have already come when he stood beside another woman and spoke vows that sealed my fate in an eternal tomb. I could not accept it. He could not belong to another while he smoldered in the marrow of my bones and pulsed through my veins.

My candle almost touched the ground, and I tightened my grip to stop the trembling in my hand. The torch on the candle glimmered hope for Bruno. My father. Massimo.

The procession was for a saint, but I petitioned my prayer higher, launched it like an arrow to land at the feet of God Himself, whom I was convinced watched and loved me. He was a father; He would hear my prayers.

The chanting of the priests droned on while I listened for my answer and eyed the sidelines for any sign of Massimo.

Chapter Twenty-Three

MASSIMO

FROM THE BALCONY OF MY room I peered down on the procession for Santa Lucia. Wails and prayers from the patrons, armed only with candles and rosaries laced through their fingers, created a miserable song. No doubt the guards surrounding the procession would try to block any music, petition, or prayer in its attempt to reach heaven. Helplessness kept an inferno stoked in my head. I leaned on my elbows at the stone rail and pounded my fists together.

Soon Barberi would have his power over me sealed and a dagger in my back. He would have me killed soon after the sham of a wedding—I had no doubt. It would be cleaner that way, less chance of complications and resistance to getting his hands on our family money. I wondered idly if Fatima knew this too. No matter how her eyes tried to steal into mine, there was more than wretched lust in her veins; there was a thirst for money to match that of a rabid dog for water.

Bile burned in my gut. I lowered my head in frustration, and the silhouette of a slender figure draped in lace passed in the procession below. I jerked to attention and watched her take the next few steps: a woman—a woman who carried her head upright and held her three-foot candle high.

As though she sensed me watching, she lifted her head to the side where I could see her clearly. Blood pounded in my ears. Marianna. The urge to dive from the stone balcony to reach her tipped me forward. I pulled back with a quick gulp of air and rushed back into the room behind me. Marianna had not left town. She was here in the vicinity. And Barberi knew who she was.

The room looked gloomy after the brightness on the balcony. My Nazi guard sat like a toad on a lily pad waiting for his prey to come close.

I walked up in front of him and stared him in the face. "I insist that I be allowed to pay my respects to Santa Lucia and participate in the procession. It is only days before my wedding and it is only customary."

The soldier took a slow draw on his cigarette while he stared at me. He snuffed the ember into the arm of the chair. The fear that Marianna would disappear into the crowd before I could reach her ticked like a bomb in my head, and I tightened my hands into fists.

The soldier stood at once and thrust his sweaty face into mine with a sneer, his teeth thick with yellow scum. "You keep those fists to yourself, *Scemo*. You can go to your ludicrous procession, but only because I am tired of this boring room. I will be beside you every step, and if you try anything wrong or attempt to get away, it will be my pleasure to shoot you—right in front of everyone if I have to."

I dashed down the steps and out onto the road before he had time to pick up his rifle; I ignored his curses and orders for me to halt. An attempt to escape would be too dangerous, but I had to find a way to lose him long enough to reach Marianna and tell her to get out of town.

It was risky to make my guard angry; he could not kill me without facing Barberi's wrath, but wounds were another matter, and he would not hesitate to shoot. A pulsing panic pushed me faster through the throngs of people who crowded the sidelines of the procession.

Altar boys set the pace of the participants and beat the drums strapped around their necks. I slipped between them down each side of the marching patrons and searched the crowd for any sign of Marianna. A sea of lace-draped heads flowed in front and in back of me. I took a hat from my pocket and pulled it down low over my head. My guard shoved his way between two monks and into the procession thirty feet behind me. Sweat beaded on my forehead.

A group of people pushed my guard out of the procession and into the sideline, his string of curses drowned out by their protests about a Nazi in their sacred parade. I ducked deep into the crowd. Devout chanters, black-robed priests swinging lanterns of smoking incense, and the mass of people all provided a way to obstruct myself from view while I wound toward the front.

Only when I was sure my guard could not be too near did I push even faster ahead. Finally I arrived behind the familiar figure that paced like an angel in front of me. My lungs burned for air and my arms longed for Marianna.

But I stopped.

I had lost any semblance of my sanity. The sight of Marianna had blown all reason out of my head. What made me think I could grab her and whisk her away in the light of day? If I was being watched, I would expose her to the enemy I was so desperate to warn her about. I stood stock still—unable to reach for her—unable to leave. People stepped around me while the drums beat like the ticking in my head, and Marianna moved farther away with the crowd. My muscles twitched.

Two women walked on each side of Marianna with their arms looped through hers. One of them looked back, and I met the dark gaze of Franca Chessari, her mouth gaping open in surprise. I raised my finger and held it against my lips to keep her silent and shook my head no, but Franca continued to stare. I turned to go, and Marianna spun around in my direction, her eyes huge. I stepped back and held up my hand.

Within seconds Marianna rushed to my side. Panicked and desperate, I did one final check for the enemy, reached for Marianna's elbow, and grasping it firmly in my hand, I pulled her against my side. I lowered my head to her ear. "Mari, it is too dangerous; step back in line—they know who you are. Get to your family and run out of town. Now. Today."

"No, Massimo, please—please."

Tears slid down her cheeks and she leaned against me for support. The chants and mumbled prayers from the crowds screamed like alarms in my head; her tears and the feel of her against me weakened my will.

I grabbed her around the waist and led her between the trees that lined the roadside. Branches bowed low over us as we darted underneath. "Pull the lace from your scarf down to cover some of your face."

Time did not move until we reached the heavy wooden doors of a nearby cathedral. I pulled one side of the door open to a rush of warm waxy air and the faint glow of candles. My arm gripped tighter around Marianna; I looked down the stone halls and passageways for any sign of soldiers, patrons, or clergy, but the church stood still and silent.

Stone pillars stood in each corner like sentinels that reached all the way to an arched ceiling forty feet above our heads. I led Marianna behind the farthest one and pressed her back against the wall. I gripped her chin in my hand, lowered my mouth to hers, and kissed her—told myself for one moment that none of the hell and nightmare that separated us was real and no one would ever have her but me.

The taste of her filled my head and stoked the fire in my chest that had consumed me since the day I had left her behind.

Marianna clung to my arms and shoulders; the fabric of my shirt gripped in her hands. She kissed me, and the cries in her throat ripped through me like a knife and brought me back to reality. I pulled away, and panic filled her liquid eyes.

"Massimo, hold on to me; just one minute is all I ask. I will die if you let go of me now."

She reached for me and I held her by the shoulders. "I saw you from the balcony and had to come and warn you. General Barberi knows your name. He knows where you live. I hoped you had left town, that you were safe. But it was insanity to risk talking to you in public. I saw you and a part of me went mad."

"Massimo, if you are mad, I am too. What can I do? My father is too sick to leave. I want to help you. We can fight the enemy together."

"I *am* the enemy, Marianna. The only reason Barberi has left you alone is because I have been in his custody. Now I have made the danger worse once again. I should have listened to the warnings in my head."

Marianna reached for me but I pressed her arms back against the wall. My determination faltered at the feel of her trembling and crying. I wrapped my arms around her, my grip so firm I feared I'd crush her. "Forgive me, Marianna. For the danger, for giving you false hope. For this whole horrible risk."

She wept against my shoulder. "Massimo, stop. I chose this too. I would do it again."

She opened her mouth to speak again and I ran my fingers down her face and placed them against her lips. "Stop, *Bellina*, shhh. . . ." I took her by the shoulders until she quieted and stopped shaking her head, her eyes wide with the final question I saw burning inside them.

"The wedding is Friday, five o'clock—in this very cathedral. It is real, Mari. Do you hear me? We can do nothing. You have no choice; you have to run. Please, I never should have—"

Angry shouts stopped me midsentence, and I pushed Marianna back around the pillar. I stepped out just in time to see two German soldiers before the butt of a rifle swung at my face. It struck me with a force that knocked me back flat on the cold tile floor, and I looked up into the bloodshot eyes of my Nazi guard.

Marianna screamed. I yelled for her to run, and the second soldier jabbed his rifle butt into my stomach and kicked me in the head. Warm blood ran down the side of my head, and the room flashed black and purple in front of my eyes. Marianna leaped onto the soldier's back and grabbed at his eyes with her fingers; he stumbled backward. He bellowed and twisted like a bull until he flung her off and grabbed her by the throat. I yelled for him to stop, and my guard stomped his foot down on my shoulder. He pinned me to the floor and pushed my head to the side with the end of his rifle barrel so I could see the soldier choking Marianna.

Rage roared from my throat, and the guard pressed harder at my temple with the rifle. "If you move or yell again, I will kill her first and shoot you in your knees."

Marianna scratched at the soldier's fingers that still gripped around her neck. He let go and belted her across the face. She stumbled backward and crumpled to the floor. I jerked my head to the side against the rifle barrel and pushed against the soldier's foot. He lifted it up and slammed it back down on my chest and pointed the rifle at the middle of my face.

I stared up into his eyes. "I will kill you if either of you touch her again."

The other soldier stepped up beside him and pointed his rifle at my chest. My guard sneered down at me and wacked me in the nose with the rifle. The warm gush of blood ran down my cheek.

The soldier stepped over me, pulled Marianna to her feet, and grabbed her face. "If you ever go near Scalvone again I will slaughter your whole family one by one and then I will kill you myself. Now go back to your pathetic little procession and act like nothing happened or I will exterminate your boyfriend too . . . or, better yet, wound him until he wishes he were dead. You traitorous Italians are a waste of the Führer's time. I wish I could kill you all."

He shoved Marianna, and she fell back hard on the floor. He pointed his rifle in my direction and stared at Marianna. "Get out now, or we will shoot him on the spot."

The slap of heavy sandals against tile grew loud; a priest ran up with a huff of breath. "What is this trouble in God's holy house? We have sanctuary."

The guard laughed. "The only sanctuary you have is what we allow you to have."

The priest ignored him, reached for Marianna, and helped her to her feet. "Come now, *Signorina*, you must go quickly."

She turned to look at me one last time as the soldier kicked me in the ribs. The priest rushed Marianna, bent and weeping, out the door.

When they had gone, my guard yanked me to my feet and pointed his rifle at my face.

"Walk."

I stumbled toward the doors, my guard beside me, while the other soldier followed behind. There was no sign of Marianna when we got outside. I sighed in relief, and my captors shoved me back to my prison.

Chapter Twenty-four

MARIANNA

FRIDAY ARRIVED AND DREAD SWIRLED in a dense fog. At five o'clock the wedding between Massimo and Fatima would take place and seal my heart in a tomb. I sat in my parents' bedroom. Papa lay on the bed and I sat beside him; his hand lay limp in mine, his calluses still thick as leather.

The trip home from the procession had been agony after the guards ripped Massimo and me apart. I'd longed to reach my father, to feel his arms comfort me like a broken-hearted child again. But to no avail. His illness had stricken him even further while we were at the procession. Thankfully Aviano had found him when he collapsed in the yard and helped him into bed.

I pressed Papa's hand to my cheek and let my tears wash over it. It had been three days, and he had not spoken since Aviano found him. No matter how we tried to awaken him, his eyelids only fluttered and never opened.

The curtains of my parents' bedroom swelled away from the window with the wet breath of an approaching storm. The sun battled the clouds outside while I set my breathing with Papa's. I coaxed his lungs to match my own, to regain a strong, steady rhythm, while my mother dozed on a settee in the corner. When Papa seemed more restful, I slipped through the door, past the hinges that whined at my departure.

I stopped in the hallway and leaned against the faded flowers of the wallpaper. I looked up at the ceiling in frustration. My throat still hurt where the soldier had choked me in the cathedral.

Today was Massimo's wedding day. No, I told myself—today was the day of his imprisonment by a woman who wanted only his power and money. I threw my head back, glad when it hit the wall with a painful thud. I wanted the pain—something physical that would overpower the agony in my heart. I squeezed my eyes shut, my hands pressed against them in fists.

My father lay helpless in bed, my mother paced the halls in worry or kept vigil at his side, my brother was gripped in the claws of war, and I could not stop the torment that ravaged my mind over Massimo. The image of him pinned and bleeding on the cathedral floor flashed constantly before me. Guilt was a sword that cut me in half; Massimo could have been killed or injured somehow for the rest of his life because he tried to warn and protect me. I had closed my ears and my eyes to his words and foolishly believed my love or my will could overpower any threat. I had insisted on holding on to him in the procession and would not let him go. The Nazi soldiers followed us into the cathedral and attacked us because of me. For days I'd relived the agony of the priest leading me away, the moment when half of me had died. I knew that somehow the other half must carry on. I slid down the wall to the floor.

Mama called my name, and I scrambled to my feet and hurried back into their room. A gray pallor had blanched Papa's face in the few minutes I had languished in the hall. Mama sat beside him in the chair she had reupholstered just last year.

I lay one hand on my father's arm and looked at my mother. "Mama, I must go find a doctor."

She lifted her dull eyes to mine and opened her mouth in what would have been a protest had I not lifted my finger up to stop her. "I know you worry about my safety, but I searched this morning and cannot find Aviano to go in my place. Siracusa is full of Nazi soldiers, but they are not officially our enemies and I will stay as far from them as possible. I must try, Mama; there could be someone with medicine or a nurse who would be willing to help. Maybe I can find Dr. Formica. You know he loves Papa and will come if there is any way he can."

She nodded her head, lifted my father's hand to her lips, and kissed it. "Go and try, Mari, God will be with you."

* * *

I stopped at our well to fill a canteen, dashed to the stable, and secured the saddle with a toss and tug of a wool blanket. I scrambled onto Tesoro's back because he would be faster and stronger than Matilda. I urged him on to town while clouds thickened and streamed like black shadows across the sun.

* * *

The hope and fear that I might see Massimo in Siracusa pressed so hard on my chest that I gasped for air every few minutes. I steeled myself; in order to protect him, to keep him safe, I had to stay away. The noise of the city was a hum in the back of my racing mind when we entered the streets. I led Tesoro to a stone watering trough to let him drink and rest. The watering trough was like a fountain; horses made of marble stood at each end of the trench, their heads tossed back and mouths gaped open like parched creatures hoping to catch the rain.

We kept to quiet streets until a truck full of soldiers, some standing at a gun mounted in the back, roared from around a corner. Dust flew from under their tires as they passed. I fanned it away and swallowed the thick grime in my throat with water from my canteen. German and Italian soldiers called out to me or whistled to get my attention. I hardly heard them and pressed on toward Ortigia, the old sector of town where I hoped to find Dr. Formica.

The streets of Ortigia were built hundreds of years ago, wide enough to accommodate only horses and carriages; they twisted like a maze on a tiny island next to Siracusa. I urged Tesoro to a quick trot across the bridge between them and down streets of old buildings as tall and narrow as crevasses through a mountain range. No laughter or conversation bounced from one window to another from any neighbors overhead. We wound our way through dank air that hung in the passageways. Shadows jumped like dark street urchins around the corners as we turned.

The doors and window of a bakery next to Dr. Formica's office stood open. I nodded to the people inside, an old man bent over a broom and two children playing on the floor with a wooden toy. The tables and chairs outside, on each side of the window, sat empty while the vegetable stand across the street gathered debris at the base of its closed shutters.

We passed the bakery and stopped in front of Dr. Formica's office and home. I held my breath and knocked on the chipped paint of the front door. Time crawled by in silence before the shuffle of house slippers behind the door gave me a lurch of hope.

One squeak of rusty hinges and the doctor's wife squinted in the brightness through the crack of the door. "The doctor is not here, *Signorina*; the Germans took him. They made him go to work on wounded soldiers even though he is so old."

She tsked her tongue and shook her gray head. "Too old, too old . . . I must go lay back down. . . . *Sono amalata* . . . I am sick, too sick. *Mi dispiace.* Please forgive me."

I took a quick breath to reply and she shut the door. I stared at it in disbelief; I had traveled miles to get here. My father could die. I stared at the door, willing the doctor to be home and to open the door with an apology for the misunderstanding. He would appear—hand me medicine, a cure, a Bible, a blessing from God Himself. I would accept anything but the final click of the door and the rustle of his wife's tired feet behind it in retreat.

I grabbed at the brass handle on the door, twisted it open, and stepped into a small entryway. "*Signora*?" The old woman, partway down a dim hallway, stopped and turned around.

I clasped my hands as if in prayer. "Please forgive my intrusion. I am so desperate. Perhaps the doctor, your husband, left some kind of medicine I could search through? A tonic, a strengthener of some sort? Your husband, Dr. Formica, knew my father. I could pay you money. Please, if there is any way you could help me."

She stared at me, the bags under her eyes deflated and puckered. "I know who you are—the fisherman's daughter. I've bought your fish at the market. *Mi dispiace tanto poverina*, I am so sorry for your troubles. Your father, he always gave my husband free fish to give to his poorest patients."

She opened her hands, palms up and empty. "They came back after they took my husband away, those soldiers. Swept everything into bags—all the medicines and bandages on the shelves and in the cabinets—and stormed off as if I was not here." Tears spread through the wrinkles on her cheeks. "I did not even get to tell my Luigi goodbye. He is too old for war."

I put my arm around the woman's bent shoulders and led her into a parlor of faded furniture. A skinny yellow cat meowed its way across the floor and rubbed around my ankles.

"*Signora* Formica, do you have food for yourself? Any family nearby to care or watch out for you?"

She nodded her head and patted my hand that lay on her shoulder. "I do not have any family, but I have good neighbors and food in our kitchen upstairs. I cook every night in case my Luigi comes home."

She started to sob, and I helped her to a high-backed chair. "I will pray every day that he will return, *Signora*." I pushed a floral ottoman under her feet. "Please be safe. I must go now. I have to find medical help for my father right away."

She raised her wrinkled hand and I grasped it in mine. The corners of her mouth turned down in a sympathetic frown. "*Carina*, all the doctors are gone to the war; only God can help your father now."

I tightened my muscles against the twist of fear from her words. She pushed the ottoman to the side and hobbled to a shelf lined with burning candles. The flickering wicks danced in the gloomy room and over the sorrowful face of the Madonna in a painting on the wall.

The *Signora* lit another candle and turned to me. "I will keep a candle burning for your father."

I thanked her and left with despair lodged like a rock in my heart.

* * *

The ricocheted ping of Tesoro's hooves on cobblestone mimicked the final click of the doctor's door behind us. Every idea to help my Papa, any hope I tried to conjure up, lasted mere seconds before it sunk in defeat. I prodded my horse with my heels for home, empty-handed and as bent and crushed as Dr. Formica's wife.

Piazza Duomo opened like a wide gulf in the middle of Ortigia. Walls of war supplies—wooden crates stacked ten feet high—stood between me and the church where I had last seen Massimo. I swallowed the ache to go inside the cathedral, to stand at the pillar where I had last touched him. My head ached at the memory of him wounded on the ground, being torn away from me. I had lost track of time, so I had no idea when the wedding may take place. The urge to bolt for home fought with a sick compulsion to stand here and wait for Massimo to come for his wedding.

I wiped the perspiration from my nose with the back of my hand. No doctor, no help, no Massimo. Tesoro would be thirsty. I stopped at a watering trough and let my horse drink, then stroked his nose and sobbed against his smooth cheek.

The afternoon had approached and the streets filled with people. In spite of the sense of urgency to get away, I had to guide Tesoro carefully not to collide with the steady crowds—some in cars, some loaded in horse-drawn wagons, piled high with belongings as if a mass exodus were underway. I wondered where they were going, what good it would do to get there.

The crowd pressed beside us and blocked Tesoro beside the tent of a vegetable stand across the plaza from the cathedral. I searched for a gap in the crowd to get away, and my gaze locked on two black cars as they pulled up in front of the cathedral. There were flowers and streaming ribbons tied to the handles of the car doors that signified a wedding. I froze.

The door of the first car opened and Massimo stepped out in full uniform. The noise of the plaza muffled. Two German soldiers stood with Massimo. My hands shook so hard I dropped the reins and slid from the saddle into quicksand at my feet. I needed to run, but could not move; I needed to scream, but had no breath.

Blurry black eyes swam in front of me. "*Signorina*, are you well? Do you need to drink?"

A woman tipped a cup against my lips. Cool water rinsed my throat while someone's hand wiped a wet towel over my face. I pushed it away and realized I was sitting on the ground. The woman patted my hand, "*Poverina . . . poverina . . .* you poor thing, it is much too hot today."

I had to get away, to run as fast as I could in the opposite direction. I mumbled a thank-you, pulled myself up onto Tesoro with shaky limbs, and took another look at the front of the cathedral. Massimo was gone—must have gone inside before a short woman, engulfed in a fountain of white lace, stepped from the other car. Tesoro staggered as I yanked his reins to and fro for balance. I pulled him to a stop and stared at the woman who must be Fatima. It was too far away to see her face. She fluffed her dress and took a handful of flowers from the woman who must be her mother. They marched into the cathedral, and I leaned forward until my face was buried in my horse's mane. I kicked until Tesoro moved at a frantic pace out of the plaza.

As soon as we were safely away, nausea gripped my stomach and I stopped and retched in a gutter. Prayer escaped me. Hope flew like ashes into the sky. I forced myself to keep moving forward to my home to help my parents, my anger buried with my cries in my horse's mane.

Chapter Twenty-five

MASSIMO

THE VULTURES HAD CIRCLED AND struck with cunning and ruthless power. I walked inside the Cathedral Duomo and down a long aisle to the steps in front of an altar: a grown man, a soldier—but a lamb to the slaughter.

The organ bellowed heavy chords through the murky passageways of the church. Alabaster saints and angels looked down on me in pity from the alcoves in the walls, their sympathy useless and any pleas in my behalf lost on the small crowd of people seated on wooden pews to watch the ceremony. A statue of the virgin wept tears of blood but offered no mercy on my behalf.

The bells in the tower chimed five times. I willed the doors of the church to remain closed. They flew open, slammed against the rock wall like a clap of thunder, and Fatima entered in a white dress that had swallowed her bulk in massive layers of starched lace. She held her father's arm, and the two of them stepped with a majesty they did not merit down the long aisle—in my direction. Dread as thick and heavy as I had endured in the battles in Africa pulled down like an anchor around my neck.

I could not see Fatima's eyes through her veil but could imagine the victorious look that must be on her face. General Barberi's stare bore a hole in my chest with each measured step in my direction, but I refused to meet his gaze. I turned toward the priest rather than watch my bride approach as was expected. The music died when Fatima stood beside me on the step.

The priest began the wedding mass, his sallow skin hanging in folds that dangled from his cheekbones. His robe spread like a web each time he extended his arms. I focused on a candle that sputtered and hissed behind him.

Fatima recited her part of the mass in a nervous twitter. My voice answered on cue like a ghost from across the sea. Freedom ebbed as the mass drew to a close and the moment for the vows approached. Bile coated the back of my throat.

I gave myself one final moment before I uttered the words that would bind me to Fatima and pronounce a death sentence on my soul; I let myself think of Marianna. Her eyes black as olives, the powdery sweetness of her skin, her courage and strength. I stumbled in place and caught the jerk of Fatima's head in my direction; I knew she feared I would run away. She was wise to fear; God willing, I would slay Satan himself to flee this hell.

A rotund woman dressed in black stepped from behind a curtain and cleared her throat. The organist held down a discordant note and the woman belted out an aria that careened through the cathedral and sheared my nerves to a raw edge. In mere minutes I would belong to the predators who surrounded me. My pulse beat like the drums at an execution.

The priest shook holy water over our heads that seared my skin. He picked up the book that contained the wedding rites and invoked a prayer that was barely audible above the woman's strident solo. The skull and crossbones, etched in the archway above him, cackled out loud and jeered at me.

General Barberi marched forward, knelt before the priest, and kissed his ring. He lifted Fatima's hand as if it was made of fine glass and placed it on top of mine. I tightened my other hand into a fist.

The soloist raised her voice in a high-pitched crescendo and wailed like a siren. The vibration shook the floor beneath my feet. Fatima's hand twitched on top of mine while I tethered my muscles into a knot to keep myself in place. I stared at the floor and focused on the love I felt for my father; I would do this for him. I could do this for him and prayed to God that it would free him.

The priest waved his hand over our heads in a blessing and opened the book to begin the vows. The soloist heaved up her chest in a deep breath for the finale and sucked all the oxygen from the room. I watched her lips move, her chin shake in a powerful vibrato, and heard nothing but my pulse jump to a frantic drum roll when she finished and stepped back behind the curtain. Fate bound and gagged me. The priest opened his mouth to commence the wedding ceremony. I bowed my head, unable to meet the gaze of my executioner.

Chapter Twenty-Six

"HALT!"

I jerked my head up and stared at the priest who looked like he had just swallowed his tongue. He shook his head and pointed at an Italian officer in front of a long row of soldiers in the back of the cathedral. The soldiers pointed their rifles at the chests of Barberi's guards. No one moved while the officer who had shouted marched with authority to the front of the church and stopped before me and Fatima. The priest stepped out of his way and gripped the book of rites against his chest, his eyes bulbous in fear.

The Italian officer snapped his fingers at the soldiers in the back and several of them closed in around the pews of people while the rest of the soldiers held Barberi's men at bay. The priest yelped like a wounded dog and lunged behind the curtain.

General Barberi jumped to his feet, his face contorted with rage. "What do you think you are doing? This marriage is sanctioned by Mussolini himself. You are all under arrest."

The officer in front of us glanced past Barberi as if he did not exist then pointed at him and nodded his head at his soldiers. Two of them seized General Barberi and fastened his hands behind his back. I had forgotten all about Fatima until I heard her scream. She darted into a nearby room then reappeared when a soldier pulled her back and restrained her. I stood locked in place, afraid to move, to speak, to hope.

The officer nodded to the soldier who held Fatima. "Take her to the car."

The soldier wrestled a screaming and whimpering Fatima to the door, and the officer raised his hand to the congregation. "Those of you who are here as spectators have no need to fear; General Barberi is charged with treason against his country, and we have taken him into custody. His guards and family will be detained and the rest of you may go."

The pews of people behind me emptied within seconds while I watched the man in charge. I had seen this officer somewhere before. His nose, the set of his eyes, even his manner seemed familiar. I had no time to think before he looked straight at me and the tension in his face eased.

"If the vows were completed, Massimo, I will help you arrange for an annulment."

My face must have reflected my shock when he spoke my name. He placed his hand on my shoulder. "Were the vows completed?"

I shook my head in spite of the astonishment that had numbed me clear down my limbs. "No, sir, I do not believe they were."

"Good, good, that makes it easier. Now we need to get you out of here."

* * *

I did not look back when we exited the murky cathedral into the brightness of day. Fatima scrambled and kicked at the soldiers as they loaded her into a car. Barberi sat surrounded by armed guards in the back of a truck that disappeared out of the plaza.

The officer pointed me toward an awaiting jeep. I jumped in quickly, and my blood began to flow again; I was filled with relief and guarded hope. The officer slammed his foot down on the accelerator, and we spun away from the church. Before I could clear my thoughts, he looked at me, grinned, and slapped my knee. "I have known your father and worked with him for many years."

"Worked with him, sir?"

He laughed. "Yes, to try to save Italy from Mussolini and Hitler. He has had me and those affiliated with me watching you, and he sent instructions through our network that this marriage was not to happen."

I took what felt like the first breath of my life. The strength and love of my father rushed through me. "Is my father still in custody—is he safe?"

"He is no longer a captive of Mussolini and is in a relatively safe place. I am afraid that is all I can tell you. Another important detail is that your grandparents are being relocated off of Sicily to a home with relatives, and your mother is with your sister in Switzerland. Rest assured that all the safety measures possible have been taken."

"I do not know how to thank you. This news seems almost impossible to comprehend."

The jeep skidded around blind corners and flew over debris in the road. Soldiers were everywhere, packed in rows in the back of military trucks that lined the streets. I had no idea where we were going but when I opened my mouth to ask, the officer raised up his hand to interrupt. I held tight to the edge of the jeep and fought to hear the man's voice above the growl of the engine.

"I am afraid there are multiple emergencies I must attend to immediately so I cannot take you anywhere you may feel you need. As you observed, I made it to your aid with seconds to spare. It would be perilous for you to go home. The safest place for you now is a hotel room with a few of our agents and soldiers. Perhaps you can be of some help if you would be willing to join with us."

"Of course I would, sir. I . . . owe you my life and the lives of my family."

A towering truck whose engine roared like an angry lion rumbled by as the jeep zipped around another corner. The officer slammed down on the brakes, and we slid to a stop in front of an old hotel, the Hotel Grande.

He grabbed a faded green duffle bag from the back seat and tossed it to me when I jumped from the jeep. "Here are a few clothes and supplies to get you by. Look in the side pocket, and you'll find papers that will show you are affiliated with me."

"Am I allowed to know your name, sir?"

"Just call me Lieutenant Bianco."

"Lieutenant Bianco, thank you once again for saving my life—and the life of my family."

"You are welcome, son. Room three-eighteen—announce who you are and who sent you so they do not mistake you for an enemy. Do not go anywhere else."

His tires spun as he drove away, a dust devil whirling in his wake.

* * *

My first impulse was to run full force to Marianna, grab her up, and take her and her family someplace safe, but Lieutenant Bianco's words had sounded dire. I darted into the hotel, my feet lighter than they had been in months.

It was almost dark, and the building appeared abandoned, the elaborately decorated foyer empty, the heavy curtains askew at the windows. It was silent, the air stale and still, my footsteps muffled in thick green carpet. I pressed a button on the wall for a light to no avail—no electricity or oil lamps in sight.

Room three-eighteen, Lieutenant Bianco had said. I climbed a wide winding staircase, thankful for dim light from windows high above the stairs and glad that the marble steps would not creak and announce my arrival to anyone I may not want to encounter.

* * *

Out of breath, more from nerves than exertion, I rounded the last corner of the stairs to the third landing. My foot hit the top step and I froze. The end of a rifle barrel poked out from behind a pillar. I raised my hands slowly over my head. "My name is Massimo Scalvone. I was sent here by Lieutenant Bianco."

A man in an American uniform stepped from around the corner, his hair as orange as a carrot and his expression grim. "Turn around and press your hands to the wall, *Italiano*, no matter who sent you."

I concealed my surprise at seeing an American soldier here in Sicily. An Italian soldier stepped out from the opposite corner with a smile on his face. "Lighten up, James, the guy has had a hard day; the lieutenant just rescued him from a bad marriage."

I did not dare move. James did not look convinced. He took a step toward me and stared at me eye to eye. "Where is your ID?"

I reached into the side pocket of the duffle bag and gave the soldier the papers. He looked at them with suspicion and then relaxed his shoulders. "Okay, Scalvone, you can come in."

The Italian soldier grinned again. "Do not pay too much attention to poor James. He is an American and his mama is so far away he's a little nervous."

James's eyes widened. "Shut up, Ronaldo; you Italians would let a stray dog in from the street if I let you."

Ronaldo laughed. "Only if he asked nicely and did not try to eat my pasta." Ronaldo slapped me on the shoulder. "You will have to excuse us, Massimo. We have been cooped up a long time in here."

My mind clicked to keep up, unsure if I was safe or about to be shot or captured by James—and confused by the camaraderie between men who were supposed to be on opposite sides of the war.

I went along with these men for two reasons: Lieutenant Bianco knew my father and, most importantly, anyone who knew the true nature and evil of Barberi had to be on the right side. I felt safer no matter the outcome; it was the end of the day, I was not married to Fatima Barberi or in her father's control, and I knew my father had managed to escape. If I could reach Marianna, I could douse the rest of the fire in my gut.

We entered room three-eighteen. A few men in civilian clothing sat at tables, reading maps and folders stuffed thick with papers. Ham radios covered tables and desks, their wires like a pot of black spaghetti spilled on the floor. Somehow the electricity worked in this room. Several soldiers spoke in both English and Italian into the microphones of the radios. Everyone seemed too busy to even notice I was there.

Finally Ronaldo tapped an older man on the shoulder. "*Mi Scusi*, Sergeant Ferro, I have Massimo Scalvone here, sent by Lieutenant Bianco. I am not sure what to do with him."

The older man looked up over the top of his glasses with a fixed scowl on his face. "I know who he is, Ronaldo." He fixed his stare on me. "You look like a soldier, son."

"Yes, sir, I am . . . just been on leave for a few weeks."

"Well, your leave is finished. We have an emergency situation here and no time to train you. But if you are a soldier you are prepared enough. We know your father and will take you on his merits. You are now an official member of our unit to overthrow Mussolini and get your Italian butts on the right side of the war like most of your people wanted to be in the first place."

He clenched his mouth closed in a grimace that accentuated his fleshy jowls, and he looked me straight in the eye. "You in?"

I cleared my throat. "If you're affiliated with my father and against Mussolini, I am in, sir. And if you are connected to Lieutenant Bianco, I believe I owe you a huge measure of gratitude for my rescue today."

The scowl on his face almost eased into a smile. "The only thing more dangerous than the Nazis is marrying the wrong woman. Glad we could help. Sergeant James will get you some gear and ammo. We will be under attack by the Americans or British sometime tonight or in the next few days, and a storm is coming. The wind and rain could ruin our plans faster than the enemy."

He stared down at a map laid out on a table in front of him. I looked at his American uniform in confusion.

"Excuse me, sir, but you are American, no? You speak Italian very well; you are here working beside us?"

The man lifted a cigar from an ashtray, bit down on it in the corner of his mouth, and laughed. "I had an Italian grandma, like many or most of our double-language men in the room. What would the Allies do without those Italian nonnas? You'll catch on, soldier; we are all in this together, and your papa is on our team. No need to worry."

Men talked into microphones in raised voices on what had to be different radio frequencies. I discerned the words, all spoken at once about paratroopers, bombers, and foot patrols. Scowling men barked out code numbers and names in Italian and English with beads of sweat trickling down their faces.

Relief, joy, and full alarm hit me like a grenade. Maybe the hell of Mussolini's reign could finally come to an end, but if Marianna had not run and left town as I told her then she was out there in the countryside alone, defenseless, with her mother and a sickly father.

Risking repercussions, I turned back to the sergeant whose thick brows now pointed downward. "Sir, I have some family, an . . . um . . . young woman and her family, just out of town here, who I must warn."

"Sorry, son, say a prayer that they are not caught in the crossfire. You could be dead by the time you hit the edge of town out alone now."

He turned his back to me in dismissal. My legs shook with the urge to run. The low whistle of wind came through the windows of the room. The percussion of explosions and gunfire in the distance rattled against my nerves. I darted a glance at the door with a split-second evaluation of how quickly I could get away and make it to the De'Angelis' home.

"Over here, soldier."

I looked up in surprise to see one of the men in civilian clothes at the table turn around and gesture for me to come to the table next to him. The man had gray hair and graying whiskers in the stubble on his face. He pointed to a piece of paper and pen on the table in front of him. "I deliver messages for the group. If you have something of an emergency, you can write a note and I will take it. I'm old, and the Nazis let me pass without suspicion."

He smiled and nodded, exposing missing teeth. I patted the man's shoulder in relief. "I do have something—a very critical message."

I scribbled the warning to Marianna to take her parents and go deeper into the countryside immediately. And then told her I had been rescued from the Barberis and my father was safe. "I am not and never will be married to Fatima. Do not hesitate to leave. In fact, run. I must help fight, but I am coming to find you as quickly as possible." I folded the paper and told the man where to find Marianna. He took my note and picked up his bag to leave.

"Do not worry; I know where this house is."

James shouted over the onslaught of the noisy room and held up a rifle. "Hey, Scalvone, you need your equipment." He stood beside a long table covered in weapons and ammunition and shoved the rifle, a belt loaded with ammo, and a canteen into my hands. No matter the explanation about Italian ancestry, it still amazed me to hear Italian spoken from a man with hair the color of carrots.

I strapped the belt around my hips and checked the rifle. "How did Italian Partisans end up working with the British and Americans?"

James crooked his head. "I thought you would know. The American OSS is backing the Italian Partisans now. Your rebels were so numerous and impressive, Mr. Roosevelt himself sent us in with weapons and equipment to team up with you."

"I knew somewhat about the alliance, but not that it had come this far." That explained the armed civilians in the room, some of them women who mingled with the American and Italian soldiers.

I picked up a helmet and put out my hand to James. "Thank you for the help. I am honored to work with you."

"Welcome to the team, Scalvone."

Sergeant Ferro rose to his feet. "Okay, men, you are a part of this operation and in on top-secret military information. This is it; God willing, this island is about to receive a kick in the pants. We play our cards right, and Sicily just may be liberated—and the Germans are not going to like it. Everyone to the jeeps! Follow me; stay together and shoot only if you have to. Spare the Italian citizens and soldiers if at all possible."

I sprinted behind several men down the winding stairway, my life and trust in the hands of absolute strangers.

Chapter Twenty-Seven

MARIANNA

I HELD ONTO TESORO'S MANE and let my sobs over Massimo and my failed mission be buried beneath the clamoring of his hooves as he galloped for home. But worry pulled me from my reverie; something was wrong with Tesoro. He limped, faltered, and pulled on the reins for control of his head. I slipped from his back and ran my hand down each leg and foot while I talked and cooed to soothe him. His right foreleg was lame, a rock wedged so deeply and tightly in his hoof that I couldn't dislodge it. I had no choice but to walk by his side and encourage him along.

The black clouds expanded their girth above the landscape, and their damp warmth blew in angry gusts of wind. Daylight slipped behind the horizon, and the silhouette of our home through the trees appeared ghostlike in the twilight. I forced my feet ahead and encouraged my lumbering horse to make it just a few more paces.

A shiver skimmed down my neck when we arrived; all the windows of our home were dark. My feet and heart stopped simultaneously . . . Papa. I bolted through the front door. The air inside was still and silent, the curtains all closed. I ran my fingertips down the wall of the dark hallway to my parents' bedroom and opened the door. Pale light came through their window, and I spotted my mother slumped in the chair beside the bed. Quiet sobs shook her slender shoulders, the knot in her hair hanging loose down her neck.

I must have gasped, because she lifted her head and looked at me with hollowed eyes. "Oh, Marianna, he is gone. What are we going to do?"

A lone candle flickered light and shadows on my motionless father. I fell to my knees beside him. "Papa . . . Papa . . . please, Papa, no . . . no . . . no. . . ."

I lit a candle that cast shadows over my father's body. I shook him and tugged at the white cotton blanket that covered him. His broad chest did not rise and fall with breath. The boom of his voice was silenced. The arms that had pulled in thousands of fish with their brawny strength and embraced our family thousands of times lay limp and lifeless at his sides.

I dropped my head down on his shoulder. "Come back. Come back. You promised all was well. You cannot go. You said we would not lose—we would never lose."

I picked up his hand, willed it to stroke my head and comfort me. The scratch of his whiskers was still so normal, so real, when I laid my cheek against his. "Take me fishing one last time, Papa. We will keep going this time. We can go so far away no war or sickness will ever find us again." I promised we'd find a clear blue horizon, full of shimmering mackerels and the warmth of a golden sun.

He did not answer me.

I stroked the calluses on his palm and placed his hand on my wet cheek. I talked to him in my heart, told him more things we could do if he would only come back. We could go to find Bruno; he was probably just on patrol somewhere, safe in the countryside. He would be anxious to come home and see us, to wrap his long arms around Papa's neck, and we would all laugh together.

The soft whimper at the foot of the bed brought me back to reality. Mama lay curled on her side, her hand on Papa's leg as she quietly cried. I put my arms around her, and she sobbed against my shoulder.

After a while the tick of the clock was the only sound in the room, the candle burnt down to an amber glow. Mama lay back down on the bed beside my father. I held Papa's hand until all the warmth had faded and laid it on his chest with a sob. My mother lay so still beside him, her face stricken white. I pushed myself to my feet to get her something to drink.

By the time I returned she was asleep. I slipped out the front door and rode Matilda to Franca's house with a prayer that her father, *Signore* Chessari, would be back from up north so I could ask him for help . . . with my father's body.

* * *

The Chessaris' maid, Alba, opened the front door. Lightning lit up the sky behind me while sheets of rain smacked against my back. She hurried me inside, wet and windblown. I slumped down on a sofa in the open entryway. Franca scurried in from the hall, her eyes wide with surprise at the sight of me.

"Oh, Mari, you are so pale. What are you thinking being out in a storm like this? The lightning could—"

She stopped short when I laid my head back against the wall and let the tears run unhindered. She sat beside me and gripped my hands in hers. "What is it? Tell me, quickly."

I tried to speak but sobs burst out of me, and I fell against her. My father had died, Massimo was gone forever, and Bruno fought the enemy face to face miles away.

"Franca, I need help. Papa died. He died, Franca; my papa is really gone."

Franca gasped. "No, Mari, no!"

I wept against my closest friend while she locked both of her arms around me and rocked me gently, as she would a child. I wiped my face with a handkerchief Alba handed me. "I was not even there when he went, Franca. My mother, my poor mama, was all alone. She is alone still. I need help. I do not know what to do with my father, and I must hurry."

Each time I said the name *Papa* a tidal wave crashed over the top of me, and I had to fight for a breath. *Signora* Chessari rushed into the room, looking as fearful and disheveled as I felt. She covered her heart with her hand. "Is there bad news of Laura?"

Franca sat straighter and held her arm around me while I tried to register the meaning of her mother's words. Franca held her hand up to her mother. "No, no, there is no word on Laura yet. But Mama, there is tragic news; *Signore* De'Angelis has died. Marianna has come, desperate for help."

Signora Chessari stared back and forth at the two of us and burst into tears. Franca stood and embraced her. The cuckoo clock that Franca's father had brought back from Germany when we were children played a merry song; a little wooden bird popped through tiny doors and chirped while the three of us cried and the wind moaned against the windows. Nothing seemed real, the room locked in a world I had never seen before.

Franca patted her mother on the shoulder, whispered something about the will of God and Laura into her ear, and my fears swelled like a wave.

"What is it, Franca? *Signora*? What is wrong with Laura, where is she?"

Franca hesitated and then looked me in the eye. "Marianna, I am so very sorry about your papa; I want to give you so much comfort, nothing but help, but we are in a crisis too. The workers in the yard told us yesterday about more aggressive bombing in the north where Bruno might be.

"Laura is gone; a note on her nightstand this morning explained she could not bear the pain of wondering where Bruno was any longer, and she had taken the car and gone into town to find information. We sent two of our workers to look for her, but they came home empty-handed. She should have been home hours ago. We have been frantic with worry."

Ice shivered through my veins. Laura, gentle Laura, heavy with child, lost in a town of barbaric men. My head throbbed, unable to contain any more fear, loss, or worry. If only I had known, just hours ago, I could have looked for her. I tried to say a prayer for her safety, but my thoughts were too jumbled. My hands trembled so hard I grasped them together.

Franca gripped my hands. "Marianna, listen to me; we will help you, and we have help for us all. Thanks be to all the saints, Papa came home this evening, and he has gone to look for Laura."

My hands still trembled beneath Franca's. She shook me. "Mari, he will be home soon, I can feel it. He will bring Laura and go for your mama." Her voice turned to a whisper. "And help with your papa."

I looked into the tired and swollen eyes of *Signora* Chessari. I reached my hand up and pulled her down on the couch beside me. "*Signora*, I can find Laura. I know the city, but I cannot leave my mother . . . or my father."

The door opened, and Franca's father entered. Rain ran in streams off the brim of his hat and down his long trench coat. He held a limp and drenched Laura close as a baby in his arms, her face tucked beneath his chin.

Elisa Chessari lept from her seat with a sob and ran to her daughter and husband. *Signore* Chessari's expression was grim. "She was at the train station. Someone told her that some of the troops were coming in. There may be danger for the baby. She told me she has been bleeding, Elisa. She passed out just before we got here. There is trouble in town. Soldiers are up in arms all over the landscape, and some may even come this way. All of you must follow me at once."

Franca stood and looked up at her father. "Papa, I will come with you, but Marianna is here because *Signore* De'Angelis . . . he died, Papa. Mari's mother is alone at their house with him, and she has to have your help right away."

Signore Chessari's gaze locked on mine, his eyes deep as a well with sorrow.

"*Che dolore*, Marianna; *Carina*, I am so very sorry. I love your father. Please wait here. I will return immediately and do what I can."

I nodded my head as the Chessari family hurried from the room; my eyes stung with new tears. *Signore* Chessari's kindness in the midst of chaos was so like my father. I clasped my hand around my throat to stifle the ache that had lodged there and wept in worry for Laura and the baby.

I could not stay seated. I paced back and forth across the marble floor and wrapped my arms around my waist. Grief wrapped its fingers like a tourniquet around my chest.

The storm raged outside when I opened the front door to look for *Signore* Chessari. Wind whipped the trees into a frenzy, the branches waving in distress. I closed the door and leaned back against it, the rumble of thunder shaking the walls.

It seemed the clock stood still for an hour before *Signore* Chessari came back and hurried through the front door. "Let's go, and quickly—there could be soldiers in the area at any time."

He ushered me outside into their car, its black silhouette visible only with each flash of lightning.

Matilda was left to roam on the Chessari property as the tires of the car slipped and spun through streams of water across the road. I looked toward Siracusa. The horizon glowed as if lanterns sat atop the city. I could not tell if it was the boom of tanks or thunder that reverberated through me.

I turned toward *Signore* Chessari, hardly able to breathe. "What . . ."

"Some sort of siege is going on in Siracusa. We must take care of your mother and father and run back to my home for cover."

The instant we stopped at my home, I flew from the car.

I found Mama still curled on her side next to Papa, her blanket laid over them both. I sat beside her, looked again at my papa, and let the tears flow and drip from my chin. "Mama, *Signore* Chessari is here to help us. We will take good care of Papa, but we must hurry. Soldiers are coming, and we have to leave right away."

She looked at me in confusion and lifted her gaze toward the door at *Signore* Chessari.

"Oh, Paulo, he is gone . . . my Adamo is gone."

Signore Chessari walked to the bed and took her hand in both of his. "I know, Camilla. Do not worry now; I will help you and take you to Elisa. God bless Adamo and help us all."

She seemed to rally a bit as *Signore* Chessari helped her from the bed. I leaned down and kissed my papa on the forehead for the last time. "*Ti amo*, Papa."

I lit a lantern and took my mother by the hand. "Come now, Mama, let us go rest on the settee in the front parlor, and *Signore* Chessari will get everything taken care of."

I blocked Mama's view when *Signore* Chessari carried Papa from the bedroom and past the doorway, my mother's blanket still wrapped around him. Purple shadows lined my mother's eyes, her elegant face and lips blanched white against the dark green couch. I gave her a pillow to rest her head.

"Mama, I need to help Franca's father for just one minute." A gold throw my Nonna had crocheted when I was a child lay at the end of the couch. I covered my mother with it and grabbed a wooden cross from the wall. "I will be right back."

My legs wobbled a bit but I ran until I had caught up with *Signore* Chessari, grateful that the rain had subsided. He turned, and I saw that he had placed my father on the long garden wagon next to the chicken coop. I longed to run to Papa's side and wished that I could carry him myself. *Signore* Chessari placed his hand on my shoulder.

"I am so sorry, Marianna, it is too dangerous to take your father to a church. We will have to bury him here on your property for now." He squeezed my shoulder. "And then we will have to go back to our home. There is a safe place there."

Pain cinched my throat tight. I placed my hand at the base of my throat and nodded my head in assent. "I thought we may need to bury him here so I brought this cross. By the pond—Papa would want to be by the pond." I could not bear the thought of leaving my father, our home, even our animals. But the boom of ammunition grew closer and louder by the moment, and I knew that we had no choice. "What about our livestock, our chickens? My gelding, Tesoro, has a pebble in his shoe."

"Run back to take care of them while I find a shovel and work by the pond. If you cannot get the pebble loose with the tools you find, it will have to wait. It is best if you turn the animals loose to graze. They will stay nearby." He looked up at the sky. "There are soldiers nearby and the rain is returning; hurry quickly."

* * *

I did as he asked, thankful when the pebble in Tesoro's hoof gave way. I freed him and the rest of the animals.

The clouds showered water on my father's grave the moment *Signore* Chessari finished the burial. Rifle fire and the blast of a tank sounded so close to our property it took my breath away. One brief prayer and I pushed the wooden cross I had taken from our front room into the ground for my precious father. I took the blue cameo necklace Papa had given me for my eighteenth birthday from my neck, kissed it, and wrapped it around the cross. I bowed my head and gripped a handful of muddy soil from his grave and sobbed. "I love you, Papa, I love you . . . *tantissimo, tantissimo* . . . so very, very much."

Signore Chessari reached down and took me by the arm. "We must leave now, Mari."

The instant *Signore* Chessari said the words, the air exploded around us. At least a dozen soldiers scrambled over our wall and sprayed gunfire that careened and whipped like serpent tails above our heads. The fields around our home lit up in streaks of fire.

Signore Chessari pulled me so fast toward the house my feet barely skimmed the wet ground. "There are soldiers all over your property; we have to get out of here now."

I pushed my legs ever faster toward the house. My lungs heaved as we darted through our dark kitchen and into the parlor, lifted my confused mother to her feet, and whisked her outside and into the backseat of the car. I jumped into the back to stay beside her. Seconds later *Signore* Chessari punched on the gas, and the car skidded through the mud out of the driveway. I stuck my head out the open window and looked back at our home, half expecting Papa to be standing there waving goodbye as we sped away.

I opened my mouth to call out a farewell, and flames burst before my eyes. The concussion of an explosion knocked me back from the window, and I cried out in surprise. My face burned like the sting of a thousand bees, and the world changed into splotches of color. I reached for my mother through a blur of images, panicked that she had been injured.

Acrid smoke filled the car and burned my nostrils. All sound was muffled and seemed far away.

Mama grasped me by the arms while her voice swam through the flood of noise in my ears. "Are you burned?"

My breath came in short bursts. "My face stings. Are you injured, Mama?"

She yelled over the roar of the car engine and the battle behind us. "No, no, I am unharmed."

The car weaved down the muddy road, and *Signore* Chessari shouted. "I think more than one tank fired at once as we passed, and you caught the heat, Marianna. Lean your head out the window so it is in the cool air— quickly."

I did as he said, held my eyes shut in the rain and wind, and prayed for the pain to subside. The pat of my mother's hand on my back soothed me and made me worry for her at the same time. I sat back and rested my head against hers. She took my hand. "How badly are you injured, *Carina*? It is so dark I cannot see you."

Images floated and weaved in a hazy blue before the headlights of the car. "It is easing now. I will be fine."

Signore Chessari turned off the lights before we were halfway there. "We do not want to light a trail for the soldiers to follow."

My eyesight was almost clear when we reached their home. My mother and I stumbled from the car to hurry behind *Signore* Chessari. He led us through their winery and into the cellar lined with enormous wooden barrels of aging wine. We stopped in front of the last barrel, and *Signore* Chessari pushed at the side of it. To my astonishment, the barrel moved and exposed a door hidden in the wall behind it. *Signore* Chessari took a lantern from a hook on the wall and led us through the door and down a steep stone passageway that smelled like the caves along the coast.

Our footsteps echoed off the rock-lined tunnel as we descended, my arm stretched out behind me to hold onto my mother. *Signore* Chessari tapped on a heavy wooden door at the bottom of the stairs.

Yellow candlelight outlined Elisa Chessari when she opened the door and pressed her hand to her heart. "Camilla, Marianna, thank goodness you are here." She reached for my mother and the two of them wept in each other's arms. "I am so sorry, Camilla. *Ti aiuto, no ti preoccupare.* Do not worry, I will be right beside you to help, my dearest friend."

She kept one arm around my mother's stooped shoulders. "We are safe here. We have supplies and dry clothes."

Signore Chessari lifted the lantern high and revealed a long, wide room of rock walls as if we had gone deep into a grotto. The air hinted of soap, yet the damp earth persisted in pressing its musty odor through the rock. Shelves filled with food, water, and several boxes stood against one wall, while a row of cots lined the other. Laura, Franca, and the twins lay asleep in the four beds near the end.

Franca stirred, pulled back her covers, and hurried to her feet. "Mari, I am so thankful you are here. You look soaked to the skin and so exhausted. I have dry clothes for you. Come with me." She handed me a bundle and pulled a curtain back at the end of the beds. "Step behind here and change. We will lay your wet clothes in the sink until we light a fire in the stove to clean and dry them in the morning."

My hands shook like an old woman's when I dressed. Franca took my wet clothes and dropped them into a deep sink next to a black stove in the corner while *Signora* Chessari led my mother behind the curtain.

Franca pointed across the room. "You see that wall in the far corner? There is a toilet behind it with a bucket of water to rinse it down. Go ahead, anytime you need to use it."

I nodded my head. "This . . . this shelter is . . . like another home."

Signore Chessari disappeared down a dark hallway at the back of the room. His wife lit another lantern, and I covered my eyes to ease the ache from the brightness. The trembling in my hands had spread to my legs. My eyes pinched each time I blinked, and the heat on my face from the explosion had not abated.

Signora Chessari led me to a bed. "Come and rest, Marianna." She looked over her shoulder at Franca. "Go back to bed quickly, *Carina*. You and Mari do not need to worry tonight; you are safe here with family."

Laura lay deep in sleep on her back in the cot next to mine. Her hand rested on the swell of her growing baby. I touched her cheek to be sure she had not succumbed to a fever. My legs twitched in relief when I sat down on my cot. I stared down at the floor; rocks that had taken centuries to form had ended up here, buried in cement and locked away from nature forever. I thought I'd drained all tears, but they came again, a trail of salt stinging my face.

Signore Chessari returned from the hallway, a long bundle wrapped in canvas in his arms. I had no strength to think through the reasons such a room would exist beneath the Chessari winery or what he had taken with him from the room in the back. Everything was clean and orderly as if someone had anticipated our arrival.

The Chessari family whispered to each other, and Franca's father stopped by the beds of each of his children, leaned down, and kissed them. He squeezed my hand and held onto my mother's.

"I wish I did not have to leave. There is so much at risk on our property, so much I need to take care of. I will return when I can, but it may be some time. Stay here no matter what. Wait for me and have faith. God be with you all."

Elisa Chessari kissed her husband and wiped at the corners of her eyes with a handkerchief, her quiet sob barely audible when the door closed behind him. I looked at my mother in concern, but she'd collapsed into slumber when *Signore* Chessari turned to go. Thank goodness for Elisa Chessari; she had wiped the mud from my mother's feet and hands and tucked her in bed like a child.

Signora Chessari blew out the candles and left one small lamp burning near the sink, its sparse light smothered by darkness before it reached the cots. My legs refused to reconcile themselves to the peace and quiet of the room and twitched against the thin mattress of my cot. Nightmares tapped at the back of my mind. I drew my knees up to my chest, wrapped my arms around them, and prayed for sleep to sink me into an abyss.

Chapter Twenty-Eight

MASSIMO

QUESTIONS SURFACED OVER AND OVER as I worked beside Lieutenant Bianco. There were so many things I wanted to know but could not voice. A silent understanding between the men ruled—the less you know of your comrades and their workings, the safer everyone will be in case of capture.

The night the Allies attacked and captured Siracusa was a frenzy of sabotaging the Nazi defenses from the rear while the British and Americans invaded. The explosions still rang in my head and muted my ears. Lieutenant Bianco now headed the operations for clearing out the Nazis who holed up like rats throughout the city and the countryside. We worked behind the lines—destroyed trucks filled with German ammunition and kept their troops from entering the city to stop the Allies.

Lieutenant Bianco supervised the various teams. I wished I knew how he had come to work with my father—if he had seen him or helped him escape. Most of all, I wanted to know where my father had been taken. But at least I could fight against the Nazis openly, free from Barberi's prison and the nightmare of a marriage to his daughter.

A deep ravine pocked with caves big enough to hide ammo or soldiers had to be inspected. We lay in a row at the top of the ravine on our bellies—me, an American named Johnson, Ronaldo, and Lieutenant Bianco. We watched like hawks for any movement below.

Lieutenant Bianco wiped the lenses of his binoculars. "I want you to know, Massimo, that Mussolini is panicked because of this Allied invasion. He is far too occupied to worry about anything that is trivial by comparison." Lieutenant Bianco looked through the binoculars into the caves. "At this point he has no idea that Barberi is in our custody and does not care if he is alive or dead."

Sweat gathered at the base of my neck. "I am glad to hear that, sir."

"But I am sorry I have to tell you that your father is not free as we were told. He had that story sent down our lines of communication so that you would cooperate that day we rescued you. He wanted to be sure you would leave with us without a fight."

I gripped my binoculars so hard I thought they would snap in my hands. "Where is my father?"

"Still held by the Germans here on Sicily. The military expect the Germans to flee the island soon and either take their prisoners with them or leave them behind. Since your father is worth a lot of money and considered a traitor, he is likely to be taken along until they get what they can out of him."

"I have to rescue him, sir."

"I know, son. I will find out what I can. Be ready to go at a moment's notice when I give you word."

Chapter Twenty-Nine

MARIANNA

A CIRCLE OF LIGHT CAME down through a pipe in the ceiling and signaled that a new day had begun. Metal pipes directed the smoke from the stove into the rocky ceiling and somewhere out into the world. I had no desire to follow it or to go outside and see an army that had stolen my life from me.

Elisa Chessari's honey-colored hair was pulled up into a smooth chignon as if a servant had pampered and groomed her for the day. She placed a pot of water on the stove, opened a metal door beneath it, and lit a fire as she had every morning for three days. The flames jumped and leapt inside while I watched from my cot.

My mother had loved and trusted *Signora* Chessari from the time she'd arrived in Siracusa as Paolo Chessari's bride. Even when the wary countrywomen eyed *Signora* Chessari with suspicion for coming from money and England and taking one of their men, Mama had walked the *Signora* through the open market, taught her the names of each fruit and vegetable in Italian, and protected her from over-zealous businessmen that might be anxious to make an extra *lira* from a foreigner. The war weighed double on the *Signora's* heart; because of Hitler's alliance with Italy, her family and friends in England would be considered her enemies.

She wiped her hands on her linen dress. "The light looks a bit muted this morning. Perhaps we will receive more moisture up top. I do need to go out again to check on the property." She studied my face. "Marianna, let us have a look at those red cheeks. Do not worry, I am sure your face will soon be soft as a peach."

The blisters on my cheeks and nose from the explosion at our property had been a surprise the first morning we'd awoken in the shelter, but the pain in my heart had overshadowed any damage on the outside of my body. I rubbed my hands over the tender areas and pushed out the memory of the pain that had caused them.

"Please do not worry yourself, *Signora*; I have used the salve faithfully."

She placed her elegant hands on each side of my face. "It is true, I do not believe you will even scar."

I braved a smile for her sake and rubbed the chills that had risen on my arms.

Chapter Thirty

MASSIMO

~❦~

DAYS WITHOUT SLEEP, TRAPPED LIKE a fox in a pit. My fingers turned rigid around the barrel of my rifle. I sat on the box that held our food supply, locked in a trance until a dry sting in my eyes set off the reflex to blink.

We'd eaten the last of the cheese and bread while rain seeped into our hideout. Ronaldo, Rush, Delong, and I hid in a dugout in a narrow valley between the mountains outside of Messina. Two other team members kept a lookout on the other side of a mountain, four Italians and two Americans all on a single mission—to save my father.

Fellow Partisans who had infiltrated the Nazis confirmed that my father was one of the prisoners still held by the Germans. The Germans planned to smuggle him off the island of Sicily through Messina and by ferry to the mainland. Luck, God, or both were on our side; the convoy to transport him and two other prisoners contained only two trucks. Most of the convoys had ten trucks or more. We also knew they were coming through this valley. And we would be waiting for them when they came.

Many military vehicles came through this way; it would be easy to stop the wrong transport trucks and ruin our chances of finding my father. Our connection in Palermo had marked the two trucks in the correct convoy with a streak of red paint on one headlight, small enough that the Germans would not notice but visible enough to be seen by our men through binoculars at close range. Cesare and Andrea watched for their approach on the other side of a small mountain. At first sighting, Cesare would tap out a signal on a transmitter connected to a receiver in our dugout by a long wire stretched over the top of the mountain. When we got the signal we would hurry into position along the ravine, ready to ambush them.

Cesare slid down the mud through the small opening into our den, his breath winded. "I ran all the way here. The wire's broken apart and shorted in the rain. We cannot send you any signals."

Ronaldo punched the muddy wall and Rush shook the receiver box for any sign of life. Without that signal we'd be blind, unable to spot the right trucks unless we stood right at the side of the road like ducks in a carnival game and stared at each set of headlights as the trucks passed. We climbed out of the foxhole and looked up the slope to where the wire went across the top. Thank goodness this mountain was small; it was really more of a large hill. And it was bare except for a few boulders and weeds that we would hide behind at the bottom. The whole area was covered in a carpet of dead grass. To be anywhere in the open would be too risky; the Germans could send scouts ahead to be sure the mountain passage was clear. We had to stay hidden in the dugout until the moment came to attack, when we could run from the hideouts next to the road.

Cesare interrupted my thoughts. "Andrea cut out the section of shorted wire but it is near the top of the hill on this side where there is no foliage whatsoever. The ends are stretched so tight they do not meet and stay together unless you hold them together, and it could short again in a second in this godforsaken rain."

The top of the hill lay completely exposed. Any man that held the wire together would be in plain sight and within reach of gunfire from anyone who passed by. But if the signal did not work, the truck that transported my father could go unidentified and pass right by us.

I ran up the mountain with Cesare and inspected the wire. Warm rain drizzled down our necks and soaked into our clothes. After weighing the options we nodded our heads in grim agreement; each member of our group would have to take a turn waiting at the top of the hill. Every time vehicles approached we would hold the wire together. The minute Cesare and Andrea recognized the marked trucks they would send us the signal and the members of my team would flash a light at the man who held the wire together so he could slide down the hill to warn us, and we would scramble into position. We would each cake our clothes and faces in mud for camouflage during our turn and pray to God that the Nazi trucks would come at night.

Two muggy days passed, the ends of the wire pinched in our gritty fingers as truck after truck drove right beside us through the mountain pass. Hours crawled; minutes stood still. We waited with empty stomachs for the critical signal to pulse down the brittle wire.

Rocks and gravel jabbed and scraped me when I lay on my belly for my shift.

I stared into a dull gray sunset with the wire held together in my fingers and must have slept with my eyes half opened because a nearby bolt of lightning snapped me awake, and I shot to my feet in the dark. I stumbled for balance and looked down the hill. Ronaldo waved a flashlight from our foxhole. Cesare and Andrea had sent the signal. It was time to move.

Sodden weeds slapped at my legs and muddied rock gave way under my boots as I started down the slope. I bent low for balance and half stepped, half slid to the bottom. I lay down under a ledge next to the road where the runoff had cut into the bottom of the mountain. The bright headlights of the first truck came around the turn, the low growl of the engine like a bear approaching its quarry. Sweat mixed with rain and ran off my soaked clothes. I panted for air while my hand held a long-handled knife in its grip and determination flexed like a muscle around my chest.

We'd dug long, wide holes in the road to slow and divide the approach of the enemy. Wet brakes squealed through the drum of rain when the first truck stopped for the deep, muddy ruts. I sucked in air, jumped in an instant to the step of the driver's door, and shattered the window with the butt of the knife. I slit the throat of the driver before he had time to reach for his weapon, ripped the door open, and pulled him from the seat onto the ground outside.

Ronaldo took care of the soldier on the other side, and I climbed into the driver's seat and slammed down on the brakes. Rush and DeLong commandeered the second vehicle, and I watched through the rain for Cesare and Andrea to make it over the mountain and take out the soldiers who guarded the prisoners in the back of each truck.

Ronaldo disappeared long enough to pull the dead soldiers into the bushes before he jumped back in the truck. "Cesare and Andrea made it. Start rolling."

My fists tightened around the steering wheel and a profound rap on the back of the cab confirmed his words; the trucks were free of the enemy. Belts screeched and tires spun in the mire before they took hold and we lurched forward.

Gunfire popped and hammered like an explosion of firecrackers. Ronaldo grabbed a rifle and leaned out his door. "A jeep—there's a Nazi jeep in the rear! They are firing on the other truck! Go . . . go . . . go!"

I stomped the gas pedal down and we fishtailed through mud that clutched at our tires. The truck bounced in and out of mud holes and ruts and flew over the top of a rise. Ronaldo grabbed hold of his seat. "The road's washed out—go left, go left."

I twisted the steering wheel hard toward a small strip of road just as the tires touched ground. The cab turned, but the rear jerked in the opposite direction. The steering wheel spun back in my hand and caught my thumb in its shaft. The dull crack of the bone echoed over the din of the engine. I slammed my foot down on the gas pedal and we skidded and slid to the other side of the road before we sank into sludge.

The flash of headlights whited out my vision; the second truck caught up with us and bounced to a stop on the other side of a bank, the jeep of German soldiers right on its tail.

I threw my door open, fought for footing in the washed-out terrain, and fell to the ground when a sharp sting that burned like fire pierced my left leg. The whistle of bullets passed by my head and pinged against the metal truck as I dove for cover and rolled behind one of the tires. Ronaldo crouched behind the other side and fired his rifle at the jeep. I fumbled for control of my rifle because of my broken thumb and took aim.

The pulse of a machine gun ripped through the air. I crawled under the truck to see where the assault came from and spotted Cesare standing at the machine gun in the back of the other truck. The scene flashed black and white as soldiers ran past the headlights and shouted in German. One by one the men fell, and the echo of bullets quieted to the soft thud of raindrops hitting the earth.

I crawled through a puddle from behind the truck on my elbows and scanned the ground for movement. A shadow moved beside the Nazis' jeep, and I slid my rifle forward and took aim from my left shoulder. I pulled the trigger, and the last German soldier dropped lifeless to the ground.

Ronaldo and Andrea ran toward me and helped me to my feet. I gripped Ronaldo's shoulder, limped straightaway to the bed of the truck, and crawled inside with my hand clutched to my injured thigh. I squinted for focus in the dark truck. "I seek General Scalvone—my father, Franco Scalvone of Foggia."

A raspy voice answered from the darkness in the corner. "Here, here, sir, he is in the corner."

Someone pulled the jeep up behind us and the headlights illuminated the prisoners in the back. Skeletal and stark white under the filth on their faces, two men gestured behind them and tried to move out of my way. A third man in back lifted his head, and my muscles tensed.

Even with a dark-stained bandage wrapped around his head and a rough beard, I knew that face. "Papa."

I put my left hand beneath his thin shoulders and lifted him to a sitting position. He reached for my face and his whole body shook. "Massimo? Massimo . . . no, no, it cannot be. It is not safe here. How did you . . ."

His words were muffled against my shoulder as I embraced him and wept.

* * *

A safe house near Messina held an assortment of medicines and bandages. A nurse who worked at a military hospital nearby made nightly calls to take care of the wounded. We made our way there in one of the trucks after the rendezvous, thankful that no other German vehicles or convoys had come our way before we'd had a chance to get away.

I rode in the back of the truck, my father's head in my lap, and the exhilaration over his safety masked the throb in my leg and hand. My comrades gave me the worst of the news after my father and I had been delivered to the safe house: Cesare had taken a valiant stand at the machine gun during the conflict and had taken out four of the enemy soldiers to save our lives. He had paid for his heroism with his own life.

My father was devastated to hear of Cesare's sacrifice. "Such a young man—a valiant soldier—he did not have to lose his life for mine. I would not have let him do it had I known."

Starvation turns the body into a state of walking death. My father looked like a marionette that dangled at the end of strings and would collapse if no one held him up. I watched the women of the safe house feed him broth with a spoon, then bathe and dress him in clean clothes.

"Papa, you would have done the same for Cesare. We cannot lessen his sacrifice by regretting it. He died a hero."

He laid his hand over mine and patted it in silence.

It was almost midnight before the nurse arrived and dug the bullet out of my thigh. I gripped my uninjured hand around a wooden dowel and bit down on a leather strap, my pain escaping in long rivulets of sweat down my body. The bullet had not hit bone, but the muscle throbbed like someone had stabbed my thigh with a knife and twisted it. The nurse bound my hand and broken thumb with strips of fabric to hold it in place. I tried not to think of the weeks it would take to completely heal. It would take at least a week before my father would be strong enough to leave the safe house. Papa was anxious to return to Foggia, to the work that proceeded there and to ensure the safety of his comrades, while my urge to go and find Marianna burned like a fever that refused to break.

When we had gathered a bit of strength, even if my father had to go to Foggia, I would go back to Siracusa.

Chapter Thirty-One

MARIANNA

THE DAYS IN THE SHELTER stitched together and passed. Candles cast elongated shadows from morning until night. We burned the kerosene lamps intermittently, careful with our fuel while we lived burrowed beneath the war.

My clothes stuck to my skin with sweat every night; terror trapped in my throat with visions of Bruno in enemy clutches, beaten and weak for lack of bread and water. I jerked in my sleep often and sat up choking on the thickness of night.

I rested easier knowing that my necklace was wrapped around the cross at Papa's grave. Maybe his spirit had watched me place it there or sensed I was near. Perhaps he was an angel allowed to break through the mists of heaven to protect me, Mama, Laura, and even the baby who kicked in her womb. Every day I urged Papa's spirit toward Bruno; save Bruno, Papa . . . protect Bruno.

At times I allowed my memory to give me the smallest flash of Massimo's face. Afterward I'd stare into pitch blackness from my damp cot—my breath labored, my arms tingling, and my face clammy. My Massimo did not exist even if his body were alive; another woman had the right to touch the skin that had warmed me, to smell the sweetness of the breath that had taken mine away, and to feel the grip of desire that had burned in the pit of my stomach. I fell limp and helpless into a void night after night.

Two weeks crept past. Laura sat beside my mother on her cot—their hair in loose braids, hands clasped together—while *Signora* Chessari wrote in her ledger at the wooden table. Franca read next to a lamp, and Damiano and Dominic passed notes and exchanged hand signals from across the room.

Damiano ran to sit beside his brother under the dim light of a kerosene lamp. They bent their heads together over a little blackboard, whispered, and drew maps with their quick, chalky fingers.

Signora Chessari roughed up their hair. "If you two spies have figured out our escape plan, you can have your race again."

They leapt to their feet, each one anxious to out-do the other. Flickers of light entered my mother's eyes when she watched the eager boys exhaust first one leg and then the other in intense hop counting. Afterward their sweaty bodies collapsed onto their cots in triumph, their moods calmed and quieted.

Some days Franca pushed me to play cards with her; I did so with scarce interest, but was grateful for her efforts to keep me busy. When my gaze drifted away one too many times, she sighed in exasperation. "Ah, *dammi la pazienza*. Come now, Mari, focus. Look at your cards and try to beat me . . . just once."

Signora Chessari and Laura prepared a lunch of panini made with canned meat and the thin bread they cooked on top of the stove. Pasta, olive oil, and beef jerky were in abundance.

They laid our plates on the marble countertop next to the sink, but my mother refused her serving. "Oh, no, thank you, Elisa. I will have mine later."

The *Signora* rubbed her hand on my mother's back. "Camilla, if you are not quite hungry, will you take the first turn reading our story?"

Mama still looked pale, her eyes sunken. But she took a book from the shelf and opened it beside one of the kerosene lamps. "*The Life and Times of Davy Crockett . . .*"

Chapter Thirty-Two

EVEN TALES OF WESTERN AMERICA held no fiery thrill for me as they once had; the shelter's stash of books remained untouched by my usual curiosity and excitement.

Mama continued reading throughout our simple meal until I insisted she come and have something for herself. Her eyes filled with tears with the mention of nutrition, as though anything that kept her strong only widened the gap between her and my father. I sat beside her at the table while she nibbled at her sandwich and watched the circle of sunlight from the pipe turn grey with cloud cover.

Heaviness pushed down on my shoulders. No sound came from above this room. No word. No help or direction. *Signora* Chessari quietly left the cellar and went up the stairs every day to see if anything had changed. But her reports were the same time after time; there was no sight of anyone and no word from the outside world. I sat my food to the side, clasped my hands together to keep from drumming my fingers and then tightened them into fists.

I tried to be grateful for our safety, to be patient, but the anxious buzz in the back of my head grew louder day by day, and I knew if something did not change soon I would fight my way up the stairs. I'd run to my home, if in fact anything was left after the burst of fire in my eyes. I touched the new skin where the cracked blisters had been.

I tapped my feet on the floor beneath my chair and counted the beats to fill my head. No matter the pull in my heart for home, I knew that if my feet were turned loose, I'd run to Siracusa. No words or vows spoken in blasphemy could keep me from Massimo. I would find him. We would get on a train to Switzerland, locate his family's money, and rip it to pieces.

Mama paused for a sip of water, and *Signora* Chessari offered everyone a tray of dried apricots and raisins. "Marianna, would you mind checking the supply of fruit leather in the back pantry?"

"Of course, *Signora*, I would be happy to."

I lit a kerosene lamp and walked down the hallway into the extra room. I had never seen such an elaborate cellar full of food, clothing, and blankets. After I straightened and moved bottles of vegetables and applesauce, I found the tins of fruit leather. I gripped two in my hands and caught a glimpse of three wooden crates, like the ones the Germans used for weapons, stacked in a corner. I put the tins back on the shelf and listened to be sure my mother had started reading to the group again.

The crates were nailed shut. I managed to scoot the top one off of the others and discovered a seam in the wall behind them—a door. With a strain of muscle I moved the heavy boxes and spotted a crack in the bottom one. I looked inside the gap and recognized the green, bumpy surface and metal pin of a grenade. I gasped in surprise and turned quickly to the door to see if anyone had followed me down the hall. I ran my hand over the hidden door behind the crates until I found a small handle on the wall next to it. I pushed it down. It gave way and swung open without a sound.

The door opened to a room of musty air and thick silence. I lifted the lantern and gasped. The room was filled with the wooden crates stacked against walls that were eight feet high. Long canvas pouches, labeled in English, lay along one wall. I untied one of the flaps on a pouch and ran my fingers down the long, cold barrel of a rifle. I remembered the night we had first arrived, when *Signore* Chessari had left the shelter with two long canvas bags just like these on his shoulder. His wife had embraced him as if it were no surprise to her that a wine maker carried military weapons.

The air in the room became entirely clear, while a calm strength started at the bottom of my feet and worked its way to the top of my head. I knew *Signore* Chessari too well to be afraid of what I was seeing. If he was involved in this war, it was in only one way: he had to be a Partisan fighting for Italy's freedom from Hitler and Mussolini. My quiet determination turned into an inferno that radiated down all my limbs.

Dominic and Damiano whooped out loud in the other room. No doubt Davy Crockett had just done something heroic. I closed the closet door without a sound and reached in my dress pocket for the pen and paper Franca had given me earlier to write to Bruno. I scribbled a note for

Signora Chessari. My hand shook as fast as my heart beat while I penned the words. I carried the tins of fruit leather back into the main room. Mama had finished her reading, and everyone busied themselves with their own tasks. *Signora* Chessari put plates away in the kitchen area.

"Oh, there you are, Marianna. Were the tins hard to find?"

"*O, no, niente problema*. Everything was just where it needed to be."

I handed her the note and watched her eyes widen when she looked down at the words.

"I want in."

* * *

July twenty-seventh. Seventeen days into our subterranean life, a deep vibration echoed down through the pipes in the tiny kitchen. Eyes widened; afraid to breathe, we gathered around the circular beam of light and tipped our heads toward the sound. There was a blurted shout in a man's deep voice, a quick reply, and then silence. Fear burned in my chest with the sound of footsteps coming down the stairway to the cellar. Someone rapped at the door, and Mama slipped her arm around my shoulder.

Signora Chessari opened the door and a draft of warm, damp air filled the room with the celestial sight of Paolo Chessari. The *Signora* ran with a cry of relief into his arms, and we all leaned on each other's shoulders in tears of joy.

The twins dashed to their father and wrapped their arms around both parents. Laura sank to the floor and wept while Franca waited her turn to kiss her father. A sob caught in my throat while I hugged my mother and held my breath for any news. *Signore* Chessari addressed us all, his eyes grave.

"We are still under siege by the Americans and British. Italian and German soldiers have been captured by the thousands all over Sicily. There are still pockets of Germans resisting the takeover, and they are hidden nearby. I have come to move you farther into the country, well away from the fighting."

His wife laid her hand on his arm. "And Mussolini?"

"Mussolini has been arrested."

Elisa laid her head against his arm with a sob while the boys jumped and yelled in celebration. I stepped forward. "Is Italy fighting against the Nazis now?"

"Our new president has not conceded or dissolved our alliance with Hitler yet. But the Allies are here on our soil and things are progressing well in that direction. God willing, it will continue so."

He lifted Laura to her feet and embraced her. "There is no news of Bruno yet, but I know he would want you to come with us to a safer place." He looked at me and my mother, his expression grave. "We will stay at Mimmo and Pasqua's home in Sortino. I brought a few soldiers with me for protection and an American army truck to carry all of you. We need to bring food and clothing."

He glanced around the room and into each of our faces. "The roads can be a bit treacherous. You women will need to take a low profile and cover your hair with scarves, and you boys will be need to be quiet and keep your heads bowed down if anyone stops us."

Dominic and Damiano nodded their heads up and down rapidly in agreement with their father, and he patted them each on their shoulders. "We must hurry now." He turned to Laura. "Do I need to carry you, Laura?"

Laura shook her head. "I am much better, Papa; I think the baby is going to be all right now."

"Saints be praised. Now we must do everything we can to keep you all safe."

My mother stepped in front of *Signore* Chessari. "Paolo, do Mimmo and Pasqua know we are coming?"

Signore Chessari placed his hands on each of Mama's thin shoulders. "I am more sorry than I can express; I must give you more news of great sorrow, Camilla . . . Mimmo and Pasqua . . . were killed in a battle. I checked on your home on my way here today and found Pasqua had already died and Mimmo was holed up on your property. They had come to help you or bring you back with them and got caught in crossfire the night I brought you here. Mimmo lived long enough to ask me to take you to their home, and I told him I would. I buried them beside your dear Adamo."

Uncle Mimmo's laugh—his political tirades—Aunt Pasqualina's passionate lectures all played in my head. To think of them silent and cold in the ground was impossible. I stared at the floor while Mama stifled her cries into a handkerchief. Franca held her arm around my waist and laid her cheek against my shoulder. "I'm so sorry, Mari . . . so, so, sorry. . . ."

I patted my hand over the top of hers at my waist, surprised at how warm she felt, and I wondered if I would ever feel warm again.

* * *

The brightness of the sun bleached the sky white. I pulled the top of my scarf down to shade my eyes with one hand and held Mama's in the other. We hurried to a green army truck with a long bed framed and covered in canvas. We placed our bags of clothing behind our backs for a cushion in the back of the truck while Laura rode in the front with her father to ease the jostling from the road.

Rain and the tracks of tanks and soldiers had muddied and pitted the roads. The rough terrain shook the truck and rocked us back and forth like an angry sea. My teeth rattled so hard I tightened my jaw and held myself against the truck sides. The Chessari vineyard, its grapevines so tall you could walk under their shelter without bowing your head, became smaller and smaller as we drove away.

I held my mother's hand and tried to rest my head on Franca's shoulder while we pitched over ruts and rocks.

Siracusa was a smoky silhouette on the bleak horizon. I longed to reach for it, but Massimo had probably left by now. The memory of him going into the church to be married sliced like a knife across the cord that held me to him.

The slopes of our property beckoned me from a distance, the tops of our cypress trees waving a silent goodbye. The breeze carried my heart to Papa and sent my gratitude to my aunt and uncle for trying to come and help us. Tears dripped down the front of my blouse. If only Bruno were here, maybe we could stay.

We traveled the entire day—nibbled on dried fruit and jerky, made brief stops under shade trees. Clouds drifted across the sun, our moods vulnerable to its shadows and rays. Scattered refugees, their stares fixed on their feet, traveled along the road—a few with wagons and horses, most of them on foot. Women, children, old men, barking dogs with concave bellies—some glanced up as we passed then stared back down at the road.

The sun sat down on the horizon. Small hope pressed me toward our relatives' home in Sortino. Mama would feel better there, Laura would be settled for having the baby. Restlessness droned in my chest and twitched in my legs. The *Signora* had stared back at me in silence when I'd handed her the note that said I wanted in. She'd placed her finger over her lips to silence me and turned away without a word. I had to go, to help, to take a stand against an army that had ripped everything out of my heart.

As soon as we arrived in Sortino, I would look for my chance to tell *Signore* Chessari that I planned to go with him to join the Partisans.

Chapter Thirty-Three

MASSIMO

I SMELLED IT FIRST—THE acrid stench of cold, dead fire. I ignored the pain from my bullet wound and bolted toward the trees that towered like ghostly sentinels around the De'Angelis property. All was silent as I scaled the wall, my shirt stuck to my skin and my lungs constricted.

I ran toward the house—to blackened, skeletal rubble that poked and stabbed at the sky—a massive pile of collapsed brick, wooden beams, and shattered glass. Charred debris tuned the wind to a high-pitched cry.

I ran to their barn, the knot in my gut already telling me I would find it empty.

A few chickens wandered the yard and picked at the earth, their tiny eyes like black orbs staring past me. Tall grass thrust its haughty fingers through tomato plants and coiled around the necks of the peppers.

The gate to the pond stood ajar. I marched full speed toward it—pushed my way through and willed Marianna to be sitting beside the edge of the deep green water. She would brush her slender fingers on the surface to tease the butterflies as they dipped to quench their thirst—look up at me, jump, and leap into my arms.

The water looked still and black from a distance when I neared. I scanned the landscape, my heart pummeling like a fist behind my ribcage. Nothing moved but the tops of trees. A stick protruded out of mounds of dirt near the pond. I stepped closer and a wall of horror rose up and choked me when I recognized the shape—a wooden cross, shoved into the middle of three graves.

I dropped to my knees in front of them, fought the urge to claw at the earth with my bare hands and gasped for air through an icy chest.

"I'm sorry, soldier. I was too late. The De'Angelis family is dead."

I whipped my head around and saw an older man dressed in black standing by the pond. His chin quivered. "I saw it with my own eyes the night the Americans came. A couple of the family members ran into the back door just a few minutes before two tanks came through the wall and shot into the house. I ran as fast as I could, but the house was gone—went up like a torch after the explosion."

He came closer, and I recognized him through the fog in my head—the man I had given the message to for Marianna in the Hotel Grande, the man who had been with the Partisans. He shifted his feet under my scrutiny and gripped his hat in his weathered hands before he extended one toward me. I stared at him—unable to process that he was there, that his words had any connection to reality.

He shifted his hat in his fingers. "My name is Aviano. I used to work for the family."

Tears ran down through his whiskers. "I came out on my bike to warn them that the British and Americans were attacking. I would've come even without your note; they'd been so good to me. But I was too late. I had to run the other way when the soldiers kept shooting. I caught some shrapnel in my side and could not come back until today."

He put his hat back on and his hands in the pockets of his pants. "I just came here to put flowers on the graves. I do not know which one is which or who put them here in the ground, but I figure the cross is for all three of them."

I riveted my attention to the cross and to the tiny glint of sun on a delicate gold chain, a blue cameo dangling lifelessly at the end—the necklace that Marianna's parents had given her for her birthday. I clutched it in my palm and held my fist to my mouth to stifle the roar in my throat. Marianna—dead—dead—dead.

Aviano backed away. "I really am sorry. God help us all."

I was hardly aware of his departure before I grasped the weeds that pushed up through the mounded earth. I ripped them loose until my hands were raw, looked up at an empty sky, and let the rage in my throat turn loose.

Chapter Thirty-four

MARIANNA

THE PARLOR WAS FULL OF ghosts. Ghosts so heavy with sorrow my muscles sagged under their weight. Aunt Pasqua's tatted doilies covered the table tops. Pictures of relatives, faded with age, all sat perfectly in place. Uncle Mimmo's transparent grins seemed to float through the walls. Now his worries over the war rang with new meaning in my heart, and I wished I had listened to him more patiently. Aunt Pasqualina's lamentations echoed from far away. Mama sniffled on the couch, and I sat down beside her.

"Mama, I know they are watching over us. Papa has his brother with him now. But not Bruno—Bruno is not gone with Papa. He may be on his way home right now for all we know."

My mother closed her eyes and nodded her head. "But we are not home to greet him. He will be lost—so confused and worried."

I handed her a handkerchief from my pocket and willed the knot in my throat to loosen.

Signora Chessari walked in and sat on the other side of my mother. "Camilla, remember that Paolo promised to find Bruno and bring him here, so do not worry."

I saw the effort it took for my mother to force a weak smile. But even forced, I would take any sign that she would be comforted and feel at least some peace here.

Signore Chessari entered the room, his hat held under his arm. "Elisa, I am going to leave Giacomo and Emanuelle with you. They've worked for Mimmo for years and are too old for the military, but they can still handle a gun in an emergency. I'll feel better knowing you have two men here. Even two old men."

She stood and took his hand. "You do not have to leave yet, do you? Please at least stay the night and eat a good breakfast, Paolo . . . please."

The crinkles at the corners of his eyes stayed tight and drawn even when he smiled. "Of course we will wait until morning, but I do not want you to worry about cooking. We have some fruit and jerky left, and that will be fine. I must get the truck back soon."

Elisa laid her head on her husband's chest, and he brought his broad arms around her.

"Do not worry; I will find out what I can about Bruno and send word like I promised. The men will help you and the twins, and you women will be safe waiting right here until I return."

He looked over the top of his wife's head at me, his eyes locked on mine as if his words were meant especially for me. I swallowed hard and stiffened my shoulders until he looked away.

* * *

A sprinkle of rain conjured up a warm mist from the pathway that wound down the side of the house. I followed *Signore* Chessari down the path with my fingers gripped around the handle of Aunt Pasqua's black umbrella. A bridge of sweet pea vines stretched across a stone arbor. *Signore* Chessari stopped in front of it, his jaw muscles flexing. "Marianna, Elisa told me; I know why you followed me out here, and what you want, and for the sake of your family I must say no. You are needed by your family, not for fighting."

"*Signore* Chessari, please hear me. I am not asking to fight in a battle, just to fight for freedom in some way—to help. Spying, taking messages, something that you know I can do. I cannot live like this anymore, waiting like a helpless child for rescue."

Rain splattered off the brim of *Signore* Chessari's hat. He shook his head back and forth, and I placed my hand over my heart. "I can feel it in here, night and day; there is something different I am to do. Something out there I am meant to help with. In Siracusa, or wherever you could use me."

His expression did not change but he nodded his head toward the house. "And your mother? She has lost your father, possibly her son. Enough is enough."

My dress weighed a hundred pounds in the rain. I put the umbrella down and pressed my palms to my eyes to push back the tears before I looked into his eyes. "I lost my father too. My mother is stronger now. Your wife, Franca, Laura, and the baby, when it comes, they will all be there for each other. Even the twins and my uncle's workers will help. We have not lost them all. I refuse to think of . . ." Massimo's face flashed before my eyes, his smile opening a chasm in my chest. I swallowed hard. "I refuse to think of Bruno as a loss; I know he will come back. My loved ones are what makes me want to do something, to help in any way I can."

Signore Chessari looked off toward the gardens that lay lush and plump down the walkway, their lust for life unaffected by the brutalities that surrounded them. His face was still grim. "How can I take you to Siracusa, a city full of soldiers at each other's throats, when you are the daughter of my lifelong friend? No . . . I must see to your safety in his place. I owe him that."

"That friend, my papa, knew me heart and soul and would want me to do what I know I must." I took his rough hand in mine and looked at him as I would my father. "I have to do something to help. Even if it is only nursing at the hospital. I know you are a part of something. It all made sense when I found the stash of weapons in the pantry. You have connections. I know you do. Just give me a chance."

"What is it you want? You will not find peace, glory, or revenge anywhere in this war, Marianna. Not with the Partisans, either. And if one of the pockets of Fascists or the Nazis find you and find out that you have a connection to the Partisans, even at the hospital . . . they will kill you . . . probably torture you first."

I took in a deep breath. "That is why I want to work through you; it would be safer. I trust you. I do not know what you do, but I know you are a man of honor and strength."

He huffed in exasperation and put his hands in the pockets of his jacket. "There is no honor in this war. Mussolini destroyed that."

"So we need all the help we can to find it and bring it back. There is honor in defending your home and the people you love or in helping the wounded. I need to find a way to help. I will find that way no matter how difficult, but I would rather it be through you."

The creases around his eyes softened, and I felt a surge of hope. "I will talk to your mother and give it some thought. I do not want to cause her any more pain or worry."

"I want to work with your help for Mama's sake, so that you will know where I am and give her messages from me that all is well."

He grimaced again. "I will consider this, but only for work in the hospital."

Patches of sun stirred the bees back to work on window boxes full of flowers. I nodded my head. "Yes, I know this is the right thing and that I need to go . . . something beckons me."

* * *

The clang of a lose shutter on the window outside woke me on the alert the next morning. I opened my eyes to a white plaster ceiling and a quiver of anticipation. I crept lightly down the marble hall and heard the distress in my mother's voice before I entered the kitchen; *Signore* Chessari must have already told her of my desire to go to Siracusa. She sounded very troubled.

"Paolo, it is so dangerous with the soldiers there, and Mari has no experience working in a hospital."

"Mussolini has been overthrown, Camilla. It does not mean that we are completely out of the control of the Nazis, especially up north, but the Americans are patrolling Siracusa and are not trying to brutalize the citizens. The British and Americans have the Germans frightened and on the run. God willing, we are on better ground."

I went into the kitchen and knelt in front of my mother. "I am only going to do things like wrap bandages and maybe clean the hospital, Mama. Perhaps I can be of some help for our soldiers who are suffering. I will not even be that far away, and *Signore* Chessari will be nearby helping too; he will look after me and maybe even bring me home for visits." I laid my hands on her knees. "Please, Mama, I need to go . . . I do not even know all the reasons why. I just know I have to go. I will be so careful you will know in your heart that I am safe."

"But where will you stay, Marianna? The homes near the hospital will never be safe enough."

Signore Chessari leaned against the counter, glanced at me, and finished a sip of his coffee. "They have a section where all the hospital workers stay, Camilla. All the soldiers, on both sides, know better than to attack or bomb a hospital or harass the people who work there."

Mama flinched at the word *bomb*. I gripped her hand as *Signora* Chessari placed calzoni on the table for breakfast. "Mama, there is no need for bombs anymore because the Americans and British are here, and they are so strong everyone is afraid to fight like before. They insist on peace."

I could see by the look on her face that she did not believe me any more than I could believe myself. But I felt desperate. A bit of color returned to her lips but guilt pressed on my chest. "I am so sorry to leave, but I have to do something. I cannot stand to see so much at risk in our lives and do nothing for it."

My mother took my hands and stared earnestly into my eyes. "*Carina*, I worry for you, for any false hope you may have about changing anything or . . . finding people."

I opened my mouth to stop her but a deep wail from outside the window prevented me. The cry had come from Laura. We all dashed from the room and out the back door. Franca came running to meet us. "She was out in the chicken coop looking for eggs."

The chicken coop was almost walled in by the grass that weaved through the partitions of wire. Laura stood locked in place in front of the nest boxes. Streams of water rolled down the inside of her legs and soaked into her shoes. She still held eggs in one hand, the front of her dress with the other. "I reached for the eggs in the top row and felt pressure in my womb. A stream of water ran down my legs."

The Chessaris wrapped their arms around each side of her, and her mother spoke into her ear. "Laura, just lean on me and your father; we are going to help you into the house."

Mama and *Signora* Chessari stayed with Laura in the main bedroom while I kept clean towels coming and boiled a pair of scissors for cutting the cord. Things moved quickly, and before the sun had set I stood at the foot of the bed, awed by the tiny miracle that lay wet and squalling on Laura's breast—my brother's son, precious and helpless in his mother's arms.

I knew then I could not go. Bruno had asked me to help his wife, and now his son was latched to Laura's breast. How could I leave a part of Bruno behind and run off to the aid of strangers?

Following a quick rap at the door, *Signore* Chessari entered the room, a smile on his face. His wife stood beside Laura and held out her hands. "Come and see your *bellissimo* new grandson."

He touched the tiny baby on his cheek before he kissed Laura on her forehead. "He is the most beautiful boy I have ever seen. God has blessed us all with a day of miracles."

Laura smiled and squeezed her father's hand. "Thank you, Papa, I have never felt so blessed in all of my life."

"I am hoping that another blessing is on its way."

We all stared at *Signore* Chessari. He lowered his brow. "Laura, everyone, a message has just come through to me; my comrades think they have heard news of Bruno's battalion. There is a chance that it is headed to the hospital in Siracusa from the mainland. Word is there are some injuries among them but most have survived. If Laura and the baby are healthy, I will go immediately to seek more details and send word."

Laura sobbed uncontrollably and held the baby even tighter to her chest. Tears flooded the room as we all embraced in hope, fear, and joy.

Mama walked up to me with a new light in her eyes. "You go now, Mari. Go with *Signore* Chessari to the hospital. Wait for your brother; take good care of him if he is wounded, and bring him back to us."

I kissed her cheek and ran from the room to pack my things.

Chapter Thirty-five

HEAVY AIR, BALMY WITH SWEAT, urine, and the metallic scent of blood, greeted me when I entered the hospital doors. I did not wait to ask for a list of any names but ran past the front desk and up and down each room and aisle of the hospital, praying for the dark eyes of my brother to be the ones that looked back at me.

An hour after I arrived at the Santa Lucia hospital, I knew Bruno was not there. Not yet, I told myself.

The first two days in the hospital, I vomited in the tiny bathroom and pulled the chain of the toilet repeatedly to drown out the sound of my sobs. Limbs ripped from their sockets. Oozing holes. The stench of rotting flesh. At times, the urge to cover my nose and the heaving from my nausea exhausted my energy.

The nurses told me I'd get used to it as I recoiled inside. I concentrated on the smell of bleach and soap and the hope that pulled me through the fog of death and suffering. Within days I could sleep through the wails of soldiers and clean up any kind of mess nature threw at me. But the restlessness that tormented me while I waited for any sign of Bruno was relentless.

By the end of the week I could contain myself no more; the need for fresh air dominated my thoughts. The patios were filled with patients, so I spoke to our chief nurse, Donatella. "Is there somewhere I could go, just for a moment of solitude?"

She smiled for what seemed like the first time since I had arrived as she wiped some blood from her hands onto a towel. "The stairs outside the kitchen lead to the roof."

I thanked her and without hesitation escaped from the chaos of the hospital and headed to the rooftop.

Siracusa glowed like golden embers had been tossed across the city. I closed my eyes in the breeze that tousled my hair and imagined the wind sweeping away the visions of suffering men and shaky hands that reached for more relief than I could supply.

The rough stone of the rooftop pitted my knees when I knelt down and cried to God to send my brother home alive. I hugged my arms around my sides and pled for him to save Massimo, even his wretched bride, if by swallowing that bitterness I could pay some sort of pittance for his safety. If only the angels who summoned the spirits of the dying from their ravaged bodies could rip the beasts of hell from the souls of evil men so they would set Massimo free. I fell forward onto my hands, my head hanging down, my tears puddled on the lifeless stone beneath me.

Chapter Thirty-Six

MASSIMO

JULY 30—LIEUTENANT BIANCO OPENED THE DOOR to room three-eighteen of the Hotel Grande and welcomed me inside. It seemed a lifetime had passed since I had last been here and joined the Partisans. I forced myself to push the sorrow over Marianna deep into a reservoir and focused on the freedom this man had given me and my father.

He patted me on the shoulder and pulled me into a full embrace. "Please sit down, Massimo; you could not have had enough time to recuperate in Messina. I want you to know how pleased and relieved I am that you freed your wonderful father and returned safely. How is the leg?"

"Healing well; the bullet went through muscle only. I thought it very considerate of the Germans to spare the bone."

"And your thumb?"

I held up my right hand. "I've never liked this thumb much—always getting in my way when I try to steer a truck in the rain."

Lieutenant Bianco laughed quietly and sat down behind a desk. He kept a steady gaze on me. "I know you are worn out, son. That rescue mission you pulled off was nothing less than a miracle—not to mention incredibly brave. The loss of Cesare Marino was tragic, but you made it a worthy sacrifice; you set your father and two other men free."

I nodded my head and gripped my uninjured hand into a fist to keep my composure. "I have been over the loss of Cesare a thousand times to see if there was anything we could have done differently. But I am eternally grateful to you, sir, for the men and supplies you provided so we could save my father and the others."

The image of Marianna's grave hit me like a tidal wave, and I inhaled deeply—I had not been there to save her.

"Lieutenant Bianco, I have one request. Please let me be of service, night and day. I am willing to do anything, go anywhere you need. I just cannot bear to be idle."

Lieutenant Bianco looked down at the map in front of him. "It just so happens that the evacuation of the German army is still going on; pockets of and spies for the Nazis still hide and even attack. We have some of our people working on cleaning out those pockets right here in Siracusa. But I think you will be needed to do more of what you did for your father if your leg and hand are well enough."

"I am well enough and anxious to be of service."

He stared at me, a deep crease in his brow. I hoped I did not look as tired as I felt. He finally spoke, "Hmm, I hope that is so, Massimo."

He grabbed a pair of glasses from a drawer and put them on before pointing to the map. "The Germans are taking their time evacuating the cities that the Allies have occupied, and they are smuggling some high-profile prisoners out with them when they do go. These are men who should have been set free; some are from other countries, and there are many Italians whom they have labeled as traitors since the Allied invasion. The smugglers take the same route that your father was on outside of Messina. If you and your team could intervene—"

"You've got it, sir. We are at your disposal."

Chapter Thirty-Seven

MARIANNA

A NOTE APPEARED ON MY cot the next day that said simply, "Alleyway, southeast corner. 10:00 pm."

I hugged it to my chest and had just tucked it into my pocket when Donatella walked into the room; her left leg always dragging just a bit behind her. She stopped at the doorway and stared at my hand that covered the note, her face stoic. She turned and walked out before I could ask her if she was the one who had brought it to me.

I found an empty alley next to the hospital at the southeast corner that night just as *Signore* Chessari rounded the corner. A shadow of sorrow masked his face and triggered a tide of fear in my chest.

"I am very sorry to tell you, Marianna . . . I was wrong about Bruno and his battalion. He has not been ordered to come back to Siracusa yet . . . soon, but not yet. I'll be watching for any news and to see if there is anything I can do."

I swallowed the news like a bitter pill but refused to give in to despair. "You are a wonderful father-in-law to my brother and a very brave man. I know you will be doing everything possible." I steadied the quiver in my chest. "I am hoping that you have also come to enlist me into more service with the Partisans. You know already that I am anxious and willing to do what is needed."

He lowered his brow. "If it was not for our desperate need for help, Marianna, I would not let you do this; but we do need another kind of help. We need someone who looks innocent—a woman to smuggle messages through the city. I think you are the person to do it. I am terribly worried about your safety; never take any extra chances, and follow your instructions to the letter. You cannot tell anyone about your connection to

Partisan activity—no Allied soldiers, no family, not even Bruno . . . when he makes it back."

Hope ran like electricity down my limbs. "Messages? Of course. What do I do first?"

"Your enthusiasm to take on danger only worries me more, Marianna. You will be out on roads by yourself where I cannot completely assure your safety."

"I have promised that I will be careful. I will follow instructions."

He shook his head with a scowl as if reconsidering, and I jumped in to reassure him. "What if I have a safety plan? If anything happens, then how can I find you?"

He exhaled loudly. "Always go to the same place—unless there are Nazi soldiers or suspicious-looking people nearby. Of course, anyone on Hitler's side is not likely to show up in public in a German uniform, but they are here, hidden in the populace and the countryside to keep tabs on the Allies with the hope of taking their control back. You need to keep your movements hidden and act as if you are out on a stroll or simple errand. So, as I said, in case of emergency and when you receive a summons, go to the Hotel Grande on Viale Tica. It has been shut down since the war, but we use a couple of the rooms. Go to room three-eighteen tomorrow night at eight o'clock. In the future you will be notified as we need you, which could be quite often. I will not be there, but an American man by the name of James will meet you."

"Do I tell him that you sent me?"

"Yes, but never by my real name."

"Then, what name?"

"I am known as Lieutenant Bianco."

I nodded my head as he continued. "You cannot use your own name outside of the hospital. From now on, among the Partisans and anyone connected to them, you will be known as Siara Como."

I hugged him, strengthened for just that moment by the comfort of family and by the hope that, at long last, I could do something active to help stop the war. He patted me on the shoulders and cleared his throat. "Marianna, I am racked with guilt for putting you in danger. If your father were . . ."

"I promise you, I will be careful. Papa would want me to follow what I feel I must do and would be grateful that you are watching over me. Also,

Signore, there were families living on the street near the open market whom we used to help . . . I wonder . . . would it be possible to check on them while I am out?"

He shook his head no before I could finish my question. "I am so sorry; all the families on the streets of Siracusa were run out or relocated the night of the Allied invasion. There would be no way to find them now."

I held my hand to my throat and closed my eyes to the tears. "If . . . if you ever hear of where any families were taken or sent . . ." I choked on the words and crossed myself. I said a prayer for the Turisis and the Silvas but comfort felt as if it were miles and years away.

"I will inform you with any news. But, Mari, just because they are moved and gone does not make them dead. There were few civilian casualties in the takeover."

I latched onto the bit of hope he gave me and nodded my head in gratitude. It was time to go. I hurried to the back doors of the hospital and looked over my shoulder for *Signore* Chessari. He stood in the shadows, his hand raised to the brim of his hat. I waved and hurried inside.

I climbed into bed on a cot in the nurses' ward. My worry and sorrow for the families on the streets haunted me, and disappointment that Bruno may not arrive soon lay like a heavy blanket over my heart. But at long last I knew I may be able to do something, to be a part of the forces that fought for our freedom. I clung to that fragment of hope and let exhaustion pull me into a deep sleep.

* * *

The time since meeting with *Signore* . . . Lieutenant Bianco passed quickly. Eight o'clock arrived and I crept through town alone, grateful that I found the Hotel Grande without any problem. The elegance of the main lobby lay beneath a shroud of dust and smelled musty. My leather shoes whispered against marble steps as I ascended the staircase to the third floor.

I tapped on number three-eighteen. The heavy wooden door gave way to a room of dark shadows. Thick curtains were pulled closed, and the only light came from the hallway. I stepped inside and checked my surroundings. Black wires lay strewn across the marble floor and led to radios on desks and table tops, where chairs were pulled neatly into place.

A black shadow filled the doorway, and my muscles froze. The shadow turned into a man who entered the room and lit a lantern. He shook his head with a tsk of his tongue.

"You are too young and skinny. Someone will catch you—snap you in half—and a whole lot of people will die."

I stood taller. "I will be careful."

"Who sent you?"

"Lieutenant Bianco. And what do I call you?"

He entered the room and sat in an overstuffed chair in the corner. "James. It's Lieutenant James, but most people leave off the Lieutenant; I was told you are Siara Como?"

"Yes, eh . . . Siara. You are an American?"

"Yes, ma'am, I am—raised by my Italian father and German mother. Not a real popular combination in this war, but the multilingual ability helps in this service. So, listen—we know they cook bread at the hospital every night. Tomorrow morning, before the light of dawn, put all the bread you can carry into bags—you will have to tie them to a bike. Take them with you to a meeting place at the end of *Viale Tica* road, all the way past the old well out of town. There is a turn there. Someone will be there waiting for you."

"Where do I get a bike?"

"Find one and take it. You will need it more than someone else does."

He handed me a folded piece of paper and nodded his head toward the door. "Do not read this; hide it somewhere on your person, and hand it with the bread to the person or people who meet you. If you get stopped, you are just delivering bread to a troop of soldiers. *Hai capito?* Got it?"

"Yes, sir."

"So go, *vai vai*."

With a quick nod of my head, which was more of a startled jump, I exited the room and darted down the stairs. I leaned against the thick curtains of the lobby wall to catch my breath. Unsure of anywhere else to conceal the note, I tucked it carefully inside my brassiere.

Sweat gathered at the nape of my neck. I dodged through the narrow cobblestone streets, away from soldiers and roaring vehicles still on patrol. There would be no time to find a bicycle in the morning. I had to do it now. I crossed myself and pled with God to help me. Just then, a man wobbled around the corner on a bike. He stopped and leaned it against a pitted wall and stumbled into a bar, already inebriated.

I ran for the bike and jumped on, my heart pumping like the first time Papa taught me to ride. I missed the pedal with my right foot and grated my shin down the rough edge of it, opening a long gash down the front of my shin. I pedaled at a frantic pace as a warm stream of blood trickled down the front of my leg and into my shoe.

The kitchen at the hospital was empty, but the loaves of bread stood in lines like soldiers at attention on top of the cloth-covered tables. Their rich scent was a ruthless assault on the pang of hunger in my stomach, but I dared not eat anything that I could take with me in the morning. I grabbed bread sacks from the pantry and set upon my task. I took only the last loaf from each row and adjusted all the others until it was barely noticeable that any were missing. This gave me eight loaves. I prayed it would be enough for the hungry strangers to whom I would take the bread.

A dull pain in my shin and stickiness in my shoe reminded me of my injury. I hid the bread in a broom closet by the back door and slipped inside a bathroom with a tub. I lifted my leg over the edge and under the faucet of cold water. The deep gouge ached and stung while the cold water washed the caked blood down the drain. I bit my lip; this was nothing in a hospital of men and women ripped to shreds by war. I dressed my leg quickly and climbed into bed for a night fraught with sleepless worry.

* * *

The cool, damp morning hung still in the air. Even the birds were still silent. The sun had not risen. No moon or lamp lit my way. Black shadows loomed in the darkness. Fear climbed up my throat. I pushed the pedals of the bicycle hard and spun the wheels against the cobblestones before they took hold and lurched me forward. Anyone who watched my first few minutes would have assumed I was dying as I gasped for air on the bike. The road and bicycling were familiar, but the terror of being caught or failing my task made my paralyzed lungs cry for relief.

I imagined a soldier around every corner; he'd shout first, and then a bullet would graze my head. I would keep going, never to give up on my mission. I slowed my breathing; I reminded myself that hundreds like me could do this—and had, in fact, done this in a much braver fashion than I. Blinded by darkness to the pits and holes in the road, I seemed to hit every one, being slammed back and forth on my bike.

The sun refused to rise and light my way. I'd left too early; the faint, distant glow out the hospital window must have been soldiers using explosives or burning something, not the brink of dawn like I'd hoped.

But getting on the bike and moving had been a relief after nightmares that caused me to jerk in my sleep. The bags of bread I'd tied to the handlebars of the bike slapped against my knees with every push of the pedals.

The old well James had told me about stood like a deserted beacon in the shadows. I sped past it but no one waited for me at the turn at the end of the road. I had been too hasty to get here, a rash mistake due to fretful nerves. I vowed to use more control, more wisdom, in the future.

Bushes and trees lined the roadway where it sloped down each side. I stashed the bike and ignored the tugs and scratches of the branches as I hid myself deep in the shrubbery. When the first glimmer of sun finally rose from behind the hills, a young man, his beret pulled down low, stepped from between the bushes up the hill.

I scrambled for the bike and pushed it just into view.

He came toward me, "Who sent you?"

"Lieutenant Bianco." I slipped the paper from my brassiere when the young man turned his head, looking for anyone who could be watching us.

He saw the paper and waved his hand in refusal. "You must be new. You pass all notes to Ivana at the next stop." He yanked three bags of bread from the bike, the fabric bags ripping as he tugged them by the strings. "Three of these are for my group. Take the path behind that olive tree to the left and watch for a flash of light." He looked around and tipped his hat. "Goodbye, and good luck."

Branches waved in his wake as he dashed back between the bushes. I got back on the bike and set my sights down the path.

A flash of light caught my eye, and I skidded to a stop. Two gangly teenagers dressed in dirty clothes jumped out from a ditch at the side of the road, grabbing me and the bike. They ripped the bread from the handlebars and pulled me onto a rough trail that was barely discernable through the shrubbery. The boys shoved my bike into the shrubs.

"Run," the one from behind me growled.

I pushed my legs harder to stay behind the leader, who seemed bent on losing me in the woods.

"Get in the truck," one of them yelled.

I spun in my tracks and spotted a truck on a dirt road. The boys grabbed me beneath the elbows and lifted me inside the tented cover in the back of the truck before I could think. Terror shot through me: it was a German vehicle. I had been abducted, taken by the enemy instead of the Partisans. The driver hit the gas as soon as I was inside. With a flood of panic I whipped around and looked out the back, wondering if I could jump out and run.

A deep female voice resonated behind me. "There is no going back. What is your name?"

My voice cracked. "I . . . am Siara."

The dimness lightened and I was able to see. I breathed easier; a truck load of Italian men and one woman—armed, quiet, and somber—sat before me. The woman handed me a beret. "Put this on and tuck your braid up inside if you can. It is better to conceal your identity whenever you're on an errand."

I remembered my instructions. "Who are you?"

"I am Ivana. You are among friends. We all fight together."

A large man in a grey jacket leaned forward, purple circles under his dull eyes, which looked into mine. "The paper you were given?"

I covered the top of my blouse with my hand, reached inside for the piece of paper, and gave it to Ivana.

The men hungrily ate the bread I had brought with me. Ivana handed me a chunk of the bread and I shook my head no. She held the piece in front of me. "Eat, even if you are not hungry; it is a law in our group. We eat when food is available, no matter the hunger."

"But I am going back and can eat all I want."

She put her hand on my arm. "You could be captured on your way and not be given any food for days; it is one of the enemy's favorite ways to break us down and get us to talk."

The bulky man leaned forward again. "Who sent you? Who was your contact?"

I was not sure if I should mention James. "Um, Lieutenant Bianco."

The men nodded their heads in approval as they ate the loaves of bread. After Ivana finished eating she smiled at me. "We work in the countryside, the hills, the sea, inside the mountains. We find and attack the German groups and individuals who hide out and try to sabotage the Allied invasion. We also do a lot of raids in the pocket of the enemy and ransack any items the Germans left behind. We take all of their ammunition, weapons, and supplies."

I saw her looking at my thin frame, and I rubbed my hands up and down my arms.

She broke her stare. "We all train in weapons and fighting. We need every rifle, every Partisan soldier to help us. Even the not-so-tough-looking ones."

I ignored the snickers from a couple of the men behind Ivana. "We need more weaponry? Even with help and supplies from America?"

"Yes, in fact more so; we must conduct ourselves like the force of power we promised the OSS. And we need to make sure that the Germans do not have the weapons or ammo to cause us any problems until they are all gone." She wiped bread crumbs into a pile on her pant leg and then ate each one carefully. "You must also be trained for weaponry. Be back Friday afternoon, three o'clock. Someone will meet you. Your training begins now. Jump from the truck, roll off the side and make your way back to your bike without walking on this road. Stay hidden."

I searched her face for any sign that she spoke in jest. Instead she focused hard on the road that disappeared at a steady pace behind us.

"I will say *go* when we slow for a turn, and you must jump without hesitation, Siara. Don't worry; we are not going that fast."

My life had hinged on the word *go* for days. Now I had to leap from a moving truck on command. We slowed for a corner, and I perched on the tailgate of the truck, my fingers gripped tightly to the edge and Ivana leaning over my shoulder.

"Go!"

Chapter Thirty-Eight

IVANA NUDGED ME FROM BEHIND and I flew, landed hard on my feet, then fell rather than rolled to my side. Rocks jabbed me in the knees as I half crawled and scrambled to the bushes.

We'd traveled only a few miles but by the time I found the bike I was covered in scratches, and a layer of dirt clung to every bead of my sweat. The scrape on my leg throbbed as I pedaled back to the hospital, numb with exhaustion.

* * *

Hitler's army fought to maintain control of Italy and Sicily and to recapture the cities the Allies had already taken: he may as well have tried to kill all the flies in the world with one flyswatter, but he was not good at surrendering. The Allies occupied some of the larger cities of the island, but some of the Nazis hid in the valleys and shadows like serpents ready to slither out and strike.

Signore Chessari . . . Lieutenant Bianco, that is, coordinated our efforts with the Americans and British to flush out the Nazis. Some days I pedaled so many miles on my bicycle to deliver communications to the various Partisan groups that my legs burned and numbed.

The first time I trained for weapons, my heart beat like a captured rabbit. Ivana emerged from the trees, kissed me on each cheek, and thrust a rifle into my hands. "Here you are, Siara. Lello will put glass bottles on the tree stumps across the field while you stand over there behind the rocks and shoot them. Benedetto will show you how."

I had used Bruno's shotgun when he'd let me tag along as he hunted doves, but this was the real thing—a powerful rifle whose name I did not even know. It made me shake just to touch it. These were the weapons that had tormented my dreams after the Nazis first arrived in Siracusa: the rifles that contained ammunition that pierced the precious bodies of brothers, husbands, and loved ones, no matter whose side you were on.

More than once I had braved a trip through town after the German invasion. My pulse had pounded in my head as the soldiers threatened, stared, and aimed these rifles straight at the chest of anyone who had displayed the slightest sign of defiance.

Ivana was the kind of young woman I wished I could be—brave and powerful as a female wolf who fights in defense of her family. They referred to themselves as The Wolf Pack—Ivana, Benedetto, and their small band of men who camped and hid in the countryside to hunt down the enemy. Lino, Giovanni, Marco, Lello, Giacomo, Antonio, and Davide—a ragtag team who subsisted on crumbs and fought with ferocity in order to someday lead a peaceful life.

Ivana wore trousers, a man's shirt, and suspenders. A beret concealed the top of her dark head, her hair tied in a knot in back. But her deep-set eyes still belied her tender and womanly side—and from the way Benedetto watched her, it was apparent he saw it too.

When the bottles were ready, Benedetto set the rifle in my hands and moved it to the proper position at my shoulder. The air in my lungs escaped in one quick gasp while my knees knocked together. I was grateful my skirt concealed them.

Kickbacks knocked me to the ground more than once, and my shaky hands missed the targets every time. Embarrassment burned clear to my ears. Ivana ignored my exhaustion and gave me only seconds to scramble back to my feet and aim again. Lello was the jolliest of the group; each time I flung backwards with my legs in the air he'd roll with laughter, then lean back on his elbows on the rocky hill to watch me try again. It helped to keep my own sense of humor even when my eyes burned in humiliation. Ivana's soldier-like dedication to our task stoked my ambition.

The grenade training was daunting. The rocks I thrust through the air in practice flipped and landed with a thud no more than fifty feet away. I would not even look at Lello, and I sighed with relief when he was busy doing something else and did not watch me.

I gulped water on our breaks and relished the rivulets that ran from the corners of my mouth and down my sweaty neck. Lunch was always bread and cheese and apples so tart I had to gulp more water to wash them down.

My neck throbbed where the muscles and bone had been punched by the backfire of the rifles. When I worked at the hospital, I buttoned my blouses tight against my neck to conceal the purple bruises along my collarbone. If only I were a stronger person, had some muscle from all of my activities, but I only became thinner as the bruises stamped my membership in this courageous army deeper into my skin. My hands ached in spite of the fact that I soaked them in cold water and rubbed them with olive oil as Ivana suggested.

Courage was a balm for heartache. Each time I took aim, steadied myself, and fired, I fought for Bruno's service to have meaning. And for Massimo's freedom, even though he may never be free to come back to me. After a few training sessions I quit jumping every time someone yelled "fire," held my aim, concentrated, and pulled the trigger with precision. I ignored my own weakness and aimed again and again, steadied my feet and legs beneath me, and put my shoulders in position.

My heart raced with joy and relief when at last the bottles flew off the stumps at the end of the field. The repeated blasts in my ears muffled sound as if I had dived underwater, but I pulled the trigger nonetheless and relished the sight of shattering glass when I hit my target. Exhilaration filled me at the end of each training, and although my shoulders throbbed, I rejoiced when I finally pulled the trigger and no longer flew to the ground.

Benedetto taught me to drive an automobile—or, in this particular case, a truck the size of a ship. Even though I was taller than many young women, I had to roll up a blanket behind my back to reach the pedals. The truck jerked and bucked like a wild horse in the beginning and gave the men plenty to tease me about. But I took to the vehicle like I had to horseback riding, and I soon experienced the thrill of controlling something so powerful and strong.

Rumors were that the new president of Italy would soon give in and surrender to the Allies. It was imperative that we help clear all resistance and let *Presidente* Badoglio see that Italy had no chance with the Axis and that we must join the Allies. He had to face the truth; the people of Italy wanted to fight against Hitler. I crawled into the back of the truck on my last day of training with an ache of fatigue that pounded through my body but with newfound confidence.

The sun sat like a ball of fire in the afternoon sky. Ivanna walked in front of our group—me and the men who had become like my brothers.

She handed me the message I had brought to her when I arrived; her reply was written on the back. I tucked it inside my chemise. "Do I need to take this tonight?"

"Yes, if at all possible."

"No worries, my friend, I will take it tonight."

* * *

The steady rumble of the truck as we traveled back to camp would have lulled me to sleep under better circumstances. Ivana and Benedetto rode next to each other in the cab, while six of us sat in the back. My hips bruised against the wheel well when the truck hit potholes in the dirt road, and I wished I did not have to wear a dress or skirt so it would be easier to move around. Ivana never wore a dress, of course, but since I had to look inconspicuous in town and women did not wear trousers, I had to stay "in uniform."

Lello passed a jug of water to Giacomo and Lino, who gulped it down in turn. Giacomo splashed some of the water up on his face and sighed contentedly. The droplets beaded on his rough black beard and dripped onto his shirt. He darted his eyes around at everyone with a smirk on his face.

"I have decided that there is no God—at least no merciful God. Here we are working ourselves to death all day long so that we can save people, and He would not send even one little rain cloud today to cover that demon of a sun. No more confessions or donations from me until He evens the score a little bit."

Davide guffawed, grabbed the jug from Giacomo's hand, and puckered his lips against the brown rim. He took a swig and wiped his mouth with the back of his hand. "The only problem is that God just does not love *you*, Giacomo. Now me, I receive my blessings in the form of women. They love me. They fall all over me and cover me in blessings."

Marco sat back in the corner, stretched out his leg, and kicked Davide in the backside. "Hey, you filthy liar, we have a lady present."

Davide tipped his hat at me with a wink, and my face burned to the tips of my ears. Marco yanked a blanket from beneath him. "Excuse our lack of manners, Siara. Davide, Giacomo, and I have lived in the woods too long now and have lost our good behavior."

The truck jostled us without pity; Davide tossed me the blanket to sit on and waved his hand toward the rest of the men. "Those of you with Lino's group—Antonio, Davide—you must behave. And Lello, just because you are the youngest, you have no excuse to be disrespectful."

Lello brought up his hand in a stiff salute. "What is it that the American soldiers say? Sir, yes, sir!"

All of the men laughed, and my pride swelled at the look of them— fathers, sons, husbands, all willing or needing to fight for our freedom. The abundance of black whiskers, shabby hair, and grimy clothes depicted the rough circumstances in which they lived. They looked like a truck full of black bears that had been rolling in the dirt. The image struck me so funny that I joined in the laughter with my comrades and splashed water on my face from the brown jug to cool down.

The road became smoother before we reached the turn where I needed to get out. Benedetto pulled to the side where I had hidden my bike and stopped. Everyone waved goodbye, and Davide hung out the back end of the truck and waved his hat.

"Goodbye, sweet Siara. Alas, we were not meant to be."

I laughed and waved as they disappeared around a curve. I grabbed my bicycle and started back for the hospital that I had begun to think of as home. It seemed strange that I had known a life before the war.

The world was never more still and sinister then when I had to be alone on my errands, and I wished, as I had many times before, that my comrades did not have to leave me out in the countryside every time. But they lived out here, and it was too risky to take me to town where they might be seen. I started my usual humming to keep myself calm and noticed that the birds had started a loud chattering. The day was slipping by more quickly than I'd realized. The branches of the trees stretched over the road, their elongated shadows like bony arms and fingers. Boulders and bushes along the side took on odd shapes as the light of day dimmed. The brisk breeze slowed to a whisper.

I pressed harder on the pedals, my hands slippery on the handlebars. I wiped them one at a time on my skirt, then gripped the bars even tighter. I forced a deep breath. *Calmati*, Mari, I told myself. *Stay calm, your imagination is the only enemy.*

But my racing pulse refused to listen to reason. The sun slipped behind a low row of hills, and panic spread like a sheet of ice across my back. My breath echoed in my ears. I stood as I pedaled, pressing down with all my might, when all of a sudden, snap!—a rope whipped up from the dirt of the road, caught like a snare in my front tire, and I flew over the handlebars of my bicycle. Both of my hands grabbed at the air. The road became the sky and righted itself a split second before I slammed down, rocks jamming into my back and knocking the breath from me.

More than one set of heavy footsteps came my way, and before I could sit up and run, someone tossed dirt into my eyes and then pulled me by my arms through the bushes. My eyes burned and flooded tears down the sides of my face. When my captors stopped, I wiped at my eyes but could not scream because of the hand that had clamped down over my mouth. I kicked and fought against the hands that tried to hold me down.

My eyes cleared enough that I stared at the scum on the teeth of a man who hovered above me and held my shoulders down, his breath as stale as day-old fish. He pinned my shoulders down while another man stood up and straddled me, a foot on each side of my arms and a rifle pointed down at my chest. I'd seen their uniforms far too many times; they were Germans, angry soldiers who slapped my face back and forth as they shouted. And I could not understand a word they said to me.

The soldier let go of my shoulders, no doubt secure in the fact that I would not move while his partner straddled and pointed a rifle at me. The two of them laughed and talked gibberish back and forth while my thoughts spun like a wheel for a way to escape. The soldier above me opened his canteen and poured water in a steady stream in my face. I coughed and blew air through my nose to keep from choking or drowning while the men roared with laughter. I turned my head to the side, and the soldier grunted in disapproval. I turned my head back, afraid that if I made them too angry they may hurt me even more.

The sound of an approaching vehicle caught their attention, and they spoke in feverish excitement to one another. The man who'd pinned my shoulders took off for the road at a run. As the soldier who was pointing the rifle at my chest watched his comrade rush away, I twisted quickly and grabbed a knife strapped to my thigh that Ivana had given me. I reached across and cut a long, deep slice in the gunman's calf before he had a chance to move. He yelled out and grabbed his leg; I rolled over, scrambled to my feet, and dashed through a thicket of bushes. I kept moving, certain that, in spite of his injury, the man would find me and kill me within seconds, but he did not follow. I stopped briefly and peeked through the shrubs to see where the other soldier had run.

A German truck idled on the road while the driver and the soldier who had held me down walked toward the back. The soldier I had cut kept screaming, and the two men left the truck and ran to find him. They had left the front door of the truck open. I made a dash for it and jumped into the driver's seat. The engine growled like a wounded animal when I shoved it into gear, but the truck jumped ahead, and I took off down the road. I glanced behind me and spotted the soldiers running toward the truck. I scooted forward to reach the pedals better and hunkered down low to avoid the bullets that smacked and pinged on the truck. At last I out-distanced the bullets and made my way toward town.

The trip back to Siracusa passed in a frenzy of fear and nausea. I stopped and crawled out of the truck down the road from the Hotel Grande and made the rest of the way through the alley on foot. By the time I arrived, climbed to the third floor, and knocked on door three-eighteen, I had no breath left. James opened the door.

"You look like you have had a difficult day, Siara."

I pushed past him and collapsed in the wide, green chair, Ivana's message gripped in my hand.

Chapter Thirty-Nine

MASSIMO

I LEARNED TO IGNORE THE times when pain spiked like someone had punched me in the leg. It was worth it. Getting shot. Saving lives. It was all worth it. My thumb protested when I forced it into labor before it had healed, but such were the demands of war. It may turn out a bit crooked, but it would heal. The only thing that mattered was helping the man who had saved my father's life and mine. So working with the Partisans for Lieutenant Bianco became my only focus.

Saving others numbed the pain over the three graves on the De'Angelis property—the ones I had not saved, the one who mattered most. Marianna floated above me when I slept, but when I reached for her she slipped away and I forced myself to my feet to carry out another mission. Our main objective: to stop the Nazis from smuggling Italian prisoners in their caravans as they retreated from Sicily. Because the Germans put on a show of "cooperation" with the Allies, the Americans and British had agreed to allot them a decent show of respect and not strip-search every convoy that passed by in retreat. But we Partisans had no such restraints.

We ran our missions back in the mountains and the valley outside of Messina where we had rescued my father. One team consisted of me; my Italian comrades, Andrea and Ronaldo; and two American soldiers who worked with us. Each time we discovered and freed an Allied prisoner of war, I obsessed over the next one—and the one after that.

It was dangerous to let me so close to the enemy. Rage stalked me like a lion set on its prey, and I could not outrun it. When reality broke through the fog, I told myself, *Focus on the objective, stay in touch with your humanity—do not kill every enemy you see—it will not bring Marianna back.*

At last the endless lines of trucks trickled down, and we returned to Siracusa to carry out a new assignment—to locate the pockets of the enemy who were hidden in the countryside and cities or incognito among our own as spies. It was a relief to return to Siracusa, to be closer to the places I had been with Marianna. Perhaps madness had taken me after all.

Chapter Forty

MARIANNA

❦

A SOLDIER RETCHED INTO THE pan I held beneath his chin. I wiped the beads of sweat from his brow and walked across the speckled marble floor to the utility room. The crude lye soap that the hospital provided diffused its acrid scent into the air and stung my skin while I washed my hands and arms up to my elbows. After one brief moment of pining for a familiar soft lavender soap, I dried my hands on a flour-sack towel and arched my back to coax the knots and bruises out of my muscles. Falling so hard on the road and wrestling to get away from the two soldiers before I escaped in their truck had taken its toll.

Donatella sounded the alarm in the hall. "All staff on alert—serious injuries coming in."

The heavy thump of fast-approaching boots bounced off the walls of the hallway as soldiers carried men toward our emergency area. Nurses in fresh aprons ran beside gurneys and makeshift cots filled with helpless men, their uniforms often shredded and burned, their eyes hollowed and bloodshot. Volunteers pushed some of the soldiers toward the emergency section in wheelchairs or even carried some in their arms.

I knew the drill; I rushed to the closet and loaded my apron and bag with bandages, grabbed a tray of instruments, and hurried to assist whoever looked my way and yelled a command over the cries and moans of the wounded men. The stench of filth and infection burned in my nose, but I worked on. I carried bowls of fresh water to one doctor and carried back the bloodied bowls from the next to be cleaned again.

Some of the soldiers lay still and silent while others stared into space as though death was their only hope. Another doctor barked a command, and I sprinted to the side of that bed, my bag of bandages and a clean tray in hand. I knew this doctor and pushed myself faster to keep his impatience at bay. He looked up from a blood-covered soldier. "Wash this one down and rip off his pant leg; his right foot has to come off immediately."

I turned to a bowl of soapy water beside me and dipped a handful of clean rags into it, wrung them out, and looked down at the soldier's face to begin my task. The floor swayed as if I stood on top of the sea. Shouts for assistance turned to a muted buzz. I dropped to my knees and lay my head on the shoulder of the wounded soldier with a sob in my throat. "Bruno, Bruno, Bruno."

There was no answer. I pulled back for another look at him and kissed his dirt-smeared forehead as tears streamed down my face. I searched for his pulse . . . one, two, three; there it was. His heart was beating.

I whispered in his ear. "Bruno, it is me, Marianna. I am here, *fratello mio*. I am here. Listen to my voice and stay with me. You are safe now; we are together. All will be well now."

I cut Bruno's pant leg back and washed thick clots of blood from the remains of his foot. Tears burned my eyes when I looked more closely at his leg: the muscles from his calf on down were shredded and black—dead. Half of his leg would have to go as well as his foot. I ran to the doctors, my chest so constricted I could barely get a breath.

I found the surgeon I knew had the best abilities and bolted to his side. "Dr. Monaco, a soldier, Bruno De'Angelis, must be checked again immediately."

The doctor glanced in my direction. "Is he dying?"

"I do not believe so. But his leg . . . I believe it is bad, sir. The entire thing may have to come off."

He wiped the perspiration from his forehead with the back of his sleeve. "He will have to wait. Do what you can in the meantime."

I grabbed more towels and a bowl of fresh hot water and washed Bruno until his skin shone in the harsh light of the room. But panic filled me once again; his skin was yellow and waxy. I opened his eyes and looked closely. The brown irises were dull, the whites like the eyes of a hundred-year-old man. Hepatitis. I teetered backward.

Bruno stirred; his eyes slowly opened, then widened in shock. "Marianna?" He turned his head, taking in the cots lined on each side of him. "Is this a hospital? What are you doing here? Laura. Where is Laura?"

He lifted his head and reached his hand toward me. I gripped it and held it against my cheek. "Laura is fine, I promise you. She is with family in Sortino, where it is very safe."

He lifted his head again and gripped my hand tighter in his. "What are you doing here? Laura, I . . . I need to see her."

"Listen to me. You know I would not lie to you, Bruno. She is well and you have a beautiful new son. You have got to stay calm and rest so you can get back to them."

"Laura? You are sure Laura . . . a baby? A boy?"

A droplet of blood rose through a crack in his lips as he tried to smile, his head dropped back on the pillow, and his grip on my hand weakened. I took his face in my hands and leaned close when his muscles shook and shivered. "Bruno, stay with me; all is well, and they are so anxious to see you. Just rest; I will get you a blanket. You will heal and be safe."

His teeth chattered as his hand groped again for mine. "Mama, Papa? Why is everyone in Sortino?"

I swallowed the ache that constricted my throat at the thought of Papa and what I would have to tell my injured brother. "I will tell you everything, I promise, but I have to get you ready for this . . . procedure to help the injury to your right foot before that doctor comes back over here and takes that scalpel to me. He is not a patient man but he is an excellent doctor."

Bruno closed his eyes. "I do not have a right foot anymore." His head lolled to the side from the strain of talking. "Tell the doctor to do what he has to do."

I could not look in his eyes for long and conceal the fear they dredged up in me. He was too weak to hear about our father before a dangerous surgery. I lifted his hand back up to my face and kissed it, washing it anew with tears as my brother lay helpless before me, his life balanced on a thin edge.

"So this is your brother; let me see what I can do for him."

The deep voice of Dr. Monaco made me jump to my feet and look up. A surge of gratitude tipped me forward to hug him, but I restrained myself and instead touched his arm.

"Yes, sir." I lowered my voice to a whisper. "His skin and the whites of his eyes are very yellow."

Dr. Monaco's examination of Bruno was quick but thorough. He nodded his head to a nurse who had run up behind me. I saw the tray

of instruments and the brown bottle of chloroform. I knelt back beside
Bruno.

"You will go to sleep and wake up in much better condition, ready to
get well and get home to your little family."

If Bruno heard the tremor in my voice, he was too weak to show it. He
drifted to unconsciousness as the doctor held a cloth, wet with chloroform,
to his nose, and called for the instruments he needed. I wept silently into
my handkerchief.

* * *

Three days later it was time to tell him. I could no longer dodge the
questions Bruno kept asking about our parents. "I see it in your eyes,
Marianna, something very sad that you are not telling me. You have been
waiting until I am strong enough. Well, I am strong enough."

I sat on the edge of his bed, the weight of sorrow pulling my head
down. "It's Papa . . . his illness became terrible. I tried to find a doctor or
medicine. We tried everything we could think of, but we lost him. Our
papa died."

I held my brother's hand while he stared at the hospital ceiling.
"When? Where is he?"

"The night that the English and the Americans invaded. *Signore*
Chessari buried him by our pond and took me and Mama with his family
to a shelter under their winery. We got away just before our property was
hit by tanks in a crossfire."

Bruno let his tears roll unimpeded. "How I wish I could have told him
goodbye." A sheen of perspiration covered his face as he softly cried. "I am
so sorry I was not there to help you, Marianna. I would have come home
somehow if there had been any way."

I nodded my head while I tried to regain my composure. I had to
tighten the muscles in my throat to keep my sobs from bursting out loud.
The man in the bed next to Bruno coughed incessantly, and I stifled my
crying to pour him a glass of water. The room was a furnace. The sun shot
through the windows along the top of the ceiling and heated it like the top
of an oven over the men.

I gave Bruno his own glass of water. "Here, drink all that you can. Papa
would want us to carry on and help each other. It is a miracle that you are
here. I can never stop giving thanks for that."

Bruno nodded and took me by the hand again. "How is Mama? It must be so hard for her to have you away from her."

"She did not do so well at first. But the help and closeness of *Signora* Chessari and the birth of your little son have done much for her spirits. I sent word that you had survived to her and Laura through a courier who tries to deliver messages to the outlying towns. I also sent word to your father-in-law; he is here in the city on business. Mama wanted me to come here when we heard that your battalion may be headed back to Siracusa. And she is comforted that *Signore* Chessari watches over me. It helps."

Bruno used the napkin from his tray to wipe at his eyes. "I have to heal quickly. Being so close and unable to go to my family is like being caged in this bed. It will heal me completely to see them again, to hold Laura and our son. Thank goodness for my father-in-law. He probably saved everyone's life the night of the invasion. I owe him deeply."

"We all do. I want to do all I can to repay him."

* * *

My life became a frenzy—hours beside Bruno, the bloodied bandages of countless wounded soldiers to change, beds to strip, pans to clean, shaky hands to hold. And nights in the woods—supplies I needed to deliver, wrapped like bandages in a knapsack on my back. Or long trips on my bike, a crucial note concealed under my clothes. On the darkest nights, the only sounds I could hear were my breath and the slip of my bicycle wheels through rocks and gravel.

Terror almost paralyzed me when a soldier spotted me and shouted or beckoned me over. I became adept at quick turns or sudden stops to conceal myself. A few times I informed the Americans who patrolled the city where they could find Germans in hiding. Unaware of my connection to the Partisans, the Americans dismissed my information; they thought me the enemy and questioned me in depth as to my intentions. It was too dangerous; I stopped trying to tell them and informed only Ivana.

I clung to the hope of seeing my brother well and on his way to Sortino. But the idea of leaving Siracusa with him was impossible now. I could not leave our band of Partisans. I was the only courier who knew the drop-off and the pickup places for vital messages that could save lives and help our country to freedom.

At night when the air seemed so still and stifled around my cot, I had moments when another truth seared its way into my thoughts: I could not leave this city where I had last seen Massimo. In spite of my tasks keeping my thoughts at a run, the pain over him never eased. Every time his image rose up from the abyss, a knife sliced my heart, and I stared at the wall or the floor, blind to everything but the ache for Massimo. His breath against my cheek, his mouth on mine, and the moment the priest ripped me away from him when we were attacked in the cathedral. It left me as shattered and empty as the moment I had lost my father, and I relived it again and again.

* * *

Tomorrow, the long row of cast-iron beds would be short the most precious of soldiers. I hurried to Bruno's side with a heart full of relief and pulled back the blanket by his foot.

"Bruno, you are healing so fast they are sending you home to Laura and your baby—to everyone. And Mama will truly be overcome with joy when she sees you." Bruno's shorter leg, still raw where they'd done the amputation, showed no new seepage. Most important, although the yellow pallor still haunted his handsome face, his eyes were not cloudy, and the quiver in his limbs had subsided. If it were not for the war he would remain longer, but his bed was needed, and being with his wife and family would heal him much more quickly than being surrounded by death and suffering.

The metal chair squeaked against the marble floor as I pulled it up beside my brother and sat down. Bruno had to go. The comfort of having him here would be torn away. The empty hole in my heart for Papa and Massimo made me long to lay my head on Bruno's shoulder and sob like a little girl. It was a healing balm to be near him.

Bruno laid his hand on my arm, the warmth of it going to my core. "Yes, the doctor came in late last night and told me the good news. I am out of the dying unit at last. They let you graduate around here if you are a good patient. I am counting the moments until I see my wife and son."

"Well, let us see if we can make you stronger for the trip today."

I scooped up a forkful of pasta and held it to his lips, but he shook his head in protest. "I am still working on my appetite."

With a tsk of my tongue I laid the fork back on his plate and stroked his shoulder to transfer some strength from my hand into his weakened muscles. Bruno surprised me and grasped my arm, a deep frown on his face.

"How am I supposed go, to rest in Sortino and get well, when I know I have to worry about you?"

I lifted my eyebrows. "I do not know what you are talking about." His grip tightened on my arm, and despite my alarm over his perceptive scrutiny, my spirits lifted. "Bruno, you are getting stronger."

"Do not change the subject. You have dark circles under your eyes and you are thin as a rail. Where do you go at night, Mari? You were rarely here helping me at night or on weekends the entire time I have been here."

I stood and smoothed his sheet over his legs with a tsk of my tongue. "I have been here every day beside you as much as possible. You must see for yourself that I am very busy. I train new aides and am helping with supply inventory. And the cleaning is enough to exhaust anyone."

The creases around his mouth and eyes only deepened, so I took an exaggerated breath. "I am afraid this war has made your imagination a little too vivid, my dear brother. Siracusa is rather boring at night unless you think soldier patrols are fun to watch. I put in a long, hard day's work, you know; I need my sleep, so you have had to live without my company sometimes."

Bruno lifted his head from the pillow. "Stop talking to me like I'm one of your helpless soldiers ready to die, Marianna, and tell me the truth. I know you are doing something secret on the side; I can see it in your eyes, and I do not want you messing around in this war. You'd better tell me what you are doing. Now."

I panicked at his discernment. If I flat-out denied it, he would see through me. Mind racing, I leaned toward him with a smirk on my face.

"*Madonna Mia*, Bruno, do not get yourself so worked up and spread your voice around where the spies can hear you. Do you want me dead by morning?"

He tried to sit up and glared into my eyes. "What are you talking about, 'Dead by morning'? This is not a situation to joke about."

"Bruno, do not get upset, I am trying to tease you. If you think I am up to something, then you had better be discreet."

I held my finger to my lips with a smile on my face and glanced around the room.

"Shhh . . ."

He laid his head back on his pillow and glared at me. "Fine, you joke and will not tell me now, but I will find out, Marianna, and whatever foolhardy thing you are doing, I am putting a stop to it."

"Well, I hate to disappoint you, but—"

"Stop it, Mari."

He gripped my hand, his eyes full of concern and his face more yellowed and waxy. My protective big brother. I swallowed my emotions, determined to protect him this time.

"Bruno, please just get well and do not worry about me. I am helping here at the hospital like a good girl. I need so much more rest these days because of my work load." My guilt lessened at the truthfulness of my words. I *was* helping at the hospital and needed more rest; I just had to omit details. I was not accustomed to keeping secrets from my brother. He had always been my confidante, my protector, my closest friend. I squeezed his hand and forced a big smile.

"By this time tomorrow you will be home."

A jab of pain hit my heart at the word *home*, and I kissed my brother on his forehead, grateful that the coolness of his skin meant that his fever was gone. His eyes, black as olives, swam in emotion. "Marianna, we have lost enough . . . please do not do anything foolish."

I embraced him, amazed at the blanket of comfort that wrapped around me. "We are not going to lose anymore; we are going to win."

The sun cast its golden haze through the hospital windows and over the walls. I held my cheek against the rough stubble of my brother's face and realized this was home. It was not a place anymore; it was the people I loved, anywhere I could find them.

Chapter Forty-One

AUGUST 24—IVANA STOOD IN FRONT OF me and the rest of her Wolf Pack under a group of olive trees. A lantern hung from one of the branches next to her, and she watched us sit down on a spot of sparse grass. Her black eyes focused on us like a hawk on its target, the message I had just delivered clutched in her hand. Benedetto rose to his feet and stood beside her, and Ivana unfolded the paper. "We have received a directive from Lieutenant Bianco. We owe a great debt of gratitude to Siara, who brought it to us in a German army truck she stole herself. Now we have an extra truck."

The group cheered and thumped me on the back; I bowed my head, a big grin on my face. Ivana smiled. "You teach a girl to steal a bicycle, and she is doomed to a life of thievery." Everyone laughed, and Ivana's face sobered. "On a more serious note, we are pleased, Siara, that you were able to escape the soldiers and commandeer their vehicle right under their noses. They will know better than to mess with our little messenger girl."

The men chanted my name: "Siara! Siara!" I covered my face with my hands and laughed with them.

James had given me Lieutenant Bianco's latest message to bring to Ivana and Benedetto, along with the directions to take the German truck I'd stolen and deliver it to them. He provided an American uniform and a helmet for me to wear as I drove the truck back out of town. I'd rubbed a bit of dirt on my face and tucked my hair up in the helmet and finally breathed when I made it to the countryside without being stopped. I'd felt safer on the bicycle.

I pulled my knees up to my chest, lifted the helmet, and shook out my hair. Davide whistled low behind me, and Ivana stared him down before beginning our instructions.

"There is a German camp of six vehicles and tents fewer than five miles from here. The largest of the tents holds a cache of weapons. We are to clean out that cache, or get as much of it as we can, and bring it in to Lieutenant Bianco. Their weapons will be used to clean out more enemy camps."

Davide snorted. "I like it; we turn around and use their own weapons and ammo on them—poetic justice."

Benedetto's face stayed serious. "As long as there is justice we will take it, poetic or otherwise."

An owl hooted and swept low over our heads, and Ivana took the lantern down from the tree. "We go at midnight tomorrow night unless otherwise notified. I will give the details then. Be ready for a quick summons with no delays in case of emergency." Her eyes focused on me. "Siara, our numbers are low for this mission. We could use your help."

I glanced at the familiar pile of knapsacks that held everyone's meager supplies under a tree. The cots were not comfortable at the hospital, but I slept in relative safety at night while the rest of my group lived in the open and packed up their beds each morning in case they had to run. I bit down on the quiver in my lip and nodded my head in agreement. "I will be here."

Lello whooped and hollered while he and the rest of the men headed over to make their beds for the night. I stayed under the tree and listened to the cries of the owl as he searched for food until Benedetto came up beside me.

"It is too far for you to walk back. I will take you to within a mile of the hospital and drop you off."

"Thank you, my friend; I 'found' another bicycle that I've been using but I did not think to bring it with me for the return trip."

We traveled back to town in silence but my thoughts did not quiet. I was well aware that my determination to defend my country and family would be difficult, but since Ivana had asked that I help them tomorrow night I knew, like never before, that I may actually have to use the weapons I had trained with. My resolve to train well and be strong seemed important, but I had always expected to stay in my role as the messenger girl. Until the day I had to cut the soldier's leg to get away I had never intentionally hurt anyone. Now I may have to pull the trigger against one human being in order to save another—to save myself, my comrades, my country. No matter the cause or need, I still shook in my sleep that night, my dreams filled with visions of my loved ones falling off of cliffs while I tried to grab their hands to catch them.

* * *

The next night I sat beneath the same tree, a rifle in my hands, ammunition strapped across my shoulder. Ivana gave us the last of the instructions and we piled into the back of the truck.

Had it been a hundred years ago and set in the West like some of my books, the circle of German trucks, jeeps, and canvas tents may have been covered wagons camped for the night on their journey across the American plains—people hidden in shadows, bows pulled back, arrows nocked.

But this was Sicily, Italy, August 1943, and this group formed their camp on the outskirts of an ancient city and defended it with weapons that could shatter entire bodies on impact. The ring of empty vehicles that circled the German camp had been placed as barricades, but worked in our favor when Ivana and I hid behind them.

The moon crouched low on the horizon as if hesitant to rise and illuminate our small band. My comrades lay on their bellies behind an embankment or crawled toward the trucks to join Ivana and me. My nerves locked up in anticipation of Ivana's signal to start our mission. Everyone dressed and covered in black; our faces, hands, and legs were smeared with coal to match the darkness of the night. We waited, seeming to count the seconds as if a clock would chime and our tense muscles could project us forward on our quest.

Our orders were to get all the ammo and supplies we could but not to try and annihilate the Germans. They were a small band hidden in this valley, but they still outnumbered us three to one. Lello listened at the ready over an embankment on the opposite side of the camp in case of trouble. If he heard any shots fired he would toss grenades away from the camp as a distraction so that we could get the weapons or at least get ourselves safely away.

A lone German guard, perched on a stool, chomped down on a hunk of bread out in front of the mouth of an enormous canvas tent. According to reports through James, this was the one filled with rows of ammunition. The guard bent his head, his hair reflecting light from a small fire nearby as I crouched behind the wheel of a jeep.

We had timed the hour perfectly. Laughter and conversation, the clang and clink of metal cups as several soldiers drank and toasted one another in a nearby tent, were helpful diversions and masked any sound Ivana's knife made as she cut a slit in the back of the tent. The guard stood and put his bread on a table. He left his post and walked over to the tent where the loud and boisterous soldiers were drinking. He opened the flap and walked inside.

The chalky coal on my face and legs itched, but I did not dare scratch or move. The moon peeked its way through the trees and cast Ivana's clothes in purple shadows as she looked my way and signaled for me to follow. The tent flap was cut and ready.

I wished I had listened to Ivana and stashed a pair of men's trousers in my pack. My skirt bunched around my hips and exposed my knees to sharp rocks and dried weeds as I crawled around the jeep and into the tent behind Ivana.

My eyes adjusted quickly to the darkness and I could make out what I needed to see: metal shelves held boxes of ammunition, canvas bags of rifles, and crates of grenades. I took a tin box down from a shelf that felt like it weighed as much as I did and carried it to the opening through which we'd just come. I handed it off to Giacomo, who would run a few yards and pass it to Lino, Davide, or Antonio, who in turn would dash over a hill and into a valley to a wagon hidden under the ledge of a rock. Ivana would hand off to Benedetto and Marco. When finished, we would all run to the wagon and pull it like a team of horses to the truck, which was hidden and covered in branches in a ravine. If anything went awry, we were to make a run for it in different directions and away from the wagon or truck.

Benedetto had been wise in his delegation and assignments; it was faster for me to take the supplies from the shelves and hand them off than to try to run with them. My arms strained under the weight of the boxes as I lifted them down, and my back muscles wrenched in protest. Any slowing, any hesitation, and the soldier would be back before we were finished. I pushed myself until my muscles burned like fire and sweat trickled from the nape of my neck under my braid.

The German soldiers sang a hearty song in their tent. Mosquitoes hummed around my face, and I batted them away after each handoff. Each box seemed heavier than the one before. I bit my lip until I tasted blood to keep my breath from a pant that would be heard by the guard if he came back.

The silence ended all at once when a dog outside the tent snarled and barked. I jumped as if a bucket of frigid water had been thrown against my back. The dog had come from nowhere but seemed determined to let the Germans know we were here. The singing in the tent stopped, and the guard ran back into the tent, a flashlight in one hand and a gun in the other. I was too far from the opening to escape, so I dived forward behind a stash of rifles. The ammunition and pistol that was strapped to my belt jabbed me in the abdomen as if I had been punched, and I had to swallow the cry that shot up my throat.

The dog continued to bark and growl. It must be a stray; no one had warned us about a dog. Whatever it was, it had interrupted our operation just minutes before it was complete. Shots were fired from somewhere outside, and the dog yelped before it went silent. The blast of grenades echoed from the other side of the camp. Lello had provided our diversion but it was too late; our guard was already in the tent, his flashlight pointed to the opposite corner as he shouted and fired his gun.

My heart beat so fast it rattled against my ribcage as I wondered what kind of an imbecile fired a gun into a tent full of ammunition. I lifted my head a fraction higher to look for a window for escape. Then I knew—the guard had not shot blindly into a tent of ammunition; he had aimed at Ivana. Blood seeped from under the hand she held over her side, but the other hand held her pistol directly aimed at the guard in front of her. The guard thrust his jaw forward in a grimace, his gun and the flashlight pointed straight at Ivana in a deadly standoff. I rolled to my back in silence, pulled my pistol from my belt, and turned back.

The soldier and Ivana still stared each other down. The soldier had his side to me. Any shot at his head and I could easily miss and hit the remaining boxes of ammunition. Better to take the bigger target and go for the body. Men shouted, rifle fire rang through the camp, and I swallowed the bitter bile in the back of my throat. I glanced at Ivana, saw that the flow of blood had increased until I could no longer see her hand that covered the wound, and her face had blanched white. A mosquito buzzed by my ear and landed on my cheek but I did not move a muscle. The German growled as if he were the dog, then steadied his aim at Ivana.

The sting of the mosquito pierced my cheek. I cocked the pistol, aimed at the torso of the soldier, and fired. A grunt of pain escaped the soldier as he grabbed his shoulder and dropped his gun. I caught a glimpse of Benedetto's arms reaching through the back of the tent and pulling Ivana out while the wounded guard scrambled for his weapon and the beam of his flashlight flipped like a fish out of water.

I felt before I heard the pounding of feet against the ground as more soldiers ran toward the tent where I lay like a rabbit in a trap. I slipped the knife from the strap around my thigh, cut a horizontal slit across the bottom of the tent, and rolled through to the outside. The next tent was so close that I was wedged between the two. I cut into the fabric of the second tent and pushed my way through into blackness. I stood to feel my way to the other side; my shin slammed into what must have been a chair, and my hip smacked against the edge of a table. I felt my way underneath the table and tried to catch my breath as I reached for the outside wall of the tent. It was loose at the bottom, so I crawled underneath the canvas and came up outside on my knees before I ran between two trucks to a group of hedges at the edge of the camp.

Bushes slapped against my face, their prickly fingers snatching at my clothes as I bent over at the waist and ran. The rattle of gunfire echoed in my head but I kept moving, pushed through the underbrush until I spotted Ivana between bushes. I ran to her side.

She had ripped the scarf from her head and pressed it into her side with one hand while she used her left to scoot backward from the camp. I wondered why Benedetto had left her there after he pulled her out of the tent. And then I saw him—face down in the dirt at Ivana's feet, his shirt soaked in blood. Lello, Giovanni, and Giacomo ran up behind a group of soldiers headed our way; their rifles blasted and knocked the three Germans to the ground. Lello helped me lift Ivana and we bolted back for the trees while the others kept firing at the Germans.

The muscles in my shoulders burned and my lungs heaved for air before we reached another copse of hedges where we could stop and rest. We laid Ivana down behind a group of boulders.

"Ivana, we are safe. Tell me . . . show me where else you were shot, quickly." I pulled at her clothes to reveal her injuries.

She did not answer. I turned her head to look at me. Her eyes were half closed, her limbs limp and unresponsive.

Lello had a bag looped across his shoulder that hung at his hip; he pulled it off and rifled through it. He pulled out a white metal box with a red cross on the top. "I have some smelling salts in here somewhere. I think she fainted as we ran."

He ripped a small packet in half and held it beneath Ivana's nose. She did not move or even flinch. Ivana was not breathing. I laid my head on her chest, unsure if the pounding I heard was my own pulse or Ivana's heartbeat. I grabbed Lello by the arm.

"Check her heart, see if it's beating. Hurry, Lello, hurry." Lello held his ear against Ivana's chest while I ripped the bottom of her shirt away and looked for the bullet hole. The wounds of many soldiers had prepared me for the sight of her covered in blood but not for the words that fell from Lello's trembling lips.

"I cannot hear her heart. I think she is dead . . . oh, please, God help us, I think she is dead."

Two Nazi soldiers came at us like mad men within seconds. Lello and I ran through a thicket of bushes and over a hill before we scaled a rock wall. We pulled the pins from two grenades and launched them back over the wall at the Germans. Everything went silent after the explosion.

We waited five minutes, listening for any sound, then jumped back over the wall and ran to Ivana. I knelt down beside her, praying for a miracle, not wanting to leave her alone either way. I checked for her heartbeat again and again, to no avail.

* * *

Two hours later we crept our way back to the German camp with the hope of finding our wounded. Lello went ahead of me while I held up to my shoulder a rifle I had taken from Ivana's body. An eerie silence lay over the Nazi campsite. Only one truck remained, its tires flattened and the rest of it covered in bullet holes.

The tent that held the ammunition had been cut to pieces, the shelves emptied and disheveled, the poles still in place. The rest of the tents were gone. The Germans had emptied and abandoned their camp.

Lello rushed back beside me. "Siara, it is not good . . . I checked Benedetto, but it is too late for us to help him. He is at rest now, probably chasing Ivana through the clouds. It is better they went together."

I buried my face in my hands to stifle my cries and choked on the dust that coated them. Lello pulled me to my feet. "I hear a truck; we've got to run, *subito*."

DAWN ARRIVED BEFORE LELLO AND I made it back to town. We parted ways at the city limits, and I prayed for the strength to push the pedals of the bike I had stolen to make it home. I stashed it in a shed near the back door of the hospital and crept inside the kitchen. I was covered in blood and dirt, but nobody here would notice it as much out of the ordinary. I went into the showers and stood beneath the shower head for a long time watching the grime, like the blood of my friends, wash down the drain.

The hospital was so busy no one would know I had not slept at all. It was my shift to work. By lunchtime my legs shook so hard I had to sit down. I had not slept for thirty-two hours. Donatella patted me on the shoulder.

"You look ill, Marianna; go to your cot and rest."

I hardly felt my cot beneath me before I fell asleep.

* * *

Somebody was shaking me. I held up my hands to defend myself and recognized Donatella.

"Marianna, there is somebody at the back door asking for you."

I stumbled from my cot, smoothed down the wrinkles in my dress, and found Lello waiting for me on the back stoop. "Lello, how did you ask for me here? I am not known as Siara. . . . "

"Just as I am not Lello everywhere. Your supervisor never told you she worked with us?"

I shook my head as the reality hit me. All this time I had thought myself so clever in my excuses to leave the hospital, but Donatella had known what I was doing all along.

"She was one of the Wolf Pack." Lello's voiced quieted. "Ivana's cousin. She broke both of her legs in a raid more than two years ago, so she does not go out on missions anymore."

"Why did she not tell me?"

"Her boyfriend died at the same raid where she was wounded; she does not like to talk about the Partisans. She keeps to herself."

I would never get used to the slap of shock and pain from news like this. No wonder Donatella put in the most work hours of any of us; we all buried the pain somehow. "So you came here to ask her if you could speak to me?"

Lello furrowed his brow. "Yes, I went back to look for the wagon of weapons from the raid in the ravine, and it is still there. The truck is too. I drove the truck you took from the Nazis here to talk to you. We could go and get the cache of weapons tonight before someone comes across it and takes it."

"Ivana and Benedetto's bodies—did you take care of them?"

Lello's eyes glistened with tears. "Yes, I had no time to dig but I put them together and piled rocks completely over them."

The warm breeze cooled the tears on my cheeks. "You say we should go for the weapons? Just the two of us? Our friends, do you know anything about the others?"

He lowered his head. "No. Everyone was too spread out and hidden and no one else came back to our camp. Right now we can only hope they all made it. But that wagon is full of enough weapons and ammo to either help us or to re-arm the enemy."

The bell atop the cathedral across the plaza rang, and I watched a group of nuns tread up the stairs and go inside. A wagon pulled up in front and four men dressed in black jumped out and lifted a coffin from the back that they carried in behind the sisters. Another wagon of people, the women's heads covered in long black scarves, followed behind the men, and one woman reached out her arms toward the coffin as if she longed to hold the person inside. Her cries of sorrow carried over to where I stood with Lello. A jeep of American soldiers passed by and honked at a dog that had run into the road. The sound echoed off the church walls and made me flinch as the dog scrambled away.

When the plaza emptied I answered Lello. "We need help. I will go to my contact place and see if there are any others who could come with us. I have never gone there without being summoned before, so I do not know if anyone will be there, but I will try."

Lello grabbed me by both arms and kissed me on each cheek. "Yes, I knew you would do it. Meet me by the old well at the end of the road with the answer. I will be there waiting, no matter how long it takes. Hurry."

I grabbed my bicycle from the shed in back and peddled quickly to the Hotel Grande.

James opened the door and pulled me inside. "You are never to come here unsolicited. It is possible that you are being followed. We already know what happened last night. Two of your men made it back and told us—a third was captured and has probably been tortured and told them everything by now. They may be looking for you."

I fell back in a chair and laid my hand on my chest. "Who? Who came back? Who did they capture?"

James sat across from me. His stare locked into mine. "Davide and Lino made it back but they are both wounded. If you search your hospital when you get back you may find them there—I sent them over after they checked in with me. But Marco . . . the Germans captured Marco." He stood and pulled me up by the arm. "Go back to the hospital. Your team is disbanded, at least for now. Stay quiet."

I pulled my arm away with a tsk of my tongue, fed up with being ordered around. "I cannot just go back to the hospital and leave this unfinished. People on my team died for this mission. Another member is waiting for me tonight. I came to get more help to go get the wagonload of weapons."

James pushed his hair straight back and grunted in frustration. "That wagon is probably gone by now."

"No, my comrade went back today and found it. And we have a truck nearby that we can load it all into. James, there are enough weapons in that wagon to make a difference to either us or the enemy, whomever gets there first."

James clenched his fist. "Lieutenant Bianco is not here. It would be up to me to give this go-ahead, and I am leery. The Germans could have discovered everything from Marco by now. You are all in danger."

"Marco would not give in and tell them anything."

James looked at me with pity. "Siara, with the methods they use, you would tell them where your own mother was hidden."

A shiver covered my skin with goosebumps, but I held up my chin.

James kept his gaze locked on mine. "You have one chance. If you cannot get it tonight, then it is finished, and there will be no other attempts. We have another group, the one who would use most of the weapons from this wagon load for their raids anyway." He grabbed a piece of paper and a pen and wrote quickly. "Take this message with you to the DiPaolo Inn in Ortigia; give it to the man at the desk named Luigi. He and another man will come with you to help."

He tried to force a smile as he handed me the message. "This is your only chance, Siara. God be with you."

* * *

Luigi stood as tall as the doorframe of the ancient DiPaolo Inn, his arms and legs as thin as the slats of wood that framed it. He wore a name tag on his suit, the sleeves too short at his bony wrists. I was thankful for the name tag; at least finding my contact had been easy. I stood across the desk from Luigi in a foyer made of stones that covered the walls from floor to ceiling.

"I have a message for you from Lieutenant Bianco."

He glanced around the empty foyer and took the note from my hand. "What is your name?"

"Siara Como."

"Ah, the little messenger girl."

My cheeks flushed as I nodded my head, surprised that I was known outside of my group.

He smiled. "Wait right here, please. Sit down and look at a newspaper like you are a guest."

He disappeared down a long hallway, and I picked up the newspaper as he directed, too nervous to read a single word.

Chapter Forty-Three

MASSIMO

❦

THREE LOUD RAPS ON THE door and Andrea shot like a cannon to his feet, his knife clenched in his hand. I had just showered and dressed and grabbed the gun I kept under my pillow. Ronaldo held his pistol behind his back as he eased the door open and Luigi walked in. "*Calmatevi*. Stay calm and nobody kill me. I just have a message here from James." He held up his hands as if in surrender, the note cupped in his palm. "Ivana's group was in a battle last night. They lost almost everyone—even Ivana and Benedetto. The only two able to go back for the weapons cache need some help tonight."

Ronaldo took the note from James, and I took a drink of water and sat down, thankful for the relief to my aching leg. Ronaldo frowned. "Who brought this? Why is it signed by James and not Bianco?"

"I do not know why it came from James. Siara brought it. The messenger girl. The one who James said is so beautiful."

Andrea stretched his neck to look over Luigi's shoulder down the hall, and Luigi punched him. "Relax, she already fell in love with me in the foyer. You are too late. James must think this is an emergency to go ahead without Bianco. He said it has to be done tonight. They need only two of us to help."

I grabbed my boots. "I will go."

Ronaldo chortled. "Are you crazy, Massimo? You have been limping all day. You stay and rest, and Andrea and I will go. No *problema*."

I put on my boots and winced when I stood up. My leg seemed determined to thwart my every move. Perhaps the bullet from the Nazis had nicked the bone after all. I pushed the pain from my mind and looked at my comrades. "If we all go it might be safer and get done more quickly."

Luigi shook his head, "James said only two. I have to watch the front desk. Unless you want to stay and work the front desk, Massimo; then I can go and help."

Ronaldo heaved a sighed in exasperation. "James said two, and since we do not have time to make a plan, it will be better if Andrea and I go. We are used to working together. Massimo, you rest your leg for the next one."

I took another drink of water. "*Va bene*; I will take the next assignment."

I watched my comrades leave and shut the door behind them with a sense of unease. Something ticked in my muscles—an anxiousness to go with them. It would not be easy to rest before their return. I settled down to sleep with my pistol at my side.

Chapter Forty-Four

MARIANNA

❧

LUIGI CAME BACK DOWN THE hall with two men who looked like they could use a shower, their Italian uniforms covered in dirt and their faces a bit haggard. The taller one walked right up to me.

"Nice to meet you, Siara. My name is Andrea, and it will be a pleasure to work with you." He bowed over my extended hand, and for a moment I thought he might kiss it.

The man behind him with the darker skin punched him in the arm and took my hand from Andrea. "Andrea is half French—we try to ignore that half. I am Ronaldo."

Andrea punched Ronaldo in return, and I felt the corners of my mouth twitch.

"Well, I will be happy to work with both of you. No matter what halves you may have."

Andrea winked at me. "She is witty and wise as well as beautiful."

Luigi stepped up. "All right, enough. It is time to go. Sorry I do not have better behaved men for you, Siara. These two just returned from Messina. They are a bit tired but they have proven their worth many times."

I smiled and nodded my head. "We will be happy to have their help."

* * *

It seemed almost obscene to breeze so easily through the evening after the violence and death of the night before. The sky sparkled like black ink sprinkled with diamonds, the air barely sighed around the trees, and the night birds lay quiet in their nests. The four of us drove right up to the wagon filled with weapons.

Ronaldo gave us the go-ahead. "Siara, stay at the wheel, the engine running. Lello, Andrea, let's fill this truck before the sound of our movements can travel."

The three men jumped and landed on the sandy ground of the wash. A cold sweat beaded on my skin as I kept watch through the windows for any danger.

It seemed mere minutes before they leapt back into the truck and we were flying over the landscape on our way back to Siracusa. I felt safer with these men than I had in a long time.

A cloud of loneliness covered the land when we passed the place where Ivana and Benedetto laid in their tomb of rocks. I prayed for them in my heart while I watched out the windows for any sign of the enemy.

Lello drove the truck and whistled in between bounces over gullies and cracks in the ground as if he were on a regular job assignment. He hit the brakes when I warned him about a pile of rocks, and he veered around them with ease. "So why did you let me drive the truck back, Siara?"

"I do not have a blanket to prop behind my back."

He grinned and pressed on the gas. "That did not seem to stop you when you took the truck from the Nazis."

"*Si* . . . I try not to let anything stop me."

Lello laughed out loud. "You may look gentle, Siara, but I believe your backbone is made of granite."

Heat flooded my face, and I winced over the reference to granite. My strength had ebbed because of Ivana's death. As hard as granite may be, it could break—even shatter.

Ronaldo and Andrea rode in the back to guard the supplies and watch behind us. When we neared the main road one of them banged on the back window of the cab in warning. Lello slammed to a stop until three taps on the window signaled the go-ahead. The trip back became an episode of nerves. Every few minutes the men in back signaled for us to stop. We drove at a crawl at times to minimize the sound of the truck and did not use our headlights. Andrea had run up to the cab during one of our stops and told us that they believed we were being followed. Yet every time we stopped, everything remained still and silent.

We had brought my bike in the truck so the men could drop me off close to the hospital. Lello stopped a couple of blocks away, and Ronaldo handed me a note after he'd unloaded my bike for me. "We will take the weapons with us. Take this note to James tomorrow so that he knows we made it back and where we took the cache."

I folded the note and tucked it in my sock. I waved goodbye to my new friends as they drove away and hurried toward the hospital. My nerves from earlier had not completely calmed, and I looked over my shoulder constantly. I was relieved when I reached the shed in back of the hospital where I hid my bike.

The lamp on the back wall of the hospital had been extinguished. Not a single beam of light reached the inside of the shed, and it reeked of unwashed bodies. I had taken my bike in and out of the dark shed many times but never noticed a smell before. A breeze stirred as if someone blew their breath on the back of my neck. I turned quickly to look, but could see nothing. I pushed the bike to the far corner of the shed, and the air warmed and thickened at my back as if someone had crept up behind me. I reached for the knife strapped to my leg just as thick arms locked around me from behind. Pain jarred through my head. Light and color spun in my eyes before I fell into a pit of darkness.

Chapter Forty-five

Jumbled dreams dipped and swirled. Waves slammed against my head and threatened to crush my skull. I forced my eyelids open to utter blackness. I lifted my hand and it bumped into rock just inches above my face. I wheezed and bolted up, smacked my forehead against rock, and fell back. I ran my hands up and down the wall above and below me and reality erupted in a cold sweat on my skin—I was in some sort of tomb, wedged between a ceiling and a bed of solid stone.

Terror threatened to drown me. I slid my hand up and checked my eyes; they were open, seemed normal, but I could not see. I spread my arms to the side, felt for walls, and hit one with my left hand. The warmth of my breath blew back on my face in short bursts. I ran my right hand farther out along the bedrock beneath me and finally curled my fingers over an edge that dropped off. Inch by inch I scooted to that side, tested every move until I was able to hang first one leg and then the other over a rough stone ledge. I twisted my shoulders and sat up. Pressure throbbed behind my eyelids. I held my hand up to my face and saw nothing. Blindness. Panic burned like acid on my skin.

I touched the top of my head and pain sliced through my skull until my teeth ached. A thick, sticky mass caked in my hair and a bump as large as an orange rose up at the crown.

A ping like a droplet of water hitting the bottom of a well penetrated the silence. I forced myself to concentrate; I had been in the shed to stash my bike when everything went black. With a quick intake of breath I reached in my sock for the message I had tucked inside. I wanted to weep when I realized it was gone.

I heard the scratch of approaching footsteps and saw the golden flicker of a torch; someone was coming. The air wrapped its clammy fingers around my throat.

The torch glowed against walls of lava rock lined with deeply carved caves and tombs. Catacombs—I had been unconscious inside a grave in the catacombs. The only catacombs I knew of were deep beneath a church. Someone had put me here and now they were on their way back. A shudder rattled my teeth together. I sucked in air as if going under water, crouched behind a low wall that surrounded my tomb, then cried out in pain and shock as I was pulled to my feet by my hair. I looked into the face of a Nazi soldier. He kept one hand wound tightly through my hair, the fiery torch gripped in the other one. He jutted out his chin and sneered in my face.

"What? Not dead? You have not moved for two days. Well, no matter, you will be dead soon."

His grip on my hair did not loosen as he dragged me over the wall across the uneven ground and headed back the way he had come. I expected the hair from my wound to be ripped from my scalp before I finally gained my footing. The soldier let go of my hair and I stumbled beside him. Each time my footsteps faltered the soldier grunted in frustration and shoved me forward to the cave floor. The porous rock scraped the skin off of my hands and knees. I cried out, only to receive a hard kick that threw me against the wall and cut the side of my cheek. Warm blood rolled down the side of my face.

"You walk in front of me; if you try to run I will shoot you down like the dog that you are."

I walked as best I could, ignored the sting of ripped skin on my knees and palms and focused on my memorized information. I knew what they would want to know and knew I had to protect my comrades, especially *Signore* Chessari. I must repeat only the script we all practiced. My legs buckled, and I struggled to keep from falling. The soldier shoved me down again. I prayed for strength when my legs refused to support me . . . *Dio mio, dami la forza.*

The winding hallways finally opened to a large room where two German soldiers sat at a table, candles lit in front of them. The older one squinted his eyes and smirked as the soldier pushed me forward.

The three of them gestured and spoke in German for several minutes while streams of thick blood ran down the front of my legs from my torn knees.

The older German lifted his head and spoke in poor Italian. "What is your name?"

My voice came out in a whisper. "Siara."

"Siara, eh? I know you are lying; you will pay for that."

He lifted a canteen and drank while water dripped down the front of his chin and onto his neck. He wiped his mouth with the back of his sleeve and stared back at me with a smirk.

"So, Siara, you are thirsty?"

I tried to speak again but my voice was locked in my throat. I nodded my head and the ugly grin spread across his face. "Good. You will die of thirst before we are finished with you. It is a horrible way to expire but very enjoyable to watch. Of course you may go quickly; you do not look so good."

Two more Germans walked into the cave and a tall one, who looked the age of my father, stared me down. He snickered, poked at the younger soldier beside him, and gestured at me. The young soldier just stared ahead. He looked familiar but my vision was too blurry and my thoughts too confused to remember where I'd seen him.

The German at the table looked like a pig with his pink skin and squinted eyes. He looked at me and narrowed his eyes into little slits. "I do not know why the Lieutenant brought you all the way down our lovely hall today, Siara. We read your pathetic little note that was hidden on you. You are an idiot used by bigger idiots to do nothing, a worthless child who will be a pleasure to kill. Still, you may know something after all. We will find out tomorrow; it is too late to start your torture now. I am tired and hungry."

His eyes turned red as he chuckled and pointed at the young soldier who stared ahead. "But our new soldier here will be more than happy to 'escort you back.' He needs to be reminded that the Führer does not tolerate weak men." The pig man moved his gaze up and down my body until my skin burned. He sneered. "Yes, he will see just how pleasurable torturing a woman can be. He will also give you a sampling of what tomorrow may bring. Who knows, you may even like it."

The other men roared in laughter, and the young soldier grabbed a rifle. He shoved my shoulder hard in the direction I was to go. My stomach heaved and convulsed at the thought of what may happen to me as the soldier poked the rifle in my back and forced me forward. "Move."

More laughter erupted behind us as I staggered from the room.

The soldier pushed me back past deep tombs, their murky doorways like mouths agape, ready to swallow their victims. The torch sputtered in his hand, and shadows bounced off the crags that hung from the ceiling. The shadows jumped and stretched over small niches and arched chambers, chiseled into rock. A rancid dampness like rotting soil lingered in the air.

My feet refused to walk in a straight line while my head floated through cloudy water, and every rasp of my breath echoed inside my ears. Fear came in waves that squeezed the air from my lungs and made consciousness fade away. Each time my mind resurfaced I would jump at the clink of the boots right behind me and teeter toward the wall. The soldier pressed his hand against the small of my back. I flinched and stumbled to my swollen knees. He grabbed me around the waist and lifted me to my feet while my arms tried in vain to lash out and fight him.

I let out a small cry, and the soldier twisted me around without effort and covered my mouth with his hand. "No, shhh, you must be quiet, *Signorina*; you must hurry."

I tried to step forward but sharp tingles started in my toes, traveled up my legs, invaded my body. When they reached my head the walls swirled in multiple colors, the floor swam and dipped beneath me, and the tunnels closed around me.

I came up for air to the cool trickle of a stream that traveled down my throat. I choked and sputtered but opened my mouth for more. The soldier held a canteen to my lips and supported the back of my neck. I gulped, and the chill of fresh water filled my empty belly.

I opened my eyes in the direction of the soldier and chanced a glimpse of his face. A long, red scar ran from beneath his left eye all the way down his cheek. I recognized him as the same Nazi soldier who had argued in our defense that day on the road when Massimo rescued us. He spoke Italian, and his voice made the faintest of echoes off of the cave walls.

"*Signorina*, I do not want to see you die, but I cannot get you out of here; there are too many guards in front of the only door out. There is a small cave through a hole in the ceiling inside one of the tombs. I can help you climb up to hide but I cannot come back. God must help you from here."

The cool water filtered through my veins and stirred my awareness. I stared at his face, too weak to doubt or fight him. He leaned the torch against a wall, placed one hand behind my back and the other under my knees, and lifted me into his arms.

I slumped against his chest and he shook me. "Do not faint again. Hold on to me while I reach for the torch."

Relief sent a small dose of strength through my limbs, and I clasped my raw hands around his neck. Torch in hand and me in his arms, the soldier ran down the winding black labyrinth, my cheek rubbing against the buttons of his uniform. Several minutes later his footsteps stopped and he lowered me to my feet at the door of a deep tomb.

Skulls coated in shiny green moss and black mold lined a wall of the small domed room, their mouths locked in a grimace, their hollowed eyes haughty and watchful. A black rat dashed and jumped through the maze of bones. Chills rattled my teeth and my legs dipped beneath me.

The soldier's urgent whisper pulled me back. "I will boost you into the cave up above. Quickly, now, you have to move no matter the pain." He lifted me by the waist onto a stone coffin beneath the cave in the ceiling. "I found this place today when they told me about you. Reach up above you and feel inside the opening for a ledge. It turns to the side and you can lay down in there. It is small. Duck your head and crawl, or you will hit the top."

I gulped in air and did what I was told. I lifted my hands into the black hole and gripped the rocky ridge inside. The soldier lifted me higher, and I grit my teeth to stifle the panic caught in my throat. I scooted on my side across a jagged surface that tugged at my dress as I searched for walls with my fingertips. The ceiling bumped my shoulder as I moved and sent a tremor of alarm through me at its proximity . . . I was wedged in the bowels of a grave while the bones of the dead watched me from below. The pain in my head accelerated, and my insides twisted and heaved. I opened my mouth in a frantic pant for air and tried to scramble back out of the cave.

The soldier pushed at my kicking feet and forced them back up inside. "No, no, you must stay here or they will kill you. I am sorry; this is all I can do. I have to escape now myself. I cannot come back. I will try to send someone to get you."

He spoke some more but I could not concentrate. The sides of the cave breathed and heaved around me as more of his words floated around my head. The echo of his boots in retreat grew faint—and disappeared.

The air around my face warmed as I gasped for breath, my nose pressed against the rocky wall. The hammer in my head spread into my shoulders, arms, and legs. Paralyzed and helpless, I let my head fall limp to the lava rock that served as my pillow. *Papa, Bruno, find me . . . find me. . . . Massimo, I am alive in a grave, come back, come back. Dio mio aiutami, please God, help me.* Mercy and defeat wrapped their wings around me at last and I let the darkness have me.

Chapter Forty-Six

MASSIMO

THE ROOM SMELLED OF DUST and strong coffee. Lieutenant Bianco's face had hollowed out since we had last met, and when I patted him on the shoulder his bones were more prominent. "You getting much food, sir? We certainly do not need you on our list of casualties." I walked to the marble-topped table, cut off a thick chunk of provolone, and took it to him.

He took the cheese and put it on the table beside him. "Thank you, Massimo. I know you just returned to town and must be tired from all the missions outside of Messina. Well done."

Lieutenant Bianco gestured for me to sit on the green chair in front of him. The hotel room had not changed much; sparse pieces of furniture and tables cast dim shadows over nests of wires and empty ammunition crates. "I apologize for asking this of you, Sergeant." He tried to smile before his brows lowered in a scowl.

I sat forward in my chair. "Apologize, sir? You have saved both my life and that of my father. Ask me anything you want."

Lieutenant Bianco rubbed his eyes and face with his hands. "Your father, Franco, is a valiant man. It was an honor to be a part of his rescue as well as yours. It is in regards to a rescue that I called you in today. But I am compelled to apologize because it may be your most dangerous mission yet—you may be walking into a whole hive of the enemy."

"I will be glad to work in any capacity; you know you can rely on me."

"Heaven knows we need reliability, Massimo." He clenched his hand into a fist on the arm of the chair. "Have you heard of the Partisan team member named Siara?"

"The messenger girl? Actually, I have, sir. I have never met her, but she seems to have a reputation throughout the operation for her courage."

His attempt to smile turned to a grimace, and he blinked his eyes in the dim light. "She was captured five days ago. We have had no information until this morning. In most cases they would have executed her by now. But I got a message this morning that a German soldier reported on a prisoner—an operative named Siara—three days ago when he surrendered to the Americans; he swore she may still be alive."

A red flush of anger deepened in his face as he stood and walked to the window, pulled back the curtain, and looked through the dirt-streaked glass. "I need you to go get her, Massimo. She is the daughter of a friend and is like my own daughter to me. And we cannot let them . . ."

I stood, ignoring the ache in my leg. "We will not let them do anything, sir. We will find her and bring her back immediately."

Lieutenant Bianco moved with more energy and grabbed a paper from the black desk next to the window. "I am not sure which holding camp the German soldier who gave us the information is in. All we have is his name—Peter Weimer. And a description: he has a long, red scar down his left cheek. These papers will clear you with any Allied soldiers or guards. Stop in the room next door and tell James to go with you—he speaks German and Italian. Siara has been coming here to get the messages from him, so he will recognize her and could help. Take all the men you think you will need, all the weapons necessary, and leave the minute you can. I know I can trust you."

I forced a smile and walked to the desk, the wind and whistle of passing vehicles outside the only sound. "You have nothing to worry about. We will take care of this and send word right away when she is safe and well, sir."

His mouth pulled down at the corners in a deep frown. "Massimo." He stopped for an instant. "She is being held by the most brutal of all, a pocket of the SS left here in hiding to spy. They are desperate and ruthless, so . . . Siara . . . may not be coherent. By now she has been beaten and starved at the very least. Only God knows what else."

I shook off the dread that shivered across my chest at the thought of the SS interrogators with a young woman. I wished I could still reassure my friend that we could bring her back in good condition. The room was silent.

"Massimo . . . if . . . if she does not answer to Siara . . . use her real name to get her to respond."

"No problem, sir, whatever you say."

"Bring her back no matter what state they've put her in; God willing, I will find a way to help her heal. She is so young, so good. Do not let her die in there, son. Do not let them have her."

I took the paper from his hand that had the information I needed. "I will bring her back, sir. You can count on me."

"God be with you, and your men, and . . . Marianna."

My muscles twitched. "Marianna, sir?"

"Yes, sergeant, Siara's real name is Marianna De'Angelis. Use it if you need to."

I gripped the paper as my heart slammed to a stop. "Sir—sir—this Marianna De'Angelis, she is of Siracusa, a fisherman's daughter?"

"Yes, sergeant, you know her then? Oh, of course, your summer with your grandparents—you could have met her."

"Yes, sir . . . she is not dead, and . . . buried at her home?"

"No, sergeant, that would be her father, an uncle, and an aunt. I buried them there myself. Marianna has been working with us for weeks under the name of Siara."

My hands shook. My chest ignited in hope and terror. Marianna was alive—living, breathing, existing in this world. Not floating like an angel just beyond my grasp. Within seconds a cold sweat sprang up on my face and down my arms with visions of horror; I pictured Marianna's deep, innocent eyes, widened in dread and fear, her delicate body wracked in pain, the lilt of her voice deepened to cries of agony or stifled screams. And all the while she would say nothing, give them nothing, regardless of her anguish—as the torture would continue on and on.

Sweat streamed down my back and face as my pulse raced like a machine gun. Lieutenant Bianco watched my reactions with a confused expression on his face. He inhaled sharply as a light of realization clicked on in his eyes. "You do know her. You care for her . . . go, go now, Massimo. You will find her; save our girl and bring her back to us."

I flew down the steps, the pounding in my chest like the countdown of a bomb.

* * *

An ancient monastery at the edge of town served as a prison, its majestic architecture a thousand years old, now broken and torn apart. A house of peace surrounded by endless, shoulder-high coils of barbed wire meant to shred the flesh of desperate men. Hordes of German soldiers, reduced to helpless beggars, paced through the wasted gardens and under the shelter of withered trees. In the furthest corner, the bodies of dead men lay in heaps, stiffened and decaying on the ground they had claimed as theirs.

I had seen it all before—the futility, the desecrated lives. All I had eyes for was one man, a German soldier who held Marianna's life in the palm of his filthy hand. My frustration built like a bushfire out of control at our slow progress in tracking him down. This was the third prison camp we had tried; if the soldier was not in this yard, my anger would detonate.

My Italian comrades and I wore civilian clothing, our uniforms stashed away until they no longer represented an enemy to the Allied armies. I showed the official papers to the guard in charge of the camp and spoke the words I had memorized in English. "We seek a private Peter Weimer for information."

Two British soldiers read through the papers and nodded their agreement to the main guard.

A lanky American guard shifted his cigarette to the other side of his mouth and opened the gate for us without a word. We walked in the dirt-packed yard, Ronaldo at my side, James, Andrea, and Luigi quiet and alert behind me.

The two British soldiers escorted us, their rifles at the ready. A Red Cross volunteer stood on a small brick platform in the middle of the yard and dipped a ladle into a wooden barrel of water that leaked into a muddy puddle. Dozens of somber men surrounded him, their metal cups outstretched in their hands for their share of the precious liquid.

James held a makeshift bullhorn to his mouth. "Weimer, we seek private Weimer for information."

James stayed beside me to translate. An older dark-haired man lowered a metal cup from his lips, wiped the drips from his mouth and chin, and stared at us. "Look in the back."

Pressure built inside my chest with every step I took toward a group of men near the far wall. We stopped a few feet from the only man with a red scar slashed down his cheek, and I stared him down. The group of men at his side scattered.

"Weimer?"

His shoulders tensed and his face paled. "Yes, I am Weimer."

Frustration and urgency seared through my veins. I locked my muscles into a knot, grabbed the German soldier by the front of his shirt, and jerked him up against a brick wall.

Ronaldo strode up behind me and clapped his hand down on my shoulder. "Easy, Massimo, we will not find Siara if he is not alive or willing to answer questions."

The German man gasped and cried out. "I speak *Italiano*. The *Signorina*? You want to find the *Signorina* I told the guards about? I . . . I did not hurt her. I swear, I helped her. I hid her."

I loosened my grip on his shirt and let him back on his feet. "Tell me exactly where she is."

The soldier panted for breath and nodded his head. "The . . . catacombs, the catacombs; I hid her. I did not harm her."

"Why the catacombs? What was she doing there?"

The soldier blinked and sucked in a quick breath. "A group of the SS has been hiding there since the Allied occupation of Siracusa. They send out spies and capture people right under the Americans' noses and bring them back to do their interrogations there. I was supposed to . . . to hurt the girl and tie her up by herself in a tomb so they could torture her the next day, but I did not do it."

The word *torture* locked a vice around my throat, and I choked for breath. Ronaldo stepped up and looked the soldier in the eye.

"Is she alive?"

The soldier shook his head. "I . . . I . . . do not know if she is alive . . . I hid her three days ago. I ran away from the SS and surrendered to the Allies."

Ronaldo looked at the soldier suspiciously. "Why? You German soldiers are all killers. Why would you help her?" He looked over at me. "This is probably a trap."

I lifted my pistol; Weimer stood taller. "I could not harm a girl. I have a sister."

Ronaldo scoffed. "Ha—most of the men here have sisters. I do not believe you." He spit on the ground and glanced at me again. "It is a trap. We might as well shoot him now for lying."

Sweat ran down the sides of Weimer's face as he looked me straight in the eye. "I am not lying. I saved the young woman. I did not harm her."

The prison yard had emptied out in our area when I'd lifted my pistol, and all was quiet. The sun burned like fire on my head while I stared him down.

He looked back at me unblinking, his eyes clear and steady.

The vice grip on my chest eased a notch and I took a step back. "How many soldiers are in the catacombs, Weimer?"

He took a deep breath. "Maybe a dozen."

"You are taking us in there to find her."

His eyes widened. "They will kill me if they ever see me again."

Ronaldo looked at me, then back at the soldier. "Was she hurt?"

"She had a bad wound on her head. The men who brought her in thought she was dead or dying and put her in a tomb for two days, but she woke up."

My anger spiked with the vision of Marianna stretched out helpless on a cold slab. "You left her there for two days without help? You did not check or try to help her?"

A glint of fear came back to his eyes. "I was not in there the first two days; I had been assigned to hide on the outside and watch for the Allies. The SS soldiers to whom I answered were angry that my questioning tactics with the prisoners were too soft, and they had kicked me out of the catacombs. Until—until the young lady you are looking for was captured. They brought me inside to force me to be brutal. I had seen what they did to women, so I found a place ahead of time in the catacombs to hide a woman if I had a chance. When your Siara woke up, the soldiers came to get me from my post outside. They threatened me. I was to toughen myself. They wanted me to . . . harm her, but I did not; I did not touch her."

I shaded my eyes from the sun with my hand and looked at him closer. "Why did you just hide her? Why did you not take her with you?"

"She could barely walk; I had to carry her. And the guards, the SS, they would have killed both of us. She was too wounded, and I had nowhere to take her."

His words slammed me in the gut. "Why could she not walk?"

"I only saw the lump and the, uh, blood on her head, and she had blood on her knees and legs like she had fallen down. I gave her water. I carried her. I swear to you, it was all I could do. It would have done no good to try to take her out of there. They would have killed us both on the spot."

The rims of the soldier's eyes reddened. "I knew I had to run and be taken prisoner or the SS would kill me. When I surrendered to the Americans, I told them about this girl so she could be helped. But it has been three days and nobody has asked me about her until now."

I turned to my comrades. "Andrea, Luigi, go and see if anyone from Ivana's group is available to help us. The more numbers we have to take over the catacombs, the better. Meet us back at the guard tower in one hour, fully loaded. We are going in."

They took off in a run and left me, James, and Ronaldo with the enemy who had tried to save Marianna's life. Weimer stood straighter now, his blue eyes dull with dread. "What will you have me do?"

"You have to come with us or we will never find her."

The long red scar down his cheek deepened to purple. I placed the pistol back in the harness at my side. "That scar looks fresh."

"I told you, no one displeases the SS without paying the price. If you can possibly keep them from capturing or killing me—I would like to see my family again someday."

My tongue thickened. "You did the right thing to . . . to try and save the girl. We will do what we can for you."

I reached into a bag for a set of civilian clothes and hat and threw them to the soldier. "Put these on so you will not be recognized as German right away."

Weimer nodded his head, stripped down right there in the yard, and put on the extra clothes. The pants came up short on his pale ankles. I checked my rifle and gear as he dressed and bit back the fear that threatened to explode at the thought of Marianna alone and injured in the dark.

"How far back in the caves did you hide her? Can you find it right away once we take care of the soldiers and guards?"

"Yes—she is in a small cave in the ceiling inside one of the tombs."

I nodded my head to James to interpret as I spoke to the two British guards who had watched the entire confrontation. "You saw the papers I gave your lieutenant at the gate, no?"

They bobbed their heads in unison.

"I have permission to take this man with us on an Allied-approved mission." They stepped back out of our way and I turned to my new prisoner. "Every one of us will be watching you. Do not try to escape. Let's go, Weimer."

Chapter Forty-Seven

MARIANNA

I WAS COILED IN A cocoon—blind, suffocated, and deaf but for the sounds that scurried away before I could identify them. I wanted to scream at the pain when it pulled me from a peaceful world of unconsciousness and wished I could place my hands on my throat and lips to know if my cries were real, but I could not feel my arms. The rocks jabbed into my skin and dug deeper into my muscles until they burned and numbed.

In my dreams I broke through the ceiling as an archangel, soared over mountains and valleys, then lost all power and plunged back down to my tomb with a scream in my throat. A faint voice from deep inside my memory hushed me each time, warned me to be still. I fell with relief into a black void time and again.

* * *

Something touched my leg, a tiny scratch on my skin, a pinch on my ankle. I fought my way through a cloud, and a thin damp rope whipped across my foot and dragged across my toes. The pinch on my ankle bit deeper and deeper until the bite brought me to full awareness: a rat—a rat chewed on my skin. Horror shot through me and the warm body of the rodent popped against my foot as I kicked it. It squealed in protest and landed with a dull thump below. Repulsion shook my muscles, and I twitched painfully against my rock bed.

I was awake for the first time in what could have been hours or days and at last comprehended words that kept floating back to me. Something that the German soldier said to me before he left me in the cave. I moved my foot once more and heard the clink of metal against a rock. Water. Light. Hope. The cave was too small, the ceiling too low for me to sit up and reach for what I prayed would be a canteen and some kind of light left at my feet. Ignoring the pain, I moved as much as I could and shook each one of my limbs to wake them up. Inch by inch, I scooted one of the objects up with my foot and knee against the wall until I grasped it with my hand. I slid my finger up the side of the metal cylinder and the yellow bulb inside came to life. A flashlight.

For the first time I could see the walls that had entombed me; there was no room to move or to breathe. Panic wrapped around me. I had to get out fast before I fainted again. I took slower breaths and scooted out inch by inch on my shoulder and hip, stopping to rest when I could not go on. The air cooled when my feet dangled out of the cave. As I moved I bumped into something that I hoped was a canteen, but I still could not reach for it. Cold sweat prickled across my skin and inflamed the thirst in my throat.

I wrapped my fingers around the flashlight, but it was impossible to sit up in the tiny cave to hold the light toward the room below so I could see. The rat was down there, and who knew what else. I rocked back and forth between my shoulder and my hip and pushed the canteen out of the cave with my knee. It fell, bounced against the stone coffin below, and rolled to a stop somewhere in the room. My hip reached the opening. I rolled onto my stomach, scooted a few more inches, and kicked in empty air, stretching my toes to find footing on the coffin below. It was no use; the German soldier had been forced to lift me to my hideout. I would have to drop at least two feet.

I closed my eyes, clamped my jaw tight, and dropped. The marble casket smacked against the bottom of my feet. I tumbled backward and slammed against the ground on my back. Flashes of a thousand fish in my father's boat flew before me, their eyes wide in shock, their mouths gaped open and gasping for oxygen. I wheezed and struggled to expand my compressed lungs and waited until the throb in my chest abated. A rusty flavor filled my mouth. I had bit my lip when I landed, and blood coated my tongue.

The flashlight had slipped from my hand when I fell. I ran my hands in the darkness all over the ground near me, and at last I found the light that was the key to my survival.

I slid the metal button forward and illuminated my surroundings. I was out of the cave and back in the room full of skeletons and starved rodents.

I stood on shaky legs and the right one buckled; my foot had bent when I landed. I stepped forward and managed a limp. I spotted the canteen at the end of the coffin and gulped three mouths full of water before I made myself stop. Ivana had lectured all of us about drinking slowly if we'd been without water. The liquid cooled and soothed me all the way to my feet. Exhaustion filled every inch of my body, and I longed to rest. I resisted the urge to lie down on top of the coffin or let myself slip back to sleep. If I were to survive, I had to stay awake and find a way out.

The flashlight flickered but lit enough for me to stumble my way. If the SS soldiers had discovered that the soldier helped me, he would be dead by now. I feared that I would come upon his lifeless body somewhere along the path. Many times I had been jolted from my stupor in the cave and hoped that the sound of shots I had heard were only a part of my hallucinations.

I wound through the passageways, lit the flashlight just long enough to estimate the number of steps I could take before I had to have light again, and walked in pitch blackness.

The next turn in the hall revealed my deepest fear as I spotted a soldier's body sprawled on the cave floor and splattered with blood. I forced myself to look at his face and exhaled in relief; it was not my rescuer. I risked the battery, used the light to search the body, and found a small revolver in his boot. I slipped it into the pocket of my dress and stumbled on.

Thirst was a rasp that scraped at my throat. There was little water in the canteen. I took small sips each time I rested against the rough walls and slowed my labored breathing. I coaxed my legs forward with the promise of five more steps, then three, then one.

Someone shouted up ahead—guttural, angry threats in German that I had come to fear and dread. I limped into the shadows of another cavern and hid behind a wall. The air filled with blasts of gunfire and pounding footsteps. I lay on the floor able to see only when the battle sparked and fires flared. Hours passed and the sounds lessened; voices became fainter, fewer, until they were gone.

Perhaps the enemy had been discovered down here and attacked. The hope that I was no longer in danger buoyed my spirits, but the weakness in my body defied me, and I could not move. My heartbeat and my breathing slowed until they were barely perceptible, and the revolver in my pocket fell to the floor.

The faces of my loved ones loomed above me: Papa's eyes the blue of the sea, his arms extended toward me. Mama and Bruno beside Laura as sunlight entered a window and lit the face of their baby boy.

And Massimo, his eyes afire as they looked into mine, his spirit giving me strength even as he drifted away from my reach. I called to him as the flashlight expired and the darkness consumed me body and soul.

Chapter Forty-Eight

MASSIMO

"SHE IS NOT HERE."

It took every ounce of my strength not to lock my hands around his neck for lying. I jumped on the stone coffin just seconds after Peter Weimer and reached inside the cave in the ceiling. It was empty. I gripped both my hands into fists.

Ronaldo and the others gathered around the room. "Massimo, if they had killed her, then her body would be with the others. Andrea and Luigi checked and she is not there. Maybe somebody—"

"Where? Where would they take her?"

Andrea wiped the sweat from his forehead. "Maybe she escaped after the SS was all wiped out before we got here. Or maybe the soldiers who raided found her and took her to the hospital."

I locked my jaw in frustration. The Americans had discovered the Germans in the catacombs and wiped them out sometime, maybe as long as two days before we got here. There was no sign of Marianna.

Peter Weimer climbed down from the coffin and stood with the others. "I had given her a flashlight and a canteen, as I told you. They are both gone. Perhaps she did climb down and escape."

We searched every nook, every inch of the catacombs until we found the flashlight and canteen that Weimer recognized as his inside a cavern close to the entrance. I gripped the canteen in my hand and faced the men in my group, grateful that Andrea and Luigi had found Lello and Davide to help us.

"James, you find our American military contact. We need to know who attacked and wiped out the SS members who were hiding down here. Lino, you and Lello go to Lieutenant Bianco and see what our other contacts may know. Meet us at the Santa Lucia hospital."

Every one of us took off at a run, jumped into jeeps and a truck, and turned to our destinations. I stood up in my jeep and called out to the rest of the men before they drove away. "No more than two hours before we meet again. *Sprigatevi*! Move quickly!"

* * *

The halls of the Santa Lucia hospital were cooler than outside but did nothing to ease the urgency that pulsed like a drum in my head. Every face looked the same—whiskered, bandaged, yellowed, and male. We searched every room, even the women's room in spite of the protests from the nuns who flapped like birds protecting their nests.

The kitchen, pantries, bathrooms, barracks; nothing. We started for the exit, defeat heavy on my chest, when Lello caught up with us. "Wait, wait . . . I may be able to ask someone for information." He bolted back toward an office we had not searched while the rest of us followed behind.

A woman, her hair pulled up in a nurse's cap, sat at a desk, her head bowed over a pile of papers. Lello marched up and shook her hand. "Donnatella." She stared back at Lello, her face locked in a grimace. "I only work in the hospital. Leave me out of whatever this is, Lello."

He laid his other hand on top of hers. "It is Siara, Donnatella; you must know she was taken." Tears filled the woman's eyes but she looked down. "I know. She has been gone for days, almost a week."

Lello let go of her hand and stepped around the desk beside her. She turned the other way and he gripped her by the shoulders. "I know how you feel about working with us. We ask only for information. We know she was taken to the catacombs and hidden there and that there was a raid that cleaned them out. Have you heard anything at all?"

Her shoulders relaxed and Lello took a step back. I reached out my hand to her. "Please, this young woman . . . Siara, we must find her."

Donnatella blinked back the moisture in her eyes. "I know of that raid; two male survivors were brought in by Father Conforte, but no woman. I would know her."

I slapped the desktop with my hand and hung my head down, my mind racing to think of the next place we could search.

Donnatella sat up straighter. "But wait, Father Conforte always helps with the wounded after raids and brings us soldiers, but he never brings any women here. If he found Siara, he would have taken her to the Santa Domenica church outside of town where they shelter only women."

We were out the door before her words could reach the other side of the room.

Chapter Forty-Nine

MARIANNA

A BRILLIANT LIGHT GLOWED THROUGH my eyelids as the angels called to me and nudged me on the shoulder. "*Signorina . . . Signorina. Opri I tuoi occhi,* open your eyes and drink now. Yes, yes, now you are waking up. It is time to drink more soup so you will feel better."

These angels were gentle and kind, but my body still ached and refused to move. The release I had prayed for in the catacombs had not come. A squeeze on my hand and consistent pats on my cheek roused me and I forced my eyelids open. Brightness shot into my eyes.

Two women hovered above my bed, their faces round and pink and their heads draped in white. Nuns—sisters. The closest one slipped her hand behind my head and lifted it up. She held a cup to my lips and tipped it so the contents trickled into my mouth. I swallowed and winced at the burn in my throat.

The sister holding the cup smiled at my success. "There you are. I told Sister Carolina you were going to make it. You have gotten stronger just since yesterday morning. I am Sister Anna, and you are a very brave young lady. What is your name, *Carina?*"

I was not sure who I should be. "Siara," I whispered.

I sipped the broth with the help of Sister Anna and asked for water. She propped pillows behind my back and ran to fill my request. Sister Carolina helped the woman in a bed next to me. My hands were bandaged but my fingers were not covered. I used them to tug on the nun's sleeve. "How did I get here? I thought I died in the catacombs."

The sister shook her head with a tsk of her tongue. "Oh no, *Signorina,* you were not meant to die. There was a battle in the catacombs a few miles from here. Father Conforte went down there to search for any survivors when it was over and found you. You are at the Santa Domenica church. Father Conforte always brings the women to us. He thought you may die before he got you to us but you are very brave and strong. We bathed you and dressed your wounds and have been feeding and caring for you while you were in and out of consciousness for two days. You do not remember?"

I shook my head, and she laid her hand on my shoulder. "All that matters now is that you heal. Do not worry."

She moved to help a woman in a bed across the aisle from me, and I tried to make more sense of my surroundings. The arched and ornate ceiling and the bells that tolled and echoed through the hall confirmed that I was in a church converted into a hospital like so many others since the war began. Wide windows spanned the entire wall across from me and revealed a long terrace and green lawn outside.

Women filled at least thirty beds in the cavernous room, their hair tangled or limp and strewn across their pillows. Some had their heads shorn and laced with rows of stitches. Faces were bruised and swollen, broken limbs were wrapped. Several sisters moved around and lifted the women by the shoulders for medicine or spoke the rosaries at their sides. Nausea overwhelmed me. My fight for freedom and all my efforts to thwart the enemy had resulted only in this; I was nothing now but another patient, stranded and alone.

All the messages, raids, and helping wounded men by the dozens— nothing I had done had changed anything. Bruno's missing leg, my papa dead from the heartbreak of war, and Massimo, a prisoner locked away from me for life. I sank into my pillow in despair. Nothing made sense anymore. The war still raged like a demon—the demon that had wrapped its claws around my life and squeezed out my brightest hope before I even joined the Partisans by taking Massimo away. A woman a few beds away sobbed into her pillow, and a shudder shook me until my teeth chattered together.

Sister Anna had gone to fill the water glasses of the women across the room. Her eyes widened, and long white robes flowed as she hurried up beside me and took my hand. "Oh my goodness, *Signorina*, you look positively ashen. Why do your teeth clatter so?" She leaned close and whispered in my ear. "I know you were imprisoned by the enemy, so I want to reassure you that you are safe here. No man will find you."

No man will find you. The words burned like a branding iron on my skin. Massimo would not find me. . . . I turned on my side and pulled my knees to my chest. The sister patted my hand and sat on a metal chair as she scooted closer.

"Siara, listen carefully. You see, this is not an ordinary hospital; it is a church we made into a sanctuary during the war for women only. Even the priests do not enter where the women are unless it is for last rites. There are dozens of people every week who come by looking for people. Some may be family members, but they could also be spies. Sister Teresa is very strict and protective in screening them. She keeps the door to this ward locked and will not let any men inside to search. You do not need to be afraid.

"When people ask Father Conforte for help in finding their loved ones, ,he is very careful. He does not ask Sister Teresa about the women patients unless the people who are searching have proof that they are really family."

She squeezed my hand tighter. "Please do not be afraid of those who took you. You have been through a terrible time, but you will heal. Look, you are awake already. We know there are enemies and traitors everywhere, so we are very careful to protect you."

I tried to calm my breathing and stop shaking but there was no stopping my tears. Poor sister Anna had no idea that her attempts at comfort and reassurance meant nothing to me. Somehow, coming back from the brink of death without any hope of being with Massimo had only brought the biggest realization back once again to haunt me: there is more than one way to die in this war.

* * *

The sun tilted west by the time my tears had peaked and ebbed. I sat up in my bed, encouraged that I could do so with a trace of energy. I wanted to leave this place, to make my way to Sortino to be with my family. I sat up and struggled my way to my feet, feeling like a baby bird on the edge of its nest. The bandages on my knees tugged at my skin, the palms of my hands were raw and scabbed over, and my head felt as if it would never stop aching again. I ignored it all, resigned to the life of pain I had been trying to outrun.

My long, white gown brushed the floor as I took the first steps, the marble tile cold and hard under my feet. I walked through a doorway at the end of the windows, my hair warming my back before the wind twisted and tugged on it. The massive arms of an elm tree hung over a lawn that expanded down a hill and abutted a fountain of cherubs and horses. Women sat on benches or in wheelchairs around the fountain, and I was relieved they were too far away to ask me questions. I walked through cool dichondra to a chair beneath the elm and leaned back against the slanted slats.

Birds called to their young while the sun burned behind dusty clouds. I closed my eyes and listened to the branches of the elm tune the wind in a soft cry that spoke Massimo's name before it carried it away from me again.

The Mediterranean looked black as a grave on the horizon, the waves rising like a demon with its arms stretched out to grab me. I let it have me, let my arms lay limp on the chair while the darkness of the sea pulled me deep into her womb.

I must have dozed again. Sister Anna had walked undetected to my side, where she stood like a white-robed sentinel next to my chair. She touched my shoulder softly with her hand.

"Dear Siara, I am so sorry to disturb your repose, but it is possible something important just came to me."

I nodded my head and wished I could escape her presence in spite of her kind demeanor. The sister looked into my eyes. "Father Conforte found me in the garden a few moments ago and gave me this."

She held out her hand, opened her fingers, and I looked down at a blue cameo lying in her palm. She rolled it over and revealed the etching on the back: *Marianna*. Sister Anna continued on, oblivious to the fact that I could not breathe.

"Father Conforte said that a small group of men came a few minutes ago and asked about a young woman named Marianna or Siara. Father Conforte scolded them and said that if they were not even sure of the name of the woman they sought, that he could not help them and he would not ask Sister Teresa."

I wrapped my arms around my waist to hold in a tremble that grew in my core. I had left this cameo on the grave of my father. I could not fathom who would have it and know to bring it here in search of me. Bruno would not know to ask about a Siara. The twittering of the birds in the tree rang in my ears as Sister Anna held the cameo up by the chain.

"The leader of the men pled with Father Conforte to give this cameo to one of us sisters to ask around. Father Conforte finally relented and gave it to me. But, Siara, if you do not know a Marianna, I will just go and let you rest."

I took the sister by her hand and clasped the cameo. "When, Sister? When did he come here?"

Her eyes lit up. "You do know her? The leader of these men said that he had a message for us to give to the Marianna that owned the cameo if she ever came here. To tell her that he is not married and that he will search for her until he finds her. He told Father Conforte that his name was Massimo."

The world spun like a carousel as I pushed myself to my feet. Sister Anna grabbed hold of my arm to steady me. "Siara, sit back down to rest. The men came just a few minutes ago, but Father Conforte sent them away. He just found me and gave me the necklace, so I came as soon as I could to find you. I had a feeling you might know something. But do you know if this Massimo is a good man?"

I nodded my head, unable to speak. The ground stopped swaying, and I hurried across the lawn and terrace and through the hall of women. My legs dipped and quivered but I pushed myself to move faster to find Sister Teresa. She sat at her desk by the hall door and stood with a start at the sight of me. I saw nothing but the walls and doors between me and Massimo. I looked at her. "Please, Sister, I know the man, the group who came looking for me just now."

Her eyes grew big. "Very good then. God be with you." She grabbed the key and turned the lock. The hall opened into a spacious chapel. I set my sight on the wooden doors that lead to the outside.

I crossed the chapel and pulled at the heavy doors. A driveway of cobblestone wrapped around the front of the church where it met with a long dirt road. I hurried over the stones to the graveled road, ignoring the dust that flew up onto the hem of my white gown and the scratch of gravel on my feet. I looked in panic down each direction and spotted a band of men, their backs to me as they walked far away toward a jeep.

I almost fell to my knees at the sight of him—wide shoulders, a dark head of curly hair looking down at the ground as he walked. My lungs heaved so hard I had to stand still to get my breath to call his name.

"Massimo."

Maybe the wind carried my voice, maybe Papa reached down from the clouds and tapped him on the shoulder, because he stopped and turned around. He tilted his head and stared. His muscles stiffened and he broke into a run in my direction.

I ran toward him, sobs racking my chest. Shouts of joy from the men that ran up behind Massimo rang over the fields. Lello, Davide, James.

Within seconds Massimo arrived. My arms reached out as he reached for me and I fell against him. I cried his name and met his mouth with mine while tears covered both of our faces. His arms were warm, real, his hands a source of power against my back. Massimo lifted me, carried me to a nearby bench, and held me in his lap. I wept against his neck, and he brushed my hair from my face and covered it in kisses.

Daylight slipped lower in the sky while Massimo and I stayed wrapped like a cocoon around one another on the bench.

The evening birds chattered and whistled as if announcing our reunion. Lello, Davide, and James each leaned down and kissed my face and patted Massimo on the shoulder. My friends stepped back, and a tall blond man in ill-fitting clothes with a long scar down his cheek walked up beside us. I gasped before I reached for his hand, my throat locked too tight for me to speak. I nodded my head up and down and pressed the German soldier's hand to my cheek.

Massimo broke the silence. "Marianna, this is Peter Weimer."

I nodded again and took a deep breath. "Thank you. Thank you, Peter Weimer, for saving me."

I looked up into his eyes, and the soldier's chin quivered. "I am very happy that you are safe, *Signorina.*"

I leaned back, pressed my face against Massimo's neck, and closed my eyes. A thousand questions lay quiet on my tongue. A soothing breeze lifted strands of my hair and swirled like ribbons around the two of us. My head no longer ached, and my arms and legs had new strength. Massimo stroked my cheek, and the Mediterranean opened its mighty belly and lifted me back to shore once again.

About the Author

Melinda S. Sanchez grew up spellbound by the characters of wonderful books—Pippi Longstocking, Laura Ingalls Wilder, Kit Tyler, Charlie Bucket, Karana, and more.

In second grade, she wrote her first book. It featured two mice that got married; the wife always wore curlers and cold-cream to bed, and the husband was in the military. By the age of twelve she was prolific in writing poetry and stories.

As an adult, Melinda lived in the picturesque country of Italy and fell in love with the people, language, landscape, and history. She met her husband there, and together they have five beautiful grown children and four perfect granddaughters. They also have a house full of dogs, cats, exotic lizards and creatures, and birds. Between the people, animals, reptiles, and birds, there are plenty of characters to inspire and keep Melinda spellbound and writing, writing, writing for a long time to come.